POINTS OF
IMPACT

BY MARKO KLOOS

Frontlines

POINTS OF
IMPACT

MARKO KLOOS

47NORTH

Text copyright © 2018 by Marko Kloos
All rights reserved.

No part of this book may be reproduced, or stored in a retrieval system, or transmitted in any form or by any means, electronic, mechanical, photocopying, recording, or otherwise, without express written permission of the publisher.

Published by 47North, Seattle

www.apub.com

Amazon, the Amazon logo, and 47North are trademarks of Amazon.com, Inc., or its affiliates.

ISBN-13: 9781542048460
ISBN-10: 154204846X

Cover design by Ray Lundgren

Cover illustrated by Paul Youll

Printed in the United States of America

For Robin, Lyra, and Quinn, my galactic center.

PROLOGUE

I've been at war for most of my adult life.

When I was a kid, there wasn't much to do in the Public Residence Clusters other than getting into trouble or watching Networks. I wasn't good at getting *out* of trouble again, so instead of running the streets, I read books and watched a lot of shows.

My favorite stuff to watch was the military shows, the ones that ran year after year. Steady casts of actors who became more familiar to you than your own family, playing hard-bitten sergeants and officers doing battle with The Enemy, whoever that happened to be in that season. Some shows were what I now know to be hyperpatriotic bullshit, and some were a little more gritty and critical of the war machine, but they all had something in common: there was always a victory in the end. It may have been hard-won at terrible cost, but there was never a doubt that victory had been achieved against The Enemy.

Turns out all those shows were full of shit.

Real war—it's not like that at all. In real war, you don't often get a clear-cut victory. Sometimes you battle The Enemy, and you both walk away from the fight exhausted, bleeding, and mentally bruised, without any clear victory to show for it, no patch of ground or objective to point to and say, "That's what we earned with the lives of ten thousand grunts and sailors." Sometimes, both sides just sort of grind to a halt because they can't keep up the fight anymore, because we've bled each other to the point where you can't continue fighting, but you've sacrificed so much that you can't just concede defeat, either. So you retreat to your respective corners for however long it takes to recover enough to fight another round.

Mars was just like that.

Three years ago, we tried to take it back from the Lankies, and they tried to hang on to it. Neither of us were successful, but neither side really got defeated, either. We lost more than ten thousand troops in the offensive. The Lankies tempted us into overextending our lines, and then they emerged from prepared positions dug into the Martian rock, an extensive tunnel network many hundreds of kilometers long. We got off that planet in time to save more than half the troops we had brought, but we ran out of time and ammunition to keep up the fight that day. In the end, we killed thousands of Lankies, nuked all the seed ships they were growing under the surface, destroyed their terraformers, and fucked up Mars for humans and Lankies alike with the help of hundreds of nuclear warheads.

But there were no ticker-tape parades back home, no moving footage of surviving settlers getting rescued by Spaceborne Infantry troops, no parade down the middle of the main avenue in Olympus City. Just a bunch of funerals, folded flags, and somber speeches, ten thousand times all over the North American Commonwealth and the Sino-Russian Alliance. We hadn't lost, but we damn sure hadn't won, either. But if we couldn't use Mars anymore, neither could the Lankies, and the incursions stopped. If there are seed ships left, they hightailed it out of the solar system, because none of our units have spotted one since the Second Battle of Mars. Three years without a Lanky seed ship sighting and some people think we may have beaten them for good, driven them back to wherever they came from.

Most of us know better. So we are preparing for the next round, all of us. NAC and SRA and all the other world alliances, pulling on the same rope even though we're still bickering and in-fighting like a giant dysfunctional family. The NAC lost the priceless *Agincourt*, but the Sino-Russians still have *Arkhangelsk*, and we have improved the Orion missiles that let us wipe out the Lanky fleet gathered above Mars. But even with the prodigious appetite of our power blocs for weapons of mass destruction, it turns out that we can run out of nuclear warheads when each of those Orions takes hundreds of nukes for propellant. Uranium and plutonium are suddenly in short supply, and the power blocs on Earth have strip-mined all their old atomic warhead stocks. All our nukes are fuel for missiles now, aimed into space instead of pointed at cities on Earth, one of the few positive side effects of the Lanky threat.

The NAC was cash-strapped even before the Lankies came. Now we're positively broke. Luckily, the European Union and the well-heeled countries of the Pacific Rim recognized that the defense of Earth is a problem for all countries, not just for the NAC or the SRA alone. So we've been getting new equipment and operating cash, along with the benefits of shared research and development.

We've trained new troops to build up our spaceborne fighting power yet again. We've used the influx of new money from the rest of the world to rearm, reorganize, and develop new gear, all while keeping a close eye on the stars. The Lankies may not be in the solar system anymore, but they're out there, sitting on the colonies they took away from us over the years. And I have no doubt that we will clash again soon. The only question is who will have the guts to strike the next blow first.

I fulfilled a promise after Mars and joined the Lazarus Brigades as a Fleet adviser, training troops and getting mixed up in PRC conflicts for a year and a half. In the past I've battled Lankies and the SRA on desolate rock piles thirty light-years or more from home, but those eighteen months on Earth were harder and more dangerous than anything I've seen or done out in the black. As tedious and dangerous as my Fleet job can get, finally going back to it felt almost like being let out of purgatory. Some of the things I saw and did when I was with the Brigades will forever weigh down my conscience. Even Halley doesn't know the full story, and I doubt I'll ever burden her with that knowledge.

But for now, I am back at my job, doing what I've been trained to do. There are still Lankies on Mars, and I'm part of the cleanup crew that steps on the roaches whenever they leave their dark hiding spots and scurry around in the light. We can't have Mars back, but we'll be damned if we let *them* have it, either.

CHAPTER 1

—— OLYMPUS HIGHWAY PATROL ——

"Contact at forty degrees relative, Captain."

The courtesy warning of the pilot yanks me out of the half-dozing state I've been in for the last fifteen minutes or so. I sit upright in my jump seat and scan the console display in front of me. The drop ship is bouncing a bit in the rough air, but after three months of endless atmospheric patrols above Mars, I can nap through anything short of a category four hurricane.

"Hang on," I say. "Checking the scopes."

The drop ship is a Dragonfly—but not a standard battle taxi model. This one is a Dragonfly-SR, a modification they cooked up just for this particular job. The SR variant has high-powered optical sensor arrays all over the outside of the hull. Lankies don't show on radar or infrared, but they can't hide from camera lenses. On the downside, the constant shit weather on Mars means that the SRs have to fly under the low cloud ceiling to spot Lankies, and that makes for long and boring patrols. Eight-hour shifts of looking at consoles and getting bounced around by the winds at low altitude. The SRs have auxiliary fuel tanks on the wing pylons instead of missiles so they can actually stay aloft for closer to twelve hours, but the limiting factor is the endurance of the human crew.

"Well, hello there, Mr. Lanky," I say when I see the familiar spindly form of one striding across the surface a few kilometers in front of our portside bow. A few moments later, the software of the optical array draws an outline around another suspected contact, and the second Lanky emerges from the haze in the predicted spot.

"Target," I call out to the pilot. "Two large hostile organisms, bearing zero-five-zero, distance forty-five hundred, speed fifty klicks per."

"They're in a hurry," the pilot remarks. "Getting skittish down there."

"You would be, too, if someone dropped guided munitions on your head every time you went outside for a stroll."

"What do you want to do here?" the pilot asks.

I think about it for a second. We generally kill surface-dwelling Lankies on sight, but the way those two are moving makes it look like they have a destination, and they're not just running from the sound of the engines they may have heard. The Dragonflies are quiet, but the Lankies that are still alive are the most careful and skittish of what's left, and there's no telling if they've heard or spotted us from over four kilometers away and three thousand feet up in the air.

"Hang a starboard turn; then come back around to port and do a loop," I tell the pilot. "Keep four klicks' separation. I want to see where those guys are heading."

"Copy that."

The drop ship tilts into a right-hand turn that momentarily takes us away from the Lankies, but the camera arrays stay fixed on our adversaries with computer precision. It's incredibly tedious and labor-intensive to flush out Lankies by skimming across the planet's surface with nothing but optics, but it doesn't tip them off to our presence with active radiation.

We nuked much of Mars comprehensively three years ago at the close of the Second Battle of Mars. Every Lanky settlement was a seed ship under construction beneath the Martian rock, and we dropped bunker-busting penetrator nukes on every one of the building sites. That sort of nuclear detonation is the dirtiest possible one because of the irradiated soil and rock that gets pulverized and then dispersed all over the place. Most of Mars is so radioactive now that our suits' Geiger counters sound like high-cadence machine guns on full auto fire. Every time we get back to the carrier after a mission, the bird gets to spend twenty minutes in the decontamination lock before we are allowed off. But the Lankies seem to be immune to radiation, because even after three years, there are still plenty of them alive underground, judging by our kill rate on the surface.

The Dragonfly-SR changes direction and banks to port for a sweeping turn that takes us around the Lankies on the ground. The targeting computer keeps the crosshairs of the observation optics firmly on the creatures as they trot across the dusty Mars soil. They don't look up or give any other indication that we have been noticed, but they move like they have a purpose. I watch them walk down a slope and into a wide ravine, kicking up puffs of ochre dirt with every step. It's hard to be sitting in an armed drop ship and drawing a bead on live Lankies without pulling a trigger, but I've learned to delay gratification. When you want to kill a lot of wasps, you don't hunt them down and swat them individually. You follow them back to the nest and then torch the whole thing.

"Call it in?" the pilot asks.

"Not yet," I reply. "Let's not spook 'em. And I want some more accurate target reference point data before we waste ordnance on just two runners."

"Your show," the pilot sends back. He sounds as tired as I imagine I do. We're at the tail end of our eight-hour patrol, one of only half a dozen SR-modified drop ships above the northern hemisphere of Mars right now, and reaction times are slow. After hour five, you just sort of mentally start checking out and looking forward to chow and a hot shower back on the carrier.

When we spot Lankies, I have several ways of dealing with them. There's a rotary launcher taking up most of the cargo bay behind me, and it's loaded with a dozen guided missiles with 250-kilogram warheads. Those are for lone stragglers and small groups, and we can launch them right out of the tail end of the drop ship. For larger groups, I can call down kinetic strikes from orbital assets or request tactical air support from the carrier's Shrikes. And if we find a buried seed ship or even suspect there may be one, I can request a nuclear strike from the carrier, which will send down a thermonuclear warhead piggybacking behind a high-density penetrator designed to deliver the nuke dozens of meters into the Martian rock before lighting off the payload. It's a nasty, brutal way to fight, but the alternative would be to lose tens of thousands of troops in those underground tunnels in close combat with a physically far superior enemy. We're done trying to meet the Lankies on even terms. Now we stack the deck in our favor any way we can, even if it means fighting dirty and leaving nothing behind but irradiated soil.

I'm the only person in the cargo hold, so there's no one to talk to while I observe the Lankies. I don't want to distract the pilots from their jobs with noncritical observations, and we keep our signals traffic with the orbital units to the bare minimum to keep our emissions signature low. So I study the plot and the camera feeds silently, letting my brain do the calculations on autopilot. We don't have Shrikes on patrol over the hemisphere right now, so there's no close-air support nearby to call upon. My plot shows another Dragonfly-SR almost a thousand klicks to our east, and a whole lot of nothing otherwise. There are three units in orbit, but only one is close to a good launch window for an orbital strike—the frigate *Berlin*, the ship that was part of our tiny task force for the commando raid into the Leonidas system three years ago. She was held together with patch welds and hopeful prayers back then already, and three years of combat ops have not improved her condition any.

The Lankies continue their descent into the wide ravine and then stroll northwest, following the course of what looks like an ancient riverbed. I pan one of the optics clusters and look at the terrain ahead of the Lankies to predict where they're headed. These days, whenever we spot them on the surface, they're never away from shelter for long. They've either always preferred the subterranean lifestyle or they have adapted to our hardware limitations frighteningly fast. Without anyone to observe the colonies they took over, there's no way to know which is true, but we'll have a tough job ahead of us either way.

"There we go," I murmur to myself when I spot the dark irregularity of a tunnel entrance just half a kilometer ahead of the Lankies. It's tucked into a sidewall of the ravine, extending a natural rift in the rock wall, and if you didn't know exactly what to look for, you'd be likely to miss it or write it off as a natural terrain feature. But when I zoom in, my suspicions are verified by the obvious Lanky footprints in the dust and soil in front of the entrance. They've been going in and out of there for a while, and they haven't yet managed to sweep their tracks effectively.

"Got a tunnel entrance half a klick ahead of the Lankies, bearing three-thirty. They'll get there in another minute at the rate they're going."

"Call in orbital?" the pilot asks. "We won't get them before they go underground, but we may bust a nest or something."

"There's no way to tell how long that tunnel is before it reaches a hideout," I reply. "Could be ten kilometers, could be fifty. Let's pop these before they get under cover. At least we'll be rid of them."

I flip the cover from the fire control of the rotary launcher and hit the switch for the tail ramp with my other hand. The ramp opens with its soft hydraulic whine that's almost immediately drowned out by the wind noise. The launcher control panel switches from STANDBY/SAFE to ARMED/LIVE.

"I've got fire control," I tell the pilot. "Putting two on the Lankies and two more into the tunnel mouth. Come to heading three-five-five and hold her level."

"Copy," the pilot acknowledges. "Coming to three-five-five and holding level."

The drop ship comes out of its wide left-hand turn and straightens out on the bearing I specified. The rotary launchers we mounted in the cargo bays of the SR models save us the necessity for a gunship nearby, but they have limitations in use. They're pig-heavy and use up almost all the atmospheric lift capacity of the Dragonflies, and they can only be fired without danger when the ship is in a specific and narrow speed and attitude envelope.

On the targeting screen in front of me, I drag target markers onto the Lankies—*one, two.* Numbers three and four go onto the entrance of the cave, programmed for a horizontal ingress. The launcher can only fire once every two seconds because the rotary mechanism needs time to move the next half-ton missile into launch position, and I want the Lankies to be the first hit so they don't have advance warning of the incoming ordnance.

"Going weapons hot," I send. "In three, two, one. Firing."

The launcher spits the first missile out the back of the drop ship. The expeller charge is just powerful enough to kick the missile out of the launcher tube and through the tail ramp opening. Then the full propellant charge fires with a loud *bang-whoosh*, and the missile takes a nosedive and streaks toward the ground, following the computer's guidance for a rendezvous with the Lankies a few kilometers off our port side. The launcher rotates with a loud whirring noise, and the next missile fires, then the next. I watch as the eight-meter missiles drop out of the back of the ship with just a meter of clearance between their unfolding guidance fins and the edges of the tail ramp opening. Like everything else we've cobbled together to fight the Lankies in the last few years, this gear and these tactics have safety margins thin enough for a very close shave.

At just under four kilometers, the supersonic missiles take very little time to reach their targets. The Lankies are still unaware of our presence when the warheads execute their top-down attack profile from only a few thousand feet overhead. The explosives in the bases of the warheads each propel two dozen superdense and needle-sharp depleted uranium penetrators downward in a narrow cone. I watch the video feed on my console with grim satisfaction. The projectiles hit the Lankies and the ground around them at many times the speed of sound. Amazingly, even the missile penetrators with all their kinetic energy concentrated on a fine point will sometimes glance off a Lanky's cranial shield if it hits at a steep angle, but the warheads fire enough of those rods into such a small space that every single missile hit on a Lanky has been a guaranteed kill so far.

These are no exception. The Lankies on my screen drop to the dirt as if someone had turned their off switch. The spray of sharpened uranium rods churns up the soil all around them, throwing up ochre-colored geysers ten meters high. I've seen the aftermath of those kinetic warhead impacts many times, and those rods will penetrate a Lanky from top to bottom and still make a meter-deep hole in the ground. It's one hell of a grim way to recycle our spent uranium, but swatting Lankies is the best use for it I can imagine.

A second or two later, the other two missiles I fired launch their warheads into the mouth of the cave. One explodes against the rock wall and disintegrates, but the other disappears into the dark crevice, and a gust of rock dust and debris billowing from the cave mouth a moment later confirms that the warhead exploded inside and dispersed its payload into the tunnel. The Lankies have been smart enough to build sharp bends into their tunnel system so we can't just clear them out with direct fire, but I wasn't counting on killing many hidden Lankies with that shot. I was betting on the explosive charge to collapse the tunnel entrance. When the dust from the impacts clears, I can see that the crevice is now filled with rock and gravel. It wouldn't keep them from digging themselves back out and clearing the exit, but they never dig an entry point twice in the same location because they've learned that we chart and observe them for easy future kills.

"Target," I tell the pilots on the flight deck. "Two kills, one exit closed."

"Least we got *something* done today," the pilot replies.

"Let's stay on station for another five and then RTB. I'm good and ready for some rack time."

"I hear that. Five minutes it is," the pilot says.

Almost eight hours in the air, four missiles expended, and two-thirds of our fuel load burned for two Lanky kills and a closed-off tunnel entrance. It doesn't seem like the result is worth the time and expense, but on average, this has been a successful patrol, and the crew gets to paint another two Lanky silhouettes onto the side of their bird. Tomorrow, I'll get to fly another patrol in the back of a drop ship, and then again and again, until my three-month rotation is up and I get to spend a three-month stretch on Earth or near it, far away from this irradiated rock and its stubborn squatters.

There's a loud metallic-sounding tearing noise coming from the right side of the ship. The entire hull of the Dragonfly vibrates and shudders. From the open hatch of the cockpit passageway, I can hear loud warning buzzers going off. Then the world goes topsy-turvy. The Dragonfly violently flips around its longitudinal axis, and I get yanked backwards into my seat. From the way I am hanging in my harness a second later, I can tell that the drop ship has flipped through a full 180-degree turn and is now flying inverted and with a nose-down attitude. We're no longer in controlled flight; we're on a ballistic arc.

"Eject, eject, eject," the pilot shouts into the intercom. His voice doesn't sound nearly as excited and panicked as I feel it should, considering we are now heading for a ground that was only two thousand feet below us when we were flying level and controlled.

The drop ship's computer takes over to save the crew. Faced with an unrecoverable aircraft attitude, it overrides all manual controls and initiates the emergency eject procedure far faster than even the best human pilot could. The straps of my harness tighten to painfully taut levels, and I can feel the leg and arm restraints wrapping around my extremities and yanking them close to the chair. Then the eject capsule shoots out of the base of the seat and ensconces me in a titanium shell in a fraction of a second. I hear a muffled explosion, and then I feel a mighty push from below. My stomach lurches with the sudden and rapid upward movement. It has been three seconds at most since the ship flipped over suddenly, and I've not had enough time to process the situation enough to get scared. The drop ship's computer thinks it's time for the crew to get shot out of the Dragonfly to save us, and I am disinclined to argue with the silicon brain of our ride.

I know I've cleared the drop ship's hull when I hear the sound of rushing wind outside. I feel the capsule arcing into the sky for a few more seconds. Then another teeth-jarring jolt announces the deployment of the capsule's parachutes. I've never left a drop ship in this particular fashion, and I don't much care for it. At least the automatic restraint tighteners managed to get all of my limbs inside the capsule before it snapped shut. The rescue capsules have a reputation for breaking arms or legs on activation.

What the fuck just happened? I wonder. But I don't broadcast that inquiry out to the pilot and gunner because I don't want to send out radio signals for the Lankies to sense. In any case, I'll find out soon enough.

When the ship malfunctioned, we were just a little over two thousand feet up in the air, so the ride down to the surface doesn't take very long. I'm blind and deaf inside the capsule for just a minute at the most before it hits the Mars surface with the bone-jarring sound of metal on rock. The rescue capsules are not nearly as well cushioned as the bio-pods, and they hit a lot harder, hard enough to send a flare of pain up my spine and punch the breath from my lungs for a moment.

The rescue capsules don't open automatically like the bio-pods do. I fumble for the luminescent release handles on the inside of the capsule and give each a hard yank in turn. The shell opens halfway and comes to a stop with a grinding crunch. I release my restraints and grab the upper and lower halves of the titanium shell to move them further apart. They budge for another few centimeters, then get stuck again. I turn on the assist servos on my armor and use their power augmentation to wrench the shell halves apart all the way.

My rescue pod is lying on its side in a rubble field. The orange triple canopy of the parachute is draped behind the pod, tangled up in the lines attached to the top of the pod roof. This is my first emergency eject from atmospheric flight, and I hope I won't ever have to repeat the experience. The bio-pods are cushy and gentle rides in comparison. But I guess getting jarred and bounced around a bit beats burning up in a flaming wreck.

The drop ship hit the ground half a kilometer away while I was descending in the rescue capsule. A huge orange-black fireball marks the spot to the north where the only orbital taxi in a thousand-kilometer radius just explosively disassembled itself all over the surface.

"Fucking fabulous," I mutter to myself, careful to keep the comms cold. The entrance to that Lanky tunnel isn't too far from here, a few kilometers at best, and we still have no idea just how sensitive these things are to radiation.

There's an emergency kit in the back of the ejection capsule. I pop open the access latches and drag the kit box out of its receptacle. Then I take inventory of the contents. One standard water module for the battle armor connector, a handheld backup radio, ten packs of emergency rations, and an M109 service pistol with five magazines, a hundred rounds in total. I take the water module and the radio, but leave the pistol and the food behind. I don't intend to stay down here long enough to need extra calories, and if a Lanky finds me, that pistol will be about as useful as a kickstand on a drop ship. If I need to shoot myself, I already have my personal sidearm in a holster strapped to the front of my chest armor, and that will do the job just fine.

I look around for signs of the pilot's and copilot's chutes. The area where our bird went down is mostly flat but craggy and run through with ravines and sinkholes. In the distance to the north, I see something orange billowing close to the ground, so I gather my spare kit and set out that way.

The environmental controls of my battle armor practically go apoplectic with warnings and bright red readouts. The radiation sensor tells me that my surroundings are radioactive enough to give me fatal radiation poisoning with less than half a day of unprotected exposure. My suit's filters report they're good for another twenty-one hours. After the comprehensive nuking we put on all the Lanky building sites, the planet is a lethal wasteland, and I have no idea how the Lankies managed to hang on month after month without dying like flies in those caves. But our own settlers hung on and waited for rescue for over a year, and maybe hope against hope is a trait that both our species have in common.

The drop ship pilot is gathering his stuff out of his own rescue capsule when he sees me coming toward him across the rocky landscape. He has taken the time to gather the orange parachute and is now stuffing the silk canopy and its attached spaghetti of nylon lines into the cavity of the open capsule.

"What the hell happened just now?" I ask when I'm in voice range.

"We lost the starboard wing," the pilot replies. "I was flying straight and level, and all of a sudden, *boom*. Came off the bird like a loose piece of trim."

"What did we have hanging off it?"

"Just the two external tanks, but those were already empty. We were on internal tanks. No weight left on the wing pylons."

"Super. Brand-new drop ship, and the wing just fucking falls off in the middle of a patrol."

"It wasn't new." The pilot finishes cramming the parachute into the empty rescue capsule and pulls the clamshell closed over the telltale orange fabric. It's standard E&E protocol, even though we're pretty sure the Lankies can't even see like we do.

I look over to the spot where the Dragonfly hit the ground, tens of millions of Commonwealth dollars and a priceless war machine converted into a black cloud and a debris field around a shallow crater.

"Material fatigue," the pilot continues.

"That ship was five years old at most."

"Yeah. But we've been flogging the shit out of those birds. That one's been flying twenty surface missions a week in this shit. High winds and radiation and all."

"Twenty times a hundred and fifty," I count. "Three thousand flight hours."

"And not in blue skies with minimal loadout. These things weren't meant to be ridden like that. They get more combat hours in a month than they usually get in two years."

"Material fatigue," I repeat. Everything's tired, man and machine, and now things start falling apart even without Lankies helping with the disassembly.

"Yeah." The pilot—a second lieutenant whose name tag says "BRASSEY"—unloads the contents of the emergency box and starts filling his flight suit with gear.

"Let's go find your left-seater," I say. "He can't be too far from here."

We look around the area for a few minutes before we see the remnants of a dust plume to our south. It takes twenty more minutes to navigate the ravine-riddled terrain to the spot where the copilot's capsule hit the ground. It's obvious from a hundred meters away that the capsule is completely destroyed and that nobody's going to walk away from this spot. The emergency chute must have failed to deploy properly, because the remnants of the capsule look like they've been stomped on by a Lanky a few times.

"Goddammit," the pilot says. He sounds bone-tired and defeated.

"Yeah," I concur. Surviving a drop ship crash and then dying anyway because the rigger for the emergency chutes fucked up on the job is a pointless and disheartening way to go. But at least it's a quick death, and in the windowless capsule, he probably never even knew that something had gone wrong.

"Someone needs to get his dog tags," Lieutenant Brassey says, in a tone that makes it very obvious he'd rather be fighting a Lanky hand-to-hand. I wasn't particularly close to the copilot, so I sigh and shrug off my pack.

"I'll get 'em," I say. "You sit and watch the neighborhood. Anything Lanky-like shows up, you let me know the very same second."

"Got it," Lieutenant Brassey says. "And thank you."

The rescue pod broke apart when it hit the Mars surface. The copilot is still strapped into the remnants of his seat, which got ripped from the base of the pod and flung a good fifty meters from the main part of the debris field. I don't need to remove the pilot's helmet to know that he's dead. There's a splatter of blood on the inside of his face shield, and his limbs are splayed out in an unnatural fashion. Still, I let my suit's sensors check for vital signs. There aren't any, of course. But the pilot's dog tags are around his neck, inside that flight suit, so I have to remove the helmet anyway.

The face underneath the helmet is young, even for a new second lieutenant. There's blood coming from the copilot's nose and mouth, and his eyes are half-opened. He has sandy-blond hair shorn into a slightly shaggy buzzcut, the standard hairdo among pilots who wear heavy flight helmets most of the day. I fish for the chain of his tags inside the collar of his flight suit and pull out the dog tag. It's a rect-angular piece of metal with rounded corners, designed to be broken in half. I take the tag in both hands, snap off the bottom half, and tuck the rest of it back into the collar of the dead pilot's flight suit, in case a grave detail is ever going to come and bury him properly. Most likely, the Lankies are going to claim him as bonus protein for their building projects, and if I had a thermal charge, I would give this poor bastard a proper funeral pyre on the spot. As things stand, all I can do is leave him where he is and hope the Lankies overlook him. He's probably not much older than twenty, and his life ended here, on this irradiated piece of shit planet, due to a technical defect that could have been caught if the maintenance guys had paid twenty seconds' more attention. Or maybe they did everything right, and a piece of steel or string of nylon rope just gave way at the wrong time. Either way, the end result is a dead pilot and a smashed capsule, and the *hows* and *whys* don't matter much at this point. I tuck the bloodied dog tag into one of my exterior pockets and turn away from this grim little graveyard.

The cloud cover over Mars is so low that it looks like I could jump up and brush the bottom of the clouds with my gloved hand. The exterior temperature is well over thirty degrees Celsius, and the cooling elements in my armor are already busy. My battery will last a week or more, and the new improved filters in the standard battle armor are now good for days on a Lanky planet, but I really don't want to stick around that long.

"We need to clear datum," I tell Lieutenant Brassey when I get back to where he is standing.

"Shouldn't we stay by the crash site so the SAR flight can find us?"

"The pods have a distress beacon built in. You know that. It's radio energy. If there's a Lanky in the area, it's like a summoning flare. We need to haul ass and call down a SAR bird from a safe spot." I look around at the red-and-ochre wasteland around me. "If we can still find one in this place."

CHAPTER 2

MATERIAL FATIGUE

I've never liked Mars outside of the big cities. It didn't lend itself to large-scale farming or growing vegetation despite eighty years of terraforming, and the Lankies have undone all our work in just a few years. Now it's the same dusty red desert as before, only with a high-CO_2 atmosphere and enough heat and humidity to make the visors on our helmets fog up. And after the big battle with the Lankies three years ago, it's a graveyard for too many of my friends and comrades-in-arms. We are in the southern hemisphere, not the northern one where I dropped during the great assault, but I still have the most unpleasant flashbacks at the sight of the barren landscape.

We have put two kilometers between us and the crash site when we see the first Lanky in the distance. It's striding across the Martian plains toward the plume of black smoke from the shattered drop ship, but it's almost a kilometer to our left and seemingly unaware of our presence. Still, we take no chances. There's a small cluster of rocks nearby, and we huddle behind it to keep out of sight.

"What do we have?" Lieutenant Brassey asks.

"For what? Fighting that thing?"

"Yeah."

"I have bad news for you. If he finds us, we're dead. Worse than dead, maybe." I think back to the scene from the Battle of Mars, when we discovered that the Lankies bring human bodies back to their tunnels. Food, protein for building—whatever they use us for, I have no interest in ending up that way. I nod to the pistol Lieutenant Brassey wears strapped to the chest of his armor.

"We get jumped by Lankies, you take your helmet off, and you check out quickly."

Brassey nods, but he doesn't look happy with the reply. A few years ago, I would have taken pity and prettied up the situation assessment for the green lieutenant who has probably never been on the surface of Mars and most likely never seen a Lanky from outside of a cockpit. But I didn't want to kindle false hope. Better a quick bullet to the brain than getting crushed by a Lanky or being dragged off to be used as organic filler in a seed ship hull.

The Lanky disappears behind a low ridge, still headed for the crash site. I scan the area ahead of us for safe spots to send a burst transmission to the Fleet. With any luck, they've already picked up the wailing from the drop ship's crash beacon and dispatched a SAR ship, but I'm not willing to wait around and hope.

"That little hill over there," I say to Brassey and point to our northeast. "Three klicks. Twenty minutes if we hustle. I'll call for pickup from there."

"Copy that," Brassey replies.

I should be scared and worried as we trudge up the hill a little while later. Climbing the featureless slope makes us visible and obvious from far away, and the Lanky disappeared from sight uncomfortably close by. But I'm more irritated and pissed off than anything else. I don't want to buy it on this irradiated rock, where no humans will settle again for a century or more. But if I do have to buy it here, I certainly don't want it to be in a pointless crash because some wrench spinner missed tightening a bolt somewhere. The most frustrating part is that the pilot is probably right, and there's nobody to blame for our current situation. Nothing makes me feel more like a powerless cog in a machine than almost dying just because a tired widget broke, and I don't even have anyone to shout at for it.

"If TacOps is on the ball, they'll see the crash beacon from the wrecked bird," I tell Lieutenant Brassey.

"That would be nice," he says and looks skyward, as if he's hoping to see a SAR drop ship appear out of the low cloud ceiling overhead right this minute and save us a bunch more legwork and a risky radio call. There were only six drop ships in the air over the whole hemisphere when we went down, and seeing one-sixth of your patrol drop off the holotable display should be a solid indicator that shit has gone sideways. But now that the CIC and TacOps consoles are frequently staffed with first-deployment trainees two months out of tech school, things some-times fall through the cracks.

Behind and below us on the rubble field, the wreckage of our Dragonfly is still burning, sending billowing black smoke into the leaden sky. I don't see any Lankies nearby, but that doesn't mean there aren't any around. They've had three years to expand the tunnel system they used for their surprise counterattack at the Second Battle of Mars, and by now they can pop out of the ground anywhere.

"All right," I say when we reach the top of the little hill. "Take over watch. I'll call down a taxi."

Lieutenant Brassey nods and turns around to keep an eye on the rubble field below. He's resting one hand on the pistol strapped to his armor's chest plate. Two pistols and a radio—not really an ideal combat load for hiking through a Lanky-infested wasteland.

I dial into the Fleet's TacOps channel and select burst transmission mode, three milliseconds, maximum transmitting power.

"TacOps, this is Tailpipe One. Romeo One-Five is down with one KIA. Requesting immediate combat SAR."

The computer in my suit compresses the message into a tiny data package and sends a burst transmission up into orbit, where NACS *Regulus* is in orbit above the southern hemisphere.

"Tailpipe One, TacOps. Copy request for SAR mission. Stand by."

I can picture the console jockey at the TacOps station in CIC disconnecting his headset and rushing over to the officer of the deck to check for available air assets. Thankfully, downed crew get priority billing when it comes to the allocation of those assets. It's important for the flight crews to know that the Fleet will spare no fuel or ammo expense to get them back if they crash.

"Tailpipe One, this is the XO. SAR mission will be out of the clamps in three minutes, call sign Angel One-Niner. ETA twenty-eight minutes. Keep your heads down and lay low."

"Copy SAR flight Angel One-Niner inbound, ETA two-eight minutes. I'll check on TacAir when he's overhead. Tailpipe One out," I send in reply. Then I walk over to Brassey, who is keeping a nervous watch on the area, fingering the pistol in his chest holster.

"Twenty-eight minutes for SAR to get here," I tell him.

"Hope they'll get here in time," he says.

"Don't hope too much. Expect they won't, and then you can't get disappointed."

"That's not a very optimistic outlook," Brassey says.

"I'm out of optimism. I traded whatever I had left for some spare rations in Detroit a year ago," I say.

Twenty-eight minutes on the surface of Mars seems like an eternity, and there's no spot on the planet that doesn't remind me of the bloody mess from three years ago. We can't settle here again, they can't move around on the surface freely, so we have a pointless stalemate now. If I had command, I'd aim the particle cannon mount of the *Arkhangelsk* at the planet and hit the fire button on the main weapons console until the reactors are out of fusion mass.

Fifteen minutes into our wait, we see more Lankies in the neighborhood. Three of them appear without warning out of a ground depression half a kilometer away, moving laterally from our right to our left toward the still-burning wreck of the drop ship. At first, they're walking in a tight group, but as soon as they are out of the depression, they spread out until there is about a hundred meters of space between them.

"Son of a bitch," I murmur. "They've learned their lessons."

"What's that, Captain Grayson?"

"Oh, they're moving like our guys would when they're on foot patrol. Space it out, so one strike or ambush can't take out the whole patrol at once."

We speak in low voices, even though the nearest Lanky is several hundred meters away. With just our pistols, we couldn't even scratch one of those things if they discover us, much less kill all three. It's hard to watch a group of them close enough for a MARS rocket or a few magazines from an M-95 rifle and not be able to do a thing. We watch the Lankies walk over to the burning wreckage. One of them stoops and seems to examine the site, while the other two stand nearby as if to keep a guard.

"Oh shit." I make a fist when I see the Lanky by the wreckage reach down and pick something off the ground. I crank up the magnification on my optics to full power to see that the mangled and lifeless body of the drop ship's pilot is now dangling from the long-fingered hand of the Lanky. The alien straightens itself out and then points its head up into the sky, looking like a dog sniffing the breeze for a familiar odor.

"Tailpipe One, this is Angel One-Niner, do you read?" I hear on the TacAir channel. The air cavalry has arrived in the neighborhood.

"Angel One-Niner, I read you five by five. We are two and a half klicks to the northeast of the crash beacon. There are three LHOs clustered around the wreckage, and they have our KIA with them. Suggest you plow the shit out of that map grid ASAP before they make it back underground with our guy. Just aim for the beacon. The hostiles are all within three hundred meters of it."

"Copy that. Starting gun run. I'll give you a thirty-second mark so you can turn on your own transponders."

"Copy," I reply. "One-Niner, you are cleared hot."

I don't see or hear the incoming SAR drop ship yet, but the Lankies have definitely sensed its presence, because they are now turning and striding back the way they came, and this time they are moving faster. I decide to throw caution to the wind and turn on all the gadgetry in my suit.

"Angel One-Niner, hostiles are now moving away from the crash site at fifty klicks, heading zero-two-zero from the beacon. I am painting them for you on TacLink. They'll know we're up here in a second or two, so hurry up."

"Thirty seconds to target," Angel 19's pilot returns. "Copy cleared hot. I've got you on TacLink."

Even after doing this a thousand times, it's still unnerving to be in the target area of an attack run in close proximity to the impact zone. The pilots know their stuff, and with our positions showing on the drop ship's TacLink screen, the chance of accidental friendly fire is low, but there are still unforgiving physics involved, and computers can fail.

Down below us, the Lankies increase their pace. One of them swings its head over to our little hill and alters its course toward us.

"Oh shit," I say. "One-Niner, make the easternmost LHO a priority target. He's coming our way, and we have no ordnance."

"Copy that," the pilot replies. "Hang in there."

I unlock my pistol from its holster and flick off the safety with my trigger finger. Between the magazine in the gun and the two spares,

I have ninety rounds at the ready, and I intend to use eighty-nine of them on the Lanky once it gets close enough. The last one is for me, a last measure of defiance. With the other hand, I pat the pocket with my PDP in it to make sure it's still there and in one piece. I can't send Halley a last message from the battlefield, but every time before I go on a mission, I write her a final note and schedule it for a delayed send. If I make it back, I move it back into draft status and cancel the send. If I don't make it back, the computer will send it as instructed. The SI grunts worked this system out years ago as a fail-safe last good-bye, and everyone else in the Fleet adopted it.

The Lanky that peeled off the little group comes directly toward us, even though we are crouching behind a low cluster of rocks. Then its steps become a little halting, and it turns its head toward the sky and then back to the two other Lankies that are now two hundred meters away from it.

"That's right, asshole. Turn around," I murmur. The lone Lanky is still almost two hundred meters away and at the bottom of the little hill we just climbed, but if it gets any closer before close-air support gets here, we'll be danger close, and our body armor won't stop tungsten-tipped autocannon shells.

One hundred and fifty meters. I take aim at the center of the Lanky's mass, knowing full well that the spitball rounds from the pistol won't do much more than annoy the thing at best.

The Lanky hesitates again and comes to a stop about halfway up the slope. Then it turns around and strides back down the hillside to catch up with its two companions. I let out the breath I'd been holding and flick the safety on my pistol again.

Up ahead, where the two Lankies are heading down into the ground depression from which they had appeared just a few minutes ago, dozens of explosions start peppering the ground, throwing up dirt and rocks all around the Lankies and carving a swath of destruction for a hundred meters. A few seconds later, I can hear the roar of the heavy antiarmor cannons of the SAR drop ship from the cloud cover above us. A second burst follows, and the Lankies disappear in geysers of Mars soil. I see a limb flying through the air, torn from a Lanky body by the joint forces of kinetic energy and high explosives, and I smile with grim satisfaction. The last Lanky changes its course abruptly, away from us and the impact zone of the drop ship's cannons. It heads off to the east in as close to a run as I've ever seen a Lanky go, taking fast strides that are at least fifteen meters long.

"One-Niner, you are on target. Splash two. The third one is hauling ass away from us."

"I see him on TacLink. Stand by. We're overhead."

The drop ship, a Dragonfly with external fuel tanks and missiles on its outer ordnance pylons, comes out of the cloud cover two hundred feet above our heads in a tight starboard turn, bleeding off speed from the attack run. Then the pilot pivots the ship and points the nose toward the fleeing Lanky, now almost two kilometers away already.

"Damn, those things can really move when they want," Lieutenant Brassey says.

Overhead, I hear a boom and a whooshing sound. Two missiles leave the launch rails on the outer wing pylons of the Dragonfly and chase after the Lanky. They cover the two thousand meters in just a few seconds and converge on the Lanky in a brilliant orange flash. The thunderclap from the explosion reaches us six or seven seconds later.

"Splash three," the pilot says. "Heads down. We are touching down on the flat spot one-three-zero meters to your direct north." He marks the spot on our TacLink, and the Dragonfly descends in a hover, chin turret swiveling from left to right and back as the gunner is keeping an eye out for more targets.

I stick the pistol back into its holster and stand up.

"Let's go," I tell Lieutenant Brassey. "Before the wings fall off this one, too."

The Dragonfly lands in a cloud of radioactive dust. The tail ramp comes open the moment the skids touch down, and a whole squad of SI troopers in heavy armor dash out and take up perimeter guard positions around the ship. Several of them come running toward us. We meet up halfway between the hill and the drop ship.

"You need a corpsman?" the lead trooper shouts. He's wearing staff sergeant insignia—the new ones, three diagonal slashes over one horizontal one—and carries the short-barreled carbine version of the M-95.

"We don't," I say. "Neither does the pilot."

"Where's the body?"

"Lankies carried it off just before you creamed them from the air. He's gone for good."

The staff sergeant shakes his head slowly and speaks into his squad channel. I take off toward the drop ship at a trot, Lieutenant Brassey in tow.

"Don't hang around," I shout back at the staff sergeant. "The neighbors are kind of pissy."

We board the drop ship with the rescue squad and strap ourselves into jump seats in the center row of the cargo bay. I give the mission control chair at the front bulkhead a wistful look—it's equipped with an emergency eject capsule, but it's the only seat in the cargo bay so equipped. If this bird crashes as well, there's no escaping for me or Brassey again. But the mission control seat is already occupied by the lieutenant in charge of the rescue flight, and it would probably be a little rude to order him out of his spot at gunpoint. So I fasten the harness of my jump seat and hope for the best. In any case, being in here and lifting off in a functional drop ship beats being stranded down there amid the corpses and the irradiated dust. I'm tired and angry, and I don't even bother to ask the pilot for permission to do my customary sensor tap so I can see the feed from the external cameras as we ascend through the cloud coverage and into Mars orbit.

We used to have a creed. We never left a man or woman behind on the battlefield, alive or dead, even if it cost us more lives to retrieve one of our own. But the war against the Lankies has turned that on its head. There's no way to keep up that pledge without immolating ourselves, because we are fighting a war against a physically far superior species that uses our own dead as organic filler. The best we can hope for is a thoroughly destructive death, to deny the Lankies the raw materials they need. On the way up to the carrier, I pull the dog tags of the dead pilot out of the pouch where I stashed them and read the embossed inscription identifying Lieutenant Whitmer, along with his serial number, blood type, and religion. At least he got to be here, on the main battlefield in the ultimate fight for human survival, and he got to make his mark instead of spending his life sucking down shitty soy rations in an overcrowded PRC shithole on Earth. And in retrospect, it was a dumb creed. When I buy it on the battlefield, I don't want other troops to get hurt or killed to retrieve my dead body, which is just going to end up a tiny pile of ashes inside a stainless steel burial capsule anyway.

The docking clamps pull us up into NACS *Hornet*'s flight deck forty minutes later. We disembark and line up for the obligatory decontamination at the decon station in the middle of the flight deck. We've been out of the radiation-shielded drop ship and on the surface of Mars, which means I get to spend an extra fifteen minutes getting my armor and gear sprayed down, then stripping out of the armor and taking multiple trips through the decon shower just in case I had an undetected leak in my armor somewhere. I pick up a fresh set of CDU fatigues at the last station in the decon facility while a Fleet doc looks me over and checks the radiation dosimeter attached to my dog tag.

"Good to go, Captain," he says. "Dosimeter's clean. Just make sure you report to sick bay right away if you start feeling odd."

"I've been feeling odd for years now, Doc," I tell him, and he grins.

Out in the clean section of the flight deck, Lieutenant Brassey is already in a clean new flight suit and fastening the tighteners on his boots.

"You heading back to flight ops before the debrief?" I ask.

"Yeah, for a minute. They'll want to know about what happened."

"Grab the biggest wrench you can find, and then beat your crew chief with it."

Brassey makes a pained face.

"Don't be harsh, Grayson. Sometimes, shit just breaks. Material fatigue, you know?"

"Yeah," I repeat, and let it go. Brassey nods and smiles weakly before taking off toward flight ops. He'll have to get in line for a new bird to fly more combat patrols down there, and part of me suspects he won't be too heartbroken if he has to do shipboard duty for a while because half our hardware is down. Metal and alloy get fatigued when they're overused without rest periods, but so do human brains.

———

Our after-action debriefing is a little more involved this time because we lost an airframe and a pilot and because we had to call on precious SAR assets to haul our asses back to the carrier. I give my version of events, Brassey corroborates it with his version, and none of it serves to put the CAG or the XO in a better mood. The XO is present because we had someone killed in action. I can tell that he's pissed off, but at least his anger is not directed at us. The CAG, the commander of the carrier's air/space group of drop ships and strike fighters, looks like he's already mentally writing the report he'll have to file for a fatality and the total loss of a multi-million-dollar drop ship.

"All things considered, you did an exemplary job," the CAG tells us. He's a major in his early thirties, not much older than I am. "You verified the pilot's status and secured his ID tag, got to a safe spot, and called down air support on the remaining Lankies. That's six confirmed kills today."

"Yes, sir," I reply. *Out of a thousand left underground,* I don't say out loud.

"We're rotating out in seventy-two hours," the XO says. "*Intrepid* is arriving on station in eighteen hours to relieve us, and we'll hand over the shop to them. Why don't you two grab some chow and rack time and then go on standby for the rest of the rotation? And go see the counselor if you need to."

"Yes, sir," Brassey and I say simultaneously.

"Dismissed. And good work down there, both of you. Despite everything else."

We leave the briefing room and go our separate ways. Lieutenant Brassey's place is down in Pilot Country, and I am not a part of that world. They'll need time among themselves to grieve the loss of one of theirs, and nobody takes that sort of thing lightly over sandwiches in the officer wardroom. I didn't know the pilot very well, despite having flown a dozen or more missions with him behind the stick. Once upon a time, I would have been social across departmental boundaries, but these days I mostly keep to myself. You get attached to people, then they die, and you have to deal with the grief and the anger.

Seventy-two hours until we head back to Earth, and there's a week of transit ahead of us after we light the engines and burn for Gateway Station. Being on a Fleet ship with nothing to do for ten days is both a luxury and a tedium. Nobody's shooting at you, but the hours trickle by at a glacial pace. There are a few major advantages to serving in an understaffed and overextended Fleet—I have a private stateroom in Officer Country, and there's no crowd at chow or in the RecFac no matter the time of day. They also restored the big comms relay between Earth and Mars, but there's nobody left on Mars to take advantage of the bandwidth. We can vid-chat home in high definition because the few garrison ships of the Olympus Highway Patrol have the relay mostly to themselves.

"What the fuck is that thing?" I ask Halley, who is coming in sharp and clear over the Fleet vid-chat link.

"What thing?"

I point at my screen. "That staff officer bar on your rank sleeves."

Halley looks at the rank insignia on her shoulders—a single star above a horizontal bar—as if she's seeing them for the first time.

"Huh. Would you look at that? How did that get there?"

"You made *major* already? You don't have the time in service yet."

"That's what I told them, too. But it goes with the new assignment I'm starting next month."

"O-4 is, what, ten years in service at the earliest?"

"Used to be," she confirms. "Ten years in service, three years in grade as O-3. I have eight in service and two in grade. They insisted. What are you so surprised about, Andrew? You got your third star early, too."

"That's different," I say, and glance at my own rank insignia, the three stars of a captain I've been wearing for three months now. "I'm a junior officer. Time in grade to make captain was only three years even before the Lanky business." I just now parse her earlier reveal. "*Wait.* New assignment? Back to teaching at Drop Ship U?"

"Thank the gods, no." Halley grins and shakes her head. "I have had my fill of classrooms and simulators."

"So where's the new gig?"

"Assault Transport Squadron Five. I'll be their new XO."

"Congratulations," I say. "*Major.* Where's ATS-5?"

"Right now they only exist on paper. They're getting assigned to a new ship. I'll be reporting to Combat Aviation School on Luna to help ferry the hardware."

"Could be worse," I say, which is of course a massive understatement. The only class of ship that fits a whole squadron of drop ships is one of the Fleet's few remaining carriers, which are the most spacious and modern units in the Fleet. Halley and I started our careers on a cramped old frigate that would probably fit into a supercarrier's hangar bay in its entirety once you knocked off all the antenna arrays and trimmed the exhaust nozzles by a few meters.

"What's your status? Your rotation should be just about over," Halley says.

"It is. We're getting relieved by *Intrepid* in a few hours, and then we're heading home. I don't have new orders yet. This ship's headed for the fleet yard, though."

"Maybe we can have some leave time together. It's been six months. Why did you have to do two rotations back to back?"

"They told me to," I say. "But yeah. Shore leave sounds good. I have no shortage of leave time."

"Then get your ass home, Captain."

"I'll tell the helmsman to step on it."

I briefly think about telling Halley about the drop ship crash and my latest close call, but then I decide to put it off until we can see each other in person. I could have died but didn't, something that has happened to us a hundred times each in the last eight years. If I talk about it, I want to be out on a walk in the mountains of Vermont, not sitting in front of a terminal screen. So I sign off with a smile, as if my last few hours have involved nothing more exciting than stubbing a toe on a hatch ledge. We do what we have to do to keep ourselves sane in this grind.

CHAPTER 3

———— PROMISES TO KEEP ————

Every time I dock at Gateway again, I'm surprised that the station hasn't yet fallen out of its orbit and rained down on the North American continent in a shower of glowing wreckage parts. I don't know what the expected service life of the station was when they opened it, but I know that Gateway is well past it. Many of the high-traffic corridors and concourses have ruts walked into the nonslip deck padding, and I've never made a transfer between two nonadjacent airlocks when I didn't pass a corridor that was closed and secured with safety barriers because of urgent maintenance. There are only so many times you can patch and weld a piece of hull section or bulkhead before the whole thing starts crumbling at the seams.

Hornet is going to the fleet yard for an overhaul, and a big chunk of her crew is leaving the ship here at Gateway to catch rides to their next commands, which means that getting off the ship is a royal pain in the ass. Thousands of crew and embarked SI troopers have to pass through the same airlock. At least Gateway isn't as crowded as I've seen it lately. With the garrison force on Mars in an established deployment cycle, we no longer have to move everything on the board at the same time. Even with all the new arrivals from *Hornet*, I can make my way along the main concourse without getting pushed along or knocking my gear bag into people.

At the transfer station, a Fleet staff sergeant and two corporals manage to look both bored and harried at the same time. I let them scan my orders, and they assign me a seat on a shuttle.

"Eighteen hundred hours," I say and check my chrono. "That's six and a half hours from now. You have no other transport going down to the biggest Fleet base on the East Coast earlier than that?"

"None that have any space on them, Captain." The staff sergeant in charge makes a vaguely all-encompassing gesture with one hand. "Look around you, sir. *Phalanx* arrived just before you did. They're doing a full crew change before they have to head for the nuke yard for a restock, so they get priority billing on the shuttle seats."

"Great. So much to do around here for six hours. Nothing you can do to get me down to Norfolk earlier? I'll strap myself to a cargo pallet if I have to."

The staff sergeant consults his terminal screen.

"Nothing open until 1800, sir."

"Fuck."

"Tell you what," he says. "If I have something opening up, I'll send you an update on your PDP. Best I can do right now, sir."

"It'll have to do," I reply. "Thanks."

Gateway doesn't have much to do for people who have to kill time. There's a single RecFac on the main concourse, but when I stop by to check it out, even the officers' section is crowded.

It appears that I'm not the only one waiting for a ride down to Earth. I duck back out of the RecFac and go to one of the chow halls. I've been an officer for a year now, and it has taken me this long to reliably steer for the officers' mess instead of the enlisted mess without having to think about it. Gateway's officers' mess is about five times the size of a shipboard one, and the food is served buffet-style. I settle in and head over to the buffet, expecting to see the usual varieties of soy-based garbage we've been eating since the exodus, but I'm pleasantly surprised to see reconstituted mashed potatoes, chicken that looks like actual chicken, and three varieties of vegetables. There are even dessert options, something I haven't seen in a Fleet chow hall in a long time.

"What's up with the luxury chow?" I ask one of the mess orderlies, who shrugs.

"It's been getting better. Haven't served any soy in two months, sir."

"Outstanding," I say and heap on another spoonful of mashed potatoes. Then I sit down at a table to message Halley while I'm eating, to let her know that I am safely on Gateway. The bandwidth this close to Earth is good enough for video, and Halley picks up after the third hail. From the background, I can see that I caught her at lunch as well.

"What about it?" she says when I pan my PDP over the plate to show her the stuff on my plate.

"It's real food," I say. "Well, sort of. Not as good as what we had before. But edible."

"Yeah. The chow has improved a lot recently. I see fresh fruit at just about every breakfast now. And real eggs, not the powdered shit."

"I thought we were broke."

"That's what I thought, too. Rumor has it that the Euros and the Aussies have kicked in a bunch of cash to keep the show going. Guess they figured out that if we get our asses kicked up here, they'll be next."

"Where are you?" I ask.

"Officers' mess at Armstrong," she says. Fleet Station Armstrong is one of the main bases on the moon, and the one with the biggest military spaceport.

"Tell me your leave went through."

"My leave went through," she says. "Heading down to Earth tomorrow."

"My shuttle out is at 1800 tonight. I have to report to Norfolk before I go on leave."

"You still don't have your next assignment?" Halley asks.

"Nope. Hope I don't get to supervise a bunch of bored corporals in the TPU while the Fleet figures out what to do with me."

"They won't. You're a podhead, not a filing clerk."

"Wouldn't be the first time I used my podhead training for folding towels."

"Well, if that's what happens, then you make sure they're the most precisely folded towels the TPU has ever seen. Now finish your chow and don't miss your shuttle. I don't want to waste a minute of this leave. Not after six months of enforced celibacy."

"You're coming in loud and clear, Major," I say with a smile and sign off.

———————

For once, I get lucky in the game of seat-assignment lotto. Not fifteen minutes after I finish my meal, the PDP in my pocket vibrates. I take it out and look at the screen to see that the transfer station has assigned me a seat on a departing shuttle at 1230. I check my chrono, which shows 12:10. The shuttle leaves from an airlock that's on the opposite end of the concourse, naturally.

"Always a fly in the soup," I mutter and shoulder my gear bag for a mad dash through the busy concourse.

The ride down to Earth is smooth and reasonably scenic, and I managed to snag a window seat in the back of the shuttle. Most of the North American continent lies under a hazy smog pall as always, but there are breaks in the clouds here and there, and even the smog can be beautiful in its own way, painted from below as it is by millions of lights. When we descend through the cloud cover, we're somewhere above the Northeast, just a few hundred miles southeast of Vermont, and I feel a surprising little pang of homesickness when I see the Green Mountains poking out of the haze in the distance. Directly below the shuttle, the supertall high-rise towers of many Category Five PRCs poke out of the haze, collision avoidance beacons blazing on their rooftop masts and painting the smog in flashing streaks of red. Every time I fly over the East Coast on the way into Norfolk, I am reminded just how densely populated this part of the country really is. From the air, the sea of fusion-powered lights stretches for thousands of kilometers. You could probably walk from Miami all the way to Halifax without stepping into a single patch of grass.

Norfolk is a gigantic base, bigger than almost every other military installation we have. Back in the days of the old United States, it was a wet-navy base, but now it's one of the three main Fleet hubs on Earth, the other two being Great Lakes and San Diego. Whoever decided the locations for the operations hubs of a space-going fleet must have had a lot of nostalgia for ocean ports, even though most of the traffic from the bases goes up into orbit and not out into the ocean. It would have made more sense to put the Fleet bases in the Rockies and ten thousand feet closer to orbit, but this is the military, and making sense is against service tradition.

The shuttle touches down on one of the many landing pads of the air/space field at 1345 hours. I hitch a succession of rides from the flight-ops building to the inner core of the base, where the base command buildings are clustered around a second, smaller airfield. Even through the ever-present smog haze, I smell the ocean just a few blocks away.

Fleet Special Warfare Group Two is headquartered in a small, dingy two-story building that looks like it may have been in service since before there was a NAC Defense Corps. There are no field units quartered here, just the administrative and command elements. The place is lousy with staff officers and high-ranking NCOs wearing mostly service Bravos, the usual staff-duty uniform with slacks and short-sleeve shirt. I am wearing mine as well, the prescribed uniform for travel and reporting to new commands, but I wear it so rarely that it feels like I'm in a costume.

The commanding officer of Special Warfare Group Two has his office all the way at the end of the building. The door is open, and I peek around the corner to see if the colonel is busy. Colonel Masoud is not wearing his service Bravos. I have never seen him in anything but his faded camouflage CDUs, sleeves crisply rolled and folded without a wrinkle, no accouterments other than his name tape and the gold space special warfare badge. I knew from the message traffic on MilNet he had been bumped in rank since Mars, but this is the first time I've seen him with the new rank insignia. I knock on the frame of his open office door, and he looks up from the printout he was reading. I drop my gear bag and snap a salute.

"Captain Grayson reporting as ordered, sir."

"Come in, Captain," Colonel Masoud says and nods at the empty chair in front of his desk. "Have a seat."

"Yes, sir." I move my gear bag out of the way and sit down as directed. I haven't seen the colonel in person since just after the Second Battle of Mars, but he always treats me like I had just been in his office earlier in the day. He doesn't waste time with perfunctory politeness, and I suspect he doesn't give a shit whether people like it or not.

"Congratulations on your promotion, Captain," Colonel Masoud says.

"Thank you, sir. Likewise. You got to skip O-5 altogether?"

"Oh no," he says. "I was already O-5 once before I had some . . . disagreements with my superiors. They restored that rank after Mars. Then they added a pay grade on top, because there weren't enough suckers around to compete for this job."

Special Warfare Group Two has four SOCOM teams under it, and there is only one other special warfare group in the Fleet, which means that Colonel Masoud is now the commanding officer of half the

Fleet's SEALs, Spaceborne Rescuemen, and combat controllers. With the shortage of senior officers in nearly every combat specialty, I suspect that he had that role unofficially already since our massive ass-kicking by the Lankies at the First Battle of Mars and that they merely made his position official and finally gave him the stars and the pay that went with it.

"How are things on Mars?" Colonel Masoud asks. I know that he has a very good picture of what's going on because he's a hard-nosed perfectionist, but I humor him anyway.

"Pretty awful," I say. "We have them contained, and we're killing them whenever they poke their heads out. But we're grinding up our gear. And the troops are just as worn out as the ships."

"Garrison duty is bad for people and machines. But we can't afford to take the pressure off the Lankies, or we'll be right back at square one in a year."

"Yes, sir. Everyone is aware of that. But double deployments are too long out there. People get tired, and then they make mistakes."

"I've argued with command about the length of the rotations, but we just don't have enough qualified SOCOM people on the roster to allow for six-month tours. Which brings me to your new orders."

He pulls a printout from the stack of papers on his desk and studies it with a frown. Then he turns toward his terminal and flicks through a few screens.

"You have been assigned to a new ship. It's classified, so you won't know the hull number or class until you report to your new duty station. You will, however, be able to deduce something from the fact that your new assignment is special tactics officer."

The special tactics officer, or STO, is the junior grade officer in charge of a group of combat controllers. To have a whole group of red hats under me, the new ship has to have at least a battalion of embarked SI troops, and more likely a full regiment. That means the classified ship has got to be a supercarrier, the only Fleet unit large enough to embark a full regiment.

"I have too few trained veterans around as it is. I don't feel particularly happy about having to loan out one of my scarce assets to someone else. But I don't have the last word on personnel issues around here, even though the plaque on the door says 'Commanding Officer.'" He shakes his head at the contents of his terminal screen.

He hands me the printout he's been holding, which is a standard orders form with my data on it.

"Enjoy your leave, Captain. You've earned some time off after two deployments in a row. On December 1, you will report to the transfer station listed on your orders, and they will arrange for transportation to your new command."

Knowing Colonel Masoud, I have the distinct feeling that he already knows the exact nature and purpose of my new command. But I know he takes pleasure in playing his cards close to his chest.

"Yes, sir." I get out of my chair and salute, then turn on my heel to leave.

"One more thing, Captain."

"Sir?" I turn around again to face the colonel.

"You need to correct your uniform."

"How so, sir?" I ask.

"I distinctly remember putting you in for the Fleet Cross after Arcadia. I also remember reading that the award was approved and issued. But your ribbon rack isn't showing that award."

I look down at the rows of ribbons on my Class B shirt. They're sorted by order of award precedence, and the item on top is the blue-white-red ribbon of a Silver Star, with a little gold star in the center to denote a second award. Colonel Masoud is looking for the black ribbon with the white, vertical center stripe that belongs to the Fleet Cross. Mine is still in the award box, where it has been since the skipper of a previous command awarded me the medal six months after Arcadia.

"Huh. Must have forgotten to update my ribbon rack, sir. I don't wear this smock a lot."

"I see." Colonel Masoud studies me for a few moments with dark eyes that don't betray any emotion.

"Captain," he says finally. "Let's skip the pleasantry bullshit for a minute. You still have a chip on your shoulder about Arcadia. Even after three years."

"I didn't know there's a statute of limitations for being angry that a third of your platoon died. *Sir.*"

"And you blame me for that. Even though you were the one who planned and executed that assault. That hardly seems fair." Colonel Masoud leans back in his chair and folds his arms in front of his chest. "We lost over a third of our entire Spaceborne Infantry branch on Mars. Do you blame command for those deaths too?"

"That was different," I say. "We all knew the plan from the start before we went into battle on Mars. We didn't use anyone as diversions."

"And troops died nonetheless, just like on Arcadia."

"Maybe fewer would have died if you had let me in on the plan. Maybe I would have planned things differently. I wouldn't have felt like we had no alternative."

Colonel Masoud sighs and unfolds his arms again. Then he leans forward and puts his elbows on the desk in front of him. He studies me over his steepled fingers.

"Captain Grayson, you are one rank away from being a staff officer yourself. If you want to stay sane, you must stop second-guessing your choices as a field commander. It's not productive. It serves no purpose. And it will mess you up in the long run. If you falter or hesitate on your next combat drop because you are thinking about the casualties on your last drop, you will not be able to function, and more troops will die."

"With all due respect, sir—I hope I never stop second-guessing myself. I'd like to think that I still have a shit left to give about the fate of my troops."

Colonel Masoud flashes a thin-lipped smile.

"Why do I have the feeling that every time you say 'with all due respect,' you don't really mean it?"

I hesitate for a moment. Then I return his smile in an equally humorless fashion. I don't want to spend my leave time in the brig, so I moderate my reply and don't give him the two-word answer that's really on my tongue.

"Because you are unusually perceptive, sir," I say instead.

For a moment, Colonel Masoud just looks at me, and I am convinced that I've managed to tip-toe right across the line with him. Then he sighs almost imperceptibly and shakes his head.

"Maybe we'll talk about this subject again when you are a staff officer. But the next time I see you in service Bravos, I *will* see that Fleet Cross ribbon on your uniform. You're dismissed, Captain."

"Yes, sir," I reply.

I pick up my gear and walk out. In two weeks, I will worry about uniform ribbons, black ops, and cloak-and-dagger stuff again. Until then, I have fifteen days of leave, far away from Lankies, drop ships, and Colonel Khaled Masoud.

CHAPTER 4

LEAVE

I always feel a disconnect for the first day or two of leave. It's like dropping off a cliff and hitting the water hard, only to feel yourself sinking in a bottomless pool. In the Fleet and on deployment, my life is structured, scheduled, regimented, and confined. I move in the tight quarters of a warship, work in watch cycles or physically and mentally grinding ground deployments, and move and live under constant supervision. Then I leave Gateway and go Earthside, and twelve hours after the end of my deployment, I have freedom of movement and unlimited travel privileges on an entire half continent, with nobody looking over my shoulder. I know where I am going and how to get there, but I feel lost and anxious at first, too much elbow room after too long a stretch in a metal tube in space.

None of the northbound shuttle flights have available passenger slots tonight, so I leave the base and take the train up to the transit station in Richmond. From there, I switch trains to a maglev going up the East Coast. It's slower than flying, but faster than staying on the base in Norfolk overnight and taking a chance with shuttle seats in the morning. But I don't mind the maglev trip so much. As the train zooms north through the Washington/Baltimore metroplex and then

Philadelphia and New York City, I have time to decompress and get used to being among civvies again, even if I stick out in my uniform and with my sidearm and gear bag. With the threat of surprise Lanky incursions removed for now, at least we no longer have to carry alert bags with PDWs and light armor, but we still have to wear pistols. I spend the time reading news on my PDP and looking at the urban landscape gliding by outside. The train cuts through some of the most densely populated ground on this planet, but it feels nowhere near as claustrophobic as the enlisted mess on a frigate at chow time. Somewhere between Philadelphia and New York City, I doze off, and by the time I wake up from my nap, the train is slowing down to pull into the Boston transit terminal. For the last leg of the journey, I have to change trains to the Green Mountain Line, and I manage to catch the last maglev for the evening with ten minutes to spare.

It takes a little under an hour to get from Boston to Liberty Falls. I take this ride almost every time I come down to Earth because I usually take the shuttle down to Homeworld Defense Air Station Falmouth, just south of the Boston metroplex. And like every time, my anxiety starts falling away when the maglev passes the Vermont line and crosses over into mostly unpopulated mountains. When I reach the Liberty Falls stop, I am still tired and a little bleary-eyed, but I no longer feel lost and unmoored. If I have a home on this planet, this is it, even though the place where I stay doesn't belong to me or Halley.

The streets of Liberty Falls are quiet at this hour, ten minutes past midnight on a weekday. It's mid-November, and there isn't any snow on the ground yet, but the air is clean and cold, and there's frost on the grass outside. In another fifty or sixty years, one of the nearby metroplexes will probably grow to swallow up this tidy little town, but for now it's as different from the PRCs as Mars is from Greenland.

At Chief Kopka's restaurant, everything is dark and locked. I didn't tell my mother or the chief when I would be in because I didn't want anyone to stay up and wait for me. The chief added Halley and me to the biometric security pad at the back door a few years back so we can let ourselves in, and I let the pad scan my fingerprints and then head upstairs to the small guest bedroom Halley and I get to use whenever we are on Earthside leave. It's a small room, with just enough space for a bed, a pair of dressers, and a desk, but it looks out over Liberty Falls's main street, and it has a private bathroom. Compared to most Fleet accommodations, it's palatial, and much cozier than a windowless berth with steel furniture that's bolted to the deck. I drop my gear bag, take off my uniform shirt, and get the PDP out of my pocket to send a message to Halley.

>Made it to the Falls.

Her reply comes back a few minutes later.

>Bastard.

>Love you too.

>If you really did, you would have spent a night on a crappy cot in the TPU on base in solidarity with your wife.

>It appears that even true love has its limits. Waiting for you while drinking the chief's coffee. Hurry up and have a safe ride down.

>Enjoy your coffee. See you tomorrow. And go to sleep. I need you rested.

I sign off MilNet with a grin. Then I undress to take a shower in the little bathroom and wash the travel grime off before going to bed. My mind wants to keep me awake with replaying the conversation I had with Colonel Masoud, but my fatigue wins out, and I fall asleep as soon as my head hits the pillow.

———————

In the morning, I wake up to the sound of activity downstairs in the restaurant. I can smell the faint scent of fresh coffee and hear the clinking of plates and the low din of conversation. I check my chrono, which shows 0638. Then I get out of bed and grab a set of civvie clothes from the dresser. At some point in the last two or three years, when our stays here in Liberty Falls became semiregular, Halley and I bought a few civilian outfits to wear while we're on leave so we won't stick out everywhere we go here in the safe little 'burber town. People here aren't used to seeing armed corps personnel in the streets. Before then, I hadn't even owned any nonissued clothing in years. After so many years in uniform, putting on civilian clothes feels a little bit like I'm pretending to be someone else.

"When did you get in?" my mother asks when I walk downstairs and into the restaurant, where she is busy setting the tables. She puts down the bundle of napkins in her hands and comes over to give me a long, firm hug.

"About 0100," I say. "Couldn't catch a flight from Norfolk on short notice, so I had to take the train. Good morning, Chief," I say to Chief Kopka, who sticks his head out of the kitchen at the sound of my voice.

"Morning, Andrew. Cup of coffee, Captain?"

"Affirmative," I say. "Very much affirmative."

He nods and disappears in the kitchen again.

"How long is your leave?" Mom asks.

"Two weeks," I say. "Two deployments' worth saved up."

"Is Halley coming too?"

"She'll be in later today. She had to stay up on Luna overnight because she couldn't get a late shuttle down."

"I'm so glad to hear it," Mom says. "It's been too long. Six months since you've been home. At least your wife makes it down here once a month or so."

"The commute from the moon is a lot shorter than the one from Mars orbit, Mom. Just the transit back from there takes a week."

"How are we looking up there?" the chief asks. He's coming out of the kitchen holding a little serving platter with a mug of coffee and a small container of cream.

"We're playing whack-a-mole with the leftover Lankies," I say. "All air missions. We fly patrols and drop missiles on anything that moves. I get to sit in a drop ship all day and look at console screens while flying through shit weather."

"I figured they'd all be dead by now."

"So did we all. But they're still popping out from under the surface. Like cockroaches. But we're much better off than the year before last."

"Those were dark days," the chief says. "The darkest."

"Mars wasn't a win. But at least it wasn't a loss. We'll get 'em off that rock, sooner or later."

I sit down in one of the booths, the customary one that Halley and I pick when we're down here, and the chief puts the serving platter onto the table in front of me.

"Is that cream?"

"Sure is," the chief replies. "Got eggs again, too. The breakfast menu is almost back to the way it was."

I pour a healthy dollop of the fresh cream from the chilled porcelain container into my coffee.

"The Fleet chow has gotten better, too. Maybe things are looking up again."

Chief Kopka smiles and does a little drumbeat with his hands on the table. "Things *are* looking up. I can source fresh milk and eggs again. And meat and pork and chicken. I don't care how they unclogged the supply chain. I'm just glad I can cook proper food. For a while there, I was sure I'd have to shutter the place. Of course, that wasn't exactly our biggest worry."

I stir the coffee, take a sip, and let out a little involuntary groan.

"Good, huh?" the chief says.

"Good doesn't cover it," I reply. "I've been looking forward to this cup for six months."

The chief has to prepare breakfasts, and Mom has to set the tables and get the place ready for opening, so I leave them to their tasks and sip my coffee leisurely while I watch the pedestrian traffic on Main Street through the window by my booth. I used to have a massive chip on my shoulder about these upper middle class 'burbers, living in relative wealth and comfort not two hundred kilometers away from the PRC where I grew up with none of those privileges. But over the years, I've come to realize that they're no more to blame or hate for their circumstances than any welfare rat, and I've stopped feeling guilty about enjoying the little luxuries of this place.

My PDP buzzes halfway through my second cup of coffee. It's not the distinct alert pattern of a Lanky incursion, so I ignore the device until I am finished with my coffee. Then I take it out and check the screen.

>About to hop on the shuttle. I'll let you know when we're skids down and I'm on the train.

>See you in a few hours.

I always have to smile at the notion of one of the Fleet's best drop ship pilots having to make the trip down to Earth in a dingy shuttle, strapped into a seat in the back next to a hundred console jockeys and wrench spinners. With her drop ship, she could ferry herself to any place in the NAC without having to take trains or go by departure schedules. The Fleet would never let her use a drop ship as a personal taxi, of course, but I'm amused at the thought of a Dragonfly landing on Main Street right in front of the chief's restaurant, and Halley casually hopping out of the cockpit like she's parking a hydrocar.

I nurse my coffee until just before eight o'clock, when the chief opens the doors of the place for breakfast. Halley and I always clear out when the restaurant opens so we don't take up space for paying customers. The chief keeps insisting that we don't owe him anything for all the food and drink we have gotten from him over the years, but between all of that and the rent he doesn't charge us for the use of the private guest room upstairs, I know that I'll give him a sizable chunk of my discharge pay if I make it to the end of my service time alive.

Most of the shops on Main Street aren't open this early, but some are. I go for a walk and look at store windows, checking out things I don't need and can't afford even though my service account has almost a million Commonwealth dollars in it after eight years of service. All of that money only gets released after I leave the military. Main Street stretches for two kilometers, from the transit station in the south to the recreational park with the little waterfall in the north, with lots of quaint little stores and public buildings in between. The library on the village green is open, and I walk in and sit down at one of the public terminals to catch up on news.

Halley sends me an update an hour later.

>On the train from Boston. ETA Falls 1045.

I log off the terminal and put my jacket back on for the hike down to the transit station, where the train will arrive to the minute in a little less than an hour. Usually I feel a pleasant anticipation when I know I'm about to see my wife again, especially after six months apart, but this time there's a fair bit of anxiety tempering the pleasure. I haven't told her about my new assignment, and I can't imagine she'll be wildly excited about me going off to another deployment again without any idea where I'm going just yet. We got spoiled being stationed Earthside or on Luna together, and only now, after my eighteen months in the Brigades and two deployments over Mars, do we get to feel the full weight of the hardships again that come with military marriages.

My wife steps out onto the little plaza in front of the transit station just as the first snowflakes of the year are drifting out of the sky. She's in her Fleet service Alphas, the slightly dressy uniform with an overcoat, and she's carrying just a little kit bag.

"You still look strange in civvie threads," she says to me after our exchange of firm hugs and publically appropriate kisses.

"I feel strange," I say. "Like I'm playing someone in a Network show. But it's comfy and warm at least."

"I can't wait to get out of this monkey suit."

"Why are you wearing your Alphas?"

"I was at PXO course for the last ten days. Monkey suit mandatory."

"What do they teach in PXO course? 'One Hundred Ways to Chew Out Junior Officers'?"

"You learn that every XO gets to kill three enlisted fuck-ups per deployment cycle, no questions asked." Halley shoulders her bag and looks around the plaza.

"Hey, look at that. Snow."

"It won't stick just yet. Ground's still too warm. Temperatures like this, we'll barely have frost at night."

"Yeah, but it looks pretty. I've seen nothing but grungy bulkheads and artificial lighting for almost two weeks."

We walk up the road toward Chief Kopka's restaurant. As always, Halley cuts through the little park in front of the transit plaza and runs a hand across the grass, which is lightly frosted with snowflakes. She does this every time we get into Liberty Falls. If they ever get rid of this park and pave over the lot, I think she'd declare war on the town government. I watch her but don't join in.

"You seem a little glum," Halley says. "We have two weeks of leave ahead of us. Perk up a little."

"I got deployment orders yesterday," I say. "Directly from Colonel Cut-Throat."

She looks up at me from her crouched position on the grass and squints.

"Not another tour of Mars."

"It's not Mars." I look past her and down Main Street, where the civvies are going about their days, unaware of all the shit that's going on millions of kilometers away to keep them safe.

"Got assignment to a new ship," I continue. "Masoud gave me their special tactics team, so it's got to be at least a space-control can."

"You got orders and you don't know where they're sending you?"

"I know this drill," I say. "It's a brand-new ship. Classified name and hull number. But Masoud says it's not going to Mars, so I have no clue. If I had to bet, I'd put money on either training for something new and stupidly dangerous, or going out of system."

"Going out of system is stupidly dangerous, too," Halley says. "The *Archie* has an Alcubierre drive now, but there's no way they'll pull the only battleship we have left off Earth defense duty. So whatever you're going in, it's going to be Lanky bait."

Arkhangelsk, still under SRA command, is now the cornerstone of our planetary defense. We have Orion batteries, of course, but the number of missiles is limited because each of them requires hundreds of nuclear warheads. The civvies on Earth need the security of being able to check the Network news feed and see that battleship moored at the SRA station or doing orbital patrols. She'll never leave the solar system without backup or replacement, even if she does finally have the ability. Her sister ship, *Agincourt,* is well on the way out of the solar system by now, with a destroyed drive system and no crew left on board. She took a hit from some seed ship wreckage at the Battle of Mars and went on an unrecoverable trajectory at flank speed, so the skipper had no choice but to give the Abandon Ship order.

"So I'll go be XO in a carrier's transport squadron, and you'll be off doing shady stuff for Masoud," she says. "Hey, maybe they'll put us on the same ship again."

"We've had that luck twice. Three times, if you count *Regulus.* Lightning's not gonna strike four times in the same spot."

"You never know," Halley says. She gets up from her crouch and wipes her hand on her jacket. "Fleet's not that big anymore. They retired a ton of the old cans we used for Mars. Too expensive to run, and they won't do any good against the Lankies anyway. We kind of blew most of our powder at Mars."

"This is the military, remember? You get a luck budget. And I think we've overdrawn ours by a lot already."

"Maybe," she says and blinks into the sky, where the snowflakes are drifting down in the cool breeze. "But mathematically speaking, you start with the same odds every time. Just wait and see where the chips fall. There's no point fretting over it because we can't do shit about it anyway."

We've almost reached Chief Kopka's restaurant, which probably has the first breakfast guests already, enjoying their coffees and their omelets made with real eggs and cheese. Halley doesn't go to the front entrance. Instead, she goes around the building to use the back door, the one that leads to the upstairs guest apartment.

"We'll get lucky again," she says with confidence. "But just in case we don't, let's get the most out of this shore leave."

She uses the biometric pad to unlock the door and nods at the staircase.

"Get your ass up there and join me in the shower, Captain. And then let's have a decadent brunch, go for a hike, and not talk a word about the fucking Fleet for a week straight."

"Tailpipe One, copy five by five," I say.

CHAPTER 5

EARTHSIDE

When you are stuck on a starship on interplanetary transit, a week and a half usually seems like a tedious eternity. When you're on leave, the same span of time flies by so quickly you'd swear someone held down a finger on the universe's temporal fast-forward button. It's late November, and winter is making its approach known with occasional snow flurries that don't stick on the ground yet. It won't be long before they do, but I'll be away on my next deployment by then, and I'll miss the snow again, for the third year running.

Halley and I spend our leave in the usual manner. We go for long hikes in the quiet autumn landscape around Liberty Falls, expanding our bubble of known geography a little every time, eating the lunches we bring along while sitting on fallen logs or granite ledges. Not only is the food far better than anything in the Fleet, but the setting for these meals is as different from officer wardrooms as possible. I've had meals outside while on planetary deployments, of course, but this isn't the same. Instead of eating cold rations while under the stress of combat, I have warm meals from thermal lunchboxes, sitting next to my wife under a cloudy autumn sky and looking over a wooded valley or babbling mountain brook with no other people in our field of vision. After a few days of open skies and the quietness of nature, I feel my tension and fatigue ebbing away as if this place had opened a relief valve in my brain.

We hike during the days. We come back in the evenings for dinner, which the chief leaves for us in our guest room upstairs in insulated to-go boxes. Then we go back out for strolls down Main Street whenever the weather is still agreeable. It has become our unwritten rule that we don't sleep with each other in the guest room while there's still someone downstairs in the restaurant—not because Mom or the chief would ever come up and bother us, but because it doesn't feel right. But once the place closes and they take off for the night, we drop our restraint.

"Do you remember what you told your mother the last time we went to see them?" I ask.

Halley wraps one of my arms around herself and places it against her stomach. We're lying in bed spooned against each other, limbs comfortably entangled, listening to the noises out on Main Street. It's a Friday night, and people are out, despite the low temperatures.

"I try to forget that visit," Halley says. "What part do you mean in particular? The one where I called her a spiteful bitch?"

"The part about maybe having kids. You told her that if you got pregnant, you'll have it tubed until we get out of the service."

"Oh, that."

"Are you really thinking about it?"

"What, getting pregnant? Not really." She looks at me over her shoulder and then rolls over to face me.

"I mean, you know the regs. They won't even deactivate the birth control implant as long as I'm in a spacefaring billet. I'd have to apply for shore duty and then get permission to get pregnant. And then we'd have to tube it anyway. Until we're done with our service."

"Unless you resign your commission and get out early."

"And give up all the separation money. All those years for nothing."

"Yeah," I say. "That wouldn't be smart."

"I can't say it's at the top of my list right now," Halley says. "Having a kid. Bringing another person into this shitshow. We've got a handle on the Lankies, but you and I both know they could be back any day."

"What about after? When we're out of the service and sitting on our back pay?"

Halley is silent for a few seconds. Then she lets out a small sigh and shrugs.

"I want to, eventually. Because I want a piece of you and me to continue if one of us buys it out there. Pretty selfish, huh? Three hundred billion of us, and I think the two of us are so special that we need to add to that number."

"Why shouldn't we? They don't have that moral dilemma in the PRCs. They get absolute shit to eat, crime is through the roof, they get free birth control, and they still have children."

"Anything true to the rumor that the Commonwealth puts birth control in the drinking water there?" Halley asks.

I chuckle.

"I don't think so. Have you seen the birth rates? They are filling up the housing as fast as we can build it. But that rumor has been around as long as I've been alive. People believe what they want to believe."

"Can't really blame them. I'd have a hard time putting it past them. Not after what the old government pulled when they packed up and left for their galactic resort."

We lie in silence for a while. After more than a week of being back in our leave routine, my brain has conditioned itself to make me sleepy at the end of our regular sequence of activities, and there's a great deal of comfort in that predictability.

"Yes, I want children with you," Halley murmurs, obviously starting to drift off just like I am. "When we're no longer riding the bullet every day anymore. When we've pried those spindly fucks out of our solar system. But for now, let's put our energy into not getting killed."

"Fair enough," I reply, even though I know that it's not even a little bit up to us. But it helps to have at least the illusion of control.

Halley's leave is shorter than mine by a day because she didn't save up as much as I did. I could stay in the Falls and spend that day by myself, but I know I'd be bored out of my skull down here alone. So when Halley packs her gear bag and gets back into uniform, I do the same.

"What are you going to do?" Halley asks as we're tucking our civvie clothes back into the dresser drawers in the guest room. "You're not due to report to Luna until Sunday."

"I'll come to Falmouth with you and see you off," I say. "After that, maybe take a train trip and see what's up at Shughart. I've got the time."

"Not that I don't like you coming along on the train ride with me, but you have a screw loose, Andrew. You could goof off here for a whole day instead. Catch the shuttle from Burlington to Luna and be there in two hours."

"Nah," I say. "This is our place. Doesn't feel right when we're not here together."

"That's sweet." She leans in and kisses me on the corner of my mouth. "Dumb, but sweet. If it were me, I'd be crawling back into bed right now and sleeping until the last possible minute."

Our ride back to Boston is probably the least tense we've ever taken together on the way to new assignments. Until we took out the Lanky seed ships above Mars, every deployment was a crisis, the fire brigade rushing to a massive conflagration and head-on into mortal danger. Ever since then, it's different. We're both still anxious because you never know what can happen out there, but the Damocles sword of imminent extinction is no longer swinging over our heads by a fraying thread.

When we reach South Station in Boston, I accompany Halley down to the government level of the station to get on the military-only train out to Falmouth, where she will hitch a ride up to Gateway and then on to her new command. I'm not much for public good-byes, but I also want to stay with her until that good-bye is inevitable.

We see each other off in our usual way—firm hugs, short kisses, and no drawn-out ceremony. I may be back here in a month or three or six, and there's no telling when we'll see each other again until we both get to our new commands and figure out just where the hell we're going and what we'll be doing. We may even be in the same place for the holidays, which would be a first. We have parted under far more dire and desperate circumstances, headed out for much more dangerous assignments. This feels so routine and low-key that it seems almost unnatural.

"See you on leave, Andrew," Halley says, and flattens the wrinkles on my CDU blouse's chest with her palm. "Don't get killed, or I'll be pissed."

"Staying away from Lankies and malfunctioning equipment. Yes, ma'am."

The military train announces its imminent arrival with a gust of air that blows out of the train tube and across the platform. A few moments later, the train glides into the station and comes to a stop gradually and almost silently. The doors slide open with a soft hiss. Halley plants a last kiss on my lips, grabs her gear bag, and steps onto the train. I take my own bag and start walking back to the escalator without looking back, which is how we like to part, pretending that the next few months of separation are no big thing. But when I get to the bottom of the escalator, I turn around anyway and glance at the train car, and I can see that Halley is looking back at me. I shake my head with a grin, and she smiles back at me, a small and wistful-looking smile. Then her train departs and glides off into the tunnel, and a few junior enlisted walk past me up the escalator, careful to give me a respectful berth. I sigh and shoulder my kit bag. Then I follow the privates and corporals upstairs, back to the public section of the station.

With almost two days until I have to report in at Luna, I have plenty of time on my hands. From Boston, the maglevs go north, south, and west, and I can take any of them for free with my military ID. I take the Lakeshore Line, which goes from Boston to Buffalo and then down to Cleveland and Toledo, where my old HD base is located.

There are still stretches of dark country, where the police and HD troops have no control and where the maglev tracks and stations are unsafe, but ever since we banished the immediate threat to Earth three years ago, those pockets have gradually shrunk in size as the Brigades pacify PRC after PRC with the help of the SI and the new government. The PRCs will never be peaceful utopias, but with the Lazarus Brigades doing the job of police and SI, the pacified ones are more calm and orderly than I have seen them in my lifetime. The Brigades keep them that way with a velvet-gloved fist, making friends and allies when they can and pummeling would-be warlords and gang kingpins when they have to. I spent months with the Brigades training the nucleus of their special operations group, and then I went into battle with them and saw half of my trainees become casualties. I used to think that nothing was as difficult and dangerous as a pod drop onto a Lanky world, but I know now that the people who volunteer for the Brigades do a duty that's every bit as hazardous, and they don't even get good food or special leave for it.

The train glides over the urban labyrinths of the many PRCs stretching west from Boston, each ring of housing clusters newer, bigger, and slightly less grungy than the one before it as we go west. Then we're in the 'burbs, which is obvious because there's a buffer of artificial greenery between the maglev track and the neighborhoods it passes by, and the noise-protection walls on either side of the tracks are adorned with murals or advertising instead of street art and scrawled obscenities.

My old home, the PRC in Boston where I grew up, was an older cluster, a Category Three, organically evolved from a bunch of poorer suburbs. A lot of the new ones are centrally planned and built from scratch. The Category Five PRCs are absolutely massive, even from a distance. The NAC government built towers a hundred floors high and clustered them in groups of four, with walls between the towers to turn each group into its own neighborhood. On my way west, I see more Category Five PRCs than ever before. They form the outer ring of the Boston metroplex, cluster next to cluster, fifty kilometers deep. The pattern repeats itself as I cross the country toward the Great Lakes.

Every time the train speeds toward another metroplex, there's a ring of neat and clean suburbs, then green belts and security zones, then Cat5 PRCs. Even closer to the city core, the Cat5s give way to Cat4s and 3s, then the old Cat2s and 1s, the ones that were always poor neighborhoods to begin with but were allowed to evolve at their own pace. And then come the inner cities, like bubbles of order and structure in the middle of a sea of unruly bustle, commerce, and living spaces for those who can afford them. And I'm gliding above it all at three hundred kilometers per hour, looking at the world below through thick polyplast barriers that are supposed to keep the noise inside the maglev track and bullets out of it. It occurs to me that I don't really know this world anymore. I grew up in a Cat3 that I left ten years ago. And I only spent two years of my adult life in that PRC, relatively sheltered years in a fairly low-crime section without many gangs. Every time I come back to Earth, the place seems more foreign to my eyes, and I feel more and more like a stranger, an alien on my own planet. As we fight the Lankies and each other among the stars, life down here goes on. But the more time I spend up in the black, in the regimented and artificial environment of military starships, the more doubts I have that I'll be able to fit back in again down here one day.

I drift off for a while in my empty compartment, and my dream is dark and unpleasant. I am back on the street in the PRC, and I'm trying to find someone or something, running through dark alleys and derelict intersections with the dreadful feeling that I am too late for something. I smell gunpowder and drop ship exhaust in the air, and there are sounds of battle all around me, but I run through the darkness without seeing anyone, as if I am following the action a step too late at every turn. I don't have battle armor or a TacLink helmet, no way to see my squad that's just somewhere out of sight in the warren of alleyways nearby. I clear corners and dash from alley to alley, but no matter how quickly I move, I can't seem to catch up.

When a noise yanks me out of my restless sleep, I startle violently. Before my eyes are even fully open, I have my hand on my sidearm, and by the time I realize that I was dreaming, it has already cleared the holster halfway. I look to my left, where someone is standing in the door of my compartment. It's a transit police officer, dressed in medium blue fatigues and wearing a lightweight helmet with a data monocle in front of his left eye.

"Whoa there, soldier. Everything okay in here?"

I stick the pistol back into its holster all the way and let the automatic retention lock engage.

"Yeah," I say. "How about on your end?"

"Just doing my walk-through. Didn't mean to startle you, Captain. Have a good evening."

"You, too," I say and sit up from my uncomfortably reclined position.

The cop closes the compartment door again and moves on down the train car, and I try to shake off the remnants of the dream. Outside, the landscape is dark. The information display at the front of the compartment shows that we're traveling along the shore of Lake Erie at 307 kilometers per hour.

I meant to take the train to Fort Shughart, for lack of another location on this side of dark country that has any relevance to me, but I decide to get off the train at the next stop, grab some chow, and see if I can hitch a ride into orbit from the base at Cleveland or Great Lakes. Whatever is happening at Shughart right now, there's nothing there for me after all this time, and nostalgic sightseeing in the 365th's old company building probably won't do anything to improve the quality of my dreams.

CHAPTER 6

──── FLEET YARD DAEDALUS ────

When I reach Gateway in yet another packed shuttle two days later, I have a rough idea of what to expect of my new command. The new ships have been top secret since they started construction on them not too long after the Second Battle of Mars, which naturally means that everybody in the corps knows about them. But as fast as news travels in the enlisted underground, the information often gets distorted and altered as it travels down the rumor chain, like in that old children's game. Halley and I have the advantage of experience, and we've both come to conclude that the new ships are an evolution of the battleships that performed so well at Mars, even if we lost one of them to propulsion system damage. Three years aren't enough to come up with a new design from scratch and get it operational. So our money is on improved *Agincourt*-class ships, hopefully with more reliable particle cannons and less vulnerable fusion engines.

The sergeant who checks my orders at the transfer desk sends me to a docking collar that's not too far from the one where my earlier shuttle from Earth arrived, which means it's not in the capital ship section of the station.

"Are you sure about this, Sarge?" I say. "I'm pretty sure my new boat is a cap ship."

He scans my PDP's code again and looks at his terminal.

"The computer says it's right, sir. Says you're going over to CAS on Luna. I'm guessing you'll catch your final ride up there."

CAS is the Combat Aviation School, where Halley taught for a few years as a drop ship flight instructor. I raise an eyebrow and take my PDP back from the desk sergeant.

"Guess I'll find out. Thank you, Sergeant."

The ship at my assigned docking collar is another shuttle, the standard Fleet utility variety used for orbital transport, so I know the next leg of my trip won't be a long one. This shuttle isn't nearly as full as the one from Earth to Gateway. I have a whole row of seats to myself, and when the hatch closes and the docking collar retracts, no more than a quarter of the other seats are full. My fellow passengers are mostly Fleet pilots in flight suits, which makes sense if we're going to CAS on Luna. There are two SI officers in the shuttle as well, sitting near the front of the ship and talking quietly between themselves. I get out my PDP and kill some time reading news and sending Halley an update on my destination and ETA, just in case she's still on Luna.

The flight from Gateway to lunar orbit only takes about an hour and a half—forty-five minutes of acceleration burn, and then the same amount of time for deceleration, with the nose of the shuttle flipped around and pointed back at Gateway and Earth. Then we flip again for the slow coast into the Fleet base at Luna, a sprawling complex of building domes housing half a dozen schools where new Fleet personnel get their first taste of low- and zero-g environments.

The shuttle doesn't dock at the main transport hub. Instead, it descends into the hangar cluster of the Fleet's Combat Aviation School.

I've been here a lot because our joint living quarters were near the CAS dome, but I've only been in the hangar of the flight school once, over three years ago at the start of the Battle of Earth, when a Lanky seed ship was headed our way and we needed a few dozen drop ships to lift troops to safety from the deck of NACS *Regulus*.

The shuttle docks in one of the many bays at the CAS hangar, and a few minutes later, we are in pressurized atmosphere on the main flight deck. When I step off the shuttle and onto the well-worn deck, I have a slightly disorienting feeling of déjà vu. A little over three years ago, a contingent of SI troopers from *Regulus* stormed out of a drop ship and commandeered pilots and ships right off this deck, and I got punched in the face by my then girlfriend. We got married back on *Regulus* just a few hours later, with a Lanky seed ship approaching Earth and everybody preparing for a last-ditch defense. Those were far more desperate days—we had no reliable weapon against seed ships back then—but I've never felt more alive than I did that night.

The flight deck doesn't look much different from the way it did three years ago. It's still crammed full of Fleet drop ships and attack birds of every model currently in service and a few I haven't seen in the Fleet in years. But it's not the Wasps and Dragonflies that catch my eye. In the middle of the hangar, four strange-looking drop ships are hooked up to refueling probes and service links. I can tell they are evolutions of the Dragonfly design, like the Dragonfly-SR models we use to flush out Lankies on Mars. But these look weightier somehow, with added bulges and domes where the other Dragonflies have smooth hull plating. The wings are thicker and stubbier, the nose turrets don't have the usual rotary autocannon sticking out of them, and I can see the telltale zits of optical sensors all over the hull.

But the design changes aren't the most striking thing about these new Dragonfly mutations. It's the paint that really makes them look out of place, a bright shade of orange that is almost fluorescent. And as if someone decided the hull paint isn't enough to make them stand out, they also have illuminated light strips on the hull. It's like the designers read the manual on how to make a ship stealthy and then made these birds exactly the opposite. The Blackfly version we rode in three years ago on Arcadia was a smaller, more agile, stealthier ship than the Dragonfly. These things take the opposite evolutionary approach. They are bigger, bulkier, and look like they're about half again as heavy.

The PDP in my pocket buzzes, and I retrieve it to check the incoming message.

>What's your status?
>On the hangar deck at CAS.
>I'm on base too. Stay put. I'll come and fetch you.

I didn't expect to see her again so soon, and her message makes me grin. I knew her next stop was Luna as well, and there aren't too many ways to get off the moon again, so there was a 30 percent chance we would leave for our next duty stations from the same spot. But I thought her long on the way to her ship, and I'm happy for the chance to see her again. There's the possibility that we got assigned to the same unit again, and the likelihood just went up considerably. But the "Duty Station" field on my orders is still just a numeric code instead of a ship name, standard procedure for assignments that have any degree of secrecy attached. I stay where I am, twenty meters away from the shuttle that is now getting serviced for the return trip to Gateway, and study the new drop ships some more. They have no squadron markings or ship name on their tails. Overall, that flight of drop ships looks like they just rolled them off the assembly floor at the factory this morning. I strongly suspect that those ships and I are headed for the same destination.

MARKO KLOOS

Halley appears on the far end of the flight deck a few minutes later. She is wearing her flight suit, and she carries her pilot helmet under one arm. I watch her as she strides across the deck with purpose and confidence, completely in her element and comfortable with her environment. She loves being in that suit, loves having a battle-ready spacecraft in front of her, and even with a year of training raw recruits under my belt, I feel like I've only started to understand how much of a purgatory it was for her to be serving in classrooms and simulators for so long instead of being on the frontlines.

"I thought you were already off to your XO gig," I say in greeting when she reaches me.

"I was," she says. "Been going back and forth ferrying new hardware to the ship."

"What ship?"

"You'll see," she says with a smile.

She nods to the new drop ships I've been studying for the last few minutes.

"What do you think of the new babies?"

"I don't know what to think. Never seen that class before."

"They're Dragonfly-HVs. We've been driving two squadrons' worth of them from deck to deck. These are the last flight. Thirty-two ships in total."

"Deck to deck," I repeat. "So we're on a carrier again."

"You'll see," she says again. "Patience, Captain Grayson. Wouldn't want to violate OPSEC."

"Oh, come on. It's not like they kept those new ships a great secret."

"All I'm saying is don't believe the rumor mill too much." She nods toward the orange drop ships. "Want to go for a ride?"

"What in the fuck is a Dragonfly-HV? Or is that classified too?"

Halley starts walking over to the flight of drop ships, and I follow her.

"HV is for *hi-viz*. You may have noticed the loud paint job."

"Yeah. That'll stand out on the battlefield like a neon sign."

"That's the point, Andrew. They even have external light markers. To make 'em as obvious as possible through, say, high-magnification optics from orbit."

"That sounds like a great way to commit suicide by enemy fire."

"Depends on what you're up against," she says.

From close up, the new drop ships look even more imposing. They lack the sleek angles of the Blackflies, but their extra bulk gives them a solid tanklike aura of indestructibility. Of course, I know from experience that no drop ship is indestructible—far from it—but these look like they can take a massive beating and keep flying.

"Who's slotted to fly 505, Sarge?" Halley asks the crew chief, who is supervising the refueling and flight prep.

"Lieutenant Garcia, ma'am," the chief answers.

"I'll take 505 out to the barn myself. Tell Lieutenant Garcia to left-seat on 507 with Lieutenant Leach."

"You need a left-seater, Major?"

"Negative," Halley says. "I'm letting Captain Grayson ride shotgun." She flicks a thumb in my direction.

The crew chief looks at me with some skepticism, and I know roughly what he's thinking. I'm in Fleet cammies, not a flight suit, and I'm wearing a combat-drop badge instead of pilot wings. I know that Halley isn't exactly breaking regs by letting me ride up front instead of in the cargo bay, but I also know she's at least stretching them a little. But the chief probably figures that he's several pay grades too low to second-guess the squadron XO, because he merely shrugs.

"Three minutes on the fuel, and two more pallets of cargo to go, ma'am. Figure skids up in five if we can get clearance from flight ops early. Shouldn't be a problem."

"Very well," Halley replies. "Let's see if we can scrounge up a brain bucket for the captain here."

"You probably have more front seat time than any other Fleet grunt," Halley says when we strap into our seats. I look for the data and oxygen hookup and connect my flight helmet.

"This is only—what, the third time I've been in the cockpit with you?"

"Sounds about right. Let's see—Willoughby . . . and Earth, three years back."

"The day we got married."

"Yeah, it was." She smiles as she cycles through her displays and goes through the preflight checklist. "But you need to be qualified for that seat if it's anything but a ferry run or a special VIP tour. Technically, the crew chief needs to remove that stick in front of you before we take off."

"You're not going to make him?"

"Nah. Just don't touch the controls."

"Not my area of expertise," I say, remembering the simulated drop ship runs they had me do in boot camp. I burned up every single one of them on atmospheric entry. Whatever Halley does with her ships is some sort of witchcraft, something that my brain isn't wired to comprehend. To me, trying to coordinate the controls of a drop ship for movement in three dimensions feels like trying to center a greased ball bearing on a dinner plate while running up a flight of stairs.

Behind us, the cargo ramp of the ship closes. I can't hear the hydraulics through the armored bulkhead behind us, but I can see the video feed from the cargo hold on the center console. When the ramp is closed, Halley listens to something in her headset that I can't hear. She sends back an acknowledgment and switches channels.

"Flight ops, Dragonfly 505. Request taxi to the active and departure clearance."

"Dragonfly 505, flight ops. Taxi to launch pad one-six via taxiway Alpha Charlie. Hold on launch pad and contact flight ops for automated launch clearance."

"Taxi to pad one-six via Alpha Charlie and hold for auto clearance, Dragonfly 505," Halley replies with the smooth routine of someone who has gone through exchanges like this thousands of times.

"You're still not telling me where you're taking this thing."

"And spoil the fun? Hell no. Just sit tight and enjoy the ride, Andrew."

We launch out of the CAS hangar a few minutes later. Even though I usually tap into a drop ship's sensor arrays when I am riding in the back, it's much more fun to sit up front and see the scenery through the cockpit windows. We climb away from the surface of the moon and the sprawl of the military base complex. Lunar orbit is a busy place, and Halley has several exchanges with space traffic control directing her onto departure lanes and alerting her to nearby traffic. Then we're away from the military bases and heading for the lunar horizon, which always seems just within grasp. Above the curve of the lunar surface, the blue-gray hemisphere of Earth pokes up, covered as usual in swirling cloud patterns. But instead of heading out in that direction, Halley banks the drop ship to port and starts a low orbit around Luna.

"I wonder whether this place would have been a good refuge for humans if the Lankies had managed to get a foothold on Earth," Halley says.

"What, Luna? It's just three hundred thousand klicks. A seed ship can make that in an hour or less."

"Yeah, but there's no atmosphere here. It's not terraformable. They don't seem to want the places that aren't already set up for them. They can flip an atmosphere and pump CO_2 into it. Can't flip an atmosphere that isn't there."

I think about her statement and shrug.

"You're probably right. But that doesn't mean they'd tolerate a human outpost in line of sight of their new digs. They'd probably scrape us off Luna just because. Would you want someone peeking over your fence constantly?"

"Shit no," Halley says. "Those things don't make good neighbors. Just imagine."

I look over at Earth, or at least the half of it that's visible above the lunar horizon, and try to do just that. I imagine an Earth crawling with Lankies—cities empty, human population mostly wiped out, survivors driven underground, and just a few ten thousand of us sitting here on Luna and getting a ringside seat to the extermination of our species. The Lankies wouldn't be able to land settlers or deploy their nerve-gas pods, but it wouldn't matter in the long run. All they'd have to do would be to park a few seed ships in lunar orbit and shoot down everything that tried to come or go. Without resupply from Earth or some other colony, everyone on Luna would be dead within a year or two at the most. On the whole, I'd rather get killed on Earth instead of having a ringside seat to the end of civilization while getting a slow execution by gradual asphyxiation.

"This isn't going to end until they wipe us out, or we kill them all," I say.

"I have no particular problem with option two," Halley replies. "It's not like they're leaving us much of a choice. They're not much for live and let live."

"No, they aren't," I say. "But we aren't, either. Not at this point. It's too much of a grudge match now."

We leave Earth and the travel lane to Gateway on our starboard side. Halley continues her low orbit of the moon, past CAS and Fleet Base Armstrong, until we are above the undeveloped part of Luna, the edge of the desirable lunar real estate that faces Earth. I've only been around the far side in windowless shuttles or drop ship cargo holds, and this is the first time I actually get to see this part of Luna from a low-orbit vantage point.

"Over there," Halley says, pointing, sometime after we've swung around to the far side.

"Is that Daedalus?"

"That's it. You can't see the installation until you clear the rim of the crater. It's three klicks high."

Daedalus is the name for both the one-hundred-kilometer crater in the center of the far side of Luna and the radio telescope we put there fifty years ago. Over here, the facility is shielded from the radio waves coming from Earth, the ideal site for a set of big electronic ears to point away from Earth. Over the years, they expanded the complex to hold an optical surveillance array and various scientific labs, but because it's not a military base, we have no business there, and very few corps members ever get to see the place in person. We don't get close enough to the crater for me to see the whole facility, but I can see the top of the radio telescope array at our closest point of approach.

"Can't cross over Daedalus," Halley says. "They get pissed off when we contaminate their quiet sky with radio chatter. Besides, that's not where we're going."

She looks up and slightly over to starboard and points.

"That is."

I follow the direction of her index finger and let out a low whistle.

"What the fuck?"

"Yeah, that was my first reaction, too."

Up in the lunar sky, a few hundred kilometers from Daedalus and quietly hanging in the black of space, a station is orbiting the far side of the moon. It's hard to tell scale from our angle, but it's larger than Gateway, although far less bulky. It's an almost graceful-looking structure in the shape of two mirrored letter *Es* joined at their spines. I've seen this type of structure twice before—at the renegade deep-space fleet yard where they built *Agincourt* and *Arkhangelsk*, and at Arcadia.

It's a capital ship fleet yard, and the ships docked on the tines of the double-*E* shape are as capital as they come.

"Surprise, surprise," I murmur.

The ships docked at this fleet yard are all of the same class, ones I've never seen before, not even as a rumor or a schematic. They look vaguely like the basic design for *Arkhangelsk*, but they're much bigger. Where the battleships look like elongated turtle shells, these new ships have long, flowing hulls with gentle curves, narrower and much longer than the remaining battleship.

"*Ottawa* flight ops, Dragonfly 505. I'm eighty klicks to the west, approaching from two hundred and sixty degrees, altitude thirty thousand. Request docking vectors and landing clearance," Halley sends.

"Dragonfly 505, *Ottawa*. Come to heading one eighty and increase altitude to fifty thousand for AILS approach."

"Dragonfly 505, turn to one eighty and climb to fifty thousand for AILS," Halley confirms and turns the nose of the ship to the right.

"How long have you known about this?" I ask without taking my eyes off the installation we're approaching.

"Two days," she says. "The whole far side has been restricted space for years now, so I knew they were up to something. They even changed a main traffic lane for Gateway and Independence to route traffic away from line of sight. All to build these things in private."

Built on the far side of the moon, this fleet yard is safe from direct observation because it never faces Earth, and the bulk of the moon blocks all radio signals that aren't relayed on purpose by the comms satellites in lunar orbit. It's the perfect spot for clandestine ship-building close to Earth.

As we get closer, the size of the ships really comes into perspective. The station has long docking outriggers, but only half the length of each ship fits onto the dock. They looked huge from a distance, but as we approach one of them from the stern end, it's clear that they're even larger than I had guessed. I've been around lots of capital ships, including the Fleet's enormous supercarriers. These new ships make even a Navigator-class look dainty. They're not any wider—I'm guessing they have a maximum dock width to conform to—but they are much longer, easily twice as long as a Navigator.

Halley lets the computer take over as soon as we hit the AILS landing-assist beam from the ship. We drop underneath the hull and approach the bottom of it, where I can see rows and rows of standard docking ports. It seems like the ship goes on forever. If I had to estimate, I'd guess it to be over a kilometer in length. The armor plating on the hull is painted in a bright titanium white, and the markings on the hull are orange and black. All the other ships in the Fleet have some form of camouflage paint, dull gray or black, to blend into space and be less obvious to optical reconnaissance. Whoever designed this ship and her sisters very clearly didn't give the slightest fuck about low-observance camo. They look like starships out of a Network show, like something that civilians expect a starship to be, all shiny and streamlined. Something about their smooth and sleek shapes reminds me of Lanky seed ships.

"What do they call this class?" I ask Halley.

"Avenger," she replies dramatically.

"That's rather martial. Why not go all out? Terminator. Liquidator."

"Destroyonator," she continues with a grin.

"Destroyonator it is," I say.

"I guess this will be the Destroyonator class in my head from here on out." She points through the cockpit glass at the bottoms of the three other ships in turn.

"That's *Mexico City. Beijing. Washington. New Delhi.* And . . ."

"Moskva," I finish for her. "All the capitals of the SRA and NAC founding nations. Cute. Very United Nations."

"Oh, you have no idea," Halley says. "It is very United Nations. I think almost a quarter of the commissioning crew is from Eurocorps. I hear they bankrolled most of this, so they get to have their people ride shotgun and learn the ropes of interstellar combat. They've got two more Avengers under construction for the Euros."

I groan softly.

"You've got to be joking. Top-of-the-line warships . . . staffed with trainees. Foreign trainees from a different service."

"All the department heads are seasoned," she replies. "And three-quarters of the crew are Fleet. The Euros have to learn somehow. And honestly? It's no different than having some fresh Fleet nugget right out of tech school."

She lets out a low chuckle as the ship's computer works the maneuvering thrusters of the drop ship to line us up with the docking clamp overhead. We slow down and come to a halt right underneath the orange-and-black outline of the docking port, piloted by the effortless accuracy of a silicon brain.

"Oh, and wait until you see the new uniforms. You're going to *love* those."

CHAPTER 7

—— THAT NEW SHIP SMELL ——

Back in the twenty-first century, before we were so many that we had to get squeezed into PRCs, the 'burbers used to go on ships for recreation. From what I've read about them, those ships were basically floating RecFacs for civilians. You didn't go on them to get to a specific destination; you just spent a week or two on board to eat and drink and rot your brain with amusements, luxurious leisure for its own sake.

NACS *Ottawa* looks like I imagine those cruise ships to have looked like. Everything is clean and gleaming, and whoever designed this class paid attention to more than just military utility. I'm not used to aesthetic touches or cleanliness on a warship, so walking the passageways of my new command feels a little surreal. I never realized just how dimly lit most Fleet ships are until I set foot on Ottawa. All the passageways and compartments I pass through are illuminated from hidden light strips in the floor and ceiling. The ship looks like a set for a Network show, not a real commissioned warship.

Halley has already been on this ship for a few days, so I check in with the ship's personnel office by myself while she goes off to wherever Pilot Country is located on this luxury barge. Then I report to the Officers' Mess Office for my stateroom assignment.

"Captain Grayson," I tell the sergeant on duty in the office and hand him my PDP to scan my orders. "I'm the new head of the special tactics team."

"Yes, sir. Just one second."

The sergeant cycles through a few screens on his terminal. The Fleet personnel on this ship are wearing a uniform I've never seen in the corps before. It's a teal-colored tunic with a low stand-up collar and spidersilk weave spaulders attached to the shoulders. On my regular Fleet fatigues, the rank insignia are on fabric loops pulled over the shoulder epaulettes. On this new uniform, they are on the slightly bulky-looking spaulders, underneath small NAC flag patches. There's a ratings badge on the left side of the sergeant's tunic chest and a name tape on the right side. Just like everything else on this ship, that uniform looks like a prop from a civvie show about starships.

"I have your assignment, sir," the sergeant says, oblivious to my curiosity at his uniform. "You're in 5-150-5 Lima."

"Is that a single stateroom or a JO jungle?" I ask, referring to the unpopular shared junior officer staterooms where three or more officers are stacked in bunks together. Due to my occupational specialty, I've had excellent luck avoiding roommates on my deployments, but every streak has to break eventually.

"It's a single stateroom, sir. All the officer staterooms on this ship are."

"You're kidding me."

"No, sir. It's a really big ship." He lowers his voice a little. "We have a running track, if you can believe that. Almost a kilometer long. It goes through half of Oscar deck. Makes a loop around the nuke silos."

"A running track," I repeat with a grin.

"Honestly, I've been on this ship for two months now and I still don't know where everything is. Do you want me to call for a guide from the Ops Department to show you around once you've stowed your gear?"

"Thank you, Sergeant, but I think I can find my way around with the guide in the PDP. It's all just counting frame and deck numbers, right?"

"Yes, sir. But I gotta warn you. This ship has a lot of frames and decks."

I climb up to deck 5 and make my way forward to frame 150 through passageways that are entirely too well lit, clean, and clearly marked. Most of the Fleet personnel I see are wearing the new teal-colored uniform. There are some civvie dockworkers busy in almost every section of the ship. I've never been on a Fleet unit that has just rolled out of the building slip, and while it's nice to know that nothing on *Ottawa* is worn out or beaten to shit, I also know that this is a brand-new and unproven design that has never seen battle.

My stateroom, compartment 5 at frame 150, unlocks with my biometrics. I haul my gear bag into the compartment, and the lighting comes on automatically, illuminating a small but well-appointed stateroom that would be good enough for a flag officer on some of the smaller ships I've served on. It has a bunk, a locker, and a small desk with a neural networks terminal, and the space between them is big enough to do push-ups or sort through gear without bumping into anything. It's not as posh as my platoon-leader compartment in the living module aboard *Portsmouth* last year, where I had my own shower and head, but I'm so pleased with the continuation of my private living space streak that having to go to the communal head and washroom at the end of the passageway seems like a small gripe.

I toss my gear bag onto the bunk to unpack it. The locker next to the bunk already has some stuff in it—three sets of the new uniforms, neatly suspended on hangers in the vertical section of the locker. I take one out to look at it. It has captain's rank insignia on the spaulders, and the name tape says "GRAYSON, A."

Behind me, the terminal on the small desk chirps with an update. I put the uniform back and unlock the terminal. Whatever software this neural network runs, it looks much more advanced than the Fleet information-management screen I am used to. Luckily, the home screen has the same layout as the old systems, so I don't have to consult a neural networks admin just to check the orders and my incoming messages. Because all our data is pulled from MilNet, all my information is exactly the way it was when I last checked my PDP, only on a much bigger screen.

There are a few color-coded updates on the screen. The green ones are general ship business with no actionable items. There is no red "urgent" but a yellow "attention required" message on top of the queue, and I open it.

TO: ALL OFFICERS ASSIGNED BCV-60
FROM: XO, BCV-60
RE: DAILY OPS BRIEFING
ALL NEWLY ARRIVED OFFICERS ASSIGNED TO BCV-60 WILL REPORT TO BRIEFING ROOM 7-100-7-Q AT 1100Z DAILY FOR MANDATORY ORIENTATION AND OPS BRIEFING BY XO OR DESIGNATED STAFF.

I check the system time, which shows that it's 1023Z. Because I have to go up two decks and forward fifty frames on a ship I don't know yet, I decide to err on the side of punctuality and put off sorting the contents of my bag into the locker until after the mandatory ops briefing.

I'm ten minutes early, but I'm not the first one in the room. Several Fleet and SI officers are already sitting in some of the chairs. I walk in and nod at the other officers—none of them are above me in rank—and sit next to a Fleet first lieutenant in the front row. He wears the maroon beret of a Spaceborne Rescueman, which makes him part of my team. The other officers are talking among themselves in low voices.

"Andrew Grayson," I introduce myself to the Rescueman. "I'm the CO of the special tactics team. Or I will be."

"Jordan Brown," he says and shakes my hand. "That makes me your second-in-command. I'm your CRO."

The CRO is the combat rescue officer, the guy in charge of the Spaceborne Rescuemen on my team. The special tactics teams are usually split evenly between combat controllers and Spaceborne Rescue, with a special tactics officer in charge of the whole team and a combat rescue officer as his assistant. I glance at Lieutenant Brown's uniform, the same standard Fleet camo I'm wearing, and scan for indicators of his experience. He has a combat-drop badge in bronze, which means that he has done more than five drops but less than twenty. He's not completely green, but not very experienced, either. Then again, there are few podheads left who are.

"How long have you been SR?" I ask.

"Since just before Mars," he says. "I got out of PJ school just in time for the big event."

"Oh yeah? What was your landing zone on Mars?"

"LZ Orange," he says. It's a test of sorts, and he passes it when I see a dark shadow flitting across his expression. I wince in sympathy. Orange Beach got hit hard by the Lankies, and Task Force Orange suffered some of the highest casualty counts that day.

"They sent armor to hit the Lankies on Orange in the rear," I say. "I was part of the recon mission for the armor company. Didn't end so well."

"Well, that armor saved LZ Orange," Lieutenant Brown says. "If you guys hadn't showed up when you did, the Lankies would have overrun us, just like they did LZ Green."

A SEAL captain in the row behind us reaches over the back of the seat in front of him and offers his hand.

"If you're the new STO, we'll be working together. I'm the CO of the SEAL platoon. Tom Rolson."

The three of us shake hands. Something about Captain Rolson's face triggers recognition, but I can't quite remember where I met him last. The podhead community is small, so I've probably done at least a drop with every active-duty SEAL who has been in the service for longer than four years. But there's a flavor of wariness that comes with recognizing Captain Rolson, and when I remember, it's an unpleasant jolt.

"You were on the Arcadia mission," I say. "On Major Masoud's SEAL team."

Captain Rolson nods.

"I was a first lieutenant back then," he says. "I was in charge of one of the two fire teams."

I try to keep a neutral expression. Major Masoud's SEALs kept to themselves for the whole mission, both before and after we dropped onto the moon, so it's not surprising that I didn't recognize the captain immediately. I tell myself that it wouldn't be fair to transfer my resentment of the now colonel Masoud to one of his former fire team leaders. And without the SEALs clandestinely setting nuclear charges on half the terraformers on that moon, we would have lost the battle and failed the mission. But part of me still wants to punch the captain in the face and out of his chair.

That was three years ago, I tell myself. Three years ago and 150 light-years away. Even though I can still name every member of my platoon who died on that mission. I carried their dog tags around with me for over a week—except for the one belonging to Corporal Morris, who took a cannon round to the upper body that obliterated everything from the waist up. But it wasn't this guy who cooked up the mission and conned the SI platoons into playing bait.

Behind me, a staff officer steps through the hatch of the briefing room. Lieutenant Brown gets out of his seat and calls the room to attention, and we all turn toward the hatch.

"As you were," the newcomer says. He's a Fleet lieutenant colonel, and he's wearing the new uniform, while everyone else in the room is in Fleet or SI cammies.

"Have a seat, gentlemen."

We sit down again, and there's some expectant rustling in the room as officers get out their PDPs for the briefing. The lieutenant colonel walks to the front of the room and puts his PDP down on the lectern. He turns on the briefing screen on the bulkhead behind him with a few taps on his PDP screen, and it activates soundlessly, displaying the ship's seal and motto:

BVC-60 OTTAWA—ADVANCE—EN AVANT.

"Welcome to *Ottawa*. I am Lieutenant Colonel Barry, the XO of this ship."

He taps his PDP again, and the screen behind him changes from the ship seal to a 3-D image of *Ottawa*. I don't know the first thing about starship design, but even I can tell that this ship and her sisters represent a major leap in warship development. Her sleek, streamlined hull and sheer size make all other Fleet units seem ancient and obsolete.

"You will be part of the first crew of the most advanced warship ever built," the XO continues. "You will be using hardware that nobody in the Fleet has ever seen because it hasn't existed until now. But before I get into the nuts and bolts of the Avenger-class battlecarrier, I have a few administrative directives."

He tugs on the bottom of his teal uniform tunic to straighten it out, even though the material has no wrinkles in it.

"If you are Fleet, you have each been issued several sets of the new Fleet battle-dress uniform, tailored to your measurements. They are waiting for you in your stateroom lockers. After you've squared away your gear and settled in, you will change into the uniform of the day. On most days, that will be Fleet Battle Dress."

I look down at the camouflage pattern of my until-now-standard BDUs. We've worn the same uniform in the same pattern for years now. Each service has its own digital camo pattern, something that makes the wearer visibly a member of their branch even from a distance. The new Fleet Battle Dress is all solid colors, and it looks as different from the old uniform as *Ottawa* does from all the other ships in the Fleet. When it comes to new tech, we've been mostly standing still except for the emergency warfighting tools—new rifles, the new battleships, the Orion missiles. After the weapons development, there was never much money left for other gear, so we've been soldiering on with the same uniform design for at least a decade now. I wonder what kind of treasure chest the Fleet found to be able to afford a top-to-bottom remake.

"If you carry a personal sidearm, your next stop after this briefing will be the armory on the flight deck level. You will turn in your weapon, to be reissued as required for combat ops. There will be no carrying of sidearms except for authorized security personnel."

There's some low grumbling in the room at this directive. I am used to the weight of my M109 in its holster on my right thigh. It has been my constant companion both on duty and on leave. More than once, I've faced a threat with nothing but that pistol, and even if its utility against Lankies is highly questionable, it always made me feel a little more in control of my own fate.

Captain Rolson behind me raises a hand and clears his throat.

"What if we have to abandon ship, sir?"

"The escape pods on *Ottawa* all have arms lockers with small arms and ammunition for emergencies," the XO says. "The lockers have electronic access control that won't release the weapons until the computer detects that the pod has been launched."

The murmurs of discontent subside only a little. The XO shakes his head at us with a frown.

"I understand that you all got used to being armed at all times. That made sense when we were still at war with the SRA and could expect boarding actions. But we are geared to fight Lankies now. And this is a ship with an international crew. Some of the Eurocorps people don't have the same experience with hand weapons that we have gained over the years. This is a firm safety rule from upstairs, and I will enforce the hell out of it, so don't give me a reason to come down on you. When this briefing is over, you will turn in your sidearms at the flight deck armory. Nobody but SP on duty carries a loaded weapon shipboard. That's an order from the CO, not a debate item."

The XO shifts his gaze back to the screen of his PDP. The screen behind him changes to a spinning diagram of the ship, with vital parts shown in cross-section.

"I know none of you are familiar with this class because nobody is until they come aboard. The Avenger-class battlecarrier is a joint project between the NAC, the European Union, and the SRA. We pooled our know-how from *Agincourt* and *Arkhangelsk* with the Euros, and this is what they came up with. Half a million tons of one-g weight, with the spacecraft capacity of a Navigator-class supercarrier and more antiship firepower than *Archie* or *Aggie*."

"Half a million tons," Lieutenant Brown repeats next to me, and I let out a low whistle. *Archie* and *Aggie* were by far the biggest ships in the Fleet when they were built almost four years ago, and the ship we're on right now has as much laminate steel in it as both battleships put together.

"We have an augmented carrier air group on board," the XO continues. "Four strike squadrons, two assault transport squadrons, a recon squadron, and a support squadron. One hundred and ten spacecraft in total. Our troop complement is one full-strength regiment of SI. We also carry sixty-four Hades-C nuclear missiles, and six Orions."

"Excuse me, sir," someone behind me interjects. "Don't those weigh fifteen thousand tons each?"

"Not the new ones," the XO says. He changes the display to show one of the box launchers mounted on the ventral side of the ship. "These are Orion IIIs. Same principle, but a quarter the weight. Shorter range, of course, and they don't hit as hard as the originals, but we can carry half a dozen with us in those box launchers, three per side. The ordnance eggheads say that they're powerful enough to crack a seed ship hull open so we can follow up with precision nukes and blow the bastards up from the inside." He pauses and grins without humor.

"Of course, we have a pretty solid plan B, too."

He spins the diagram until we see the ventral side of the ship— engines at the rear, docking locks for the drop ships amidships, several batteries of rail guns mounted in single turrets—and a long armored bulge that extends from the middle of the ship all the way to the bottom of the bow section. When the XO rotates the animation, we see two muzzles poking out from the bow, spaced maybe twenty meters apart near the centerline. I've seen a muzzle like that underneath *Agincourt* and *Arkhangelsk*. Where the old battleships had one particle cannon each, this ship has two of them, mounted beside the longitudinal axis, and they look a great deal bigger than the ones on *Aggie* and *Archie*.

"There's plan B," the lieutenant colonel continues. "The Orions are for standoff range. These are for knife fighting. Double the range of the old models, and twenty percent more energy output. And because we have two of them, we also have double the rate of fire. Each gun has its own reactor dedicated to it, so we can fire the Alpha mount while the Bravo mount recharges, and vice versa."

I remember the troublesome particle cannon mount on *Agincourt*, which eventually contributed to her loss in battle above Mars. It looks like they've learned their lessons about the peak power draw of those cannons. The reactor capacity of this ship must be immense if they can dedicate two fusion reactors just to the main armament.

"I know most of you are veterans of Mars. Some of you were at the Battle of Earth. You know how it feels when there's a Lanky seed ship in weapons range. But the days of running from them are over. I am not even slightly afraid to go up against a Lanky unit in this ship. We have armor plating that resists their weapons, and we have the firepower to kill their seed ships. We've halted their advance. And now it's time to push them back."

I've heard the *rah-rah* motivational baloney a thousand times before, usually right before a mission where everything goes to flaming shit in a hurry, but as the XO goes through the general capabilities and features of the Avenger-class ships, I can't help but be impressed. The Euros shelled out a lot of money to aid in the construction of these six ships, and they are stuffed with top-flight technology from bow to stern. But I also know that the Eurocorps has little off-Earth warfighting experience. They don't have colonies outside the solar system, so they've not had to go into battle against the Lankies until just recently. It feels good to think we have the tools to meet the Lankies on equal footing, but as I look around in the briefing room, where some of the chairs are still covered in plastic and the paint on the bulkhead looks like it dried just yesterday, I am keenly aware that I'm about to ride into battle on a half-million-ton experiment. If I've learned anything useful at all in nearly nine years of service, it's that the battlefield is not a great environment to work the bugs out of your gear.

When the briefing is over, I grudgingly do as ordered and go down to the armory on the flight deck level to turn in my pistol and the two spare magazines I've been carrying on my person for years now. Walking back up to my stateroom, it feels strange not to have the familiar weight of the M109 in its retention holster on my upper thigh. It's amazing how quickly a two-pound piece of polymer and steel can become part of you. After a few minutes without a sidearm, I already miss the stupid thing, even if it was a pain in the ass sometimes, clunking into chairs and hatch frames all the time.

Back in my stateroom, I continue unpacking my personal gear. At the bottom of my bag, there's a small biometric hand safe just like the one I gave Chief Kopka a few years back for safekeeping. I open the lock with my fingerprint. Inside, there's an antique pistol, issued to the US predecessor of the NAC Defense Corps. It's an M17, chambered in a now-obsolete cartridge. Its polymer frame is scuffed and worn, the original finish of the metal slide and barrel have faded from phosphate black to light gray, and it's about twice as heavy as a modern service pistol and useless against battle armor. But I know from experience during my eighteen months with the Lazarus Brigades that when you shoot someone with this pistol, they will promptly fall down and die. I got this weapon as a parting gift when I left the Brigades a year and a half ago, and I'm not turning this one into the armory to get melted down.

The safe is just big enough for the gun, two spare magazines, and a fifty-round box of that obsolete nine-millimeter ammunition. I close the safe, and the lock activates itself again with a soft click.

It's not really insubordination, I tell myself as I store the little hand safe in my locker's valuables compartment. I did turn in the issued pistol as ordered, after all, and I won't carry the old gun out in the open. But there is absolutely no way I'll go into battle on an untested ship with an untested crew without fuss-free access to a weapon. When the Combat Stations alert blares and everyone around you loses their head, it's too late to be standing in line at the armory to sign out your pistol.

CHAPTER 8

—— AN UNPLEASANT REUNION ——

Four days after I report to *Ottawa,* the ship leaves the anchorage for its shakedown cruise to Fleet Base Titan, over a billion kilometers and a six-week journey away. I do my regular observance of Earth on the viewscreen of the terminal in my stateroom, but most of my view is obscured by the bulk of Luna, and I notice that our departure vector keeps the moon between us and Earth until our home planet is just a muddy green-gray dot in the distance.

Ottawa is so different from any of the ships I've served on that I almost feel like a brand-new nugget on my first deployment. The ship is so large that it has half a dozen officer's wardrooms spread out over the kilometer-long hull and its twenty-odd decks. It's not just that everything is new and works as it should. There's so much open space in the common areas that it feels like a shore-based building, not a warship. Space is always at a premium on Fleet ships, so all this elbow room feels decadent and a little wasteful. But I can't say I dislike being able to stretch out a bit.

My duty station is the STT office in the SOCOM section of the executive deck, which has both an officer wardroom and an enlisted mess within twenty frames of my office. But whenever I can, I duck down to the officer's wardroom on the flight deck level, where the pilots and flight-ops officers eat their meals. It's less formal than the executive-level wardroom—pilots wear their flight suits instead of having to dress in the uniform of the day just to grab a meal—and the atmosphere is more casual. Most importantly, it's where Halley usually eats, and we have a bit of leeway to synchronize our lunches.

———————

"How do you like the new monkey suit?" Halley asks between two bites of salad. The officer's wardroom down here is buffet-style, and I've not seen such a variety of fresh greens, fruit, and real meat and chicken since the early days of our service careers.

I look down at the blue-and-teal ensemble I am wearing.

"Honestly? It's pretty comfortable. And you can't get it to wrinkle. But I still think it doesn't look very martial."

"Yeah, they do look a bit like leisure wear. The flight deck crews call them blueberries."

"New uniforms. No sidearms. A brand-new ship that has everyone checking deck layouts on their PDPs. And speaking of PDPs—have they made you trade yours up yet?"

"Haven't had the time yet," Halley says.

I reach into the leg pocket of my new uniform trousers and pull out my PDP. Then I place it on the table between us. Halley picks it up and turns it around in her hand. Where the old PDPs were built for ruggedness, with thick shockproof polymer shells, the new one looks like it'll break in half the first time I drop it on the deck by accident. It's a transparent piece of whatever super-ionized heavy-duty glass they use for handheld screens right now, and the glass slab is surrounded by a thin metal frame.

"This weighs absolutely nothing," Halley says. "A mess fork is heavier than that thing."

"Too much new shit, all at once. I'm used to my old crap. At least I could work everything without having to think about it. Now I can't do even basic stuff without reading a tutorial first. It fucks up my work flow."

"Cry me a river," Halley says. "I'm on my seventh drop ship–type rating in as many years. At least you can't kill yourself by hitting the wrong button on your PDP."

"A fair point," I concede.

"Besides, not all changes are bad. Did you find out about the alcohol yet?"

"What alcohol?" I ask. Fleet ships are dry underway by policy except for special occasions. When a cruise exceeds six weeks and becomes an official deep-space deployment, crew members are allocated two bottles of beer, but that's the extent of alcohol consumption on NAC warships away from the dock.

"The RecFacs have bars. We're allowed one drink a day. They scan your tag to make sure you don't double-dip. And you can't get a drink if you're up for watch rotation within six hours. But yeah. One real drink per day. And it's not even that fizzy soy shit."

"Why are you just now telling me this?" I ask. "I missed four drinks already."

"I just found out about it today from one of the crew chiefs. Been too busy to check out the RecFac."

"Real booze on a Fleet ship. That's a drastic change I can live with."

"They say it's because of the Euros on the crew. Apparently, they have that policy on their own ships, and we adopted it. To keep the allies happy."

"It'll keep our guys happy, too," I say. "They'll mutiny when they go back to a regular NAC boat with a dry-ship policy."

The officer wardroom doesn't look as cozy as Chief Kopka's restaurant, but it's a far cry from the ones on the other Fleet ships. There are booths all around the perimeter of the compartment and tables and chairs set up in rows in the middle, spaced apart far enough that everyone has room to move. The wardroom booths and tables are about half-full with officers eating their lunches. Most of them are in flight suits, but there are a few officers in blueberry uniforms. Looking around, I see mostly NAC patches on the uniforms, but there are a few Eurocorps officers in the mix. I see a German flag, a Swedish one, a Union Jack, and a French flag.

"Do you have any Euro pilots in your squadron?" I ask Halley.

"No ship commanders," she says. "None of them are rated on our birds. But flight ops has three Euro observers."

Halley has been different since we came aboard *Ottawa*. I haven't had many opportunities to see her—she's in Pilot Country, my duty station is almost at the other end of the ship, and the Fleet doesn't allow joint berthing for married couples on warships. But whenever we do have meals together, she's been in a good mood—confident, happy, and content. I never fully realized how much the shorebound training duty was wearing on her all these years. Seeing her in her element and knowing that we're on the same command again has improved my mood greatly as well, even though we're working five hundred meters apart and have a quarter million tons of alloy and titanium bulkheads between us.

I take another bite of my mashed potatoes and look over Halley's shoulder at some newcomers stepping through the hatch of the officer's wardroom, and my good mood instantly evaporates. One of the pilots walking in looks unpleasantly familiar. It's a face I haven't seen in three years, one that I hoped never to see again except in a MilNet message about lengthy prison sentences at Leavenworth.

"You have got to be joking," I say and put down my fork.

Halley turns around to follow my gaze. Then she mutters an obscenity under her breath.

The pilot, who is now making his way to the buffet line to pick up a tray, is a Shrike jock. I don't have to read his name tag to know that it says "BEALS." He was part of the renegade fleet that ran off to Arcadia. I know him because he was behind the stick of a Shrike that almost shot down the Blackfly drop ship with my entire platoon in it. Only Halley's last-second intervention saved me and thirty-six SI troopers from becoming a smoking hole in the ground on that moon. Halley shot his ship out of the sky, but he ejected and became our prisoner. To this day, I don't think he knows that he was about half a second and five pounds of trigger-finger pressure away from getting his brains blown out by Master Sergeant Fallon. Seeing him standing in the chow line, loading up his tray with food, I find myself wishing I hadn't countermanded my order and stopped Sergeant Fallon at the last moment.

"Son of a bitch," I say. "I was hoping that bastard was pounding rocks somewhere."

"That amnesty," Halley replies. "Thank our president."

After Arcadia, the new NAC leadership issued a general amnesty for almost all military personnel who were part of the renegade fleet. We couldn't afford to lose that many trained specialists right before Mars, and I suppose they didn't want to give a few thousand weapon-trained people a reason for a major grudge. Only the old administration, the civilian leadership who gave the orders, ended up on trial, and they all went to prison for high treason. But people like this Shrike pilot got a free pass, even if their actions resulted in the deaths of legitimate NAC troops—*my* troops.

I shove my meal tray toward the middle of the table and get out of my chair.

"I'll be right back," I say to Halley. "Gonna go for some dessert."

"Andrew," she says, but I disregard the warning in her voice. I step around the table and walk over to the buffet line.

Captain Beals sees my approach out of the corner of his eye, but he barely has time to start turning toward me. I slap the meal tray out of his hand from below, and it flips up, bounces off the corner of the buffet counter, and clatters to the floor, spraying mashed potatoes and fried chicken everywhere. The captain flinches and takes a reflexive step backwards.

"Hello again," I say. "Remember me?"

Beals's expression goes from surprise to anger to wariness in the span of two or three seconds. All around us, the conversations in the wardroom cease.

"Yeah," he says. "I do." He flicks some mashed potato blobs off his flight suit. "The lieutenant with the psychopathic master sergeant."

"I'm glad you remember. Because I remember the body bags we brought home. Thanks to you and your flyboy friends."

There's anger flaring up behind the captain's eyes now, and his jaw muscles flex.

"You started the shooting. At the airfield that you ambushed. We filled our own share of body bags. Don't get all righteous with me, Captain."

"Only, what we did was legal. What you did was treason. And we just broke your Shrikes. *Your* patrol started killing people. The first KIA was ours."

"That was *three fucking years* ago," Captain Beals replies. "Bad shit happened. People died. On both sides. We all just did what we were told. You want to pick a fight over this *now*? It's *done*, Captain. All done. We all bled together at Mars after."

He bends over and picks up his meal tray. I have to fight the urge to take a step forward and drive my knee into the side of his head and then beat him with that tray until he no longer moves. But then I'd take up residence in the brig and spend a decade or more in Leavenworth, which would be far more punishment than this yes-sir fighter jock got for killing NAC troopers. And the amnesty means that we're all back on the same team now, absolved of all the awful things we did to each other.

"Captain Grayson," Halley says behind me. I hadn't noticed her leaving her table and walking up behind me. "Cool your jets for a bit and back off. That's an order."

I look back at Halley and take a deep breath.

"Yes, ma'am," I reply. Then I take a few steps back from the counter, and Halley steps into the space I just vacated.

Captain Beals puts the tray back onto the counter and takes another plate, ignoring the mess I made with his food tray just a few moments ago. He looks at me and shakes his head with a tiny little smirk that raises my blood pressure all over again.

"You, too, Captain," she says to Captain Beals. "Grab your tray and find a quiet corner. And if you see either Captain Grayson or me in the wardroom in the future, I'd suggest you sit as far away from us as possible."

"With all due respect, you can't tell me where to sit in the officer's wardroom, Major," Captain Beals says. "You're the XO of the second drop ship squadron, not the XO of this ship."

Halley closes the distance between them until they are standing almost nose to nose.

"And three years ago, when you were trying to shoot down my husband and his platoon, I was on your six in a drop ship and blew your ass out of the sky. You almost made me a widow. You damn near killed thirty-six mudlegs. I don't give the slightest shit about wardroom etiquette when it comes to you. I don't care if you go crying to the XO. If you see my face in spitting range, you give me a wide berth, Captain. Now *beat it*."

Captain Beals looks at Halley, then me. He probably realizes that he can't win a physical confrontation—Halley alone could probably put him in the infirmary, and my mood is foul enough for me to help put him into an ICU back at Gateway—and he can't pull rank because Halley is a major with the clout of an executive officer. My confrontation with Captain Beals is a clear violation of wardroom etiquette, but both he and I know that protocol won't keep me from breaking his nose. He takes his tray, turns away, and walks off to the other side of the wardroom without giving us another look. The conversations in the room pick up again gradually.

Halley lets out a long, sharp breath. Then she looks at me.

"Come with me, Captain," she says and nods to the wardroom hatch.

Outside in the passageway, she turns around and fixes me with an angry glare.

"You need to control yourself a little better than that, *Captain*," she says, with heavy emphasis on my rank. "You know I wouldn't have shed a tear if Sergeant Fallon had shot that smarmy fucker on Arcadia. But the rest of the officer corps doesn't know what went down between us. You can't physically assault another officer. Not in full view of everyone else, in the wardroom."

"I didn't assault him. I just smacked the tray out of his hands."

"You were two seconds away from grabbing one of those trays and planting it in his skull."

"Edge first," I say. "You remember that day, back on Arcadia? Blackfly Three shot all to shit? Lieutenant Wood and the crew chief dead, and three of our grunts with them."

"That wasn't Beals's bird," Halley says.

"No, but it was one of his squadron buddies. And he would have made the strafing run, too." I pound my fist against the nearby bulkhead.

"All of this was a mistake," Halley says. "The amnesty. They should have kicked them all out. Now we have half the Fleet holding a grudge against the other half."

She holds my gaze with hers and shakes her head slowly.

"But you have *got* to mind yourself. Whatever happened when you were with the Brigades, whatever shortened your fuse and removed that safety catch from your mouth and fists, you are still a Fleet officer. You can't start a fucking tavern brawl in the *officer's wardroom*. That's not you, Andrew."

"I know, I know." I exhale sharply and unclench my fists. "But seeing him there, flight suit and all, getting chow . . . They didn't even reduce him in rank. My guys may have to rely on close-air support from him if we get into a fight."

"He was an O-3 when we ran into him on Arcadia," Halley says. "He's still an O-3. He'll never pick up major. You know that the renegade fleet people got bumped down to the bottom of the lists for promotions. And if he fucks up on the job, he'll lose the wings and count screw washers for the rest of his career."

"If he fucks up on the job, people get their heads blown off by cannon shells," I say.

"And if that happens, I'll put my boot between his shoulder blades to hold him down while you shoot him in the back of the head," Halley replies. "And we'll go to Leavenworth together. But until then, let the shithead do his job."

She glances back at the wardroom hatch.

"He's had a big fat scarlet letter on the back of his flight suit since Arcadia," she says. "And he's standing still in his rank. That's enough punishment for now."

I think back to Arcadia, to a cool morning on the grassy plains of that beautiful moon where Blackfly Three, shredded by a dozen cannon shells, was burning so fiercely that we couldn't even get the bodies of the pilot and the crew chief out of the ship. I remember the blood-smeared, green body bags that held the three grunts from Third Platoon who bought it on that same strafing run. Two seconds of pressure on a Shrike's trigger button, and five lives snuffed out. Lieutenant Wood, Blackfly Three's pilot, got a Distinguished Flying Cross and a promotion to captain posthumously, and he'll stay at that rank forever now as well. It's laser-etched into the tiny stainless-steel plaque that's affixed to his burial slot.

"That's the point," I say. "It's no punishment at all. It's just a fucking number freeze in a personnel file."

Halley looks at the wardroom hatch again. Two lieutenants step out and give us brief curious glances before walking off down the passageway.

"He'll get his in the end," she says. "One way or another. Karma is a metric bitch."

CHAPTER 9

TALKING STUFF OUT

The worst stress in the military is not the kind you feel in combat. Everything is so fluid and hectic in battle that you don't have time to dwell on things or take an inventory of your emotions. You mostly just react. It's not even the aftermath of battle, when you lick your wounds and count your losses. The worst stress is the kind that builds up over months and years of combat ops, the low-level shit that grinds you down slowly but steadily until you find that you can't fall asleep anymore without popping pills or having a few drinks. But every ship in the Fleet has a doctor to hand out pills and a psych counselor for working out mental aches. I usually have Halley as a sounding board, but some of the stuff going on in my head is best left to a neutral party to sort out. So the day after I almost brain Captain Beals with a mess tray and get reprimanded by my wife for it, I seek out the psych counselor in the medical department on *Ottawa*. I don't care about pissing off the brass anymore, but the shrink appointment was Halley's advice and insistence, and she's about the only person other than my mother I don't want to upset needlessly.

The medical corps psychologist looks too young to be in the military, let alone a graduate of any medical school. She's wearing her auburn-tinted hair in a bob cut that falls down to chin length. On the street in Liberty Falls, I'd peg her for a college student, but she has a doctorate diploma on the wall of her office, and she's wearing second lieutenant pips on the spaulders of her Fleet uniform. Her name tag says "SAULTS, M."

"I have to say that you're not exactly what I expected here," I tell her.

"How so, Captain?" She smiles at me, revealing straight and even 'burber teeth.

"Well, most Fleet shrinks are twenty years in, burned out, and looking forward to that retirement payout."

"You're worried about my experience," she says. "I get that a lot."

I shake my head.

"No Fleet shrink has combat experience anyway. You're all trying to fix conditions you've never seen for yourself."

She leans back in her chair and looks at me with a slight smile.

"Then what are you doing here, Captain Grayson? Why did you ask for an appointment?"

"Because it helps," I say. "Talking stuff out. Sometimes."

"That's an unusual attitude," Dr. Saults says. "From a podhead, I mean."

"How so?" I echo her earlier question.

"The more gung-ho and macho the occupational specialty, the less you guys are likely to talk about what bugs you. Like it's a sign of weakness. Like it's something you should be able to handle yourselves."

"I used to think that," I say. "Until a few years ago."

"What made you change your mind?"

"I got married," I say, and she grins.

"And I had a few rough patches," I continue. "Not with the marriage. With the combat drops. Scraped past death a few too many times, in really bad ways. And then a mission went sideways, and I lost a lot of guys under my command. But I had my wife to talk to. And it helped.

But she's in the Fleet, too, and when we're deployed, I don't have a sounding board. And there's stuff I don't want her to know. Stuff I don't want to burden her with."

"Well, that's what we Fleet counselors are here for," Dr. Saults says. She gets up and walks to the beverage dispenser in the corner of her little office. "Can I get you some coffee, Captain?"

"That would be great. As long as it's not decaf."

"Decaf is an abomination, and serving it to someone should be considered a human rights violation," she says. Then she puts two cups into the dispenser. The machine hisses and fills the cups. Dr. Saults takes them and puts one in front of me as she sits back down.

"Thank you."

"You're welcome. And now let's talk about what's bugging you so much right now that you come to a Fleet psych counselor without having been ordered by your CO."

"Is that so rare?" I ask.

"For podheads? Oh yeah. I see ten to twenty people a week. Three-quarters of them are nuggets on their first real deployment who are scared and homesick. Some people just want to chat over a cup of coffee. But you're only the fourth SOCOM guy I've seen in a year. And the first one that showed up voluntarily."

"This boat has a few thousand people on it, and only thirty-five SOCOM personnel," I say. "I'd be surprised if you saw another one of us on this deployment."

"Well, I guess I'll have to get the most out of this visit," Dr. Saults says, and takes a sip of her coffee. "What do you want to tell me, Captain?"

I tell the Fleet shrink about almost having planted a mess tray in Captain Beals's head and then say, "I was hoping he'd make a move and try to hit me first. So I'd have an excuse to pound him into the deck. Truth be told, I would have done it anyway if my wife hadn't been there to stop me."

"And does that bother you?" Dr. Saults asks.

"Nope," I say. "The only thing that bothered me about the whole incident, from start to finish, was the way my wife reacted. That's why the little bastard still has a full set of teeth in his mouth."

"What did he do that made you despise this guy so much?"

"Well, that's a longer story," I say.

"I'll be here all day," she replies. "You want to share it, go ahead."

I backtrack to the Arcadia mission to give her the proper context. I talk her through the whole timeline, including the battle we fought at Arcadia City to try to capture the former president, and Major Masoud's surprise nuking of the city's main fusion plant. I thought that three years would be plenty of time to start forgetting some of the details, but as I recount the whole mission beat by beat to Dr. Saults, I find that it's all still just as easy to recall, as if it had happened last month. She listens to my monologue, asks the occasional clarifying question, and looks appropriately concerned and disturbed at all the right places in my narrative. When I'm finished telling her about the Arcadia mission, my cup is empty, so Dr. Saults gets us both refills from the dispenser.

"That's why I wouldn't lose any sleep at all over Captain Beals's death or if he lands in the infirmary," I conclude. "He went with the renegades. He willingly killed my comrades. And when he had the chance to fix his shit, all he did was pick the side he thought had the best chance of winning."

"You take it personally. Because he tried to kill you."

"And my wife. But she turned out to be a better pilot. Shot his ass down."

"You said there's stuff you're not telling her. That you don't want to burden her with. Did that stuff happen at Mars?"

"Mars was a shitshow," I say. "Everyone went through the same wringer there. Everyone who came back, anyway."

I take a long sip from my cup. It's the standard shitty Fleet coffee, and I am not particularly fond of that swill, but holding the mug gives my hands something to do.

"After Mars, I spent a year and a half Earthside. Down in the PRCs, with the Brigades. Mars was a nightmare, but it was just a forty-eight-hour nightmare."

I put my coffee cup down in front of me and look at the diploma on the wall behind Dr. Saults's head.

"When I got there, we were still raw from Mars. But I still felt like a Fleet officer. I knew my slot. I spent time training people for the Brigades. But then I got roped into combat missions, because there's no such thing as a neutral observer when the bullets start flying down there."

"Who did you fight? I thought the Brigades had everything well in hand now?"

"They do. In the cities they control. And they're gaining ground every day. Block by block. But some of those gangs are hard cases, and they don't want to let go of their turf."

"I see. And you went to battle against the gangs."

"Eighteen months," I repeat. "And for the last six months, I did stuff every day that would get me a court-martial if I had done it in the Fleet. I killed people who didn't deserve to die. Let people live who damn well needed a bullet between the eyes. And at the end, I didn't feel like a Fleet officer anymore. To be honest, at the end I wasn't sure whether I was pointing my gun at the right people."

She studies my face as I talk, and I know that she's looking for telltale behavioral signs from her Psych 101 textbook: averted eyes, changed volume or tone of voice, halting delivery, that sort of thing. But I mostly feel exhausted and numb when I think about the Brigades and my time in the PRCs, so I keep a carefully neutral expression. I know this game because the Fleet shrinks already put me through that wringer after I returned to regular service, and I could tell they were searching for evidence that my mental pottery had cracked irreparably.

It should feel weird to be sitting in this office and telling all this stuff to someone who looks like I have ten years of life experience and eight years of service on her. But I know that this is her job, and it feels better saying these words in front of a live human who can at least feign empathy than keeping them percolating in my skull unsaid, or writing them down in a PDP file that nobody will ever read.

"What did you do after you got back?" Dr. Saults asks. "You had a psych eval, obviously."

"You know I did. It's probably right there in my file." I nod toward the transparent frame of her terminal screen. "And I lied my ass off. I was just glad to get back to the regular Fleet. Took a month off at home in Vermont, but then I went right back to it."

"You've done a lot of combat missions," she says. "More than most. More than anyone I've seen in this office this year, I think."

"I've been in for nine years," I say. "Seven as a podhead. I was up to over three hundred drops before Mars. And I've done five or six Lanky patrols a week over Mars for a year. I've kind of lost count of the total, to be honest."

Dr. Saults looks at her screen and zooms in on a data field.

"Five hundred and twenty-nine," she says. "That's just official corps numbers. Not counting whatever you did for the Brigades."

I let that number roll around in my head for a few moments. I went into combat for the NAC over half a thousand times, and I've spent almost my entire adult life in the military. Many of those missions were milk runs, with no shots fired and clean rifles turned back into the armory. Many were dangerous, my team going up against SRA marines or Lanky concentrations. Some were so stressful and hair-raisingly scary that they each probably took a year off the rest of my life. But the ones I get to revisit in my dreams most often are the dark and bloody ones, the events your brain insists on playing back to you in high definition whenever you encounter a sound, smell, or sight that reminds you of them.

"They got us by the balls, don't they?" I say.

"What do you mean?" Dr. Saults asks.

"I don't know how to do anything else. I know how to direct air traffic. Use and fieldstrip every small-arms system in the corps. Call down airstrikes. Do a spaceborne drop onto a barren rock from a hundred thousand klicks away. But that's it. I know how to break shit and kill people. Lankies, too. But give me two weeks of shore leave, and I'm barely functional."

"What do you do when you're on shore leave?"

"Go home to Vermont. Sleep a lot. If my wife and I get leave together, we go hiking in the mountains. You know, anything where you don't have to breathe filtered air or listen to fusion engines while you're going to sleep. You want to hear something odd?"

"Sure," Dr. Saults says.

"On our first long leave together, we stayed at a friend's place in Vermont, out in the country. First few days of the leave, I had trouble falling asleep because it was too damn quiet. No engine noise. No 1MC announcements. No boots tromping around on the deck."

"I have the opposite problem," Dr. Saults says. "I have to put in earplugs and turn on the haptic alert on the bunk. Otherwise I'll be up for two hours after rack time."

"Get out while you can," I say. "I mean it. Do your minimum time to pay them back for your psych degree, then get the hell out. Before you end up living your whole life in watch cycles. Before they have their hooks in you so firmly that your only option is to keep re-upping."

"Why does it sound like I'm the one getting counseling here?" Dr. Saults says with a smile.

"It's not counseling. It's friendly advice. Relaying experience."

"I appreciate the advice," she says. "But I don't plan on doing this forever. I want to go back home and work in pediatric support. I did, in fact, join for the free degree."

"No shame in that. I joined to get out of the PRC. That's why the corps never had a problem with recruitment before the Lankies. No shortage of PRC rats trying to move up."

Dr. Saults is a second lieutenant, which is the standard rank for new doctors joining the Fleet after med school. It also means that she has less than two years of active service, which in turn means that she has never been on a ship in combat ops against the Lankies. She's never even seen one outside of Network or MilNet footage.

"I don't have any problem sleeping anymore," I say, to steer the conversation back on comfortable ground for this green medical officer. "In the Fleet or down on Earth. In fact, I'm always tired. I could go and hit the rack right now for a nap, and I'd be out in two minutes flat. But I have some trouble controlling my anger these days. It's like I'm always pissed off about something, and it doesn't need much of a spark to light my fuse."

"Since you got back from your tour with the Brigades, you mean."

"Yeah."

"Why do you think that is?" Dr. Saults asks. She's back in her therapist mode, probably glad she can go through her psych-school script of mental-health evals.

"I'm not sure. I mean, I worked on detached duty for eighteen months. I had two Fleet officers with me, but I was the ranking team member. The next person I had to answer to was a thousand miles away in an office at Norfolk. And then I got back, and they stuck me on combat patrols over Mars for two deployments, back to back. Have you been on a ship assigned to orbital garrison, Lieutenant?"

"No, I haven't," she says. "I did my residency down at Great Lakes. But *Ottawa* is my first space deployment."

"Oh, man. No wonder you still need earplugs," I say.

I lean forward, plant my elbows on the desk in front of me, and rub my eyes.

"Orbital garrison duty is the pits. If you manage to get yourself assigned to a ship bound for Mars, you'll be busier than a mess cook at dinnertime. Eight-hour patrols in terrible weather, and we're flying over what's left of the biggest colony we've ever had. We get a decontamination session after every patrol because the planet is so radioactive now from all the nukes we used that it practically glows on its own. We see Olympus City on some low-level passes, and every time I remember what it used to look like, and it makes me want to puke. I try not to think of how many millions died down there. How many were used as protein chains for those fucking seed ships they were building all along." I pause and down the rest of my coffee, which is still hot enough to make the action uncomfortable.

"And we do that *every fucking day*. For *months*. Sometimes we get to kill a Lanky or two from the air. Sometimes I get to call down another strike, kinetic or nuke. Fuck the place up even more. Go back to the carrier, decon, debrief, take a shower, grab some chow, go to sleep. Get up the next morning, and do it again. And most of the time, I'm just staring at a screen and getting bumped around in the shittiest weather you've ever seen. Boring the shit out of myself, logging flight hours over an irradiated graveyard."

The concern on Dr. Saults's face is the most genuine I've seen since we started our talk.

"If you've done that for two deployments in a row, I can understand your mental state one hundred percent."

I very much doubt that, I think, but nod anyway.

"Have you tried antidepressants? They usually work well for PTSD-related symptoms."

"I was on pills for over a year. From just after the Battle of Earth until just after the Arcadia run."

"And did you feel they helped?"

"Some," I say. "I think it was mainly because I thought they would. But I used them too often, and I washed them down with liquor. They made me feel kind of lethargic. Like I had no energy left, emotionally. And I didn't want to keep going down that route. So I stopped taking them."

"There's new medication out now that works much better and doesn't have the side effects," Dr. Saults says. "I'd like you to try it out."

She turns her attention to her screen and taps in a few entries.

"In my professional opinion, you have PTSD, which is common among frontline personnel." She looks at me again and smiles curtly.

"My unofficial opinion is that you also have a massive case of burnout, which is even more common among combat troops that have been in for as long as you have. I'll send a scrip for you to the ship pharmacy. That'll help you in the short term."

She smiles again, but this one is a wry sort of smile that looks a bit out of place on her young face.

"And for the long term, you should probably take the advice you just gave me. Think about getting out while you can. Before you end up needing those meds and that liquor just to function. Or before you don't listen to your wife and actually do take someone's head off with a mess tray."

I fake a sheepish smile and get out of my chair. Dr. Saults thinks she's seen enough of my mental state to take a stab at a fix, but I haven't given her a glimpse of the really fucked-up areas in my head yet. I know that if I did, she wouldn't put me on meds; she'd have me committed or push for a medical discharge from the corps.

I leave Dr. Saults's office and walk to the end of the passageway. Then I check my shiny, new transparent PDP for directions to the pharmacy. It's on the same deck, five frames forward and three compartments to starboard. The elevator bank that will take me back to my office is nine frames back, the opposite direction from the pharmacy.

I think for a moment. Then I tuck the PDP away and turn around to head to the elevators. I'd rather be anxious and awake than relaxed but drugged up with whatever wonder chemical they cooked up now to keep the cogs in their machine running smoothly.

But as I stand in front of the elevator bank a minute later, I realize that I'm already thinking about that allotted drink tonight and that I'll just try to take the edge off with something else. And one day, I'll either try to work a spaceborne landing while half-drunk, or I'll bash the skull of someone like Captain Beals into a bulkhead. There are plenty of Arcadians on this ship—troops who were part of that treason, but who have been given a chance at redemption during Mars and who are now at least no longer outcasts. Not to the rest of the corps, anyway. But I lost men and women, almost lost my wife, and I won't ever fully forgive and forget.

That's not you, Andrew, Halley had said when she read me the riot act after the incident with Beals.

When the elevator door opens, I don't get in. Instead, I turn around to go back to the pharmacy, to pick up whatever Dr. Saults prescribed. If it nudges me back toward the way I was before even a little, it'll be worth the try. And if it doesn't, I have a private sink in my stateroom that will send those meds right to the ship's recyclers. But I know I want to reduce the chances that my wife will ever look at me again with the same disapproval as she did just an hour ago outside of that wardroom.

CHAPTER 10

EARTH TO TITAN

The SOCOM detachment on *Ottawa* consists of two teams. One is the SEAL team, sixteen men led by Captain Rolson. The other is my special tactics team, made up of eight combat controllers and eight Spaceborne Rescuemen. My second-in-command, Lieutenant Brown, is in charge of the PJs, as the Spaceborne Rescuemen are nicknamed for reasons that are a little fuzzy and have something to do with their nucleus as airborne rescue medics in the old US military. I'm in charge of the entire team, but I'm also the operational leader of the combat controllers. I know that this is the standard organizational setup for an STT in a SOCOM detachment on a carrier, but I still can't shake a feeling of inadequacy as I walk into the briefing room for the first STT briefing on this deployment. There are seventeen men and women sitting in the chairs of a briefing room that could hold fifty, and I get a little pang of worry when I see just how small the STT is compared to the SI complement on *Ottawa*. But even though we are almost useless without the SI's firepower behind us, the SI can't do their jobs without SOCOM.

Lieutenant Brown calls the room to attention when I step through the hatch. I could issue an "As you were," but I let him do the full report and announce that the STT is complete and ready for briefing as ordered.

The first meeting sets the tone for a command, and I don't want to appear too casual. I've commanded more troops before—the platoon for Arcadia numbered almost forty SI troopers—but these are all relatively seasoned troops in an extremely demanding occupational specialty. No matter what their rank, nobody in this briefing room has spent less than two years training before being assigned to an operational command.

"Thank you, Lieutenant," I say when Lieutenant Brown has finished the formality. "Have a seat, ladies and gentlemen."

Everyone takes their seats again, and I walk up to the lectern at the front of the room and pull out my PDP to glance at the unit roster.

"I am Captain Grayson," I say. "I will be your CO for this deployment. You all know we will be the STT for the Seventh Spaceborne Infantry Regiment and the Fifth and Eleventh Assault Transport Squadrons. That's twelve hundred troopers and sixty-four drop ship crew counting on us to not fuck up when the hammer drops."

The STT troopers look at me attentively. When we go into battle, the combat controllers will do their regular job of jumping in with the first wave and calling down air and orbital support. The job of the Spaceborne Rescuemen is to pod-launch in whenever a drop ship goes down, to patch up survivors and defend them against threats before the SAR flight can lift them out. Of the two jobs, Spaceborne Rescue has the slightly longer and harder training track, and the men and women in this room don't carry enough body fat between them to fill up a coffee cup if you suctioned it out of them. The lowest-ranked member of the group is a combat controller staff sergeant, and the highest-ranked ones are two master sergeants, one from each occupational specialty.

"This one is a new one, even for me. Looks like the combat controller team is getting a permanent station in CIC," I continue. "It's called Tactical Operations, and it will be staffed by a qualified combat controller at all times. We will work out a watch rotation for everyone to make sure that every red hat in this group gets equal time in that chair.

The hardware is all new and shiny, but the software is the same we're all used to. So it'll be like running a big admin deck from a cushy seat."

One of the combat controllers raises a hand.

"Sir, there's eight of us. With the watch cycle, we're going to get our schedules all out of sync within five days."

"There's nine of us," I say. "I don't exempt myself from the rotation. Don't get me wrong—I'll swap one of you into that CIC seat on the fly if I have to pay attention to something else, but we're splitting the rotation nine ways."

I see approving nods from the combat controller section. I am a red hat by training, but as a special tactics officer, I'm not strictly a combat controller anymore because that's an occupational specialty reserved for enlisted personnel. But I've spent so much time wearing the scarlet beret when I was enlisted that it's hard to think myself as above these guys, even though I am four pay grades above the highest-ranking one of them and get to eat in a wardroom instead of a mess.

"Here's how it's going to go. This is a shakedown cruise, not a combat deployment. We're doing joint training with the whole team whenever we can. As most of you have probably discovered already, this luxury barge has everything you're used to from a shore installation. We have dedicated PT facilities, a shooting range just for SOCOM, and our own TacLink simulator with combat controller software. The CCT will get up to speed on the new hardware and rotate through the battlespace control station in CIC. The PJs will do whatever it is you guys do for training. I'll leave that up to Lieutenant Brown, but I assume it involves running that mile-long PT track with an anvil under each arm."

The troops in the room laugh.

"Only one anvil, but held at arm's length," Lieutenant Brown corrects me from the first row, and the team laughs again. I feel very much at home with this group—they've all sweated and bled in training about ten times more than the average SI grunt, and we're part of a very small club, one with a high mortality rate in combat.

"Word has it we're doing a large-scale live-fire exercise after we refuel and restock at Titan, if this thing makes it there without major bits falling off unexpectedly. We have at least five weeks until then, so we'll use that time to make sure that we hit it out of the park. You know the drill. I'll be sending out the roster for this week shortly, and we'll get to work. Any questions?"

"Sir, are we going to sim the pod launches or do live ones?" one of the combat controllers asks. She's the only woman on the team, but she's taller than half the guys in the room. Her name tape says "LANG, E.," and she's wearing staff sergeant stripes.

"They said live-fire, so I am assuming we'll do live launches, too," I reply. Sergeant Lang returns a satisfied nod. Simulated pod launches don't involve any pods at all—you just take a ride in the lead drop ship wave, and the computer determines by algorithm if the simulated pod from the ship made it onto the planet. If the computer says that it didn't, you get to step off the drop ship and count as a casualty the moment your boots hit the dirt. It's much cheaper and far less risky than an actual pod launch, but it doesn't count toward your official drop total, and it's boring as hell.

"You all know your jobs. Daily orders in this briefing room at 0700. Stay in shape, keep the edge honed, learn the new stuff, and take your downtime when you're off the clock. But stick to the booze limit if you're going to drink. We all know there's no one-drink limit on engineering moonshine, but I want a sharp team. Let's use the hell out of that fancy running track that goes around the missile silos. Because we all know that the console jockeys on this boat aren't going to set foot on it."

I hear a resounding chorus of "Aye, sir!" all over the room.

"All right. Let's get to it and make use of the transit time. Any issues or questions, you know where to find me or Lieutenant Brown. *Dismissed.*"

On the Network shows I watched as a kid, the starships always had a bridge with windows on the top or front of the ship. In real life, that's the dumbest thing you could do to a warship. You don't need windows because you have optics all over the hull, and polyplast panels would be a weak spot in the armor. More importantly, you'd place the operational heart of the ship at an obvious and vulnerable spot, easily targeted and destroyed by a single rail-gun round or missile hit. On a real warship, there is no bridge, just a combat information center. The CIC is in the middle of the ship, surrounded by as much laminate armor as possible. I'm used to the CIC being like a bunker, an armored citadel with hatches and its own life-support system, but like everything else on this ship, *Ottawa's* CIC bucks tradition. The compartment is bigger than the hangar deck on the first frigate I served on. The modular control stations all along the walls of the CIC make the compartment look even bigger than it is. In the other Fleet ships, the consoles are clunky things in heavy shockproof mounts. In this CIC, they are almost graceful-looking minimalist designs with huge transparent screens. There's the usual command pit with the holotable in the center of the CIC, and a large situational display takes up almost the entire forward bulkhead.

I report to the XO in the command pit and then take over the TacOps station for the first time. It's plain that the consoles on this ship are brand-new. On this particular station, the touch screens don't even have fingerprints on them, and I have to remove the protective liner from one of the control surfaces. Then I activate the stations, and the screens in front of me turn on instantly. I have one in the center, two angled ones on the left and right, and one more overhead, mounted to the control station rack and tilted down to face my seat. I'm used to having to wait twenty or thirty seconds while the tactical control system comes fully online because it has to poll information from so many different sources, but this system just jumps into live status as soon as I put my hand down on the control surface for access authorization.

We are not in the middle of a planetary assault, and I have no ground attack craft or drop ships to direct, so I start familiarizing myself with the capabilities of the integrated systems of this ship. Everything I tap into responds with lightning speed. Compared to every ship I've served on before, the neural network speed on this thing makes the systems on the older ships feel like working with cans on a string. On the flight deck, most of the drop ships are powered down and their systems cold, but a few of them are hooked up to service umbilicals, and I can tap into their onboard systems in a blink to look at the flight deck from the cameras on their hulls.

It takes me a few minutes to arrange the screens into my preferred layout and save the setup to my user profile so the other combat controllers who will be cycling through this seat can't mess with it. The big situational display at the front bulkhead of the CIC shows the plot, *Ottawa* creeping along a trajectory line to intercept the orbit of Titan, Saturn's largest moon and location of the biggest Fleet base in the outer solar system. The holotable in the center of the command pit shows the tactical display, a sphere around the ship that shows everything out to a hundred-thousand-kilometer radius. I don't need the plot on my smaller display— the relative location of the ship in the solar system is of no importance to tactical ops—but I do like to have the tactical display mirrored on my overhead screen, so I set it to duplicate the holotable display. The screens on the sides are for air assets and their inventories, camera feeds, and other nuts-and-bolts stuff that lets me keep an eye on resources. The center screen right in front of me is for my TacLink display, where I will spend most of my time once we have birds in the air and targets to engage.

With the system access afforded by my console, I check out the weapons systems of *Ottawa* for the first time to see what kind of firepower we'll be able to call down. Controlling the weapons is the domain of the various weapon officer stations, but I can see the assets we have so I know their status and their availability for orbital strikes. I scroll through the available systems and let out an involuntary low whistle. *Ottawa* has a dozen ventral rail-gun mounts, each connected to enormous magazines of three hundred rounds per gun. Amidships on the top of the hull, there are missile silos to port and starboard of *Ottawa's* dorsal bulge, thirty-two Hades-C guided antiship missiles with thermo-nuclear warheads on each side. But the nukes aren't the biggest punch this ship can dish out. That's the pair of ventrally mounted particle cannons that run almost half the length of the ship and the six Orion III missiles in their armored box launchers. Going over the weapons systems of *Ottawa*, I know why the SRA got exactly as many ships of this class as the NAC. This ship is nothing like we've ever put into space before. In direct combat, it could probably take on the entire remaining Fleet and blow it into stardust. But everything about the *Ottawa* is clearly designed to kill Lanky seed ships and scrape them off occupied planets, not to take on other human-crewed warships.

As I study the three-dimensional image of the ship on my screen, I am once again struck by how much the shape of the design reminds me of a Lanky seed ship. It doesn't have the length or sheer mass of a seed ship, but it shares the almost organic, flowing shape of the hull, without a right angle anywhere. It also doesn't radiate the menace of the flat-black Lanky ships—the hull is painted titanium white with orange-and-blue markers here and there. It's a pretty ship, as far as a warship can be called that. But it's undeniably powerful-looking, and after my quick inventory, I know that *Ottawa* has enough destructive power tucked away under that gracefully flowing white armor to back up that impression. If seed ships are monsters, this thing is a monster killer. And we have three more just like it almost ready for their own shakedown cruises at Daedalus.

We went from an ass-kicking to a stalemate, I think. *With more of these, we can finally return the ass-kicking in kind.*

If they work as they should, an unbidden voice in my head cautions me. I remember how quickly *Agincourt* got taken out of the fight three years ago above Mars even though we did everything by the book. That was an expensive beta test for the battleships, and I hope they learned the right lessons from them, because I do not want to find out what it feels like when you launch out of *Ottawa* in an escape pod, no matter how cushy they made the damn things.

CHAPTER 11

———— A PLEASANT REUNION ————

The trip to Fleet Yard Titan takes six weeks from Earth. The running track sandwiched into the space between the nuclear missile silos is exactly one kilometer long. Two days before our arrival at Titan, with Saturn already looming large behind the ship even at low magnification, I have run that kilometer two hundred times, five kilometers per day.

The track would be a thing of luxury on a shore installation. On a warship, it's an unimaginable opulence because it's thousands of cubic meters of empty single-use space. It has a firm padded surface and a white line down the middle, and it's wide enough for two people to run abreast if there's nobody faster coming up from behind to claim the space. I'm sure there are emergency-use plans for the space when it is needed, but right now it's just a long ellipse of a passageway, uninterrupted except for a slight narrowing of the track for bulkheads every now and then. It's air-conditioned and quiet, and the ability to run for almost half a kilometer in a straight line without having to stop or turn alleviates some of the twitches of claustrophobia I usually get on a spaceship, even after years of deployments. It also counteracts the side effects of *Ottawa*'s officer's wardroom, which has the best food Halley and I have had in years outside of Chief Kopka's little restaurant.

In an unusual display of design smarts, the running track is connected to the ship's main gym, where some motivated SI troops are currently doing weight work on the benches. The weight bars don't have weights hanging off them—racks full of ten- and twenty-kilo steel plates would be a hazard on a ship that can pull over ten g's of acceleration, artificial gravity or not—so they are connected to computerized uprights that generate the programmed weight via electromagnetic resistance. It lacks the satisfying feel of lifting real steel, but it's much better than having to take three-month breaks between lifting routines.

There's a small vestibule connecting the gym to the running track that's the only way on and off the track not involving an emergency hatch. I've been running with three of my STT sergeants for our regular prebreakfast 5k, and we trot up into the vestibule at the end of our fifth round sweaty, out of breath, and ready for coffee and eggs. Just as we enter the vestibule, the hatch from the gym side opens, and three SI officers step out and fill the space from the other side. We wear PT gear, and the Fleet issues black workout shorts while the SI uses green ones. The workout shirts in both branches are black, with simplified rank symbols on the upper sleeves—one fluorescent horizontal stripe for junior NCOs, two stripes for senior NCOs, one round pip for junior officers, and two for staff officers—to quickly identify pecking orders in interunit PT gaggles. The three SI troopers coming out to use the track all have the same junior officer pip on their sleeves as I do, and I nod at them from my hunched-over position as I catch my breath.

"How's the weather out today?" one of the SI officers asks. Her voice stirs a faint memory in my brain, and I straighten up to get a better look at her. From the way her eyes widen in surprise, I see that we recognize each other at the same moment.

"Andrew Grayson," she says. "Son of a bitch."

"Hansen," I say. "How have you been?"

When I saw her last, we were both in battle armor and bleeding, a scary, hot summer night almost nine years ago that now feels as distant as if someone else lived through the event. Then-PFC Hansen was one of my squad mates in Bravo Company, 365th Autonomous Infantry Battalion, Territorial Army.

"I've been all right," she says and grins. She has lost the ponytail—in fact, her hair is now a short cut better suited for vacuum-rated battle armor—but she still looks much the same as she did when I first walked into the squad room at Fort Shughart nine years ago, even if her almond-shaped eyes have a few more wrinkles in their corners, and she looks like she's packed on about five or ten kilos of muscle since then.

"We served together in the old TA," she tells the officers next to her, and they nod at me. "He was one of my squaddies."

"Green as a pair of PT shorts," I confirm.

"Why don't you head out and get started?" she says. "I'll catch up with you in a second."

"Go ahead and hit the showers," I dismiss the two sergeants behind me, and they nod and step through the hatch into the main gym. Hansen's two companions walk out onto the track and then trot off for their first counterclockwise round of the ellipse.

"So you're SI now?" I ask. "And you made officer."

"Yeah, I got shuffled to the space monkeys during the Mars buildup," she says. "You know, when they retrained half the HD branch to SI." She glances at the junior officer pip on her shoulder. "And I think everyone who's been in for as long as we have is either an officer or dead by now."

"How's the shoulder?" I ask. Hansen's shoulder joint took a round that night in Detroit, and Sergeant Fallon told me in the hospital at Great Lakes afterwards that Hansen's joint got replaced with an artificial one.

"It's fine. Works as well as the old one. They could have at least given me a power boost upgrade or something, but no dice."

"Yeah, I hear you. I missed the perfect opportunity for a cutting-edge knife hand." I look at my left hand and wiggle my fingers. The three outboard ones will never not feel weird, sort of muted and numb, like a local shot of anesthetic that has almost but not quite worn off. "Got those shot off. By a civilian security cop, if you can believe that. Embarrassing."

"I'd like to hear the story behind that," Hansen says. "And whatever happened to you after Detroit. I heard from Sergeant Fallon you got shunted over to the navy, but that's about it."

"Let's catch up," I suggest. "What's your current command?"

"I'm the CO of Charlie Company, First Battalion, Seventh SI. What about you?"

"I'm in charge of the special tactics team."

"Podhead," she says with a grin. "You couldn't find yourself a nice console jockey job after that mess in Detroit?"

"I tried. Got bored. Guess I'm not the console jockey type."

"I guess not." She looks at her chrono. "Listen, I want to get my laps in before chow and orders, but I'd love to catch up. You on a watch cycle?"

"We make our own team rotation for the CIC seat," I say. "Everything else is grunt schedule."

"Let's sync lunch or something. How about 1145?"

"I can do that. Which wardroom?"

"Where do you usually eat?"

"Flight deck level. But I can come slum in Grunt Country."

"You've got the credentials." She taps me on the chest with the back of her hand. "Holy shit, I never expected to run into anyone from Bravo/365 again. See you at 1145."

"Affirmative," I say, and watch her as she walks out onto the track and starts running. If anything, she's in better shape than she was in the TA, and she was already lean and mean back then. It's a strangely elating feeling to run into someone who has been part of my service history almost from the beginning, almost as long as Halley. Maybe that means some of us will make it through this meat grinder after all.

I spend the morning in my office in the SOCOM section, sorting out training schedules and CIC coverage when I'd rather be at the firing range. The higher your rank, the more administrative bullshit gets shoveled onto your plate. I suspect that staff and general officers must have a terminal screen in the head as well so they can respond to administrative messages even when they're on the throne.

At 1130, my reminder alert goes off, and I shut down my terminal screen and check myself in the mirror before heading out to Grunt Country.

In the SI officer's wardroom, everyone is wearing the standard SI battle tunic with its distinctive camo pattern, and when I walk into the wardroom, I stick out right away as the only person wearing a Fleet uniform. The blueberry suit is as different from the SI cammies as you can get. At least the old Fleet cammies had roughly the same cut as their SI counterparts, even if the camo pattern was different. But the new suits are radically something else, and as I walk up to the buffet and put food on my mess tray, I feel like some boot camp recruit who mistakenly ended up in formation wearing his PT outfit while everyone else is in battle dress. I don't see Hansen at any of the tables yet, so I sit down at an empty one and pick at my salad while I wait.

Hansen comes in a few minutes later, wearing faded but crisp-looking SI cammies, sleeves folded tightly and neatly over her biceps in the traditional way the SI maintained from the time they were called marines. Hansen spots me and nods. Then she gets her food and comes over to join me.

"I just had a flashback to that fracas in the enlisted chow hall back at Shughart," I say when she sits down. "Remember that one?"

She chuckles.

"Oh yeah. When those marines tried to cut into line at chow. That was the most fun meal I've had in the TA. Took half a platoon of MPs to get that place under control once the mashed potatoes started flying."

Hansen's tunic bears captain's rank insignia and a combat-drop badge in gold, just like my new Fleet uniform. She looks like a proper grunt, while I still think the new uniform makes me look like an actor pretending to be a starship captain on a second-rate Network show.

"And then the sergeant major chewed out the grunts who were there but didn't fight," I say, and we both grin.

"Never thought I'd trade in that green beret for a maroon one," Hansen says.

"Do you miss being HD?"

"Nope. That's why I jumped on the offer when they asked for volunteers for the SI at first. Three months later, I got out of SOI on Luna, and then it was no longer optional. They just went through the HD battalions and pulled whoever they needed. *Here are your new orders, have fun in space.* At least I got the early volunteer perks."

"As much fun as we made of the space monkeys, and now we're both here," I say.

"After you were gone, things turned to shit. Not all at once, but gradually. We just ended up getting more and more riot alerts. Three a year, then one every other month, then four or five in a month. And taking a beating all the while. That was right before the PRCs turned into a raging garbage fire. You have no idea what it was like in the end. I figured space couldn't be half as dangerous, even with the Lankies."

"I have a good idea," I reply. "I did eighteen months with the Lazarus Brigade as an instructor. Loan from the Fleet, to get their own Combat Controller School off the ground."

"Ouch," Hansen says. "You couldn't get me back into a PRC at this point. Not if you promised me a Medal of Honor and a three-story house in a gated 'burb for it. Give me the choice between dropping into a nonpacified PRC or onto a Lanky-controlled moon, I'll take my chances with the Lankies."

We eat our food and trade rough timelines of our service histories from the last eight years. Hansen switched to the SI only three years ago as a sergeant first class, and one of her volunteer perks was her pick between a senior NCO slot or an officer commission. She went the brass road, and it turns out we both made captain rank at roughly the same time, six months ago. In peacetime, turning an NCO rank into O-3 within three years was impossible, with so many troops choosing to remain in the corps and competing for limited billets. But the corps was bled white after the Lankies took Mars, and trained personnel were suddenly hard to come by. It takes three months to turn a raw civilian into a soldier, and then three more to make him or her a basically competent fire team member. It takes years to train a combat controller or Spaceborne Rescue specialist. You can train a new rifleman or build a new drop ship much more quickly than you can replace an experienced infantry company commander or drop ship pilot. Hansen, Halley, and I got pushed up the ladder quickly because too many of the people above us had fallen off.

"So you're married to your boot camp girlfriend," Hansen says with a grin when I get to that part of my own narrative. "I've heard of that happening, but I've never known anyone who's done it."

"She's on *Ottawa*, too," I say. "She's the XO of one of the drop ship squadrons."

"I am not surprised. It's like they put all the seasoned people they had left onto their shiny new toy. The Seventh SI is one of the few regiments left that isn't mostly green troops fresh out of SOI."

"You were at Mars," I say, and she nods.

"LZ Yellow. The Seventh did all right. Compared to what some of the other regiments suffered, I mean. We had three hundred dead, half the rest wounded. I had a platoon in Delta company. Held the line and gained fifteen klicks of ground before the emergency dustoff."

She stabs her next piece of chicken with a lot more force than necessary.

MARKO KLOOS

"God, we were feeling so fucking good about ourselves. We were pushing them back. We were killing them by the dozens. We were gaining ground. Until that TacLink screen went nuts with orange icons. On our flanks. In the rear, the parts we thought we had already cleared. But you know the story."

"Yeah," I say. "Same at LZ Red. They were dragging out the carrot so we'd stick our heads far enough out of the LZ. And then they had us in the bag."

Hansen picks up the cup of bug juice next to her plate and downs about half of it in what seems like one gulp.

"Drop ships and close air saved our asses on the retreat," she continues. "They were piling Lanky bodies all around us. At some point, we had the whole regiment in a bubble half a klick across, defending in all directions. And the drop ships—I've never seen anything like it, not in the PRCs, nowhere. They used everything on the external racks, shot every last round out of their cannons, and put down their birds a hundred meters in front of advancing Lankies to pick up platoons without even putting skids into the dirt. And most of us got off. None of the drop ship jocks in that squadron will ever have to buy drinks again as long as anyone from the Seventh SI is in the same room."

The Battle of Mars is technically the Second Battle of Mars, because the first one took place when the Lankies came in four years ago and wiped out the colony along with most of the Earth fleets. But whenever someone in the corps talks about Mars these days, it's shorthand for the battle that took place a year later, the combined assault on the Lankies with everything the Earth's alliances could throw at them—Operation Invictus. It has become the defining landmark of our service histories, the one big operation where almost everyone in the spacebound branches of the corps participated. It's also a demarcation line between the veterans and the untested. If you don't have the ribbon for Mars on your Class A smock, the simple orange-red one with the three white

122

stripes down the middle, you are green regardless of what rank you wear. You may be a sergeant or a first lieutenant, and you may have even pulled a garrison deployment above the nuked remains of the battlefields on Mars, but if you got out of your tech school or the School of Infantry even a day after that battle, you have not seen real combat.

When two vets of Mars get together, they invariably compare landing zones, and everyone knows which beaches got hit hardest. Red, Orange, and Yellow Beach got pounded but held the line until the end. Blue and Purple had to join up and fight back-to-back to make it off that rock. And you rarely ever meet a veteran of Green Beach, because it got overrun by the Lankies when their space control cruiser hit a mine and couldn't keep the minefield open for orbital fire support. A whole regiment of SI landed at Green, with a full SRA marine regiment along-side them, and the ones who survived could fit into three drop ships with space left over for a few cargo pallets. Green got it the worst by far, but no beach was easy, and every regiment got a severe mauling. We went to Mars with twenty thousand SI, SRA, and Eurocorps marines and came back with eleven thousand, five hundred. The SI contributed over eight thousand men and women, and fewer than five thousand returned, a quarter of them wounded.

"Can't believe you were down at Yellow while we were stacking Lankies at Red," I say. "I wonder if any more of the old squad are SI or Fleet now."

"Not that I know of. After you were gone, Corporal Jackson went MIA on a mission in the PRCs. I hear she joined the Brigades, but you know the rumor mill. I didn't buy it, because come on. Corporal *Jackson*?"

"She did," I say. "She's General Lazarus's head of security. More than that, I think."

"No way." Hansen narrows her eyes and squints at me in an apprais-ing sort of way. "Are you fucking with me right now?"

"Nope. Had quite a few drinks with her when I was with the Brigades. She's a colonel now. You join the Brigades, they make you an officer in a hurry if you have prior experience in the corps."

"Well, fuck that. They could offer me twenty-star general and my own personal city block, and I'd decline. I can't believe she jumped ship. Or you know what? I think I can."

Hansen slugs the rest of her bug juice like it's a shot of liquor.

"Priest didn't re-up after Detroit. Took his money and got out after his first four. I think losing Paterson and Stratton fucked him up a little."

"It fucked us all up," I say. "I would have stayed with the squad. But they didn't give me the choice."

"Yeah, the sarge told us all about it after she got back from Great Lakes. I hear you two were the best of pals in the hospital. I wonder what happened to her. She dropped off the radar after they broke up our platoon and spread us around. I think they stuck her into the 330th."

"After a month in the brig, if I recall correctly. For disobeying orders."

"How do you know that?"

I just shrug with a smile. "She told me the tale."

"What? *Where? When?*" Hansen looks genuinely puzzled. "You met her after you left the TA?"

"They shipped her battalion out for garrison duty to get rid of them. We ended up on the same carrier, going out to the frozen-ass end of nowhere. And she was my platoon sergeant on the Arcadia mission three years ago."

"*You* were on that mission? The one where a company of SI and a handful of podheads tippy-toed into the system and made the whole garrison surrender?"

"I had one of the platoons in that company."

"Well, fuck me." Hansen shakes her head. "Your career officially turned out way more exciting than mine, I think."

124

"Excitement is overrated," I say. "Could have stood a little less of it sometimes."

"Well, it's your own damn fault, chowderhead," she says. "You could have stayed in your console jockey job. But you just had to run off and become a podhead."

"My wife called it the nutcase track. Of course, she's flying drop ships, so it's not like she has a leg to stand on."

"Nutcase track. I like that." She looks around in the room and sighs. "I don't know if I could do that. Being married to another grunt. Or pilot. Seems like it would be a lot of work to keep things going when you're deployed most of the time. Even without the constant chance of death."

"It's only hard when we're apart," I say. "When we're together, it's no work at all."

"But you're apart most of the time. I just stick to having fun on leave. And every once in a while, you end up on a ship with a decent pick of guys for the temporary space husband position."

Space husband and *space wife* are the corps terms for dalliances on deployment. Everyone knows they happen, and the brass tolerates them grudgingly, as long as you stay outside your direct chain of command. Deep-space deployments are long and both dangerous and boring at the same time, and there's not much that can prevent those temporary bunkmate hookups from happening. It's easier to keep things discreet the higher up in rank you climb because the senior noncoms and officers often get private berthing, but I know that even the junior enlisted find ways to stray on deployments, because humans are humans, and we do what we're coded to do. I've been able to spend most of my leaves with Halley, and we've been deployed together more than once, so I've never felt the need to stray. But I've always felt some attraction to Hansen, and for a moment I wonder what would happen if Halley wasn't on *Ottawa* right now and my former squad mate made an advance. We're the same rank and not in the same chain of command, so nobody would bat an eye. But despite the lingering remnants of physical attraction, I dismiss the thought almost immediately. I only served for a few months with Hansen when we were both in the TA, and after eight years, we're practically strangers to each other again. Halley and I have managed to build a relationship despite everything the corps has thrown at us, through many separations, and the mere thought of risking everything we have for some brief fun is not even remotely in the cards. I've almost lost her in battle a few times, and at this point, I could weather the loss of a limb better than losing my wife.

The PDP in my leg pocket lets out a little chirp. I pull it out to check the screen.

"I'm being summoned," I say. "Being in charge is a pain in the ass sometimes."

"Don't I know it," Hansen says. "Hey, it was good to catch up, Andrew. Let's hit the RecFac sometime soon and continue this. I want to know more about that crazy-ass mission you were part of."

"We'll be on this boat for a while," I reply. "Plenty of chances for drinks, I think."

I get out of my chair and pick up the tray with my half-eaten lunch on it.

"Never thought I'd see your face again, especially not on a Fleet ship. Life's full of surprises, huh?"

"Yeah," she says. "Only in our line of work, they're usually unpleasant. Good to have exceptions to that rule every once in a while."

I put my tray into the recycler rack and walk out of the wardroom. I don't know if it's the knowledge that someone else from my first unit has gone through almost the same stuff and survived or the meds Dr. Saults prescribed, but on the way back to SOCOM Country, I feel better than I have in days.

My good mood evaporates when I get back to my quarters a few minutes later. I can see that something isn't quite right when I step into the passageway leading to my compartment. The door of my stateroom is open, and a Fleet staff sergeant is standing astride the threshold talking to someone inside. My stomach drops a little with foreboding when I see that the staff sergeant is wearing a black armband that says SF. He's a master-at-arms, a member of the Fleet Security Force, the branch tasked with shipboard security and law enforcement.

He hears me coming and turns around. As I expected, he's wearing the badge of a master-at-arms on the chest of his blueberries, just above his name tape.

"Captain Grayson?" he asks.

"That would be me," I confirm. "What's the problem, Staff Sergeant?"

Instead of replying to me, he sticks his head into my stateroom and talks to whoever is inside. Then he looks back at me and points into the stateroom.

"The security officer would like a word with you, sir."

The staff sergeant makes way for me, and I step across the threshold and into my stateroom. Inside, there's a Fleet officer standing in front of my open locker, and when I see that my private compartment is open, I know why he's here. The officer is wearing captain rank, and his blueberry tunic sports a master-at-arms badge as well. His name tag says "DAVIS, R."

"Captain Grayson," he says. "Please confirm for me that this is your locker."

"It's my stateroom," I say, unable to hide the irritation in my voice despite the knowledge that I'm most likely in big trouble. "It follows that it's my locker as well."

"We did a walk-through scan of the officer quarters," Captain Davis says. "The millimeter-wave sensors indicated the presence of a firearm in your stateroom, so the master-at-arms called me to open your cabin to conduct a lawful search and investigation."

He turns to the locker and pulls my M17 pistol out of the personal compartment. The slide is locked to the rear, showing that the weapon is unloaded. Then he reaches into the compartment with the other hand and pulls out the stack of full magazines.

"Any reason why you would have an unauthorized firearm in your locker, Captain?"

"That gun is personal property," I reply. "Part of my weight allowance. It's a gift from a different service."

"Even if personal sidearms were authorized on this ship, they would have to be registered with the master-at-arms and stored in the ship armory," Captain Davis says. "If they *were* authorized. Which they are not."

"My mistake," I say. Behind me, the master-at-arms shifts his position a little and crosses his arms in front of his chest.

"I'm afraid I can't leave it at that, Captain. I'm going to have to report this. By authority of the commanding officer of this ship, you are hereby ordered into confinement in your stateroom until I have reported this infraction to the CO for further determination of your status," Captain Davis says.

He sticks the pistol magazines into the leg pocket of his trousers. One slips out of his grasp and clatters to the floor. He reaches for it, but it's closer to me than to him, and I snatch it off the ground and hand it to him. Behind me, I can tell that the master-at-arms has assumed a slightly alarmed posture. I smile grimly. Neither of them are combat grunts, and they don't look like they spend much time in the ship gym or a SIMAP ring in their free time. With the anger I feel right now, I could probably mop the floor with both guys in ten seconds flat, but that would just get me into even deeper shit. Maybe it's the stuff Dr. Saults prescribed, but I find it a little easier to just open a mental valve and let some of that pressurized rage escape, enough to keep me from doing something stupid. Still, it's disturbingly satisfying to imagine what it would feel like if I grabbed Captain Davis and bounced his head off the edge of my locker a few times for taking the pistol my friends in the Brigades gave me as a parting gift when I left.

"Understood," I say. "You go do what you have to do, Captain."

Captain Davis steps around me and out of my stateroom. I walk over to my desk and sit down in front of it, intentionally failing to pay attention to them as they close my door and lock it with their master access fobs from the outside. Then I sigh and turn on my terminal screen to check my updates, trying to ignore that sinking feeling in the pit of my stomach. I may spend the rest of this deployment in the brig. The strange thing is that I wouldn't care at all if it wasn't for the fact that Halley will be upset. The meds do a fine job leveling out the highs and lows of my emotional state. Maybe too fine a job.

———

They must be bored up in CIC today, because the wheels of justice grind exceptionally quickly today. Not even an hour after the start of my confinement to quarters, the access panel outside lets out a chirp, and my door unlocks with a soft metallic clanging sound. When it opens, the staff sergeant master-at-arms is standing in the threshold.

"Captain Grayson? Follow me, please. The skipper wants to see you."

"Great," I say. "Let's go."

I stand up and straighten my uniform. Then I follow the master-at-arms out into the passageway. Whatever they have in store for me, at least they aren't under orders to cuff me, which relieves a little bit of my anxiety.

I half expect to be led straight to the ship's brig, but the master-at-arms takes me up to the command deck instead. He walks me past the CIC and down a passageway I haven't walked before. Then he presses the access-request button, and a few moments later, the door unlocks.

"I have Captain Grayson for you, ma'am," the master-at-arms says.

"Send him in," Colonel Yamin's voice says from inside. "And then wait outside until I call you back in, please."

"Aye, ma'am." The master-at-arms moves aside and gestures for me to go, and I walk across the transom and into the compartment beyond. This must be Colonel Yamin's day cabin, the spot near the CIC where she takes a break and does private business while she's off watch but not on free time.

"Good afternoon, Colonel," I say.

"Not such a good afternoon, I think," Colonel Yamin replies. She is sitting at her desk and tapping around on a data pad. Then she looks up at me, puts down the pad, and nods at the chair in front of her desk.

"Close the hatch behind you and sit down, Captain."

"Aye, ma'am." I close the door and walk over to the chair. As I sit down, I see my M17 on the pile of printouts stacked on the right side of Colonel Yamin's desk. She picks it up and tosses it onto the desk space between us.

"What the hell is this shit, Captain Grayson?"

I could give in to my natural reflex to be a smart-ass and tell her that it's a US M17 service pistol, but Colonel Yamin has never struck me as the kind of officer willing to tolerate smart-assery.

"It's a sentimental item," I say. "That pistol was given to me after my exchange service with the Lazarus Brigades. It's an obsolete souvenir."

"It still fires bullets. And you kept it in your locker with several full magazines. Don't tell me you had intended it to be just a paperweight, Captain."

"No, ma'am. It's mostly a keepsake. But I won't tell you that I didn't consider its value in an emergency."

"You're not green, Captain. I remember you well from *Phalanx*. We had a brief talk on the observation deck right before the battle."

"I remember. I gave you a bunch of shit over Arcadia."

She looks at me with the slightest hint of a smile flickering in the corners of her mouth.

"And do you still have the same reservations about the former renegades?"

I consider her question and shrug.

"About some of them. Not about you. You skippered a cruiser. You didn't try to kill me or my troops."

"I'd like to think that I wouldn't have followed that order," she says. "But I did follow others I shouldn't have obeyed. But those are my consequences to deal with, not yours."

She pats the pistol on the table.

"Talking about following orders. You aren't a nugget fresh out of officer school. You know that sidearms, personal or issued, aren't allowed on this ship. The XO briefed you about that when you came aboard, did he not?"

"He did, ma'am. I just chose to interpret the order in a flexible way."

"You are an officer. You're one rank away from being a *staff* officer. You know good and damn well that we can't just 'choose to interpret orders in a flexible way.' If everyone starts doing that, we might as well turn the corps into a debating club."

On the way here, I had consigned myself to the idea of an extended brig residency, and I don't want to give the skipper an excuse to lock me up and throw the access fob out of an airlock. But all things considered, the situation is a little absurd, and I can't help venting my discontent.

"I will take the consequences, Colonel. I skirted the regulations on purpose. You can't let that slide, I know. But the whole thing is dumb as hell."

Colonel Yamin's eyes narrow a little. She sits back in her chair and lightly taps her fingertips on the tabletop.

"How so, Captain?"

"We've been carrying sidearms on ships for years now. Everyone's used to it. We know the things won't do shit against Lankies if we end up ejecting onto a moon. But it's a badge of independence. Of being able to have a tiny say in your fate if things go to shit. And it was a big thing when we all started carrying. After the exodus, I mean."

"Go on," Colonel Yamin says.

"It was a sign of trust. Like command didn't treat us like idiot children. Or potential mutineers. It was egalitarian."

I make a gesture that encompasses the room.

"And then we get posted to *this* cruise liner. And I have to give up my sidearm because command doesn't trust me not to put holes into the hull, or shoot some trainee by accident in the fucking mess hall."

The anger takes over just a little, and I start talking faster and with more volume.

"My job is to shoot out of a launch tube carrying enough firepower to kill Lankies. To blow up drop ships or armored vehicles. On the battlefield, I have a control deck in my suit that lets me drop megaton-size warheads from orbit. If I fuck up, I'm nuking a civvie settlement or a whole battalion of SI. And once I'm back on the flight deck, my superior officers don't trust me with a fucking *fléchette pistol*. That doesn't make even the slightest sense. Not to anyone who has lost body parts for the corps."

I hold out my left hand and wiggle my fingers. The three leftmost ones are very well-constructed artificial digits, but under the light of the CO's day cabin, they look a little off. I know they'll never feel normal again. It'll always be like someone coated them lightly in liquid wound dressing.

Colonel Yamin says nothing for a little while. She just studies me with those hazel eyes of hers. I had the thought when I first met her on *Phalanx* three years ago, but it pops up in my head again—she looks remarkably like an older version of Halley. It occurs to me that I keep comparing other women to my wife, the steadiest and most reliable benchmark I have in my life.

"There are so few of us left," she says finally, in a soft voice. "So few that made it all the way through the grinder. SI or Fleet. My brother would be a major by now. Maybe an XO on a frigate somewhere. The things they make us give up . . ."

She sighs and visibly pulls herself together. Then she takes the pistol off the desk and puts it on a shelf behind her.

"I understand your points. But I can't overlook your intentional violation of safety regs on my ship, Captain."

I steel myself for what she's about to say next. I can only hope that the brig has decently comfortable bunks. Maybe I'll get to trade the captain's pips for enlisted stripes again.

"However, I will not keelhaul a decorated combat veteran," she continues. "Not for two pounds of polymer and steel stowed safely in a locker. I'm giving you nonjudicial punishment. Forfeiture of three months' base pay, and a reprimand in your personnel file. And your alcohol allowance is canceled for the rest of the deployment. Are you appealing this NJP?"

My head feels light with relief for a moment.

"No, ma'am," I reply. "I accept the punishment."

"Very well," Colonel Yamin says. "I will inform the master-at-arms. And don't give them a reason to haul you in here again. You just used your one goodwill credit with me. Don't fuck it up."

"Understood, ma'am."

"Dismissed, Captain."

Well beyond my expectation, I leave the CO's day cabin without handcuffs shackling my wrists and still wearing O-3 rank on my uniform. I've still not entirely absolved the colonel for siding with the renegade fleet four years ago, but for the first time, I find myself conceding that people like Captain Beals may be the exception rather than the rule among the renegades.

CHAPTER 12

EXOS

We dock at the Titan fleet yard two days later, after six weeks of riding the shortest trajectory to Saturn. Despite the high-energy run, our deuterium is still at 85 percent when we dock at Titan, which means that *Ottawa* has by far the biggest fuel capacity of any ship in the Fleet. Everything about this thing is built for the purpose of long, autonomous deep-space patrols without the need for tagging along a supporting task group.

The fleet yard is not a regular space station, so there are no facilities for off-duty loafing, no RecFacs or other amusements. We don't even leave the ship. Our regular watch and training cycle continues while *Ottawa* tops off her tanks and takes on more supplies and equipment for whatever we're about to do next. I know we're not heading back to Earth yet because we've only been in space for six weeks, but if they intend to see how far an Avenger-class can go on a single load of fuel, this deployment may turn out longer than even the pessimists are anticipating.

On our second day in the dock at Titan, the entire special tactics team is scheduled for a block of training time on the flight deck. The schedule item comes from the XO, but it's low on detail when I try to figure out what we'll be doing down there. All it says is "Technical

Familiarization," so I suspect they have some new and shiny gear for us to check out. The dress for the training block is specified as full battle armor. I send the duty roster update to all STT members and tromp down to the flight deck in my armor when the time comes.

"That is some science fiction shit right there," Lieutenant Brown comments wryly when he sees what's waiting for us lined up in the middle of the flight deck. A bunch of civvie techs and some Fleet wrench spinners in working coveralls are swarming around a dozen machines that look like what would happen if a power loader could mate with a light armored vehicle. They are heavily beefed up exoskeletons, standing about three meters tall, painted in the same titanium white and orange hi-viz pattern as the ship and its drop ship complement. The Fleet officer in charge of this training block is a captain from the logistics and supply group.

"Welcome, gentlemen," he says to us when we have gathered in front of the semicircle formed by the dozen exoskeletons on the flight deck. "You are here to get your basic familiarization training for the XM-5500 power amplification combat system. The Seventh SI Regiment has been picked as a field-test unit for these babies, and you as the supporting special tactics team will have to be familiar with the systems in case you ever have to use one."

He points at one of the exoskeletons behind us.

"If the test goes as the tech division hopes it will, the SI companies will see their fourth platoons turned into heavy-weapons platoons, each equipped with four of these."

There's some incredulous grumbling in our group.

"Four exos to replace thirty-six grunts with rifles and rocket launchers," one of my Spaceborne Rescue sergeants says. "Sir, we've tried going the mech route before. Years ago. They suck in combat."

"The mech prototypes didn't fare well against *human* opposition," the civilian tech next to the logistics captain says. He has a Fleet access card clipped to his white coveralls that has the name "HIGGINS" on it. "That's true. They were too tall and obvious on the battlefield."

"Missile magnets," the sergeant adds. "You couldn't go prone in them, and they had a shitload of trouble on uneven terrain."

"These aren't the old mech prototypes," the civvie tech says. "These are much smaller, more power-efficient, and built for a different job. They're for fighting Lankies, not people."

He walks over to the nearest exoskeleton and pats the frame with one hand.

"Titanium and carbon fiber laminates. They weigh a third of what the old mech prototypes weighed, but they can lift almost as much weight. We figured that no amount of armor or shock resistance will stand up to a Lanky in direct-contact CQB, so we didn't even try. It's designed as a lightweight force amplifier, not a walking tank. You'll be able to run five times faster and lift twenty times more than you could in your battle armor alone. You'll have four times the oxygen endurance and a built-in power source to keep your suit topped off. And you can carry a lot more *bang*."

He points at the arms of the exoskeleton and taps the underside of the forearm.

"Standard rail mount for crew-served weapons. We designed self-contained pods for weapons and ammunition, and the loadout can be changed in five minutes as needed. And fully loaded and with troopers in them, they are still light enough that four of them fit into one drop ship."

Inside the semicircle of exoskeletons, there are various weapon and gear pods lined up in a row, and Mr. Higgins walks down the line and points out each one in turn. It's clear that he is fully versed in military hardware and obviously a defense R&D contractor.

"We had to make some concessions to portability, but most of the heavy weapons used by the SI are readily adaptable to pod configurations. Here we have your standard twenty-five-millimeter autocannon. We had to shorten the barrel a bit to make space for the ammo cassette and still remain within the pod's size limit, but it's not going to make a difference to terminal performance at the ranges you typically engage Lankies while on foot."

"How many rounds in the cassette?" Lieutenant Brown asks.

"Twenty-four. I know that's a downgrade from the standard hundred-round cassette the crew-served versions have, but this one doesn't need a three-man crew. Standard ammo load will be twelve silver bullets, twelve high-explosive dual purpose. You can switch the feed on the fly, just like on the crew-served version."

Now the murmurs among the STT troopers sound approving. Grunts love their guns, and the prospect of being able to carry around vehicle-grade firepower strapped underneath your forearm makes those exoskeletons look a lot less dumb than they did just a few minutes ago.

"We also modified the MARS for use with an automatic loader," Mr. Higgins continues as he moves on to the next pod, which has the unmistakable blunt muzzle of a MARS unguided rocket launcher sticking out of its streamlined nose. "Because of the size of the rockets, you only get three shots, one in the tube and two in the underbarrel magazine. On the plus side, the loader is really fast, so the reload time is two and a half seconds."

The civvie tech goes through all the other pod options laid out in front of us. There are some that sound useful, like an enhanced sensor and designator pod that would increase my reach for direct target marking fourfold over the designator package built into my armor. There's a small-caliber rotary cannon complete with its own power source and a twenty-five-hundred-round magazine of caseless ammunition, a forty-millimeter automatic grenade launcher like the ones mounted underneath our M-66 rifles but with higher-pressure propellant charges for more range, and even a pod that fires fifty-meter bursts of flammable gel that burns at a thousand degrees once it leaves the muzzle. Most of the pods seem to be more proof of concept than operationally viable loadouts. I can't see myself trying to take on a squad of infantry with a minigun pod mounted to a three-meter-tall exoskeleton that can't go prone or use anything smaller than a single-story building as cover. I would get off maybe half the magazine in the pod before someone dropped an antiarmor missile on me or shot me out of the exo frame with rifle grenades.

After the show-and-tell, we get to try the exoskeletons out. The techs and instructors show us how to climb up into the frame, which is made to interface with standard battle armor. The PACS controls are as simple as they could be. There are handgrips inside of stabilizer sleeves on the lower arms of the PACS, and I stick my arms into the sleeves and grasp the control grips. The sleeve senses the position of my hand and the pressure I put on the sticks, and the articulated metal fingers on the end of each exo arm replicate my movement. I make sure I have enough clearance to either side and take a few cautious steps forward. Exoskeleton tech must have improved a great deal in the last few years, because unlike the power loaders I've tried before, there's almost no lag between my movement and the suit's translation of it. The suit probably weighs well over a metric ton, but it feels almost weightless because the high-powered servos are doing all the work. One of the techs keeps pace with me as I walk the PACS down the flight deck slowly. We are on the centerline of the deck, and the nearest aircraft are lined up fifty meters away, so we have a lot of free space in case one of us goofs up with the suit.

"How does it feel?" the tech asks. "It looks like you've figured it all out already."

"Not so different from a power loader," I say. "Feels better, though. Much smoother."

"You're fully gyro-stabilized. The suit will stay upright unless you tell it not to. Try stepping up your pace. Just stay on the centerline."

I take slightly longer steps, then start striding. The movement is so effortless that it feels like I could run without a problem, so after twenty or thirty meters of striding, I break into a light trot, and the PACS obliges. It's like all my muscles are suddenly supercharged.

"There you go," the tech shouts behind me, already left in the dust by the speed I've put on just with a careful trot. I can see maintenance crews and pilots turning and watching me from the sidelines as I pick up speed and break into a full run. The suit feels like it's barely there. I make it a hundred meters down the flight deck in what feels like no time at all. Then I slow down and come to a stop before I get too close to the anxious-looking Shrike mechanics and their ships lined up at the stern end of the deck.

I turn around and give a thumbs-up to my group, and the suit replicates the gesture. Two more troopers have mounted their exos and are now walking down the flight deck in my direction, in the same careful way I started my own jaunt. I go down on one knee, and the PACS lowers itself and plants its knee joint onto the deck. There's no weapon pod attached to either of the exo's forearms, but I extend my right hand anyway as if I had a gun to aim. The PACS tracks and copies my movement smoothly. Set up like this, it feels solid enough to make a very stable gun platform.

I get up and stride back to the now-broken semicircle of exoskeletons. Halfway back, I pass my sergeants in their own PACS, both of them with big grins on their faces. I walk back into the semicircle and park the PACS where I had started it.

"What do you think?" Mr. Higgins asks.

"That's some really nice gear," I say.

"Run up to eighty klicks per hour, lift a ton and a quarter, jump five meters high. If we'd had the funding and the R&D for these things nine years ago, things would have been different with the Lankies."

"I don't know about that." I hit the quick-release on the harness buckle and step back down onto the deck. "With a thousand of these per regiment, maybe. I'm not sure that four per company is going to turn them from 'nice to have' into 'essential.'"

I look back at the PACS and pat the ballistic liner on the inside.

"I still want one, though," I say, and Mr. Higgins grins.

After a lecture and demonstration of the suit's full capabilities by one of the engineers, we spend another hour with the PACS, running up and down the flight deck and using dummy gun pods to try out the targeting systems. Even with a hundred-kilo pod attached to the arm of the exoskeleton, it doesn't feel encumbering. The servos are powerful and almost dead silent, which makes the PACS feel more like a physical extension of my body than any other power augmentation gear I've tried. Unlike our battle armor, which is only power-assisted, the PACS can use its servos autonomously. There's a gun-calibration target painted on one of the flight deck bulkheads so the drop ship computers can zero their aim, and I tell the dummy gun on my arm to fire a simulated three-round burst at each as fast as possible. When I let the aim go automatic, the PACS swings my arm to the first target, the second, and then the third, all in under two seconds. The techs tell us that you can even set a course on your TacLink screen and let the suit walk it on autopilot in an emergency.

"In an emergency," Lieutenant Brown says and winks at me. "The second the grunts get wind of that feature, they'll be taking long naps on patrol."

"Shit, *I* would," I reply. "You can always have the computer wake you up if anything pops up on TacLink."

When our orientation session ends, I leave the PACS behind with some reluctance. For years we've been fighting the Lankies mostly as infantry on foot because we didn't have a deployable mobile armor system that's small enough to fit into a drop ship and big enough to be useful for anything. These aren't as capable as a mule or that awesome little Eurocorps recon vehicle, but they're much better than walking into battle on your own two feet and hauling just what your armor's passive power assist can bear. These PACS are evidence that R&D is still on the ball and trying to come up with better ways to kill Lankies, but part of me is a little pissed off that we didn't have these three years ago at Mars already. Even with the immediate threat of extinction, government bureaucracies grind as slowly as ever. If we could put the people in charge of budgets and equipment purchases into battle armor and make them go on every combat drop with us, it would take just a week or two for new gear to be approved and issued.

CHAPTER 13

EASY MODE

"Attention, all hands. This is the CO."

I'm just finished with my morning ablutions when the voice of Colonel Yamin comes over the 1MC, and I sit down in front of my terminal screen to dry my face and listen to what the skipper has to announce. We're three days out of Fleet Yard Titan with full tanks and supplies, and the rumor mill has been abuzz since we undocked. Halley is predicting a high-speed run back to Earth, but I don't think we would have taken on fuel and consumables at Titan just for a run back home. This ship has immensely long legs, and they'll want to see how far they can stretch them.

"The ship has taken on provisions and reactor fuel for the next stage of our shakedown cruise. We will proceed back toward the inner system at full military power to stress-test the reactors and verify fuel consumption estimates. Providing we don't have a reason to head home for repairs, we will then test the Alcubierre drive by making a transition out of system."

My stomach sinks a little at the news. We've had ships out of system a few times in the last three years to scout out and reestablish contact with some of the colonies we knew to be safe before the Battle of Mars.

But those expeditions have been high-risk missions due to the chance of an extrasolar encounter with the Lankies without our best weapons. The first-generation Orions don't fit into any ships and can't make Alcubierre transitions under tow, and *Arkhangelsk* couldn't leave the system because she has been the cornerstone of our planetary defense network until now.

"To test this ship's long-range capabilities, we are making a transition to the Leonidas system," the CO continues. "Once we arrive in-system, we will commence a planetary assault exercise. We will enter Leonidas, scout the system, proceed to the Arcadia colony, and execute a by-the-book practice assault on simulated enemy positions in and around Arcadia City."

I finish drying my face and put the towel aside, trying to parse the information I just heard.

Leonidas.

"You have *got* to be joking," I say out loud into the empty stateroom.

It makes sense from a technical perspective—Leonidas is known to be a safe colony, and it's the furthest Alcubierre trip we can make by a long shot—but the prospect of returning to the place where I lost a quarter of my platoon and nearly became a widower fills me with immediate dread. Three years ago, it was under control of the renegade NAC government, and I was part of the commando mission that stealthed into Leonidas to reclaim our assets. As beautiful as Arcadia is, I had hoped never to see that place again in person. The nuclear demolition charge the SEALs set off at the main fusion plant outside of Arcadia City was small, only a kiloton and a half, but the surface detonation was dirty, and the radiation levels in the city will be back to normal in about a hundred years.

"Because the transition into Leonidas takes three watch cycles, we will not be at combat stations until an hour before our arrival. Until then, it's business as usual. All department heads will start the operational planning for the exercise, and training cycles will be maintained until we start our transition to Leonidas. That is all for now. CO out."

I stay in my chair and stare at the blank screen of my terminal for a few moments. Then I turn the screen on and bring up the situational display. The little icon labeled "BCV-60" in the center of the screen is a few million klicks from Saturn, and the broken line of our projected course trajectory loops all the way back into the inner system. I'm gratified to see that our return trip doesn't take us anywhere near Mars, because I've seen enough of that graveyard to last me for the rest of my service time.

Ottawa is the nicest and most luxurious ship I've ever served on, but everything about it seems just a little too easy. The network access is instantaneous, and we have so much bandwidth that we can send video messages to each other instead of being restricted to low-data text. After years of bitching about cramped accommodations and lousy food, it seems stupid to object to the great chow or the space we have, but for me, all those factors come together to make *Ottawa* feel unreal, as if she's a floating RecFac with really awesome battle simulators, not a proper warship designed for combat. Even the firing range in Grunt Country follows the pattern. It doesn't even have a live-fire section where I can burn actual propellant and shoot real projectiles. The whole range is set up for sim guns only, with holographic targets and racks full of training versions of our regular armament. The sim guns look and feel just like the live-fire versions, and the gas charges in the sim rounds do a good job of producing realistic recoil, but it's different when you know there's just a low-wattage laser beam coming out of the muzzle instead of a saboted dart.

When I'm off duty, I spend as much time with Halley as we can both manage to free up at the same time. But after ten weeks of deployment, I find that I am bored and stressed at the same time. I've had the deployment blues many times before—you learn to deal with it after almost ten years of bouncing around the settled galaxy in Fleet ships—but this spell feels more severe than the ones before it. I don't crave combat and danger, but it seems pointless for all of us to be out here, taking the Fleet's best equipment and her most qualified personnel on a three-month joyride to the outer planets and back. I don't admit this to Halley, but when we're back in the inner system and hours away from our planned Alcubierre transition to Leonidas, I am looking forward to being out of the solar system again for the first time in almost four years because there's a chance something might go wrong.

"Now hear this: Alcubierre transition in T-minus thirty. I repeat: Alcubierre transition in T-minus thirty."

The 1MC announcement sounds as casual as if the XO had just announced a foreign-object damage sweep on the flight deck. For the first time in my Fleet career, I've heard the Alcubierre transition announcement without a preceding Combat Stations alert. Every time a Fleet ship transitions into a different system, the crew is at combat stations, because you never know for certain what you'll pop into when the ship comes out of the chute in the target system. This time, however, it's just an inconsequential heads-up from CIC, which only serves to add to the general feeling of disconnectedness I've had ever since I set foot on this ship.

I continue the briefing I was conducting when the 1MC announcement interrupted my train of thought. From the expressions on the faces of my special tactics team, I can tell that some of them share my minor consternation at this change in routine.

"Thirty minutes until go time," I say. "Well, sort of. We'll be in transition for twenty-four hours. And the action on the other side of the chute is all in our heads. But other than that, it's just like going to war."

The senior NCOs chuckle a little at this and exchange amused glances.

"Anyway," I continue. "This op is a standard by-the-book orbital drop. We are dumping the whole regiment in and around Arcadia City in a single wave with both drop ship squadrons while *Ottawa* provides orbital support. The regiment will have overhead cover from the strike squadrons, so there'll be plenty to do for the combat controllers."

I bring up the list of unit assignments on the screen behind me.

"Master Sergeant Taggart, you're dropping with Alpha Company, First Battalion. Master Sergeant Garcia, Alpha Company, Second Battalion. Sergeant Winters, Bravo Company, First Battalion."

I go down the list by team seniority and distribute my combat controllers so that each of them is assigned to a company command section and each company has one combat controller to drop with it. Last on the list is Delta Company of the Second Battalion, and the last unassigned name on my unit roster is Staff Sergeant Lang, the only female member of the combat controller detachment.

"Sergeant Lang," I say. "You'll be going with Second Battalion's Delta Company. The CO is an old friend of mine, Captain Hansen. She knows her business. Make sure you show her that we know ours as well."

"Aye-aye, sir," Staff Sergeant Lang replies. She glances down at her PDP to copy the data, her face serious and earnest. At her rank, she came out of Combat Controller School not too long ago, which means that she's never done a combat drop because we haven't dropped anywhere since Mars. The combat controller training track is extremely demanding, both physically and mentally. Eighty percent of trainees wash out for various reasons. The fact that Sergeant Lang has the red beret in her leg pocket proves that she's tough as a bag of bricks and mentally resilient. But I know what it felt like before I did my first actual drop, so I roughly know what goes on in Sergeant Lang's head, even if we're only preparing for a training drop.

"Once we are in-system, we'll check in with the local garrison, and from then on we'll be in full war-game mode. System recon, followed by a shortest-time burn to Arcadia and full regimental assault. We're going to come in hot and fire from all tubes, so to speak. The area around Arcadia City is a restricted no-go zone for a hundred klicks around, so it's all our playground to shoot at simulated Lankies. The radiation on the ground, however, isn't simulated. Those of you who haven't had to do decontamination routines lately will have a great chance to get familiar with them again."

I put some fake cheer into my voice with that last sentence, and I'm rewarded with some groans and low-volume grumbling. Decontamination routines are tedious, and they occur by nature at the very end of the mission, when you're back on the flight deck after a drop, tired and sweaty and ready for some chow and twelve hours of uninterrupted sleep. But there's no way to just simulate the decon stuff on this drop because the dirt in and around Arcadia City really is irradiated.

"I have word from upstairs regarding pod launches," I continue, and everyone's attention is back on me in a snap.

"The brass has decided that we will do *simulated* launches. The combat controllers will land with the command elements of their assigned companies, and we'll let the computer decide if your pod cratered or not. Sorry if you were hoping to add to your drop total for the next level."

This revelation gets an even unhappier reaction than the news about decontamination. Pod launches are dangerous, but they're our bread and butter, the distinguishing mark of our professions, and most large-scale exercises involve live launches. Because of the danger, every pod launch counts toward the total, whether it's in exercise or combat. The staff sergeants in my group all still have the pod device in bronze above their combat-drop badges, which is awarded at five pod drops. The silver level means twenty drops, and the gold level is a long climb to fifty drops. The last three years were not a good period for adding to the drop total. It's a small and inconsequential thing to an outsider, but being able to exchange the bronze pod device for a silver and then a gold one is one of the last rites of passage once someone makes it through combat controller training. The day you go "all gold"—when you add a gold pod device to a gold combat-drop badge—you have to requisition drinks for the entire podhead detachment on your boat.

"It's a sim launch, so familiarize yourselves with your assigned company zones and check in with the company commanders as soon as you can, preferably before we transition into Leonidas. Ride the bus down, check with TacOps whether your simulated pod made it down in one piece, and then go to work. There'll be four strike squadrons overhead looking for something to do, so keep them busy, and let's not have any midairs. Those are bad and will get you demerits."

The NCOs reward this comment with low chuckles.

"I've sent out an update with the rotation schedule for the CIC station all the way through the drop. That's it for the combat controllers," I continue. "Now Lieutenant Brown will take over and cover the Spaceborne Rescue portion of this program."

I nod at Lieutenant Brown, who gets out of his chair in the first row of the briefing room and steps up to the lectern. I yield the spot and sit down in the chair he just vacated. While the lieutenant goes through assignments for his eight Spaceborne Rescuemen and their tasks in the upcoming exercise, I take notes on my PDP and exchange a few messages with Halley.

He looks so damn young, I find myself thinking while Lieutenant Brown is giving his NCOs their marching orders. As a first lieutenant, he has been in the service for less than four years, and unless he spent a few years after college just loafing, he's twenty-five at the most. I only have half a decade on him, but right now, I'm the old man in the room, and only the two master sergeants on my combat controller team look like they have more years in service and more hours on the clock than I do.

Back when I joined, captains and majors were *old guys*. I anticipated many things when I enlisted, but becoming one of those old guys was not among my expectations. When we graduated boot camp, Halley and I seriously thought we'd just get out after our first term and take the money. When I think of those two naive, starry-eyed kids we were back then, I feel a great deal of pity for them. They thought they had pulled the winning lottery ticket, thought they had the universe by the balls. Instead, they got chucked into a meat grinder. And we're not those kids anymore. We're just what made it through that grinder eventually, pounded into different shapes.

On a whim, I send to Halley:

>Ever feel ancient?

The reply comes back just a few moments later:

>Every damn day.

CHAPTER 14

WAR GAMES

"Alcubierre transition complete in five. In four. Three. Two. One. Transition complete."

The feeling of low-level bone ache particular to Alcubierre transits disappears as soon as we come out of the chute. After three years, I had forgotten how much I dislike that sensation, which feels like sitting in a dentist's chair for hours on end.

"The board is green. All departments reporting ready for action."

"What's our fuel status?" Colonel Yamin asks.

"We're at seventy-one percent reactor fuel," the XO replies after consulting a terminal screen.

Damn, I think. The old frigate *Berlin* was down to 11 percent after the same transition, and that was with fully topped-off tanks before going Alcubierre. We just made a run to the chute all the way from Saturn, and we're not even half-dry after the transition. Either the ship has super-efficient reactors, or a quarter of the hull by mass is reactor fuel.

"Passive sensor sweep," Colonel Yamin orders from her position in the holotable pit. "Astrogation, get me a fix, please."

"Aye, ma'am," the astrogation officer says. A few moments later, the holotable plot changes to display our current location in-system. I hold my breath for just a moment, but no orange icons pop up on the situational orb in our neighborhood.

"Transition successful. We are in the Leonidas system, right where we planned to be."

"Looks like the shipyard managed to put the Alcubierre plumbing in right," Colonel Yamin says. "1MC line, please."

"1MC is open, ma'am."

"Attention, all hands," Colonel Yamin says into her headset, and I know that her amplified voice is presently coming out of every speaker and PDP on the ship. "This is the CO. Welcome to the Leonidas system. *Ottawa* has just completed a one-hundred-and-fifty-light-year transition. Let's see what this puppy can do when we take off the muzzle. All hands, carry out your assigned jobs like we have some real Lankies out for our hides. Fleet Exercise Pegasus commences *now*. CO out."

The scenario on the holotable looks eerily familiar. The plot on Portsmouth looked almost the same when we crept into the system with the SOCOM task force over three years ago, but this time the location of the colony is included in the plot. On the SOCOM mission, we had to spend a good while sniffing around to find Arcadia, which was built to orbit quietly and incognito around the third moon of the third planet, tucked away in the inner system behind the asteroid belt that orbits Leonidas.

"Check the rotational direction of Outpost Campbell and send them a hello on low-power tight-beam when they are facing our way. They probably already know we're here, but it's nice to knock."

Outpost Campbell is a listening post on a large asteroid at the outer edge of the belt. It's set up to monitor incoming traffic to Leonidas and serve as an early warning system in case of Lanky incursion. Three years ago, I was on a drop ship that landed several SI squads on the outpost to prevent it from transmitting a warning back to Arcadia. The asteroid rotates in its orbit, so it only faces the inner system and Arcadia every seventy-one minutes. It's a tactical defect because it means any potential incursion would have a seventy-minute head start in a worst-case scenario, as Outpost Campbell is blind to traffic coming into the system while the listening station faces the wrong way. But it also means that any message traffic is shielded from anyone coming from the direction of the Alcubierre chute because a few million tons of asteroid block the signal completely.

Three years ago, we used their blind spot to approach the station from their dark side with a stealth drop ship and successfully boarded and neutralized it. Since then, it has been rebuilt and enhanced to serve as a forward observer, early warning system, and target designator for Arcadia's Orion battery. Orions are too big to fit into ships for Alcubierre journeys, but their components aren't, and Arcadia has plenty of water for warheads and an orbital shipyard to assemble Orions in-system. Other than Earth, it's the only one of our settlements with a meaningful autonomous defense against seed ships, and we've been settling the place steadily with volunteers over the last three years.

"Outpost Campbell is acknowledging our Fleet transponder code," the comms officer says. "They are replying with an all-clear, ma'am."

"Very well. Let them know we're about to start our scheduled exercise, and to tell Arcadia Control on the next rotation that we'll be inbound at a hard burn as soon as we've finished our recon sweep."

"Aye, ma'am."

"Warm up the recon birds and float 'em out. Live-link mode. I want six to either side of our projected course to Arcadia, one hundred and eighty degrees on the system ecliptic." Colonel Yamin marks the paths for the drones on the holotable's display. "I want to make sure there isn't anything stirring in the inner system that's not broadcasting Fleet ID. Run them out as far as they go."

The recon drones, like almost everything else on this ship, are brand-new hardware put together with liberal Eurocorps assistance.

Eurocorps has the best recon tech on Earth, and until we were all looking down the barrel of species extermination, they weren't really keen on sharing their technological edge with us or the SRA. But now that we are trading money and tech for experience, all the gear designed to keep the smaller European military punching above its weight on Earth is starting to come in very handy against the Lankies.

"Launching drones from tubes one through eight, live-link mode. First flight is on the way," the lieutenant at the electronic intelligence station says. "Loading for second flight."

"Now we wait," Colonel Yamin says. She studies the plot intently, even though there's nothing to see except for the slowly changing scale markers and the blue drone markers forming an umbrella shape in front of our projected course to Arcadia. "It wouldn't do to get jumped by a seed ship out here while we have the whole regiment on the ground with exercise loads in their guns."

"No, ma'am," the XO agrees, and I can practically see him shudder at the thought.

The second wave of drones leaves the tubes thirty seconds later and joins the swarm that's heading outward from the center of the plot in a hemispherical formation. Over the next half hour, our sensor awareness bubble doubles then quadruples in size as the passive reconnaissance systems of the drones scan the space ahead of them and transmit their data back to the ship. The drive systems on the drones are so shielded that only their burst transmission updates make them visible on our plot. I try to pick them up with the sensors on the ship, but no matter which spectrum I use, the drones are invisible once they're further than a few kilometers out. With that sort of stealth technology, those drones would be lethal for a sneak attack if they were passively guided missiles with antiship warheads.

I find myself wondering how many Eurocorps ships have a few of these babies armed with warheads in their tubes as insurance policies. *Ottawa* has electric reactive armor and a state-of-the-art active defense system, but anything else in the Fleet would be a rapidly expanding cloud of debris if you floated a dozen of these stealth birds into it. The Euros may only have corvettes and frigates for their in-system patrols, but I find that I don't want to see how well our bigger ships would stand up against them in a fight.

For the next few hours, we coast toward the inner system while the recon drones speed out to their maximum range. Their scan hemisphere soon covers Arcadia and the planet it orbits, Leonidas c. One of the drones passes within five hundred kilometers of the planet's fleet yard and diligently transmits back the force composition of the docked ships. I'm amazed to see that even though the transmitters on the docked ships are cold, the drone identifies each ship not just by type but also by hull number and name. There are six ships docked at Arcadia at the moment—the frigates *Lethe* and *Acheron*, the space-control cruisers *Gladius* and *Olympia*, the fleet support tender *Manchester*, and the carrier *Pollux*. Together, that system garrison fleet represents the Fleet's biggest offensive punch outside the solar system. But even though they're modern warships and undoubtedly stuffed to the gills with nuclear ordnance, they'd be cannon fodder against a seed ship or two without the Orion missile batteries in orbit around Arcadia.

The drones are almost at the end of their run when another blue icon pops up on the screen, ten million kilometers away from Arcadia. The drone identifies the contact as the frigate *Styx*, out on a patrol in the inner part of the system between Leonidas c and b.

"That's the whole board," the electronic intelligence officer announces. "Recon birds are at the end of their leashes."

"Bring 'em back in and hold them at Arcadia," Colonel Yamin orders. "We'll pick them up once we get there. No point wasting the fuel if we're going to meet them halfway anyway. Helm, lay in the shortest-time course to Arcadia and hit the burners. Full military power."

"Aye, ma'am. Going to full military power."

With our fusion engines running at full power, *Ottawa* leaps out of her holding position like a runner out of the starting blocks. Before super-efficient fusion reactors made artificial gravity systems possible, spaceship crews had to weather the acceleration of their ships strapped into crash couches, which limited the effective acceleration of a ship to whatever its human crew could endure. There's still a limit to what the arti-grav deck plates can compensate without sucking all the power from the fusion reactor, but it's considerably higher than stone-age space-travel physics allowed.

"Accelerating at twenty-one g's. Time to turnaround burn for Arcadia is one hour, eleven minutes."

"Steady as she goes," Colonel Yamin says. "Now let's get ready for this war-gaming business and pretend like we have an enemy to fight."

When I was on a similar approach to Arcadia in a stealth drop ship three years ago, we were coasting in to save fuel and avoid detection, and the run took a tedious twenty-three hours. *Ottawa* at full throttle makes the same trip in less than a tenth of the time. An hour and eleven minutes into the burn, the ship turns to point the engines at our destination and slow down again for the second half of the trip.

We're in extrasolar space, so we don't simulate a full attack run on Arcadia with shipboard weapons, keeping the eyes in CIC on actual space and not computer-generated enemies. For the sake of the exercise, we assume a starting scenario that already had *Ottawa* successful at defeating the seed ship or ships in orbit and skip straight to the spaceborne landing. Thirty minutes before we reach our geosynchronous parking spot in orbit above Arcadia City, the XO kicks off the action for the attack squadrons and Spaceborne Infantry.

"Now hear this," he says into the 1MC. "T-minus thirty to drop. All ground units, board your assigned transports. I repeat, all ground units, board your assigned transports. Stand by to launch the first strike wings."

The sequence is generally the same on every large-scale assault, but I usually observe it from the flight deck level as I get ready to drop with the lead elements, or in the pod launch bay if I take the express elevator. Thirty minutes before the drop, the SI platoons assembled on the deck board their drop ships, and the first squadron of Shrikes goes into the launching clamps. As soon as we reach our push-off spot in orbit, the first two Shrike wings will launch and fly ahead of the drop ships to sanitize the LZ ahead of them. Then the first wave of drop ships will follow, sixteen ships with one platoon each. Depending on the ground situation after the first wave, we will either follow up with the same force composition for the second wave or launch the second flight of sixteen drop ships right away without Shrike escorts.

After months of nothing but simulator training and maintenance, I know the pilots are itching to put their birds to work and clock some real flight time, even if the rounds in the guns are all exercise ammunition. Under normal circumstances, I would prefer to ride in the first wave and get some fresh air instead of staring at console screens in CIC. But this is Arcadia City we're using as an exercise ground. They abandoned it when we blew up the fusion plant with a nuke, and almost all the buildings are undamaged, so it makes for a big and realistic urban-combat training center. But when I do prestrike recon with the superpowered optics of the ship's sensor suite, I can still see the scorch marks on the concrete of the admin plaza where missiles and cannon shells crisscrossed flight paths during our quick and furious battle down there. I'm sure they didn't bother patching up the admin building after the prisoners were secured and the casualties evacuated. The building's dome-shaped concrete roof is mostly undamaged, but I can still picture the main hallway the way it looked at the end of the battle, and I know the cannon shell holes in the corridor walls have not been filled in.

My platoon lost eight troopers in those corridors and six more on the plaza. Sometimes my nightmares still feature the private from Second Squad, Kowalewski, who got blown to bits by a cannon shell right in front of me. I have no desire to go back there and do a sightseeing tour of the battle scars we took and inflicted. I lost over a third of my platoon to see the mission through, only to see the new administration pardon almost all military personnel involved in the mutiny. The president and his cabinet—at least the ones who ran to Arcadia—were put on trial and convicted of treason, and they're serving lifetime sentences in one of the NAC's maximum-security prisons, which in my mind doesn't constitute much of a punishment. They should have just dropped the whole lot in the middle of a PRC.

I tap into the camera feeds from the hangar and watch as the launch clamps pick up the Shrikes of the first attack wave, twelve ships in total. One after another, the clamps lower the attack ships into the launch bays, orange warning lights flashing overhead. The control I have from this CIC station is amazingly fine-grained. I can move my field of view seamlessly through the hangar while the computer switches me automatically from one optical array to another. I can even check the feeds on the powered-up Shrikes and their pilots' helmet-camera feeds. There are almost too many data points for me to pick from, and after a while, I rearrange my screens to my usual feeds. I know the tech is designed to make my job easier, but this much information could be overwhelming to someone right out of Combat Controller School and turn them into micromanagers when they need to see the big picture most of the time.

"Attack ships are in the clamps. Fifteen minutes to launch," the XO announces.

The shot clock superimposed on the large situational display on the forward CIC bulkhead keeps counting down the time. I watch Arcadia stretching out underneath the exhaust nozzles of our fusion engines, more Earthlike than Earth, green and blue with wispy white cloud fields. The weather is clear in our LZ, and the temperature on the surface is a perfect twenty-one degrees Celsius, a balmy late-spring day.

"Strike Squadron Two, you are locked for drop in T-minus fifteen," I send to the attack birds. "Weather over the LZ is clear, two-one degrees, wind three knots from local south-southwest." I mark the LZ on my screen and send the information to the computers of the waiting Shrikes. "Your target area is LZ Alpha Charlie. Secure LZ and engage hostiles if present. Let's give the grunts a ten-klick safe zone."

The pilots send back their acknowledgments one by one. I know that down in the hangar bay, the outer hatches of the drop bays are opening, the last step before the launch. The burn maneuver was perfectly timed—we coast into orbit well within the safe speed margin for a combat drop.

Fifteen minutes later, the shot clock on the CIC display goes to 00:00:00 and blinks red. *Ottawa* is right in the middle of the orbital launch window.

Easy to nail the mark when you're not floating into a minefield, I think.

"Light is green," Colonel Yamin says. "TacOps, initiate the drop."

"Aye, ma'am," I reply and switch to the flight-ops channel.

"Light is green," I relay to the Shrike pilots. "I repeat, light is green. Manual drops at pilot discretion. Drop when ready. Good hunting."

For the drop, I watch the composite feed from the optical arrays on the planet-facing side of the hull. This is the sort of footage the Fleet would use in recruiting videos if they did any. A dozen hatches have opened on the smooth armor belly of *Ottawa*, and one by one, a dozen mean-looking attack craft drop out of those hatches and turn their noses toward the orbital insertion path before lighting up their engines. I share the feed in a window on the bulkhead screen and chuckle as more than a few heads in CIC swivel around to watch the brief show.

"Shrikes away," I announce when the last attack craft is out of the clamps and shooting toward the surface of Arcadia. "Time to target is nine minutes, thirty seconds."

The optical gear on this ship is unbelievably powerful, and the new high-visibility white-and-orange paint scheme on the Shrikes makes them easy to track accurately without a single watt of active radiation. I have no problem keeping twelve different lens arrays on twelve individual Shrikes, so I get to monitor a dozen fiery entries into Arcadia's atmosphere. The Shrikes trail bright tracks of hot plasma on their brief trip toward the surface until they are in denser air and slow enough for atmospheric operations. Even from this far away, I can still zoom in on each individual ship closely enough to read the wing markings.

"Simulation is running on all off-ship systems," the tactical officer says.

With the networking and the processing power possible in modern battle armor and ships, we can turn twenty-five square kilometers of ground down there into a massive simulator environment. It's the same technology I used with my boot camp platoons in training back at Orem, only at a much larger scale. In simulator mode, the drop ship and Shrike sensor suites show the pilots targets that aren't there, so they can fire rounds that don't leave the barrels. The battle suits and shipboard computers do all the processing work, and everything links together via TacLink in a big distributed network with many contributing nodes. Much like in boot camp battle sims, the troops going down to Arcadia will see whatever it is we want them to see on their helmet visors and targeting screens. It's cheaper and less dangerous than live-fire training, and I know from experience that the virtual enemies look very believable, with sights and sounds all rendered impeccably lifelike. The shock absorbers in the boot soles of the SI grunts even try to duplicate the ground tremors you feel when a Lanky is taking a step within a quarter kilometer. The recruits in boot camp usually love sim exercises because it's exciting and makes you feel like you're in combat. Those of us who have seen real battles know better. It's still a big improvement over running around and firing blanks at nothing. But without the fear of death, it makes combat and war almost fun, and that's the simulator's biggest departure from reality.

The first wave of drop ships leaves the clamps a few minutes later and follows the Shrikes into the landing zone.

"Tallyho," the lead pilot of the Shrike squadron says into the TacAir channel when the Shrikes are ten kilometers out, five thousand feet above the ground and barreling along at six hundred knots. "Ten-plus LHOs in the open. All ships, mind your intervals and follow me in."

"Sierra flight, you are cleared to engage," I send. "Weapons free."

The Shrikes form up into a wedge-shaped formation that brings all the ordnance racks to bear on the LZ at the same time. Then they ripple-fire the exercise ordnance on their rails. The blue-painted air-to-ground missiles never leave the ordnance rails in reality, but the pilots' visors and TacLink screens show two dozen missiles streaking toward their targets. More than half the simulated Lankies milling around in Arcadia City are hard kills instantly as they fall to the Shrikes' guided missiles. The simulation put two dozen Lankies on the ground, and eleven of them survive the first wave of incoming ordnance through sheer luck or improbable evasion skills. In reality, almost all of them would be dead, but there's no point making an already easy simulated environment even easier.

The Shrikes pair up and take turns making strafing runs on the surviving Lankies with their heavy autocannons. Three more Lankies fall in the first wave, four more in the second, and the rest eat it in the third. When the last flight of Shrikes thunders overhead and kicks up the radioactive dust in the streets of Arcadia City, all simulated targets are down, and the LZ is clear for the drop ships. The Shrikes climb to fifteen thousand feet and start a racetrack-shaped loitering pattern, ready to be called down again if the need for close-air support arises.

The drop ships come in fifteen minutes behind the Shrikes. The sixteen ships split into groups of four to form company-size units and deposit their infantry passengers in four different spots spread around the periphery of Arcadia City. The SI troopers leave their drop ships at a run and start taking covering positions.

I don't know what the sim has in store for them, but I know that this can't be the extent of their tasks for the day, and I'm not disappointed. A few minutes after the drop ships unload their troops, the computer shows two large groups of Lankies converging on Arcadia City from the north and south. They pop up on the Shrikes' screens at the limit of our ten-kilometer exercise bubble.

"Hostile contacts, incoming from zero-one-zero and one-eight-three," the squadron leader sends, and a few hundred TacLink screens down on Arcadia update with the target data from his Shrike. "Sierra flight, pair up and intercept."

The Shrike squadron immediately reacts and splits into two groups of three pairs each. They race north and south to stop the Lankies before they can reach the city, but the simulation has thrown a lot of Lankies at our landed SI company, at least fifty in each group. The Shrikes engage with their external ordnance and cannons. For the next ten minutes, they make attack runs on the Lanky groups and whittle them down slowly, but I can tell from their rate of advance and the frequency with which individual target icons disappear that it won't be enough. To make things worse, the sim decides to make things even harder and send smaller groups of Lankies following the first wave. The company's drop ships join the fray when the Shrikes have spent all their ammunition, taking down Lankies one by one with cannon fire, but the distance between the Lankies and the closest SI troops on the edge of the city shrinks rapidly.

"Sierra flight is Winchester," the Shrike squadron leader announces. "Heading back to the barn for rearming."

To save fuel, the flight of Shrikes will not actually climb back into orbit and do the entire docking and rearming procedure. They do have to disengage and fly out to three hundred kilometers away and thirty thousand feet high before the simulated weapons on their racks will reset to fully rearmed status. Shrike flight Sierra will be out of the battle for a good fifty minutes, and the troops on the ground will lose the scenario in the meantime.

"TacOps, this is Alpha Charlie Ground Actual," the lieutenant colonel in charge of the SI battalion sends. "Requesting follow-up close air ASAP."

"Oscar flight is in the clamps and on the way," I reply.

Things are going topsy-turvy for the ground force even before the Second Battalion is safely on the ground. Whoever programmed this exercise into the simulator doesn't believe in easy mode. The Lankies advance to within a kilometer of the first line of defense ten minutes before the second wave of Shrikes is due over the LZ, and even with the repositioned companies, there are only eight platoons on the ground in front of each Lanky approach. When the Lankies cross the eight-hundred-meter line, the platoons' MARS gunners open up with simulated silver bullets. Even without the feed from the Shrikes or drop ships, I have a perfect top-down view of the battle from my chair high up in orbit. The Lankies in the two attack waves start dropping again in the face of well-aimed fire from dozens of MARS launchers, but not every shot is connecting, and I can see from the kill ratio that the SI platoons will be overwhelmed even if they score a 100 percent hit rate with every round. The second wave of Lankies has caught up with the first wave and reinforced their numbers, and there are still close to a hundred in each attacking group. The distance between the SI lines and the advancing Lankies shrinks to six hundred meters, then to five hundred, then four hundred.

"Tailpipe Four, Tailpipe Seven, you have incoming close air," I send to the combat controllers embedded with the companies on the northern and southern defensive lines. "Call sign is Oscar flight."

My two combat controllers, Sergeants Taggart and Graff, send back their terse acknowledgments and check in with the inbound Shrikes. They split the incoming squadron between the northern and southern perimeters and mark target reference points right in front of their defensive lines, then clear the Shrikes for their attack runs. I watch the aerial ballet from my high vantage point and in air-conditioned comfort, but if it wasn't for the fact that I'm looking at Arcadia City right now, I would rather be pretend-battling on the ground than sitting up here in front of a console.

The first pair of Shrikes from Oscar flight dive down into the fracas and cut loose with their cannons, not wanting to risk friendly-fire hits among the SI from stray missiles. Almost immediately, my comms on squad, platoon, and company channels light up with frenzied warnings.

"Whoa! Oscar Three, abort!"

"What the hell is he doing?"

"TacOps, those were live rounds!"

On my camera feed, I can see a line of impacts kicking up big geysers of dirt right in front of our southern defensive perimeter, not fifty meters from the nearest friendly position. A second later, a pair of Shrikes zooms through the overhead shot. With the relative boredom of the last few hours, the sudden rush of adrenaline makes me sit up with a jolt.

"Oscar Three, abort, abort, abort," Sergeant Graff sends on the TacAir channel. "Be advised that you are firing war shots."

The feed from the TacAir channel is on low volume on the overhead speakers, but that transmission makes every head in CIC turn.

"Who is firing live rounds down there?" the XO asks.

I toggle into the TacAir channel.

"Oscar flight, abort. Repeat, abort your attack runs. Hold your fire. Weapons cold. I repeat, weapons cold. Someone in your flight has live ammunition loaded. All attack craft, come to heading zero-nine-zero and climb to ten thousand."

Both the XO and Colonel Yamin come rushing over to my station.

"Who in the hell is firing live rounds?" the XO repeats.

"Oscar Three has war shots loaded," I say. "I've given abort and hold orders to the whole squadron."

"This is not good." Colonel Yamin leans in to look at my console screens. "Halt the exercise. Make the Shrikes secure their weapons."

"Already did, ma'am," I reply.

The tactical officer stops the simulation, and the orange icons representing the approaching Lankies disappear from my TacLink screen instantly.

I switch to the command channel. "All units, this is TacOps. Did that burst hit anyone down there?"

It takes a few tense seconds for the company commander to reply.

"That's a negative, TacOps. But that was a close one. They dug a nice new trench in front of the company line with that cannon."

"Copy that. Shrikes have been pulled out. Safe all weapons and stand by."

I switch back to the TacAir channel where a dozen concerned Shrike jocks are undoubtedly waiting to find out what the hell is going on.

"Oscar flight, be advised that ground troops are okay. No casualties on the ground. Just landscaping damage."

At least one of the Shrikes in the holding pattern has live ammunition in the magazine for the autocannon, which is a major violation of safety protocols. On all cold exercises like the one we are running right now, the magazines get loaded with practice rounds, which are blue in color and inert except for built-in laser emitters to count hits. In almost ten years of service, I've only ever seen live ammo on a cold exercise ground once, and that was in rifle magazines that had been in unchecked pouches on an unlucky trooper's armor. Nobody got hurt, but the trooper in question still got demoted a rank and reprimanded. If war shots ended up in a Shrike's gun, at least three pairs of eyes failed to notice them, and three people are in very deep shit right now.

"Oscar flight, point your guns in a safe direction and check your loads. Oscar Three, hold your fire and keep your weapons on safe."

"Affirmative, TacOps," Oscar Three's pilot replies. He sounds more than a bit unhappy.

The remaining Shrikes test their firing cycles one by one. When Oscar Nine fires his weapon, I hear a curse over the TacAir link.

"Goddammit. TacOps, Oscar Nine. I have war shots loaded, too."

"Affirmative. Oscar Nine, safe your weapon."

The other Shrikes send their all-clear. I turn to Colonel Yamin.

"Ma'am, Oscar Three and Nine have live rounds loaded. The rest of the flight has exercise munitions in the magazines."

"I want all Shrikes recalled and all drop ships on the ground right now. Have the crew chiefs check the magazines of those cannons. And tell the grunts to check their ammo."

"Aye, ma'am." I relay the CO's orders to the drop ship wing and both Shrike squadrons in the air.

Colonel Yamin turns to her second-in-command.

"XO, send the master-at-arms down to the flight deck with a security detachment, have the chief of the deck pull duty logs, and secure the Shrike maintenance crews responsible for arming Oscar Nine and Oscar Three."

The XO walks off to pick up a handset, and I let out a long breath. I haven't seen if the brig on this ship is nicer than regular Fleet brigs, but I know that at least six wrench spinners are about to find out.

The safety checks take three hours, and both Shrike squadrons return to the ship to get their magazines emptied and double-checked. By the time everyone has been declared free of live ammunition, the exercise has come to a grinding halt. But we still have a battalion on the ground and a whole drop ship wing with them, so the CO decides to give the go-ahead to continue with half the scheduled units. The tactical station modifies the sim to account for the lack of air support from Shrikes and only half the planned personnel count on the ground. While the troops on the ground are still twiddling their thumbs and waiting for the action to restart, one of my combat controllers, Master Sergeant Garcia, walks into CIC and over to my station. I check the clock on my terminal and find that I am at the end of my watch.

"Ready to be relieved, sir?"

"Boy, am I ever," I say. "You heard the whole commotion earlier, I trust."

"Yeah. We were in the drop ship hold for two hours. Not much to do but to listen to radio chatter and check video feeds."

"Well, they'll be restarting the sim in about fifteen, so your arrival is impeccably timed, Sergeant Garcia." I get out of my seat and take my stainless coffee cylinder out of the cup holder on the side of the console. "All yours."

I stretch a little and grimace at the mild pain in my lower back.

"For fuck's sake. I went to Combat Controller School so I wouldn't have to sit on my ass for eight hours at a stretch anymore."

Sergeant Garcia gets into the seat and brings up his console layout.

"Well, sir, I hate to tell you that you got the worst of both worlds now. All the sitting of a console jockey, and all the sweat you had to spend to get the beret."

"Tell you what, Sergeant," I tell Garcia in a low voice. The colonel and her XO are over in the command pit and engrossed in a discussion. "If I ever look like I'm having a good time up here, I want you to drag me down to the flight deck, put a rifle in my hand, and place my ass on the next drop ship to Shitsville."

Sergeant Garcia chuckles. "I'll keep it in mind, sir."

CHAPTER 15

SHORE LEAVE

The exercise that was planned for one day got extended to three: one for the botched day with the live-fire incident, one for a thorough safety check and briefing, and another for a proper two-battalion exercise. Up until this moment, rumor had it that the CO was pissed enough to cancel the expected twenty-four-hour liberty for the crew on Arcadia, but it seems Colonel Yamin doesn't want to punish the whole crew for the safety lapses of four maintenance techs. The ships with the live ammunition in their magazines had been pulled from Ready Five status just an hour before the exercise, and the maintenance crews only put practice rounds on the rails and neglected to check the ammo cassettes. Word in the passageways has it that the crew chiefs were too busy distracting themselves by impressing a trainee from Eurocorps. I don't know if there's any truth to that rumor, but I do know that the XO gave both maintenance crews a dressing down that could be heard even through the armored bulkheads for twenty frames in either direction.

Because of the size of *Ottawa*'s crew complement, liberty must be taken in shifts to make sure that no more than a third of eligible personnel are away from the ship at any time. Halley and I got assigned to Alpha watch for our twenty-four-hour stretch of fresh air, one of the few perks of serving on the same ship while married. So when the XO announces the liberty schedule, we meet up in the flight deck mess at 0700 for a quick breakfast before the drop ship ride. We are in the uniform of the day, blue and teal as usual. From the way Halley carries herself, I can tell that she would rather be in her flight suit, which is what she wears almost all the time when she's on duty.

"Now hear this: liberty to Arcadia for eligible personnel will be in effect at 0900 hours for the Alpha watch. All eligible personnel assigned to liberty watch Alpha who wish to leave the ship for their twenty-four-hour liberty will report to the officer of the deck on the flight deck level by 0830 hours. Announcements for Bravo and Charlie liberty watches will follow at 1900 hours and 0700."

"I don't know why they won't just let us wear whatever we want," Halley complains over toast and scrambled eggs.

"You know why. We're going to be moving around among civvies, representing the Fleet. Let them look at some pretty new uniforms and give them the feeling that they're in good hands."

"Fuck that. Most of them are still the same people that left the rest of us in the shit three years ago." She looks down at her blue tunic and smooths out an imaginary wrinkle. "And I wouldn't go so far as to call these things pretty."

"They're kind of growing on me. The temperature regulation works well. I can't seem to break a sweat in them. And they don't crease, no matter what you do to them."

"Yes, but I don't feel very warlike in blue pajamas," Halley grumbles.

"Well, the uniform of the day is set. It's the price you'll have to pay for some clean air and blue skies."

We clean off our plates and return our trays to the recycler rack. Then we make our way to the flight deck to report in to the OOD, the officer of the deck.

Today's OOD on duty is a young first lieutenant, junior to both of us in rank, but we salute him first as we report in because the OOD represents the commanding officer's authority, which means that everyone except the CO is subordinate to him when it comes to reporting onto or off the ship.

"Permission to go ashore granted," the OOD says to us, and we grab our day packs and head across the deck marker and onto the flight deck to find our drop ship for the ride down.

If Halley looked uncomfortable at breakfast in her blueberries, being strapped into a cargo hold jump seat instead of up front in the driver's seat makes her almost miserable-looking.

"We've been riding in the hold together lots of times down on Earth," I say when I notice her flexing her hands and looking at the forward bulkhead with a tense expression.

"Yeah, but that's different. I don't fly those things as part of my own job. If I'm on a space-rated drop ship, I want to be in control of the stick."

When the drop ship is lifted off the deck by the launch clamps, almost all the seats in the hold are full. I see mostly blue uniforms, but there's a section in the outer starboard row where half a dozen SI NCOs have clustered together, seeking strength and protection in numbers. The cargo hold is alive with the din of many low-volume conversations, which all simultaneously get louder when the pilot turns on the drop ship's engines.

"Commonwealth Defense Corps Holiday Cruise Lines," Halley says. "Now accepting passengers for exciting off-world excursions."

"Eat authentic Fleet chow. Tour a battlefield. Pet a Lanky," I continue her pitch, and she laughs.

"At least we get paid for this," she replies. "Eventually. If we're lucky."

We touch down on the airfield at the Midland settlement. The original five colony settlements on Arcadia are built in a north-to-south line starting with New Eden in the north of the continent, then Tranquility, Arcadia City, Midland, and Landing in the south, all spaced roughly two hundred kilometers apart between settlements. We made Arcadia City uninhabitable when we blew up its fusion plant with a dirty nuke, so its population of ten thousand had to be dispersed across the other four settlements in the short term. Now that we've started a proper settlement program down here in earnest, several more colony towns have sprung up in a second north-south line to the east of the original settlements, all started by the new NAC leadership and staffed and populated with handpicked, experienced people and their dependents on a volunteer basis. You'd figure that nobody would volunteer to settle a new colony 150 light-years from Earth while the Lankies are still out there snatching colonies and making more seed ships, but I hear that when the Arcadia settlement project was announced, the list of applicants was close to a million names long.

When the tail ramp of the drop ship opens, a host of unbidden memories shoulder their way to the foreground in my brain. The temperature on this moon is always in the perfect range, low- to midtwenties Celsius. The skies are almost cloudless today, and I squint as Halley and I are walking down the ramp and onto the concrete drop ship pad at Fleet Air/Space Station Midland. I'm glad to see that we didn't go to Tranquility to the north of Arcadia City. That's the place my platoon wrecked with rifle fire, MARS rockets, and demolition charges during our distraction operation three years ago, when Masoud and his SEALs used us as a diversion so they could plant nukes on the terraformers on this moon. We killed half the garrison at Tranquility in the process, and even though I know we were in the right and they fired first, I'll always regret having been instrumental in the deaths of so many people from what should have been our own side. I don't want to spend liberty in a town where I may run into the families of those troopers.

"The blue in the sky is different here," Halley says. "Huh. I never noticed that the first time we were here."

"That's because we didn't have time to sightsee," I say. "And we moved at night most of the time anyway."

I look up at the sky and concede that she is right. The atmosphere here on Arcadia feels Earthlike, but it refracts light differently. The blue is darker, which makes the white clouds stand out more. It looks like the view from a helmet visor with UV filters and contrast turned up a few notches. Completing the reminder that this isn't Earth is the planet hanging on the horizon and taking up a good slice of our field of view—the ever-present Leonidas c, the blue gas giant to which Arcadia is tidally locked.

The Fleet base looks like a mirror image of the one at Tranquility. It has the same runway and hangar layout, and the control center building obviously came from the same prefab assembly line as the one we shot up three years ago. I do a rough count and see about two squadrons' worth of Shrikes lined up in the open hangars. Up on the control tower, a big NAC flag stirs in the light breeze.

"We have twenty-four hours of fresh-air time," Halley says. "What do you want to do down here until tomorrow morning?"

"Find a place that serves on Fleet credit, get tanked, and then look for a quiet and cozy spot out in the green to, you know, talk. Or whatever it is we feel like doing."

"That sounds like a brilliant idea, Captain Grayson," she replies with a satisfied nod. "I think I'll let you stay in charge of event planning for this one."

The military compound around the airfield is much bigger than Tranquility's base was three years ago. There are four multistory barracks buildings, vehicle sheds, a mess hall, and even a small RecFac. But

I'm not too interested in spending my twenty-four hours on this moon rubbing elbows with other officers in yet another RecFac, so Halley and I decide to take a stroll into Midland, which is just a kilometer away from the base. They terraformed this place to perfection in the twenty years since they started this colony in secret. The air is the cleanest I've ever breathed on any colony except maybe New Svalbard, and the soil is dark and smells heavily earthy. With just a little bit of water, I could probably grow something just in the dirt stuck to the bottom of my boots. The only thing that looks a little out of place in this bucolic scenery is the road going from the base to Midland. It's made of asphalt and wide enough for two-way traffic, and it occurs to me that I've never seen an asphalt street on a colony planet.

"Yeah, you're right," Halley says when I share this thought. "The most I've seen is that quick-lay concrete weave they can run off the back of an automatic paving unit. Wonder if they have the facilities to make asphalt locally."

"I doubt they spent the money to ship pavement to this place from a hundred and fifty light-years away. On the other hand, they brought a few ten thousand seed packs and saplings out here years ago already, so who knows."

"Watch us turn the corner into town, and it's Liberty Falls, complete with waterfall," she says.

"Fucking government dependents. We have to weigh our possessions before each deployment, and they get to bring a portable suburb with them."

Whatever else they can do on their own out here, agriculture is very much among their capabilities. There are farm plots on either side of the road, lush green produce growing in fields of that rich-looking soil. Automated watering units make their rounds between the rows. Water is such a scarce resource on most colonies that the sight of it spraying freely from twenty-meter dispenser booms is more alien out here than a Lanky seed ship. On the far end of the field toward the town, there are half a dozen big greenhouses with solar panel arrays on the rooftops.

"This is what I thought it would be like before I joined," I say.

"The colonies? Yeah, me too. Not those barren, dusty shitholes we keep fighting over most of the time."

"Barren, dusty shitholes, or frozen balls of ice. Nothing like this. I can see how they wanted to keep it for the chosen few."

From the direction of the base behind us, a pair of mules comes down the road at low speed. The mules have their gun mounts trained to the rear, and there are eight or ten Fleet personnel sitting on the rear deck of each vehicle, using the long barrel of the twenty-five-millimeter autocannon as a handhold. It's a minor violation of safety regs usually only tolerated in combat, but I suspect that the garrison doesn't want to deal with lots of disgruntled troops who were looking forward to a day out on the town and don't want to wait for the garrison mules to make the twentieth round-trip. The troops on the rear deck of the mule are all talking and laughing, obviously having a good time on their improvised hydrobus. The mules pass us and continue down the road, whisper-quiet except for the hum of their knobby honeycomb tires on the asphalt.

Halley and I watch as the mules disappear around a bend in the road in the distance.

"Hey, let's change plans a little," she says.

"What did you have in mind?"

"Skip the 'getting sauced' part of the day and the tour of the town. I'd rather not walk around in a settlement packed full of Fleeties on liberty. If there are watering holes there, they'll be full of blueberry uniforms."

"Yeah, I think you may be right." I scratch the back of my head and look around. "Well, what are we going to do instead?"

Halley pulls out her PDP and turns it on.

"I wonder if they have MilNet coverage out here already."

She flicks through a few screens and grins.

"Son of a bitch. They do have MilNet. And not just a local one, either. Full satellite coverage, military and civvie bands."

"You're joking." I take out my own PDP, and sure enough—I have a satellite-based data signal to MilNet.

"Son of a bitch," I echo Halley's sentiment. "All the comforts of home."

"Probably better than home," Halley replies. "Satellite coverage is high-bandwidth. And they don't have to share it among a lot of terminals out here. I bet the data throughput is five times what we get anywhere else."

Most colonies only have local networks run out of their central admin buildings, little network bubbles for each settlement for local comms and canned information. The settlements and bases in the solar system have delayed live links to the actual network because their admin facilities can pass traffic on to the big comms relays between the colonized moons and planets. But this is the first colony I've seen that has its own global satellite network.

"They were really planning for the long term," I say.

Halley brings up a local map and zooms in on our position. Then she pans the map around a bit and studies it.

"Looks like there's a road bearing off to the left right past those greenhouses. The map says there's a lake three klicks down from the intersection. Let's go there and dip our feet in the water. I haven't been to a lake in a while."

We pass the row of greenhouses, and the road leads over a short bridge spanning a brook. The water looks almost unnaturally clear. Just past the bridge, there's a gravel path bearing off to the left and disappearing behind a low hill a kilometer away. We turn onto the path and leave the road behind us.

"All right, so the blueberries aren't all bad," Halley says. "I should be sweating like a bastard right now, walking around in the sun like this."

"It's self-regulating. The air-conditioning in CIC is always cranked up, but I've never been cold up there."

The gravel path runs along the brook for three-quarters of a kilometer. It's not a wide brook, narrow enough that we could probably jump across it if we took running starts. The sound of the water burbling is one of the most peaceful and relaxing things I've heard in a long time.

A few hundred meters down the path, we pass the last of the greenhouses. On our left, across the brook, the vegetable fields we saw earlier stretch out into the distance, dozens of hectares of food crops growing in the warm light from Leonidas. On our right, there's a grassy meadow and the first signs of the nearby settlement half a kilometer in the distance.

"It's so quiet," Halley says. "All you hear is the breeze. I don't even hear any animals."

"They didn't bring anything living but tree saplings, food crops, and livestock embryos with them," I say. "Not even pets. I read up on it a while back. The place doesn't have any wildlife. They didn't want to introduce anything into the ecosystem uncontrolled."

"It needs birds. And insects."

"Bugs will come soon enough, I think. All it takes is for someone to bring in stowaways in their personal luggage when they resettle here. I'm shocked they're not already knee-deep in house flies and mosquitoes."

The brook veers off to the right toward the fields, and we start climbing the low hill in front of us. This part of Arcadia is all rolling plains and hills. On the eastern horizon, the nearby mountain chain where we played hide-and-seek with the garrison's Shrikes looms in the distance. Between the settlements and the mountains, there are pine forests running all the way to the foothills of those mountains, planted from seeds and saplings decades ago, when this place was still top secret and only known to the highest levels of government. They intended for it to be a new Earth, a backup plan for the NAC's most elite members to make a new start with their families in case things completely went to shit in the Commonwealth. Faced with Lanky extermination after the loss of Mars, they just jump-started their exodus and pulled the trigger a decade early.

"I wonder how the old residents feel about their new neighbors," I say. "The new settlements. Imagine the horror when they found out it was all unwashed middle-class 'burbers."

"Fuck 'em," Halley says. "They don't like it, they can ask for passage back to Earth. This place is way too nice for them anyway. If I had my way, everyone who took a one-way ticket to paradise while the rest of us were about to get wiped out by the fucking shovel heads should be forcibly relocated to a penal colony crammed into a deep crevice on Mercury."

We reach the top of the little hill and pause to take in the view. In front of us, there's a lake stretching out to the east, fringed by clusters of pine trees. On the southern shore of the lake, we see what looks like a pump station, although there are no water pipes going away from it and ruining the view. *They buried them for protection*, I think. *Or aesthetics.*

"Now there's a pretty sight," Halley says, huffing slightly from our brief but brisk ascent. "You have to travel wide and far on Earth to get a view like this."

The lake looks close by, but it's so large that it's just an optical illusion. It takes us another twenty minutes until we are finally at the shoreline. The only thing spoiling the scenery a little is the pump station a hundred meters to our right. It's a small, low-slung building that operates without emitting any noise to the outside world, but it still stands out in a picture-perfect view like this one. We walk eastward along the shoreline, away from the pump station. The water is lapping against the pebble-strewn sand shore in a slow, lazy, almost meditative cadence.

When we're well out of sight of the road and in the middle of a little pine forest, Halley sits down on a patch of grass near the edge of the water. The breeze rustling the tree branches carries the faint smell of pine resin and earth. She unzips her blueberry tunic and peels it off her shoulders. Then she lays it down flat behind her and lies back on it with a content sigh.

"Now this is not so bad."

I do likewise and lie down next to her on the ground. The grass and moss underneath us are a perfectly soft cushion. I close my eyes and inhale the fresh air. It's even cleaner than the mountain air in our little Vermont town, if that's possible.

"What are we going to do after this?" Halley asks. I look over to her, and she has her eyes closed and her hands folded on her chest.

"What do you mean, after this? This deployment?"

"No, after this job. After we get out of the corps, I mean. Whenever that will be."

"I've not really thought about that in great detail," I say. "I figured we'd take our money and get a place in Liberty Falls somewhere. Maybe give what's left to Chief Kopka and my mom. For all that free room and board we've been getting from the chief."

"Mmmm-hmmm." Halley's agreement sounds provisional.

"Why? Did you have something else in mind?" I ask.

"I don't know. Just thinking about options. Before all the shit with the Lankies started, you got a free ride to a colony planet with your honorable discharge. Don't you remember that from recruit orientation?"

"I must have been distracted by the total babe they assigned as my bunkmate," I say, and she smiles without opening her eyes. "No, I don't remember that."

"You had to have two full terms complete at least, but then you were exempt from the lottery if you wanted to go. Automatic winning ticket. I think the lottery allocation for vets was like five percent."

"Well, that all came to a screeching halt anyway. No more lottery. Or colony flights, except to this place."

"Yeah, but who knows? If we can push the Lankies back with these new ships, we may start the whole thing again. There are still a few colonies out there that haven't been flipped by the shovel heads," Halley says.

"You think we'll still be around when that happens?"

"We've made it so far. And things aren't as grim as they were right after they took Mars. When we had no way to fight back. It's different now."

"Until they show up in the solar system again, with two hundred seed ships. Or with something else. We've come up with new weapons and tactics. Who says they can't do the same?" I ask.

"Yeah, in that case, we'll be screwed no matter where we are." She takes a deep breath and lets it out slowly. "And that's a big fat *maybe* anyway. For now, let's just be happy that we aren't in mortal danger and enjoy the scenery."

We lie in silence for a little while. With nothing but the soft breeze and the sound of water lapping against the nearby shore, it's so serene that I could fall asleep in a minute if I allowed myself to drift off. Halley reaches over and takes my hand in hers.

"What were you thinking?" I ask. "About after."

"I don't know yet," she says. "I do know that I want to be as far away from my folks as I can get. Vermont would be a good start, I suppose."

She rolls on her side to face me, and I turn my head to look at her.

"But a colony. A place like this, anyway. Can you even imagine? Remember when we went down to Willoughby on the drop ship, and we talked about just taking the drop ship and disappearing on that planet, and nobody would have a clue where we went?"

"Yeah, I do," I reply.

"This colony has fewer than a hundred thousand people on it, and it's more than half the size of Earth. It's practically empty. We could live in a settlement or let them put up an off-the-grid prefab out in the sticks for us. Drive the buggy out into town every other week for necessities."

"It's not going to stay this empty."

"No, but they're only settling fifteen thousand people a year here. One new settlement every year. If we go out far enough, it will be a long time before we have neighbors again," Halley says. "Just think about it. The *quiet*."

"I *am* thinking about it," I say. "Gotta say, it doesn't sound terrible."

"Not terrible at all," Halley says. She squeezes my hand lightly and lets go. Then she clasps her hands over her chest again and lets out a content little sigh.

I think about what she just proposed. Leaving Earth behind after our service time is up. It really only means leaving our families behind because we don't own any property except for a few sets of civvie clothes, but I know that she wouldn't lose any sleep over putting 150 light-years between herself and her parents. I only see my mother on leave anyway, and by the time we're out of the service, she may not even be around anymore. People who spent most of their lives in the PRC have a shorter lifespan than 'burbers and the upper class. I love my mother, but it's probably a mistake to tailor my retirement plans to her life. And if I had the choice between Arcadia and Liberty Falls right now, I'd be very tempted to pick the colony. Most of the NAC would kill someone for a shot at life on a clean, empty planet with abundant natural resources, in a system far away from either human strife or Lanky incursions. If we ever get that choice, it will be more than 99 percent of the population gets.

It's warm and peacefully quiet here in the pine grove, and we don't have anything else to do for the rest of our stay. When Halley starts breathing regularly a few minutes later and then starts snoring lightly, I decide to join her in a nap and let my brain drift off for a little while.

Never waste an opportunity for taking a leak, grabbing chow, or taking a nap while in the military—you never know when you'll get the chance for another one.

When I wake up again a little while later, I blink and look at the pine needles on their swaying branches overhead for a little while. Then I check my chrono. We've been asleep out here for over an hour, and I am tempted to just go back to sleep and add another hour to the total because this is the most peaceful environment I've ever been in. But my stomach is starting to rumble, and I sit up to check the day pack for the ration bars we brought with us.

Next to me, Halley is still asleep with her mouth slightly ajar. I watch her for a little while and marvel at how little she has changed since boot camp ten years ago. Time has been kind to her, even through ten years in filtered-air environments and many high-stress deployments. There are some gray streaks evident in her hair in the sunshine, and she has little wrinkles in the corners of her eyes. But the familiar slope of her nose and curve of her jaw are as clear and defined as ever, and I could trace both from memory while half-asleep or fully drunk.

I bend over to wake her up with a kiss.

Both of our PDPs go off simultaneously with their politely urgent alert-message tones. Halley wakes and jerks her head up in surprise, and I have to pull back my own head so she doesn't smash me in the teeth with her forehead by accident. I fumble for the PDP in my leg pocket and pull it out of its pouch.

"What the fuck is it *now*?" I grumble and activate the screen.

This time, it's not a text alert, but a voice message from the XO of *Ottawa*. It plays as soon as the device senses that I am looking at the screen. Next to me, Halley turns on her own PDP and looks at it with a squint.

"This is the XO. All corps personnel, return to the nearest military installation for immediate return to *Ottawa*. All liberty is cancelled. I repeat, make your way to the nearest base as soon as possible and report in for transport back to the ship. Do not stop to smell the flowers on the way back. We are preparing for departure. XO out."

"Well, that's nice," I say. "Don't tell us *why* or anything."

"Lankies?" Halley suggests.

"I don't think so. He would have told us so, and the ship would be at combat stations with the remaining crew already. They wouldn't wait for everyone to get back to the ship."

"I hope you are right."

I know that the XO wouldn't cancel liberty and recall us unless he had a really good reason, one that won't result in mutinous rumblings from the majority of the crew. But I still feel cheated out of a full day down here with Halley. We got a walk and a nap, and now it's back to the barn already. But the second and third liberty shifts didn't even get that much—they're still up on the ship and waiting for their turn.

We gather our day packs and put our tunics back on.

"We're going to have to double-time it back," I say. "It's just three klicks away. We can run that in twenty minutes."

"Fifteen," Halley says.

"*Someone* is confident in her aerobic conditioning," I reply.

As we shoulder our packs and get ready to run back to the base, Halley looks at the clear and inviting water of the lake with an almost mournful expression on her face.

"Well, fuck. We came a hundred and fifty light-years, and I never even got to dip my feet in the water."

CHAPTER 16

URGENT DISPATCH

The ride back up to the ship takes twenty-five minutes from takeoff to skids down on the flight deck, but everyone in the ship is tense and anxious, so it feels much longer than usual before we are back on *Ottawa* and out of the cargo hold.

"I'm going to CIC," I tell Halley once we check ourselves back in with the OOD. "They'll tell us what's happening soon enough, but if I find out anything above and beyond the 1MC update, I'll let you know."

"Please do," Halley says.

She hugs me briefly. Her uniform tunic still smells like fresh air and grass. If this is to be our last happy moment together, it isn't a bad one. But I don't tell her that because she's anxious enough as it is. The crew chief and pilots either didn't know the reason for the liberty cancellation, or they were under orders not to tell before we could be given the official word.

Halley heads for Pilot Country, and I go up to the command deck to relieve the combat controller on duty at the TacOps station. If we are looking at another crisis, the best way to stay in the loop is to be in the same compartment with the ship's commanding officer and XO.

The mood in the CIC is tense but not panicked. As soon as I walk in, I glance over at the holotable and the tactical orb projected directly above it. When I see that all the icons on the display are blue, I allow myself a small sigh of relief. Whatever the problem, it's not a Lanky seed ship bearing down on us from somewhere in the system. Otherwise we'd be at combat stations and running target solutions already.

"What's going on?" I ask Staff Sergeant Wilcox as he clears the TacOps station for me to take his place.

"Nothing good," he murmurs. I see him glancing at the CO and XO, who are standing at the holotable, engaged in quiet conversation. "The skipper's about to go on the 1MC," he says.

"Go and fill in the rest of the STT," I say. He nods and turns to walk out of the CIC.

I sit down and bring up my console screens, as pointless as it is without any tactical assets in the air. Most of our drop ships are back on *Ottawa*. There's a flight of four ships coming up from Arcadia and almost in the docking pattern, but nothing else is showing in orbit other than the fleet anchorage and its docked ships. None of the situational screens in front of me give any hints about the nature of the emergency. All ship systems are in the green, the plot shows only NAC ships, and we're not at combat stations, so the problem is somewhere in that wide swath of possible scenarios between "utter calm" and "Lankies in weapons range."

Ten minutes later, the drop ships are on the deck, and the orbital plot is clear of traffic.

"All air assets are back in the barn, ma'am," the flight-ops officer says. "All personnel present and accounted for."

"Helm, bring us about for a least-time course to the Alcubierre point," Colonel Yamin says. "Go to full military power."

I try to not hold my breath when she picks up her headset and puts it on.

"1MC line."

"You are go on 1MC, ma'am."

"Attention, all hands," Colonel Yamin says. She pauses and takes a deep breath before continuing.

"I regret having to cancel shore liberty for all personnel, but we have an emergency. Two hours ago, the cruiser *Durandal* entered the Leonidas system and transmitted a Fleet priority message to us directly. Three days ago, a NAC Fleet supply ship, the *Concord*, entered the solar system to relay an emergency message from the colony of New Svalbard. It seems that after three years of relative quiet, our enemy is once again on the offensive. *Concord* reports that the long-range sensors at New Svalbard picked up several approaching seed ships with direct course for the colony. *Concord* was in orbit above New Svalbard at the time and immediately did a hard burn for the Alcubierre node to send warning to the rest of the Fleet. Their escort, the destroyer *Michael P. Murphy*, remained behind to defend the colony despite orders from the task force commander to remain with *Concord* and vacate the system."

I have a sudden and heavy sense of dread in the pit of my stomach. A single destroyer doesn't stand much of a chance against a Lanky seed ship, never mind several of them. If that action took place three days ago, that destroyer is likely a debris field by now. I bring up the data sheet for the *Michael P. Murphy*: "BLUE-CLASS DESTROYER, 9,500 TONS, TROOP COMPLEMENT 358 OFFICERS AND ENLISTED."

"I will get right down to it," Colonel Yamin continues. "The Fleet has ordered us to return to the solar system and immediately proceed to the Alcubierre transition point at best speed. We are to enter the Fomalhaut system and engage and destroy any Lanky presence there. There are more than three thousand civilians remaining on New Svalbard, along with a battalion of SI in the garrison at Camp

Frostbite. They will hold the line while they wait for the Fleet to send reinforcements, and we will make sure they will not wait and fight in vain."

She pauses again, and I imagine that the total silence in CIC is echoed in every other compartment of the ship.

"*Ottawa* is the only ship on the board right now that can stand up to Lanky ships in battle. *Arkhangelsk* can't make Alcubierre journeys, and she's tasked with the protection of Earth. None of the other Avengers are fully ready yet. So this is all on us. If we don't come to their aid, the colony will fall, and the SI troops on that moon will be wiped out. We will come to their aid, because that's exactly what this ship was intended to do. I realize that this is one hell of an end to a shakedown cruise, and I wish we had a few more weeks to tighten the bolts, but almost four thousand lives depend on us having our act together. We'll just have to accelerate the honeymoon a little."

Colonel Yamin studies the plot in front of her while she is speaking, and she looks as grim as I've ever seen her. I remember that she was in command of a cruiser at the First Battle of Mars, when the Lankies jumped the orbital garrison and wiped out most of the Fleet ships there. I don't have to wonder if the ghosts of that event are still haunting her sleep regularly.

"When we get to the solar system, we will rendezvous with a Fleet supply ship to take on fuel and offload the civilian contractors and Eurocorps trainees. Once we have topped off our tanks and restocked our necessary supplies, we will use a shortest-time trajectory to the Alcubierre node. None of the other ships in the Fleet can keep pace with *Ottawa* at top speed, so we will be entirely on our own. But that is what this ship was built for, after all. Use the transit time to train hard. The next time you hear the Combat Stations alert, it will not be a drill."

The situational plot in front of me mirrors the tactical view on the holotable display in the center of CIC. I don't feel any acceleration, but *Ottawa* is already burning hard to leave orbit. Our course trajectory curves right back to the Alcubierre node a few hours away. We are heading back to the solar system with our foot firmly on the accelerator.

"I have utter confidence in this ship and her crew. Three years ago, *Agincourt* and *Arkhangelsk* destroyed several seed ships in direct combat. *Ottawa* has twice as much firepower and five times the armor protection of that class. This ship was made to blow apart seed ships and kill Lankies. So let's go do just that. CO out."

Colonel Yamin taps the side of her headset and pulls it off her head. It was a good motivational speech, but I can tell from her expression that she may not feel quite as confident as she just sounded. But the CO's worries are her own, and I look away and focus on my screens again before she can notice that I'm looking at her.

"Six more months," she says to the XO.

"Ma'am?"

"Six more months, and we would have had another Avenger ready. I'd love to have *Washington* on our starboard when we get to Fomalhaut. Hell, even *Moskva* or *Beijing*." She sighs and shakes her head. "Well, no point standing here and wishing, I guess. Put a Ready Five on the deck, nuclear-strike package. I want all departments reporting combat ready by 1800. Let's go to war."

We enter the Alcubierre chute to the solar system three hours and thirteen minutes later at maximum safe speed. In regular space, *Ottawa* is several times faster than the next-fastest ship in the Fleet, and she can keep up her full-throttle burn for much longer than any other ship because of her multiple reactors and immense fuel tanks. But an Alcubierre transition can't be accelerated, so we'll be in transit back to the solar system for almost twenty-four hours, a whole day lost to the physics of interstellar travel.

My watch in CIC ends at 1800. Before I gather my stuff and leave the station, I send a message to all special tactics team members to call them in for a briefing in two hours. Then I leave CIC to get a shower and some chow. The knowledge of our upcoming battle adds to the discomfort I'm already feeling from the Alcubierre transition, which makes even the good food in the officers' wardroom taste more bland somehow.

"Well, I have good news for those of you looking to add to your combat drop total," I say when everyone is assembled in the briefing room. Some of the troops chuckle at this, but the younger staff NCOs can't work up more than nervous smiles.

"Those of you who have dropped against Lankies before, you know the dance. If New Svalbard is crawling with Lankies already and we get the seed ships out of the way, we'll most likely do a pod launch. There's a garrison on the ground, but the Lankies were on approach to the moon three days ago already, and I don't know how long the battalion at Camp Frostbite will hold out against landings from multiple seed ships." I don't mention *Michael P. Murphy*, because everyone but a starry-eyed optimist already knows the destroyer is gone by now if they stood and fought.

"Question, sir."

"Yes, Master Sergeant Garcia."

"Are we keeping the same unit assignments we had for the exercise drop? Might be good to drop with company sections we're already familiar with."

"I don't see any problem with that, unless any of you have objections."

The STT members all murmur their assent.

"Well, that's decided, then. Company assignments remain the same as before. Who here has been on New Svalbard before?" I ask.

Only Master Sergeant Taggart's hand goes up.

"I did a rotation at Camp Frostbite when I was right out of Combat Controller School, sir."

"So you know the environment. For the rest of you—picture Antarctica, only slightly less hospitable in the winter."

I bring up some orbital recon pictures of the SI facility at Camp Frostbite and the nearby town of New Longyearbyen.

"The good news is that this is the most fortified colony we have out there, from a physical point of view. Most of their essential infrastructure is underground. They built it that way because of the weather, not because they expected Lankies at the time. But everything there is built tough. The admin building is the only Class Five colonial hard shelter in existence, for example. That'll be a really tough nut for the Lankies to crack."

I bring up a schematic of the tunnel network underneath the town.

"This is the underground portion of the facility. It's under fifty meters of ice and permafrost. Virtually every building has one or more escape shafts that connect to those tunnels. They have food storage and fuel down there to last for a while. But they won't be able to hold out indefinitely, especially if the Lankies are around for long enough to start digging their own tunnels. I want you to study the layout of that infrastructure and get very familiar with it. Because if we have to go down into those tunnels, you won't have time to find a local guide or read a map. If their network is down, you won't get TacLink, either, because you'll have fifty meters of signal block over your heads, so don't assume you'll be able to rely on it. Even the local peer-to-peer link can get spotty down there."

I bring up a map of Camp Frostbite. I was down there for the last time four years ago, and the place has seen eight deployment cycles since then. The troops we brought on *Midway* are long off that rock, but many of the civilian colonists I knew are probably still there.

"That's the garrison. We've been keeping a full battalion there for over four years now. It has its own drop ship squadron and attached light-armor company. If New Svalbard is attacked, the mission of Camp Frostbite is to respond and neutralize the attack away from the town if possible. If the town itself is threatened, the garrison will fortify the town and hold the perimeter until the cavalry arrives."

"What do we do if the garrison is gone?" Staff Sergeant Wilcox asks.

"That's up to the CO. But I'm guessing they'll task us with sanitizing the town and establishing a perimeter around the airfield so we can lift out the civvies. That's what I would do anyway. Assume our mission is going to involve those tunnels one way or another."

The combat controllers and Spaceborne Rescuemen go over the schematics and ask occasional questions while I explain the layout of the tunnels and the composition of the garrison force. But as they're taking notes on their PDPs and paying attention to the briefing, I can't help but think that we are planning a funeral. If the Lankies have landed on New Svalbard, the colony is probably lost unless we can kill every seed ship and every last individual. And if they've had time to go underground by the time we arrive, we'll be lucky to get the colonists out and leave in one piece.

"Once we're in-system, we'll know more about the opposition. We don't know how many Lanky ships are in orbit, or if they've landed their pods already. All of this is contingent on in-system recon once we get there. Expect a prebattle briefing, but familiarize yourself with the likely battleground as well as you can before we get to Fomalhaut. The old-timers will be able to confirm that when things start to happen, they'll happen quickly. Exercise, test and triple-check your gear, and get enough food and rest. If we land, it'll be the biggest military op in three years. We will jump in with the best gear in the locker, and with the best ship in the Fleet above us in orbit. Let's put all that to good use and kick the shovel heads off that moon."

I conclude the briefing, and the NCOs all file out one by one. The younger sergeants, the ones who haven't been in battle yet except for maybe a few garrison patrols over Mars, look properly somber and pensive. The old salts are most likely worrying, too, but they've learned to hide their fears.

I'm the last to leave the briefing room. When I step into the passageway beyond, Halley is leaning against the bulkhead nearby, arms folded.

"I like the way you run your briefings. You've turned into someone who really knows his turf. You know I find competence dead sexy?"

"You listened in on the briefing?"

"You left the door open a crack. I was looking for you, and the computer said you were in that compartment. When I heard you talking to your NCOs, I figured I'd listen in while I wait."

"And what's your professional assessment?"

"Of the briefing, or of your grasp of the tactical situation?"

"Whichever," I say.

"I would have had nothing to add. We go by the book regardless of what we find on the other end of that chute and do our best. Do you really think there will be colonists left to save?"

"Have you been to New Svalbard?"

"Three or four times. But only for water stops. I've never actually been on the surface."

"They're a tough bunch down there. And they have a fortified underground city and a whole battalion of SI to hold off the Lankies. I'd say their odds to hold out for a week or two are better than even."

"Let's just hope this ship punches in its advertised weight class, or we won't even get into orbit," Halley says. "Did you have chow yet? I'm starving."

"I'll join you," I say, even though I already ate. We have twenty-three hours of Alcubierre and a few days of solar system transit left, and I figure I should seize every chance I have to sit down with Halley, just in case things go sideways in a bad way once we reach Fomalhaut. There's always coffee in the wardroom, and my evening run can wait thirty minutes.

CHAPTER 17

WAR STORIES

When we come out of the Alcubierre chute on the solar system side, there's a welcoming committee waiting for us. The supply ship *Hampton Beach* and the cruiser *Excalibur* are on station a few thousand kilometers from the transition point. There's no overhead 1MC message welcoming us back to the solar system. After we take on fuel and supplies here, we won't be stopping anywhere else until we reach the outbound Alcubierre point beyond the asteroid belt. Our trajectory has us foregoing any gravity assists from Earth or Mars in favor of a shortest-time flight path at full burn. We've used up an astonishing amount of reactor fuel already on this shakedown cruise, and it's amazing to see that even after millions of kilometers at full burn and two 150-light-year transitions, *Ottawa*'s reactor fuel tanks are still at almost 50 percent.

"Now hear this," comes the announcement twenty minutes later. "*Hampton Beach* is coming alongside for replenishment. All CONREP personnel, stand by for connected replenishment operations."

A few moments later, the XO chimes in on the 1MC.

"This is the XO. All civilian contractors and Eurocorps members, this is your port of call. Report to the OOD at the main transfer lock on deck one if you are looking for transportation back to Gateway and Earth. This will be our one and only transfer stop before we enter the chute to the Fomalhaut system. Anyone who isn't off this ship by the time we detach from *Hampton Beach* is going out of system again in four days. I repeat: all civilian and Eurocorps personnel wishing to transfer to Gateway at this time, report to the OOD at the main transfer lock on deck one by 1130 hours. XO out."

———————

The mood on the ship has flipped dramatically since we left the Leonidas system. It seems that everyone got a sudden and forceful reminder that *Ottawa* is really a warship. When I go for a run on the track later, it's noticeably more crowded than before, and most of the newly motivated runners are junior enlisted. Even the chow halls and RecFacs are more subdued than before. I get a grim satisfaction out of the evaporation of some of the more casual attitudes among the Fleet crew, but I can't help feeling some sympathy for the junior members of the crew. They got four days' notice of their first battle, and I know from experience that the worst thing about going to war is having time to think about the upcoming fight.

In the middle of my five laps around the nukes, someone hails me from behind.

"On your left," a familiar voice says. I move all the way onto the right lane of the track, and Hansen pulls even with me.

"You know, we're probably wasting time out here," she says.

"How so?" I reply, trying not to pant.

"Never fought a battle where my running stamina made a difference," she replies. "If you're tired, the armor servos pick up your slack."

"Makes me feel better. To know I can still move if I have to. Servos or not."

We run along at the same speed. Every few dozen meters, we have to switch to single file to pass someone else chugging around the missile silos, but Hansen pulls even with me again every time. Before too long, it's a wordless competition—we fall into a rhythm of switching formation and reforming, fluid and efficient. Sometimes, the company and staff officers in the SI slack off a little on the fitness training—they tend to be older and burdened with more administrative nonsense, after all—but Hansen is not one of those slackers. When we finally finish our laps and switch to a trot and then a walk into the entrance vestibule, I am out of breath and sweaty.

"We've got four days until the ball drops," Hansen says. "If you're free this evening right after chow, why don't you come down to Grunt Country? We can head to the officer RecFac on deck three and grab a drink. Time's running out for catching up and talking about old times."

"Yes it is," I reply. "How about 1800?"

"See you then," Hansen says. "Deck three, frame one seventy-five."

"Copy that. Eighteen hundred at three one seventy-five."

The replenishing process usually takes a few hours, but we stay attached to *Hampton Beach* for close to six hours, an unusually long amount of time for a ship whose skipper is in a hurry to get somewhere. I'm in the middle of a four-hour watch in CIC when we finally detach the replenishment collar and maneuver away from *Hampton Beach* to light up our main engines.

"Now hear this: underway replenishment operation complete. We are commencing our transit to the Alcubierre point. Closest approach to Earth will be in two hours, thirty-eight minutes," the XO announces on the 1MC.

"That's our last stop in the system unless something essential falls off this ship," he says to Colonel Yamin. "Reactor fuel is at one hundred percent. We've cleaned *Hampton Beach* out of all their medical supplies and rations. Ammo magazines and stores are full, but we took on a few tons of small-arms ammunition and two hundred AGM-551s for the Shrikes."

"Let's hope we won't have to go through all that ammo when we get to the far end," Colonel Yamin says. "Helm, resume plotted course to the node. Get us up to full burn."

"Aye, ma'am. Resuming course, all ahead full."

My perception of the ship's gravity does not change, but the numbers next to *Ottawa's* icon on the main plot do. The ship starts accelerating again at over twenty meters per second squared, and the velocity reading next to the icon starts clicking up decimal points rapidly. I check the bigger plot at system-level zoom and see that our turnaround point for the reverse burn is two-thirds of the way between Earth and the asteroid belt. We'll be at turnaround in two days, and at the Alcubierre node in four, much faster than I've ever made an Earth transit to the node without using liberal gravitational help from either Earth or Mars.

"Report from the OOD on the numbers for offloaded personnel, ma'am," the XO says.

"How many did we transfer?" Colonel Yamin asks.

The XO brings up the report screen on his PDP and shows it to Colonel Yamin, who looks at it and then nods with a satisfied smile.

"Good for them." She picks up her handset and motions for the comms officer to open a 1MC line. "All hands, this is the CO. We have offloaded seventeen civilian contractors to *Hampton Beach*. None of the one hundred and twenty-five Eurocorps members on this ship have taken the offer to transfer back to Earth."

She pauses and looks around in CIC, where everyone present either smiles or nods approvingly.

"As your commanding officer, I won't tell you to intentionally violate regulations," she continues. "But if you want to buy a Eurocorps ally a drink with your alcohol allocation tonight at the RecFac, you will find that nobody's going to look closely. That is all. CO out."

It's an unexpected morale boost to learn that our Eurocorps allies have decided to a man and woman that they're in it for the duration, even if that means going into harm's way along with the rest of us. I would have been tempted to take the ride off the ship, but I know that Halley and I would have decided the same way if the assignments were reversed.

I send to Halley:

>Between that and Mars, I'll have to stop making fun of the Euros.

A little while later, she sends back:

>Let's not go too far with the international brotherhood thing. But they can have my beer chit tonight.

After chow, I head down to Grunt Country, the section of the ship where the Spaceborne Infantry detachment is berthed. A regiment of SI has two battalions, with four companies per battalion and four platoons per company, almost twelve hundred grunts in total. All of them are trigger pullers, because the Fleet is handling their logistics, equipment maintenance, and administrative tasks. The SI berthing and office spaces for the embarked infantry are usually among the most crowded on a warship, but *Ottawa* continues its streak of breaking conventions. The compartments down here are spacious and the passageways wide enough for three troopers to walk abreast.

Hansen is in her company commander office, talking to a gunnery sergeant who's standing in front of her desk at parade rest. She sees me peeking into the compartment and gives me a little wave.

"That should get things sorted, Gunny. You have your waypoints. Dismissed."

"Yes, ma'am," the gunnery sergeant says. He turns and leaves the compartment. On the way past me, he gives me a respectful nod.

197

"Good evening, Captain."

"Evening, Gunny."

I walk into Hansen's office compartment. The bulkheads are barren of decorations. On Earth, where troops don't have to worry about the weight of their personal possessions, a lot of company-grade and staff officers usually have an ego wall in their office, plaques and awards and pictures of previous units. SI and Fleet officers on deployment don't get the luxury of an ego wall, and the practice is so typical for shorebound pencil pushers that most of us wouldn't adopt the practice even if we were allowed three tons of possessions on deployment.

"That's the worst part about officer rank," Hansen says. "All this admin bullshit. Don't you just want to put a round into your terminal screen sometimes?"

"Once or twice a week," I say.

"Then you have more patience than I do." Hansen gets up from her chair and shuts her screen down with a tap.

"Ready to go and get some drinks?" she asks.

"Am I ever. Lead the way, Captain."

The RecFac closest to Grunt Country is a unified compartment, with separate sections for officers and enlisted. From the sounds coming from the enlisted side, the place is pretty full on the other side of the partition, but the officer side is agreeably empty. We walk to the bar and collect our drinks—soy beer for her and alcohol-free malt beer for me, part of my penance for the unauthorized gun. There are four or five junior SI officers sitting in booths and nursing their allowed beverage for the day, and Hansen and I have no trouble finding a quiet booth at the end of the room in front of the big bulkhead screen that shows the space outside. It's not as impressive as the domed ceiling in the Fleet's officer facility, but it beats looking at bulkhead paint.

"Did you get rid of the ponytail when you switched to SI?" I ask. The ponytail was her trademark feature back then, an unusual style that tip-toed right on top of the line of a uniform rule violation.

"Oh no. I cut it off long before then." She runs a hand through her short blonde hair. "I let it grow even longer after you left the 365th. At one point, I even braided it."

"So why'd you chop it?"

"CQB is why," Hansen says. "Got into a tussle one day out in a PRC. Three guys jumped me while I was in the middle of a mag change. One of them grabbed that braid and used it as a handle. Tried to make my head an integral part of the pavement."

"Didn't go well for him, I'd imagine."

"No, it did not. You know the knives they issued back in the TA? Those big, heavy piece-of-shit telescoping blades that nobody ever bothered packing for drops? Well, after Detroit, we all carried them again. Mine was still factory sharp. Took the guy's hand off right at the wrist. And after we got back to base, I cleaned it and used it to cut that dumb-ass braid off."

"God, we were so full of it," I say.

"Ain't that the fucking truth." Hansen takes a long swig from her bottle. "I want to go back in time and shake the shit out of the little moron I was back then."

"She wasn't you yet," I say. "We're not those kids anymore."

"I guess not. To be honest, the time at Shughart is just kind of a blur these days. I try not to think about it too much. Everything, and I mean *everything* went to shit not a year after you left. Jackson and the sarge gone. The rest of us getting split up and sent to new units. When they looked for volunteers to switch to SI, I signed so fast that my pen left a contrail."

"Sergeant Fallon told me about the unit getting broken up."

"Yeah, about that. How in the *fuck* did you get her to serve as your platoon sergeant?"

"I asked nicely. And she felt like she owed me one, I guess. But after Arcadia, I don't think you could get her back into space if you told her at gunpoint."

"I want to know what went down there," Hansen says, and there's a trace of excitement in her voice. "On the Arcadia mission."

"You've probably heard all about it on Fleet News Network. Or the enlisted rumor mill."

"Yeah, but they only give the official version on the Network. And the rumor mill just distorts shit. You were on the ground. I don't know anyone else who was."

"I had a platoon of SI under me. We got to the system, did recon, and landed a company on that moon with four of those new stealth drop ships. My platoon and I played hide-and-seek with the local garrison for a few days. The commanding officer saw fit to use us as a diversion so his SEAL team could plant nuclear demolition charges on most of the fusion reactors. And it worked."

I tell her the broad details of the mission, filling her in on everything but the unpleasant details I don't feel like talking about—the relay station, the escaping shuttle I ordered destroyed, the men and women we lost in that last-ditch assault on their main command-and-control facility. She lets out a low whistle when I get to the part where the nuke goes off and Masoud broadcasts his ultimatum to the garrison forces.

"That is some hardcore planning and execution," Hansen says. "One company and four drop ships, and you got a reinforced battalion and a carrier task force to surrender. I always wondered about the details."

"They had no choice. Masoud would have blown up every single fusion reactor on that moon. Nobody is willing to chance a bet when the stakes are that high. And he wasn't bluffing."

"Like I said, hardcore. Man, I never got to do anything half as ballsy. I would have volunteered for that mission in a heartbeat."

"You probably would have done better than I did," I say. "I'm not an infantry platoon leader. I'm an air-traffic controller with a gun and a radio. But they were short on podheads at the time."

"It sounds like you did just fine," Hansen says.

"I don't know about that. But I'm still here. Some of the troops that came along aren't."

"But you got back, and you got the job done. That's war, Grayson. People die all the time. You're in charge of anything other than your own pair of boots, you're bound to lose people. Comes with the rank. For us grunts, anyway. Some of those console jockeys in CIC can probably make it all the way to staff officer without putting anyone's ass on the line."

Hansen takes another swig from her bottle.

"Ah, fuck it. We're all between a rock and a hard place. I figure ten more years, and then I've earned that lifer bonus."

"What are you going to do when you get out of the corps?" I ask.

"I don't know yet. Maybe get a place in the 'burbs somewhere. Get fat on civvie chow. See if I can find someone I can live with. It's gotta be a veteran, though, because I've got precisely fuck-all in common with civilians. Last time I was home for leave, my mother wanted to fix me up with this guy." Hansen smiles and shakes her head at the memory.

"He was nice enough. Good-looking, too. But man, it's like we were talking different languages at dinner. We had no common point of reference. He had a nice body, though, so at least the evening wasn't a total wash."

"They have different priorities. They can't relate to the shit that we do up here. Of course, I can't relate to theirs, either. I mean, when you've seen what we've seen, can you still pretend like any of that civilian bullshit is a big deal?"

"I'd tell you not to date outside your own species, but it doesn't look like you have to worry about that," Hansen says.

"Yeah, I lucked out. Ten years and counting."

"What about you?" she asks. "What are you going to do? Try to make it to twenty years for the big payday?"

"I don't know," I say. "Maybe. Podheads are usually burned out by forty. Too much stress. Physical and mental. If I stay in much longer, I'm gonna have to go lifer just for the medical care after retirement."

"They really have us by the balls, Grayson. The more they spend on training you, the more use they want to get out of you. At least we have stars now." She puts her bottle on the table between us and turns it slowly with one hand. "Easier to resign a commission than to get out as enlisted. You don't have to wait for that contract to end."

"And you forfeit bonuses and medical care," I say.

"Yeah, that too. But at least it's a quick way out. They can't quite make the noose so tight that nobody can slip out of it."

"It all depends on what my wife wants to do. If I want out and she wants to stay in, or vice versa, we have a bit of an issue."

"Well, there's one advantage to being single," Hansen says. "I don't know how you do it, with all the hoops we have to jump through for the corps. And she's on the same ship?"

I nod.

"I wouldn't want that. If this thing gets shot to ribbons by the Lankies, you'll both snuff it."

"Honestly?" I say. "We would both prefer it that way. Going out at the same time, I mean."

Hansen looks at me as if she can't decide if I am joking. Then she shakes her head and takes another sip from her bottle.

"See? Marriage is weird. I think I'll stick with space husbands. Three months at a time is about as much commitment as I can handle."

"Marriage is great. It's the one thing I have to come back to every time, no matter how shitty things get out here," I reply.

"I don't think I am cut out for it," Hansen says. "Good for you if you are, though." Her gaze locks with mine for just a moment too long, and I quickly take a swig of my drink.

"I'm fraying at the edges, I think," I say to change the subject. "Mentally, I mean. Do you ever get stressed out enough to want to take someone's head off?"

"Every other day," Hansen says with a smirk.

"You ever see the shrink about it?"

"Hell no. That shit isn't for me." Hansen takes a sip from her bottle and puts it down on the table with emphasis. "I know what bugs me. I don't need assistance from some rear-echelon psych quack. All they do is pump you full of meds."

I don't want to tell Hansen that I let them put me on meds because I know that she'd see it as a sign of weakness. Too many grunts are caught up in the mind-set that a frontline soldier should be able to manage that sort of thing on their own, that seeking help from a professional is somehow unbecoming. I know that she's wrong to dismiss it out of hand because the stuff I am taking really helps—it evens out the highs and lows for me—but I don't want to have that discussion with Hansen right now because I know she wouldn't appreciate it.

"Hey, that's what they made booze for, right?" she continues and raises her bottle to eye level.

"That's the truth," I feign agreement, and touch my bottle to hers.

We talk for a while longer, mostly reminiscing about the time we were at Fort Shughart together, but I find that the old memories have started to fade. Revisiting them with Hansen is not making them any more defined. We only shared a few months of service time as squad mates, and it all ended in a clusterfuck of epic proportions when Stratton and Paterson got killed and I had to transfer to the navy. Hansen already had a year of service and veteran status when I joined the battalion as a raw recruit, so even the experience we shared at Shughart wasn't the same for both of us. And since then, she has gone her own way and built up her own catalog of victories, regrets, and nightmare material. Still, talking to her feels good because it makes me feel like Halley and I are not statistical aberrations, that there are others out there who have made it through ten years of war against the SRA and then the Lankies. That way, I don't feel like we're just unusually lucky and due to get our tickets punched any day now.

"Now hear this," the announcement comes over the 1MC just before 1900 hours. "We are now in the closest-distance window for high-bandwidth network traffic to Earth. *Ottawa*'s neural network will be low-latency for the next three hours and forty-five minutes."

This is a cue for the crew of *Ottawa* to contact their loved ones on Earth via live link if they want to have a direct video talk without long delays. It's hard to have a conversation when you need to wait fifty seconds for your transmission to get to the other party, and their reply another fifty seconds to get back to you. For the next three hours and change, many of the crew will avail themselves to what will be the last opportunity for face-to-face conversations before we go into battle.

"I should take advantage of this," Hansen says. We've long finished our allotted beer for the evening, and she's been toying with her bottle for the last twenty minutes. "Call the folks, give them an update. It's been three months."

"Yeah, me too," I say, even though I don't have anyone to call on Earth. Mom has a dependent account, but there's no secure military terminal in her place, and she has to go to the nearest government facility to check for messages from me. There's no way for me to get her on a live link unless she happens to be in front of a terminal when I call, and that's almost impossible to orchestrate.

We get out of our chairs and dispose of the empty brown, plastic bottles in the recycler chute.

"It was good to see you, Grayson," Hansen says. "Glad you're still sucking down air."

"Good to see you, too," I reply. "Let's do this again after we get back from Fomalhaut."

"Count on it," she says.

She gives me a brief hug, and we part ways. She's heading back to Grunt Country, and I turn the other way in the passageway to go back up to the command deck. Her body language during our conversation, the way she leaned toward me and met my eyes with hers as much as possible, told me that she'd be more than receptive if I applied for the current space husband position in earnest, Halley or not. But our talk has reinforced to me just how well Halley and I match each other after ten years, and how comfortable we are with each other's flaws and idio-syncrasies. Hansen's subtle cues are flattering, but I don't intend to use them as anything but a little ego boost.

Halley opens the door of her stateroom after the second knock. She's wearing a T-shirt, and the upper part of her flight suit is tied around her waist by the sleeves.

"Hey," she says. "Take a wrong turn somewhere?"

"Nope," I reply. "I'm off until the 0600 watch. What about you?"

"Same here."

"So let's spend some time together. Away from the chow hall."

"In here? That's against regulations," she says with a lopsided smile.

"We're going into battle against the Lankies again in three days," I say. "We ought to spend the next two nights in the same stateroom together. Just in case they oversold us this hulking piece of Euro tech and we end up stardust. Fuck the regulations."

"You rebel," she says. Then she grabs me by the front of my tunic and pulls me across the threshold and into her stateroom. "Let's be rebels, then."

CHAPTER 18

AVENGER

"General quarters, general quarters. All hands, man your combat stations. Set material condition Zebra throughout the ship. This is not a drill."

I finish fastening the latches on my vacsuit right before I get to CIC. Everyone in the ship's command-and-control center is in a vacsuit as well, a visible reminder that we are about to transition into known hostile space and a possible Lanky ambush. We have spent the last three days on a high-speed run through the inner solar system, and now we are six and a half hours into our Alcubierre transition. I know that the reason for the vacsuits is a possible depressurization if we get perforated by a seed ship and that the vacsuits will keep us alive until the problem is fixed or we get the order to abandon ship in the escape pods. But the CIC is in the middle of the ship, in the most well-protected part, and if we have Lanky penetrators coming through this armored compartment, I know that the vacsuits will be mostly ornamental.

"Alcubierre transition in T-minus thirty," the XO announces.

"And then seven hours to showtime," Colonel Yamin replies. She's studying the plot on the holotable with much more intensity than the display deserves. We are approaching the transition point, but there's nothing to see on the situational orb except for the lone icon labeled "BCV-60" because all ships are blind and deaf during Alcubierre transitions. *Ottawa* has performed exactly as advertised, and we haven't lost any parts, major or minor, on our full-throttle run through the inner solar system. Even the fuel consumption estimates were within half a percent of our actual use, and I hope that the ship's flawless performance history so far will extend to her weapons systems and armor once the first shots are fired.

Colonel Yamin waits for the Combat Stations alert to fade out. Then she grabs a handset and opens the 1MC circuit.

"All hands, this is the skipper. We are thirty minutes from transitioning into the Fomalhaut system. It's highly likely that we will run into a sizable Lanky presence around New Svalbard. Our job is destroying any Lanky forces threatening the colony and the safe evacuation of the civilian population if needed. This is the toughest and most well-armed ship in the Fleet. Let's put her to good use and get our people out of there. And if we have to crack a few seed ships to get the job done, that is fine by me. It seems the Lankies didn't learn their lesson from Mars. We will make sure it sticks this time."

She hangs up the handset and straightens out the front of her tunic. The CIC is quiet except for the low whisper of the air-conditioning system and the soft hum of the consoles.

"Warm up the Alpha and Bravo mount reactors and set the particle cannons to standby mode. Energize the reactive armor and the active-point defense systems. I want us to be ready for a brawl as soon as we come out on the far side."

I watch our progress on the display. Thirty more minutes, and we will be in hostile space, engaging seed ships in direct combat for the first time in three years. We have greatly improved our ship designs in that time, and I sincerely hope that the Lankies haven't done the same and we don't run into a seed ship that's twice as large as the ones before it and five times as hard to kill. But it doesn't even take a newer, tougher seed ship to kill us—if the Lankies have set up a patrol right at the Alcubierre point, they can engage us in the first few moments of our presence, when we are at our most vulnerable because we're going from blindness to daylight again. And if they've parked a seed ship in the middle of our trajectory right outside of the transition zone, we'll smack right into it.

I get out my PDP and dash off a message to Halley.

>I love you. See you on the other side.

>In this life or the next. If it's Option B, save me a spot in the mead-hall.

I smile and tuck the PDP away again. We're not religious, but we've discussed the idea of an afterlife before, and Halley and I concluded that Valhalla is the best afterlife of all the mythologies we've read about. Fight all day, feast all night, and only grunts allowed. Maybe you get to go to whichever place you like best, and maybe Odin has upgraded Valhalla to include automatic fléchette rifles.

Colonel Yamin walks over to the command chair and sits down. Then she straps herself in with the five-point harness every chair in CIC has installed. The XO does likewise, and the few personnel in the CIC who have not yet taken their seats follow suit.

"Combat illumination," the CO orders, and the lights in the room switch from soft white to a low amber. If we get a hull breach and lose power, it will be easier for our eyes to adjust to the darkness as we head for the escape pods. Being trapped on a disintegrating ship has been one of my nightmares ever since Halley and I got stranded on the broken *Versailles* over eight years ago, so I know the route to the nearest escape-pod bank exactly by number of steps both running and walking. The likelihood of successful escape from this deep inside the hull is marginal, but I suppose the comfort of having the pods nearby is the high-tech secular version of a belief in an afterlife.

The shot clock on the front bulkhead counts down with clinical precision. Twenty minutes, then fifteen, then ten. Finally, we're just a few moments from transition, and it feels like everyone on the ship is holding their collective breath. As always, I spend the last few seconds of the Alcubierre trip thinking about Halley, because I want her to be the last thing on my mind if we end up disintegrating against a seed ship as we leave the chute.

"Transition in five. Four. Three. Two. One."

The low-level ache pulling at my molars disappears, and I take a long breath. Coming out of Alcubierre is always like that feeling when your leg falls asleep and then wakes up painfully and slowly—not debilitating, but unpleasant enough to dread the experience a little right before you know it's going to happen.

"Transition complete, ma'am," the helm station reports.

"Astrogation, give me a fix. Tactical, full scan of the neighborhood," Colonel Yamin orders.

I look at the situational display floating above the holotable. A few seconds later, a new 3-D grid with coordinate markers overlays the tactical orb.

"We are in the Fomalhaut system, ma'am. Right on the marker. The neighborhood is clear out to a hundred thousand klicks. No contacts."

Colonel Yamin unbuckles her harness and stands up again. She walks over to the holotable and flicks the situational orb around with her finger. I release my harness as well and duplicate the situational display on one of my screens.

"Let's float out the drones and get a full picture before we contact New Svalbard and make our presence known with radio waves," the CO says. "Full spread, spherical coverage. Go active mode on the drones. We can't afford to miss anything. If we have to engage, I want to be at the outer edge of our weapons envelope."

"Aye, ma'am."

We launch one flight of drones, then another, then a third and fourth. On the tactical display, forty-eight drone markers accelerate outward from our position in all directions, and the awareness bubble on the situational display slowly expands. With every passing kilometer the drones put between themselves and us, I feel a little better about our odds. The more distance we have between the Lankies and us, the better our chances of survival. The electric reactive armor of *Ottawa* is supposedly designed to withstand the kinetic energy of the Lanky penetrators, but I'm not especially eager for us to put that specification to a test in a live-fire scenario.

———

Forty-five minutes into the drone run, the first contact pops up on the tactical display.

"Drones 8, 15, and 41 are within passive detection range of New Svalbard," the tactical officer says.

On the plot, at the edge of our awareness bubble, a circular icon in a crosshair blips into existence. A second later, the computer tags it with the label "NEW SVALBARD," and a dotted line marking the moon's trajectory across our sphere of awareness appears on the plot.

"New contacts, bearing three-four-four by positive ten relative to drone 15. One . . . two . . . three bogeys in orbit around New Svalbard. Designate Sierra-1 through 3. Telemetry from drones 8 and 41 confirms hostile contacts."

"Give me a direct feed," Colonel Yamin orders. "Put it on tactical."

A square window superimposes over part of the tactical orb on the holotable. It shows the camera feed from the nose array of drone 8, which is pointed square at New Svalbard. The moon is still almost a million kilometers from the drone, but the optics are so powerful that it looks like the drone is ten minutes from orbit. The computer has superimposed orange targeting brackets over three familiar shapes gliding across the backdrop of clouds and white-and-blue ice. The seed ships are flat black, almost impossible to spot in empty space, but against the light background, the drone camera has no problems tracking them from nine hundred thousand klicks away. The tactical display dutifully updates itself with three more icons around the one for New Svalbard. The new icons are signal orange, a color that no skipper wants to see on her ship's tactical orb. But for only the third time since Mars, a Fleet unit is advancing toward those orange icons on purpose.

"Turn off the drives on drones 8 and 15 and let them coast in. Let 41 run out to the maximum telemetry range so we can get a picture of the dark side of that moon." Colonel Yamin pans and zooms the display, then switches to the tactical view.

"We have three bogeys and six missiles. That's not a bad ratio. Get me Orion firing solutions for all three bogeys. Let's hope that's all they brought to the party."

The computer calculates firing solutions for our Orion missile battery and displays them on the tactical screen a few moments later. The Lankies don't give any indication that they are aware of either *Ottawa*'s arrival or the presence of our drones. I'm still not used to seeing offensive firing solutions and target locks on Lanky seed ships. It feels like we're out hunting, putting a crosshair on a dangerous predator on the prowl.

"Anything from New Svalbard?" Colonel Yamin asks.

"The drones are picking up low-power comms transmissions on the surface, but nothing distinct. From the signal strength and ELINT signature, I'd say they're suit-powered transmitters," the lieutenant at the electronic-warfare station replies.

"So we're not too late. There are still people down there," she says.

"Yes, ma'am."

"Bogeys Sierra-2 and 3 seem to be in geostationary orbit, ma'am," the tactical officer chimes in. "They're right above the equatorial temperate belt. Bogey One is in high orbit above the northern polar cap."

"That's a problem," the XO says. Lieutenant Colonel Barry draws a rectangle on the tactical display and magnifies a slice of the live camera feed from drone 15. The two seed ships in orbit around the moon's equator are no more than ten ship lengths apart, seemingly at a standstill in front of the snow-white backdrop.

"How so, XO?" Colonel Yamin asks. She steps next to him and looks at the window he just magnified.

"These two bogeys are geostationary almost right above the colony," he says. "If we launch Orions at them, they'll break apart, and we'll have deorbiting wreckage all over that stretch of the continent. And that's only if they hit."

"I see what you're saying," Colonel Yamin says. "That's a shitty backstop for a thousand-ton block of Pykrete moving at a few ten thousand meters per second."

"If one of the Orions misses and hits the continent near our colony . . ." The XO leaves the sentence unfinished.

"Megaton-level surface impact," Colonel Yamin continues. "I see your point."

She studies the tactical display with a frown.

"We could take a chance and close to knife-fighting range," she says. "Hopefully they'll turn toward us when they see us coming, and we'll have clear shots with the particle cannons."

"Three fast-moving hostiles at a range of twenty thousand klicks or less," Lieutenant Colonel Barry says. "That's shaving it too close. If the mounts fail to recharge fast enough or break down on us, we'll be rubbing shoulders with the Lankies while our pants are down around our ankles."

"I'm open to other ideas," the CO replies.

"We can cut down the odds a bit," the tactical officer says.

"How so, Captain Baye?"

The tactical officer walks from his station into the command pit, picks up a light pen, and points at the holotable display.

"Bogey Sierra-1 is giving us a perfect broadside shot right now. Last time we hit them, above Mars, we launched from stealth, right? If we show them we're here before we launch, they'll start maneuvering, and the Orions aren't that nimble. But once the first Lanky goes up, they'll know we're in the neighborhood. So we take out"—he marks the bogey's position above New Svalbard—"Sierra-1 with an Orion first. Cut down the odds. If that one misses from this angle, it'll go off into space or hit the northern polar region."

"If we blow up Sierra-1, the other seed ships will turn our way and come sniffing us out," the XO says.

"They may give us a bow-on shot away from the colony," Captain Baye says.

"We will have five Orions left for the other two bogeys," Colonel Yamin muses. "And if they start to bob and weave too much for the Orions, we have the particle cannons. We have two barrels ready to go. We can take on two seed ships at once."

She expands the tactical plot in front of her and highlights the red track leading from the icon labeled "BCV-60" to the Lanky seed ship above the northern pole.

"No point giving away our advantage. We drop the first Lanky from long range, we cut the odds down by a third before the main event even starts. We'll deal with the other two as the situation dictates. Warm up the Orion launcher and get one of the big birds ready to fly."

"Aye, ma'am."

I am monitoring everything through my console screens, but this is not my part of the action. TacOps only comes into play once the drop ships and attack birds are out of the clamps and on their way down to the moon. It's hard to be a spectator right at the cusp of battle, but at least I know the CO knows her job. Still, there's always an element of uncertainty in war. I want this battle to begin because I know that once I am busy, I have no time to be scared.

MARKO KLOOS

"Tube six, fire."

Ten minutes later, *Ottawa* fires the first war shot of her service career. When the expeller charge launches the nuclear-propelled three-thousand-ton Orion III missile out of one of the preloaded launch tubes, the vibration makes the deck under my feet rumble. I watch the launch on the external camera and find myself wishing that this won't also be the last war shot of *Ottawa*'s service career.

"Tube six is clear. Bird away," the weapons officer announces.

On the plot, a light blue icon in the shape of an inverted *V* appears right in front of *Ottawa*. It accelerates away from the ship at three hundred meters per second squared, following the red line that leads from *Ottawa* to the Lanky seed ship above the north pole of New Svalbard.

"Bird is running normally. Nuclear pulse propulsion initiating in five. Four. Three. Two. One. *Ignition*."

The expeller charge, a simple solid rocket booster, serves to get the missile out of the launcher and to a safe distance from the ship so the nuclear propellant can take over. When the Orion III is thirty klicks away from the ship, the first of hundreds of small nuclear charges lights off right behind the missile, and the Orion III starts its acceleration run, picking up speed faster than any spaceship or conventional missile could hope to match.

The Orions are a brute-force method to get a heavy payload to fractional light-speed velocity in a very short amount of time. With the particle cannons of the battleships, we have another weapon that can crack a seed ship's hull reliably, but the particle mounts have very short range, and they draw a lot of energy. The Orions don't have a range restriction—they will accelerate until they run out of nuclear charges and then stay at their velocity until they hit something. Their only limitation is the fact that they're minimally guided and that the target needs to be visible to the launching platform before the launch.

Right now, three of our stealth drones are functioning as forward observers, feeding optical targeting data back to the ship. It's the same tactic we employed in our successful strike against the Lanky fleet at Mars, only with a single ship performing the tasks of the entire strike force.

For the next eleven minutes, I can't do anything but watch the track of the Orion as it races across the gap on the plot between our blue icon and the orange one labeled "SIERRA-1." The image from the drone cameras is even better now because the drones coast ever closer to New Svalbard even as they are keeping the seed ship locked from three different vantage points.

"Thirty seconds to impact," the tactical officer says. "Bird is running true."

The Orion III streaks past the drone line of deployment and into their field of view like a very motivated and angry firefly. In the dark of space, the brilliant chain of nuclear explosions trailing the missile marks its flight path in a dramatically obvious fashion.

"Twenty seconds. Bogey's course and speed unchanged."

Colonel Yamin is holding on to the edge of the holotable with both hands, and her grip is so tight that I can see the white of her knuckles. The Lanky seed ship is still making its slow and steady round of the polar region, oblivious to the destructive energy we are hurling at it.

"Update on Sierra-2 and 3," she says.

"Still in geostationary equatorial orbit. No change in course or speed."

"Ten seconds to target. Nine. Eight. Seven . . ."

Colonel Yamin leans forward and expands the window with the live feed of Sierra-1 with both hands.

"For Darius," she says in a low voice.

"Impact," the tactical officer announces. "Waiting for delayed visual confirmation."

At this distance, the radio signals from the drones take almost twenty seconds to arrive back at *Ottawa*. The entire CIC crew stares at the visual feed that still shows the Lanky gliding through space for an agonizingly long period. Then the display washes out with a bright flash. When the camera filters kick in and show the same section of space again, all we see is an angry-looking iridescent cloud of radiation and debris.

"That is a *hit*," the tactical officer says, his voice rising to a shout on the last word. "Splash one. Sierra-1 destroyed."

The CIC erupts in raucous cheers. I make a fist and tap the edge of the TacOps station's frame a few times.

When the initial impact cloud has dispersed a little, I can see that the seed ship didn't disintegrate entirely. What's left of the oblong hull looks like no more than half of the intact ship, and it's clearly a defunct wreckage. We watch the decapitated Lanky ship tumble and drift toward the moon's north pole, out of control and without any semblance of coordination. The Orion III doesn't hit quite as hard as the original design but it seems that it hits plenty hard enough to assure a mission kill.

"All right, people," Colonel Yamin says when the cheers have died down. "Let's not open the cold beers just yet. That's one out of three."

"Sierra-2 and 3 are still in their orbits," the tactical officer says. "They either didn't notice the fireworks, or they don't care."

"Contact New Svalbard. Send them a tight-beam transmission announcing our presence and intentions. Maybe a few ten thousand watts of radio energy will get the shovel heads to notice us. Warm up tubes one and three."

"Aye, ma'am. Prepping tubes one and three for launch."

"New Svalbard System Control, this is NACS *Ottawa*," the communications officer enunciates into his headset. "We are on an interdiction and relief mission inbound your position. Do you read?"

For several minutes, there's no reply, and the comms officer repeats her message several times. The mood in CIC goes from jubilation to subdued concern. If there's nobody left alive on New Svalbard, we came all this way with the throttle wide open for nothing.

Then there's a burst of static on the overhead speakers, and an excited-sounding voice acknowledges our message.

"*Ottawa*, New Svalbard System Control," the voice says. "We read you loud and clear. Thank the entire fucking pantheon of gods."

I grin at this exclamation, delivered in the slightly twangy drawl the colonists down on the ice moon seem to have adopted as their local accent. It has been five years since I set foot on that moon, but I still remember the inflections.

"System Control, *Ottawa*. What is your status? Be advised that we have engaged and destroyed one of the enemy ships in orbit and that we intend to close in with the other two and engage."

"*Ottawa*, System Control. Understood. We are under sustained attack by Lankies on the surface. They landed four days ago on the northern plateau, and they've advanced to within two kilometers of the city. The garrison is holding the perimeter, but they are short on almost everything. The Lankies have destroyed Camp Frostbite. The drop ships at the airfield are out of fuel and ammunition. We have three thousand people underground and in the admin center."

Colonel Yamin grabs her headset and takes over from the comms officer.

"System Control, this is *Ottawa* Actual. We are on the way with help. Stand by for updates. Can you relay comms to the commanding officer of the garrison?"

"Stand by, *Ottawa* Actual."

There's a thirty-second silence on the channel beyond the message delay. Then a female voice comes on. This one sounds gruff and more than a little tired.

"NAC task force, this is Major Archer, garrison commander. Please identify."

"Major Archer, this is Colonel Yamin, NACS *Ottawa*. What's your situation on the ground?"

"Colonel, it's good to hear you're inbound. We are holding the line, but barely. My platoons are stretched thin on the ground. We're low on ammo, the drop ships are dry, and half my mules are destroyed. The ones that are left are down to a few dozen rounds each. If we don't get relief soon, the Lankies are going to push us back into the center of the town, and they're going to take the airfield and destroy the comms arrays. Tell me you have a battalion on the way and a drop ship wing loaded for bear."

"I can do you one better than that, Major. We have two battalions and four strike squadrons. As soon as we are in orbit, we are sending reinforcements and close-air support your way. Hang in there for another two hours."

"Copy that, Colonel. Best news I've had all week. I'll pass word to the battalion," Major Archer replies.

Colonel Yamin takes her headset off again and hands the channel back to the comms officer of the watch.

"Status on the other two bogeys."

"Still in their orbit, ma'am. They haven't budged."

"So we do it the hard way. Let's get this battlewagon on the road. Helm, set course for New Svalbard, all ahead full."

"Aye, ma'am, all ahead full," the helmsman replies.

Ottawa burns her main engines and starts advancing into the system at twelve g. As usual, I don't even feel the forces that would have me flat against the bulkhead and gasping for air without the artificial gravity. Only the rapidly increasing number next to our tactical icon shows that we are underway again, racing toward the Lankies that are killing our friends and comrades. I've never been in a position to save a colony from Lanky invasion, and even though I'm still fearing the impending close quarters battle, it feels good to be the cavalry for a change instead of running from the seed ships. I wonder if Lankies can feel anything like fear. If they can, I hope they feel it in spades once they notice that we are coming for *them* this time.

CHAPTER 19

CQB

An hour and a half later, we have closed half the distance to New Svalbard and turned the ship around for our counter-burn. The Lankies are still holding their geosynchronous station, unaware or unconcerned that a NAC warship is bearing down on their position.

"New drone contact, bearing two hundred by negative eighty-three," the tactical officer calls out. "Ma'am, it's the *Michael P. Murphy*."

"On the holotable," Colonel Yamin orders. A second later, a display window overlay opens on top of the tactical screen, showing the distinctive angular shape of a Blue-class Fleet destroyer.

"They're running silent. No active transmissions, no running lights."

"I would too if I was in a destroyer right now," Colonel Yamin says. "Ping them once with a low-power tight-beam. See if their radios are broken or if they just haven't spotted us yet."

The comms officer does as ordered. Whatever the *Murphy* is doing out there, they won't be able to miss the active radio energy bouncing off their hull. A few moments later, they respond in kind with a tight-beam signal of their own.

"Unidentified ship, this is NACS *Michael P. Murphy*. Please authenticate."

"Send our Fleet ID and put me on that tight-beam channel," the CO orders.

"You are go on tight-beam, ma'am."

"*Michael P. Murphy*, this is NACS *Ottawa*, *Ottawa* Actual. We thought you guys were a debris field right now. I am glad to see that's not the case. What is your status and intent, over?"

"*Ottawa*, this is *Murphy* Actual. We are combat ineffective. Be advised that there are three Lanky ships in the area around New Svalbard. We engaged them, but they landed a few hits before we could get out. Main sensor array is down, we have no radar or lidar, and we have expended all our ordnance and lost the rail-gun mount."

"*Murphy*, be advised that the number of enemy ships is down to two. We are aiming to reduce that count further in about an hour. If we aren't successful, make for the Alcubierre node at best speed and transition out of this system. You did what you could. Let *Ottawa* do the heavy lifting."

"*Ottawa*, *Murphy*. I have no particular objections to that plan. I sure hope you know what you are getting into."

"Affirmative, *Murphy*. Stand by for updates. And if you hear our crash buoy, get to the node and get the hell out of the AO."

"Copy that, *Ottawa*. Good luck and Godspeed. *Murphy* out."

Colonel Yamin focuses her attention on the plot again, where a new icon labeled "DD-655" has appeared at the edge of our awareness bubble, on the opposite side of the sphere from the marker for New Svalbard. *Murphy* is coasting passively in the general direction of the Alcubierre chute, her fusion engines idling to reduce her radiation and thermal signature. If they have lost their main sensor array and radar to battle damage, they are flying mostly blind, and without a rail gun or missiles left in their magazines, they're largely defenseless except for their point defense cannons. But they're still largely in one piece, which is an outcome I wouldn't have bet money on.

"Bogeys are still geostationary. They're glued to their orbits," the tactical officer says.

"We need to start thinking about prying them loose from their parking spots," Colonel Yamin says. "Give them something to worry about."

"The plot is clear for five million klicks past New Svalbard at least," Lieutenant Colonel Barry replies. "We could go full power on all transmitters and blast them with noise. They're sensitive to radio energy, right? If we drop stealth and go active, they'll pick us up for sure."

"Make them come about and head our way. Force a head-on engagement with two seed ships," Colonel Yamin muses.

"We won't get clear shots at them if they stay in that orbit. If we lure them out, at least we have a safe backstop and room to maneuver. The particle cannon won't care whether we get a broadside or a head-on shot."

"And head-on they can't use their broadsides."

"They can try to go for a ramming kill, but we know that our ship is more nimble than theirs. We should be able to kill them outright, and avoid them if we can't score hard kills on the first pass."

"We have the mobility and firepower advantage," Colonel Yamin says. "So let's dictate the terms of the engagement for once."

She studies the plot for a few moments, but I can tell that she has made up her mind. I reach over my shoulders and pull down the straps for the safety harness to buckle myself back in.

"All right. We are going active. Comms, broadcast at full transmitting power. And let's ping some radar off their hulls. We won't get a return, but maybe all those megawatts will tickle them."

"What would you like me to broadcast, ma'am?" the comms officer asks.

"Oh, I don't know. How about you pull some music out of the data banks? Let's give the shovel heads a sampling of Earth culture. Put it out over FM and AM bands. And drill them with a nice focused tight-beam on top of that."

"I like it." The comms officer grins and turns his attention to his screens. "One musical sampler from Earth coming right up."

A few moments later, a rousing classical music piece comes out of the speaker on the comms console. The communications officer smiles and turns toward the holotable.

"Pouring out Earth culture at fifty megawatts on all frequencies, ma'am," he says.

"I like that music," Lieutenant Colonel Barry says. "What is that, Wagner?"

"Yes, sir. *Ride of the Valkyries*. Nineteenth-century opera."

"Put it on shipwide speaker for the crew," Colonel Yamin says. The XO looks at her with an amused smile on his face, and she shrugs in reply.

"Might as well charge in with style," she says.

"Aye, ma'am." The comms officer's grin gets a little wider. He taps a few screens, and then the music comes from every overhead speaker.

"The crew on *Murphy* will think we've lost our shit," I say, but I can't suppress a grin myself.

I'm pretty sure we're the first Fleet unit actively trying to get the attention of the Lankies, and I'm *very* sure we're the first ones to do so by deliberately blasting classical music at them.

We carve our way toward New Svalbard, decelerating gradually in our reverse burn. At first, it doesn't seem like our systemwide entertainment program has any effect on the Lankies, but a few minutes after the start of our broadcast, the two orange icons at New Svalbard subtly change position on the tactical plot.

"They heard us," the tactical officer says. "Sierra-2 and Sierra-3 are leaving orbit and coming about. They're accelerating."

"Nice of them to take the bait," Colonel Yamin says. "Cut the overhead speakers. Keep sending on all frequencies. Let's lure them out far enough for an ass-kicking."

"Bogeys are now CBDR. I'd say we got their attention."

CBDR—constant bearing, decreasing range—means that the bogeys are heading directly for us, which leaves no doubt about their ability to locate the source of radio transmissions. I watch as the distance between the center of the plot and the approaching Lanky ships shrinks a little more with every passing minute.

"Aspect is still bad for an Orion shot," the tactical officer warns. "Bogeys are still right between the moon and us."

"We'll be below minimums for the Orions in a few minutes anyway," the XO says.

"Flip the ship. Target lock both bogeys for the Alpha and Bravo mounts," Colonel Yamin orders. "Get the reactors up to full power."

The lateral thrusters on the ventral side of the ship fire a long burst, and the ship rotates on its transverse axis to present the bow-mounted particle cannons to the approaching seed ships. When we are facing the moon and the seed ships between us and New Svalbard bow-on, the dorsal thrusters counter-burn to arrest our rotation.

"We have locks on Sierra-2 and Sierra-3," the tactical officer reports. "Tracking targets. Closing speed is eleven hundred meters per second, increasing."

The two Lanky seed ships are close enough to *Ottawa* that the high-powered magnifying lenses on our optical array could spot hull rivets if the Lankies had any. The two hostile ships look like a pair of sharks on the prowl to me—lethal, streamlined forms out for an easy meal.

"Fifty thousand kilometers and closing fast."

"Open fire at twenty thousand. Lock on Sierra-3 with both mounts and blow that son of a bitch to pieces," Colonel Yamin says. Everyone is back in their seats and strapped in now. In less than a minute, we will be in weapons range, and so will the Lankies. This won't be a sucker punch from a million klicks away, but a knife fight in a toilet stall.

"Forty thousand."

I check the tightness of my harness straps and the fasteners on my suit. *Ottawa* is an enormous ship, but the seed ships are still three times as long, and they probably have ten times our mass. If one of them decides to ram us head-on at these closing speeds, we will burst apart like an overripe piece of fruit.

"Thirty thousand."

"Alpha and Bravo mounts show a green board," the weapons officer says. "Reactor power to full pulse afterburner."

"Set both mounts to one-second burst," Colonel Yamin orders.

"One-second burst, aye. Entering weapons range in three . . . two . . . one."

"*Fire.*"

The lights in CIC dim very slightly. Deep inside the ship, the two particle cannon mounts that run the entire front third of the hull focus more destructive power than humanity has ever managed to concentrate on one spot. I stare at the screen that shows the live video feed of the two Lanky ships barreling toward us almost side by side, with no more than ten kilometers of space between them.

The impacts from the particle cannons light up the display and wash it out completely. The drone cameras are tracking the Lankies from three different angles, and those auxiliary feeds show the hull of seed ship Sierra-3 disappear in a supernova of radiation and glowing particles.

"Direct hit," the weapons officer announces in a jubilant tone. "Target destroyed."

"Closing rate is too high," the tactical officer warns. "Sierra-2 is going to pass us ten klicks to port."

"Evasive action," the CO shouts. "Dorsal bow thrusters, down forty degrees."

"Negative forty degrees, aye," the helmsman replies. The bow of *Ottawa* begins to swing downward in reaction to the approaching Lanky, but the closing rate is so high that the seed ship covers the distance between us before we have altered our trajectory significantly.

"All rail-gun batteries, go to automatic mode and engage the enemy," Colonel Yamin orders. "Full broadside, maximum rate of fire."

The metallic clanging from the rail-gun mounts reverberates through the hull as the projectiles leave their magnetic rails at several thousand meters per second. The Lanky appearing on our portside looms over us, so immense in size that the ten klicks between us still feel close enough to almost scrape hulls.

"Incoming ordnance," the tactical officer yells. "Threat vector two-seven-zero."

"Roll the ship," Colonel Yamin barks. "Turn our dorsal armor toward them."

"Aye, ma'am," the helmsman replies. "Rolling the ship."

The Lanky penetrators aren't nearly as fast as our rail-gun projectiles, but they have much more mass, and our hull isn't twenty meters thick. I've been on ships that have been hit by those dense organic projectiles. They make two-meter holes in whatever they hit, and they go clear through the armored hull of a warship from port to starboard or bow to stern. Even though I know that *Ottawa* has been built with this scenario in mind, I still grasp the armrests of my chair hard enough to make the metal creak.

"All hands, brace for impact," the XO shouts into the 1MC.

The cloud of penetrator darts envelops *Ottawa* like a fierce hail. I can hear the impacts of the darts on the armor, interspersed with the sounds of many minor explosions. *Ottawa* shudders under the onslaught but plows on, and the Lanky ship is astern of us in a matter of half a second. Then there's a second series of impact sounds from the bow and starboard front of the ship.

"Passing through the debris cloud from Sierra-2," the tactical officer says.

"Damage report." Colonel Yamin's grasp on her armrests doesn't look any more gentle than mine. But we still have air in the compartment, and we didn't blow up in a reactor explosion, so I loosen my grip just a little.

"Several hull breaches," the XO reports. "Compartments open to space at frames 180, 224, and 366. Whatever hit us didn't go all the way through. No hull breaches forward of frame 180."

"The dorsal armor saddle deflected everything," the CO says. "Send out the damage control parties. And kick me in the teeth the next time I expose our flank and stern armor."

"Sierra-3 is starting to come about again," the tactical officer says. "He's spinning and counter—*burning*? I don't know what. But he's decelerating."

"Coming back for another pass," Colonel Yamin says grimly. "Let's let him have a second serving, then. Status on the Alpha and Bravo mounts?"

"Eighteen seconds until charged."

"Can we open the distance to use another Orion?"

"Doubtful," the XO replies. "Not at their acceleration rate. He has to close with us to point blank because he doesn't have long-range ordnance. And we have to close with him because we can't open the gap again."

"We'll let him have both barrels," she proclaims after a glance at the tactical display, where the distance between us and the seed ship is still widening. "Lateral aft boosters, full thrust. Bring us around and go to full counter-burn, all-ahead flank."

"All-ahead flank on rotation, aye."

I check my harness again to make sure I am strapped in with no wiggle room. The artificial gravity field is great for low-gravity maneuvers, but when the ship is pushed to flank speed turning and burning, things can get very bumpy.

Ottawa flips end over end again until our exhaust nozzles are pointed at New Svalbard once more. The distance between us and the Lanky has opened up to fifty thousand kilometers again in the span of twenty seconds, but our rate of divergence is slowing drastically as both ships counter-burn to put on the brakes. It's like a slow and awkward joust with heavily armored knights and lances, but we're on a rain-slick frozen lake, and the horses are on skates.

"The active defense system vaporized over half the incoming penetrators," the XO says. He scrolls through the screens on the display in front of him. "The reactive armor deflected most of the rest. The civvie contractors are going to piss themselves with joy when they find out."

"For more reasons than just that one," Colonel Yamin replies.

For the next few minutes, we bleed backward velocity while the Lanky seed ship does the same. The distance between us opens to sixty, then seventy, then eighty thousand kilometers. *Ottawa* is first to the punch. When we have arrested our rearward slide and fly in the opposite direction of our ingress, the Lanky is still on the brakes and gliding away from us.

"We have a red light on the Alpha mount," the weapons officer cautions. "Malfunction on the magnetic containment field. Alpha mount is offline, ma'am."

"What about Bravo mount?"

"Still online and charged."

"Damn it. Cut the main propulsion. Stand by on Orions. Get a firing solution on Sierra-3 and launch when ready."

"Full stop, aye." The helmsman pulls the throttle levers in front of him all the way to the idle position.

"Ma'am, we're under half the minimum range for the Orions," the weapons officer objects. "They may not crack his hull if they don't impact with enough speed."

"I've read the user manual, Lieutenant. Now float out the bird. Unless you're comfortable betting your life that Bravo mount will not malfunction in the next five minutes."

"Aye, ma'am." The weapons officer blanches a little and returns his attention to his screens.

"It may not destroy him, but it may crack him open. Or rattle his cage enough to break off," Colonel Yamin says.

"Sierra-3 is starting to close the gap again," the tactical officer reports. "Bearing zero degrees by zero, CBDR, ninety thousand klicks and closing."

"Tube one is locked on target and ready to fire. Firing in three. Two. One. *Fire.*" The weapons officer looks at the colonel. "Tube one is clear. Bird away, ma'am."

"Very well. Keep that Bravo mount locked on target in case we miss."

The Orion III starts its acceleration run thirty kilometers in front of *Ottawa's* bow. Once again, the display lights up with a chain of nuclear explosions that blind the cameras momentarily with each burst. Our frontal sensors can't see through all the radiation and electromagnetic noise from the nukes detonating between us and the seed ship, but the auxiliary feeds from the drones give us a perfect picture from several different angles.

The Orion covers the distance between us and the seed ship in a relative blink. If the Lanky ship senses the incoming warhead, it doesn't have much time for evasive maneuvers. Less than ten seconds after the launch, the twenty-five-hundred-ton Pykrete warhead of the Orion III slams into the bow of the Lanky ship at several thousand meters per second. The bloom from the impact is far less spectacular than a hit from the particle cannons because there's no flare of gamma radiation. The warhead just bulls against the hull of the Lanky with brute kinetic energy. The impact cloud disperses, and for a second or two, the seed ship looks untouched. Then a big piece of the frontal hull slope tears off and starts spewing a trail of debris in the seed ship's wake. It reminds me of the results of the desperate action of NACS *Indianapolis* a few years ago above Earth, when we had no Orions or particle cannons to take on the approaching Lanky seed ship, and Colonel Campbell decided to turn his ship into an improvised kinetic warhead.

"Direct hit on Sierra-3," the tactical officer announces. "He's damaged. We cracked the hull, ma'am."

"Wonder if they have spall liners on their ships," Lieutenant Colonel Barry muses. "There's got to be armor shards tearing from bow to stern in that thing right now."

"Sierra-3 is still holding course and maintaining acceleration."

"We didn't quite hurt them enough," Colonel Yamin says. "Weps, open Hades silos one through four. Nuclear-fire mission authorized. Hand off target marking to the nearest drones and aim for that crack in the hull. Fire when ready."

"Aye, ma'am. Opening silos one through four."

On the sides of the forward hull, right next to *Ottawa*'s heavy dorsal armor saddle, four silo hatches open silently. Each of those silos contains a heavy nuclear-armed missile for antiship or surface-bombardment use. Against an intact seed ship, they're a waste of good plutonium. But I know from the Battle of Earth that if we hit that hole in the hull, the atomic warheads will tear the ship to pieces from the inside.

"Distance sixty thousand, still CBDR."

"Firing missile silo one. Three. Two. Four. Missiles away."

Another low rumbling sound reverberates through the hull. On the plot, four light blue inverted V icons leave the center of the display and head toward the incoming seed ship. They aren't as fast as the Orions, but the distance is shrinking steadily, and the missiles cover the gap in just a few minutes. The seed ship plows through the radiation debris from the nuclear propellant charges the Orions left in their path, damaged but still intact enough to put a hurting on us.

The Hades missiles meet the remaining Lanky seed ship forty thousand kilometers away. Two of them detonate against the undamaged portion of the hull in impressive but ineffective fireworks. Another Hades shoots past the gash in the hull and misses the Lanky by what looks like a few meters at most. But the last Hades disappears into the seed ship through its broken exterior. A second or two later, the hull of the Lanky ship heaves outward, and the entire dorsal front quarter of the ship bursts open. I know that the seed ship hulls are impervious to radiation, but that works both ways, because the gamma radiation from a half-megaton warhead just bounced around in that hull and cooked everything in it several times over.

"Sierra-3 is still CBDR," the tactical officer warns. We may have just killed everything in that ship, but the hull is following the laws of physics, and absent any other physical influences, it will continue on its trajectory.

"Evasive action," Colonel Yamin orders. "All-ahead flank, forty-five degrees by zero. Get us out of the way."

The helmsman acknowledges the command and throws the throttle lever all the way forward again. I try to watch the plot and the cameras at once as we swiftly move out of the path of the incoming seed ship. When Sierra-3 barrels through the space we occupied not too long ago, we are five hundred kilometers away and accelerating. If the seed ship spews out penetrators as it hurls past our point of closest approach, we're too far away to detect them.

"Bring us about," Colonel Yamin orders. She looks like she just aged five years in the last few hours. "Track that bastard and prepare for follow-up shot with the Orions."

"He's on a collision trajectory with New Svalbard," the tactical officer says. He hurries to the holotable and brings up the trajectory projection for the seed ship.

"Where is he going to hit?"

"Right here." The tactical officer points to a spot on the northern plateau, four hundred klicks away from New Longyearbyen. "If he doesn't break up in atmo first."

"He won't," Lieutenant Colonel Barry replies. "He'll make a crater the size of Central Park when he hits."

"Comms, warn the garrison they have incoming wreckage. Let them know the approximate impact point so they don't wonder why they suddenly have a minor earthquake."

"I don't think they're going to overlook that hull coming through the atmosphere, ma'am. Not even from four hundred klicks away."

I let go of my armrests and let out a long, shaky breath. The whole engagement only lasted a little over three hours from the time we launched our drones, but it feels like I've run a marathon through a live-fire range even though I didn't move from the TacOps station once.

The seed ship hull is clearly out of control. It enters the upper atmosphere of New Svalbard and begins a drag-induced rotation around its vertical axis. It makes the trip through the atmosphere broadside on, a lifeless, ragged three-kilometer lump of alien matter trailing bright contrails of superheated gas on the way down. Our cameras track the seed ship until the wreckage disappears in a cloud bank. A few minutes later, a huge thermal bloom billows up on the infrared spectrum.

"Impact," the captain at the electronic-intelligence station calls out. "They went in hard. I'm transmitting the site coordinates to System Control."

"The plot is clear," the tactical officer says. "We have no hostiles within twenty million klicks."

The cheers in CIC are much more subdued than after our first kill. We won, but *Ottawa* is still bleeding air, and we're down one of the particle cannons, our main anti-Lanky firepower at short range. And if we had hull breaches, we probably have casualties as well. *Ottawa* has performed much better against the Lankies than any ship before it, but this short and violent battle should serve to dispel any illusions among her crew that the war will be a cakewalk from now on.

"Tell *Michael P. Murphy* that the coast is clear. Have them make best speed to New Svalbard and rendezvous with us in orbit." Colonel Yamin lets out a percussive breath and runs her hand through her hair. "The day is not over, people. In fact, we've only just started."

She walks over to the holotable and changes the scale of the display to show only New Svalbard and its immediate vicinity.

"Tell the SI regiment to get ready for a drop. We are landing the Second Battalion first. Keep the First Battalion in reserve for now. And I want the first attack wing out of the clamps and on their way to provide close-air support in thirty minutes."

I send a priority alert to my special tactics team and order them to get into battle gear. Then I send a direct message to Master Sergeant Garcia, my second most senior combat controller. He's assigned to Alpha Company of the Second Battalion, and I order him to relieve me in CIC thirty minutes early so I can take his spot on the drop ship. I'm familiar with the territory down there, and I feel that I've spent enough time watching events while sitting on my ass in an air-conditioned command center. I don't know if the people I knew five years ago are still on that moon, but I want to be in the first wave of the rescue mission. We fought for the civilian administration on New Svalbard, and we paid for their continued right to exist independently with the blood of good men and women. This is the place where I met my friend Dmitry for the first time, and where I firmly bonded with Master Sergeant Fallon over the most potent cocktails in the settled galaxy. And if there's a fight going on to keep the Lankies from stomping it all flat, I'll be damned if I sit in the second row for it.

CHAPTER 20

GHOSTS IN THE SNOW

It feels good to be back in battle armor. Securing all the fasteners and triple-checking connections and suit functions is the routine that signals my brain I'm about to go to war. I've been wearing nothing but blueberries or a vacsuit ever since I got on this ship, and I never realized just how much I missed the armor and the feeling of readiness and competence it bestows until just now. It's like wrapping your hands and putting on gloves right before you step into a SIMAP ring.

When my armor is sealed and all diagnostics show green, I go back to my locker and open the personal compartment with my biometrics. I take out the ancient M17 pistol and stick it into its holster on my chest, right above the magazine pouches for the carbine. I tuck the loaded spare magazines away into their respective pouches. Then I close the locker and leave my stateroom to go to the armory by the flight deck.

The flight deck is abuzz with hectic activity. Several platoons are already lined up behind drop ships for transport, and when I cross the deck threshold, four Shrikes are in the clamps and on the way to their launch bays simultaneously. Their stubby wings are loaded to capacity with air-to-ground missiles and cluster munition canisters. I am carrying an M-95 instead of my usual lightweight PDW buzzgun—there's no doubt that we are facing a standup fight against superior numbers, and if the perimeter gets breached, I want to be able to shoot back with something more effective than a people-shooter.

"Alpha Company?" I ask a trooper in the nearest gaggle.

"Yes, sir. Third Platoon."

"Where's First?"

The trooper points at the drop ship on the far end of the line, which is being boarded already. I jog over to the tail ramp and follow the troops into the cargo hold.

The senior officer in the hold is the company commander, a captain named Porter. He raises his helmet visor when he sees me and gives me a slightly puzzled look.

"Captain Grayson," I say. "I'm the STO. I'll be your combat controller for this drop."

"What happened to Master Sergeant Garcia?"

"He's probably sipping a nice hot cup of coffee up in CIC right now," I reply. "I'm more familiar with this AO than Sergeant Garcia, so I decided to replace him for this mission."

"Fine by me," Captain Porter says.

I take my seat at the controller console by the back bulkhead, stow my weapon in the clamp, and plug my suit in. Then I activate the consoles and do the customary check-in with the pilot for permission to access ship systems. Finally, I check my comms back to the CIC.

"Talk to me, Garcia," I say on the TacOps channel.

"Radio protocol, Captain," Garcia replies with a soft laugh. "But you are coming in loud and clear."

"The command element of Alpha Company is going to set up on the airfield. Once we are skids down, I'm going to make a beeline for the tower and get the bigger picture from there."

"Godspeed, Captain. And don't get killed. If Taggart becomes the new senior combat controller, he'll be absolutely unbearable."

"Copy that," I reply, suppressing a chuckle. "I'll check in from the ground. Tailpipe One out."

The Dragonfly's tail ramp closes swiftly and almost silently, and the illumination in the hold switches to combat red. The screens in front of me automatically adjust to the darkness. I bring up my usual combination of plot and external camera views. The ship I'm in is assigned to Assault Transport Squadron Eleven, not Halley's ATS-5. It occurs to me that even though I've flown in a drop ship with her behind the stick several times, she's never actually been my pilot on a proper ground-assault drop.

We are in the clamp a few minutes later, briefly hovering three meters above the hangar deck for our quick ride to the drop bay. I look around for the ships of ATS-5, but I don't see my wife in or near any of them. They are tasked to ferry down the reserve battalion in case we need it, so she will launch in the second wave if at all. But once I'm on the ground and she's overhead in her drop ship, she has to become just another air asset to me, an aerial weapon for me to direct onto a target. I want to believe that I can make that switch in my brain, despite my better knowledge. But Halley is the best pilot I know, and she can take care of herself while she's in the air and behind a stick.

The clamp lowers us into the launch bay, which closes above us. Then the doors of the launch bay open, and there's nothing but space underneath the Dragonfly.

"Three. Two. One. *Drop*," the pilot counts down. On *drop*, the clamp overhead releases the ship, and the Dragonfly goes into brief free fall. The grunts in the hold do their customary whooping, as if we're cresting the biggest hill of a roller coaster track. I close my eyes until the drop ship has left *Ottawa*'s artificial gravity field and my stomach stops trying to slide up my throat.

Clear of the ship, the pilot swings the nose around and takes formation lead for the flight down to the surface. New Svalbard looks just the way it did when I saw it last five years ago—glacial plains of thick ice, mountains capped with snow, and swirling white-gray cloud fields. It's easily the least hospitable place I've ever been to, and yet I've always liked the harsh and austere beauty of it.

"Check out the event at two seventy, four hundred klicks off," the pilot says. I tap into the portside array and look in the direction he indicated. A huge dark cloud is rising a few hundred kilometers in the distance. I've seen many high-energy kinetic impacts over the years, and it's remarkable how similar they look to mushroom clouds from atomic detonations. The wreckage of the Lanky seed ship hit the continent with enough force to throw up a few hundred thousand cubic meters of superheated ice and rock, and all of it is going to come raining down on the moon again over the next day or so.

"Garcia, Grayson," I send to the TacOps station.

"Go ahead," Garcia says.

"Advise the skipper that we need to sanitize the crash site ASAP. I'd love to say that nothing could have survived that impact, but after Greenland I wouldn't bet money on it."

"Already on it, Captain," Garcia replies. "I just tasked two flights of Shrikes to burn it out with nukes."

For a moment, I am taken aback at the notion of nuclear bombardment of the crash site. New Svalbard is an ice moon, and potable water is its main reason for being. Before the Lankies, it was one of the NAC's main water stops. Setting off nukes on this moon will make much of the ice useless and deny us this resource for the next fifty years or more. But then I remember Greenland again, and the unexpected hardiness of the Lankies even under fifty meters of ice. If any of the seed ship's passengers survived the crash, they'll be entrenched under the surface in a few weeks, and they'll have another seed ship rising from the ice in a year.

"We got a little break with the weather," the pilot sends back. "Broken clouds over the target area and light winds below five thousand. It'll be a little bumpy in the higher altitudes, though, so tell the grunts to buckle in and hang on."

I relay the message to the troops in the cargo hold and make sure my own harness is on as tight as possible. When a drop ship pilot tells you that the flight is going to be a little bumpy, strap in firmly and prepare to lose a filling or two.

I thought I remembered the shitty weather above New Svalbard, but five minutes into the atmospheric part of the descent, I am still surprised by the pounding the drop ship is taking. The temperate belt around the moon's equator usually has slightly warmer air above it than the mountain air to the north and south—a result of the terraforming process—and the cold winds from those regions are often fierce. The bouncing and the jolts go from awful to worrisome the lower we are in the atmosphere. When the Dragonfly leaves the cloud coverage at five thousand feet above the deck, the pounding subsides, and I say a quick thank-you prayer to the weather gods for not scattering the ship all over the glacier below.

I'm not mentally prepared for the suddenness of being low above a battlefield lousy with Lankies again. We come out of the clouds, and there are dozens, maybe hundreds of Lankies spread out over the glacier below as far as I can see. They walk singly or in small formations, with wide gaps between the individuals. All of them are heading in the same direction as the drop ship, toward the town of New Longyearbyen, sitting on the glacial plain thirty klicks to our west. My fingers run on autopilot as I bring up my TacLink screen and designate target reference points as fast as I can place them on the screen.

"TacOps, Tailpipe One," I send to Sergeant Garcia, this time using proper radio protocol. "We have what you can call a target-rich environment down here on the glacier thirty klicks east of the town. I am updating TacLink."

The pilot of our drop ship doesn't bother slowing down to engage. There are plenty more Lankies in front of us, and the Dragonfly bobs and weaves as the pilot fires his cannons or launches missiles at targets of opportunity. Behind us, the other drop ships of our flight come out of the clouds one by one, and their pilots start picking off Lankies as well. But the free-for-all doesn't last very long. Thirty seconds after we come out of the clouds, our drop ship flight heads into another weather front, and this one looks like it's a wall of windblown snow from twenty thousand feet all the way to the ground. The shaking and bouncing resumes as the Dragonflies get tossed around again like corks in a swift current.

"Zero-zero visibility up front," the pilot sends. "I'm flying by radar altimeter. We have eighty-knot crosswinds. If this shit goes all the way to the airfield, prepare for an interesting landing."

As soon as we're in the soup again, the Lanky contacts on my TacLink screen fade from bright to light orange, signifying contacts that are no longer actively observed. Lankies don't show up on infrared or radar, so they're practically invisible in weather like this until they're right on top of someone. Behind the drop ship flight, several Shrikes rush toward the target reference points I marked earlier to drop cluster munitions blindly. But the Lanky formation was widely dispersed, and they can walk at fifty klicks an hour when they want to. Without a chance to thin them out from the air, they'll hit the defensive perimeter at New Svalbard unobserved and with minimal engagement time for the defenders.

"TacOps, Tailpipe One. Advise the ground commander he has a company's worth of Lankies incoming from the south-southeast. They're hiding in the weather and advancing toward the settlement. Close air can't get an accurate bead on them."

"Copy that, Tailpipe One. We're going to drop kinetics on their probable route of advance. Keep your heads low and don't backtrack."

The weather improves as we get close to the settlement, but not by much. When we cross the outer defensive ring in front of the spaceport runway on the western edge of the town, visibility is half a kilometer, and the winds are still strong enough for the pilot to have to rely on the spaceport's automated landing assist instead of trying to fly it in by hand. The computer takes over the controls and puts us down in the middle of the drop ship landing pad on the first approach, but with no small amount of sideways skidding and rapid thruster corrections.

When the tail ramp opens, cold air gushes into the cargo hold. The landing pad outside is covered in swirling snow. The last time I was here, it was planetary spring, and the weather was cold, but not unbearably so. But as I step out onto the pad, the temperature readout in my suit shows twenty-five degrees Celsius below zero, with eighty-knot winds that add up to a windchill factor of fifty below zero. I lower my helmet visor to keep the bitingly cold wind out of my armor and let the built-in heaters do their job.

There's a welcoming committee at the edge of the drop ship pad. We walk out to meet them, and I salute the highest-ranking officer among them, an SI major who must be the commander of the garrison battalion. Captain Porter does the same next to me, and the major returns our salutes and waves us away from the noisy drop ship pad.

"I'd say we're glad to see you, but that would be a massive under-statement," the major says. "Major Coburn, garrison commander."

"Captain Grayson," I reply. "I'm the STO. This is Captain Porter, the CO of Alpha Company."

"Let's go inside and out of the wind," Major Coburn suggests. The control center is less than a hundred meters from the landing pad, and we trot over to it, slowed down by the eighty-knot headwind that pushes into us like an insistent invisible hand.

Inside the control center, we remove our helmets, which are already frosted with snow and ice. Major Coburn looks like he has had a very rough week. His face sports a stubble that's two days old at least, and his eyes have dark rings under them.

"Situation," he says. "This is day seven since they showed up in orbit. At first, we hit the landing sites with our Wasps and tried to contain them far away from the town. But twelve drop ships aren't enough to hold back Lankies at three different footfall sites. The ordnance bunkers at Camp Frostbite were empty in three days. The fuel lasted until day *four*."

We walk through the ground floor of the admin center. There are no civilians in sight, just SI troopers in battle armor. Major Coburn leads us up the staircase to the top of the control tower. The last time I was here, a missile from a Shrike blew up the fuel tanks not a hundred meters away and took out most of the windows in the tower. They've long since been repaired, but from the shopworn look of things up here, it looks like that was the only substantial repair this facility has seen in the last five years.

The major activates the holotable in the middle of the room and brings up the tactical map. From up here, I have a good view of most of the airfield and the city. The snow is blowing through the streets and piling up against the buildings, and there's no activity on the roads at all. I know that the admin building is a kilometer to the east, but the blowing snow obscures it from view, with only the occasional red blip from the anticollision light on the building's roof antenna array visible through the swirling mess. Two pairs of Shrikes thunder over the town at low altitude and head off to the north. Major Coburn looks up from his display and grins curtly.

"Never thought I'd see that sight again," he says. "Beautiful."

He expands the map view and waves us close.

"All right. The Lankies keep up probing attacks with half a dozen individuals at a time. They come in, get bloody noses, and disappear back into the weather. We can't hold the whole perimeter with what we have left, so I concentrated the defense in a few key locations. Greenhouses, food-storage silos, the fusion plant, and of course the airfield. It will be a lot easier now that we have reinforcements and more air support."

He zooms the display scale until New Longyearbyen takes up half the plot and marks the locations he just mentioned on the map.

"There's no frontline anymore. Not in this weather. They push on one side of the city, we feed in reinforcements and kill a bunch, and they go back into the snowstorm and repeat the same shit on the other side of town half an hour later. The Lankies are no longer coming in dumb like they used to, and that worries me."

"They're still taking a lot of pointless casualties," I say. "Every time they poke you, they leave dead bodies behind."

"It's only pointless if there's no method to it," Major Coburn says. "I still want to think they're dumb as bullet ants, but they're smart enough to move only when we can't see them coming from a thousand meters away. It totally negates our range advantage. And we're expending a shitload of ammunition every time we stop a probe."

"They were plenty smart on Mars," I reply. "And Greenland. They may not think like we do, but they're not dumb as bullet ants. They can lay ambushes. Respond to changes in tactics. Find ways to neutralize our technology advantages."

"Yeah, I think we're in some deep shit. We may not be able to hold on to this moon."

"Where do you want my platoons?" Captain Porter asks. "We have my company on the ground right now, and Bravo Company is due on the pad in five minutes."

"I would love for your company to reinforce our four outposts. Send a platoon each to the greenhouse complex, the food silos, and over to the fusion plant. I have a strung-out platoon at each. They're badly in need of relief."

"Copy that. We're on the way," Captain Porter replies. He switches over to his platoon-level command channel and walks off as he starts talking to his platoon leaders.

"We saw a big group of Lankies on the glacier shelf to the southwest on our approach, thirty klicks out. If they are in a hurry, they could be here in half an hour. I suggest we send Bravo Company to reinforce the southern end of the airfield, sir."

"I'll bet you a bottle of booze they won't be coming from there now that you've observed their approach. But let's send a company down there anyway. Push comes to shove, they can play mobile reserve. Whoops—hold for one second."

He holds up his hand and listens to a transmission over his command channel.

"Copy that, Lieutenant. I am sending reinforcements your way right now. The first company from the relief ship is on the ground."

Major Coburn turns to me and points his thumb over his shoulder to the northeast.

"You got here in the nick of time. The Lankies are making a push toward the greenhouses, and my guys are almost out of MARS rockets. Tell Captain Porter to send a platoon that way ASAP and support the position."

"I'll go with them. I know where the greenhouses are."

I hurry down the stairs and hail Sergeant First Class Kaneda, who is the combat controller for Bravo Company and who is riding in the lead ship of the second drop ship flight about to touch down.

"Tailpipe Two, Tailpipe One."

"Tailpipe One, go ahead."

"Sergeant Kaneda, make your way to the control tower as soon as your boots are on the ground and coordinate CAS from there. I am going with Alpha's first platoon to hold back a Lanky push."

"Copy that, sir. Coordinate CAS from the control tower. Good hunting."

Out on the landing pad, First Platoon is loading into the cargo hold of their drop ship again, and I follow them up the ramp. I don't bother with the controller seat at the front of the bulkhead and grab the nearest available sling seat to buckle in. The pilot guns the engines and goes skids up even before the tail ramp has fully closed.

"Check the map for the round structures a quarter klick north of the northeast edge of the city," I tell the pilot. "That's the greenhouse complex."

"Copy that," the pilot replies. "ETA fifty seconds."

The drop ship lowers its nose and picks up speed rapidly, and a few moments later, we are racing across the domed rooftops of New Longyearbyen at criminally low altitude. I have flashbacks to that day five years ago when I was passenger in a drop ship over this town, about to take part in a mutiny to prevent some desk-humping one-star general from seizing civilian assets for military use. The greenhouse complex we are racing toward was one of those assets, and now I have to help defend it against a different enemy altogether, one that can't be made to back down.

The greenhouses, four of them, are big domes made from alloy latticework and triangular polyplast panels. They rise thirty meters above the surface of the glacial plain half a kilometer from the edge of town. I know from my short time on this moon half a decade ago that the greenhouses are essential to the food supply chain of the colony, providing fresh fruit and vegetables for thousands of people.

We make a pass above the complex, and the pilot brings the drop ship around to face north, toward New Svalbard. At least ten eggshell-colored Lankies are advancing out of the snow squall a few hundred meters in front of the greenhouses and almost invisible in the weather. Because of their long limbs and their strange joint arrangement, they never look particularly fast, but I know the ones below us are striding along at fifty klicks per hour. The pilot cuts loose with the automatic cannon mounted on the starboard side of the hull bottom. Then he follows up the burst with guided missiles from the wing pylons. They streak out into the swirling white landscape and connect with the first two advancing Lankies. The first one takes a missile to the chest, right below the neck. The Lanky falls forward and hits the ground in a billowing plume of snow. The second one lifts its arm and raises its four-fingered hand, as if it wants to swat the missile out of the air. The warhead hits its upper arm and blows it in half. I watch in fascinated horror as the lower arm of the creature tumbles to the ground end over end. The Lanky wails loud enough for me to hear the sound over the wind and the gunfire from five hundred meters away through the hull of the drop ship. The cannon fire that follows rakes the Lanky from chest to knees, and it falls down thirty meters in front of the advancing line.

Underneath the drop ship, I see the muzzle flashes from several rifles. Another Lanky stumbles, then rights itself and continues its speedy stride. Then there's a missile launch from the right of the hovering drop ship. I switch my helmet view to the starboard array and see that the greenhouse domes have platforms at the top, and there's a two-person MARS rocket crew on the one to the right of us. Their rocket covers the distance to the lead Lanky in a second and a half and makes it stumble again. It falls forward and crashes into the snow face-first, sliding a dozen meters on the snow-covered ice.

I switch to the TacAir channel without bothering to check for assets in the airspace above the town. I know we have a dozen Shrikes overhead looking for something to shoot at, and this is as worthy a target for their ordnance as any.

"TacAir, Tailpipe One. Requesting immediate close-air support. Hostiles in the open, four five zero meters northwest of the greenhouses. I am marking the TRP. Weapons free, weapons free. Everything to the north of the first line of houses is hostile."

Ahead in the snowstorm, the remaining Lankies turn one by one and stride back the way they came, leaving their dead behind on the frozen ground between us and them. When a pair of Shrikes rolls in

245

twenty seconds later and strafes the ground in front of the greenhouses, the Lankies have passed back into the cover of the weather, like gigantic ghosts from a truly fucked-up nightmare. The explosive rounds from the cannons churn up the ice and snow, but none of them connect with anything that isn't dead already.

"Tailpipe One, TacOps. The Shrikes are having dwelling time issues down there. You have a visibility bubble of less than half a klick, and they have to fire blind before they clear the low ceiling."

"We'll have to shift the close air burden to the Dragonflies for now," I reply.

The pilot pivots his ship around and puts down the skids a hundred yards to the south of the greenhouse complex, skidding sideways in a heavy wind gust at the last seconds and dragging the starboard skid across the ice for a few meters. I hold my breath and wait for the ship to flip onto its side and explode, but it stays upright and settles on all three skids just a moment later. For once, I am glad not to be in my controller seat by the bulkhead, because when I unbuckle and grab my rifle, I am among the first troops down the ramp.

The garrison's SI troopers are deployed in a pitifully sparse firing line directly in front of the two greenhouses making up the north-facing side of the complex. I do a quick headcount and come up with fewer than twenty—way too few for a platoon, even counting the rocket crew on top of the greenhouse on the northwest corner. The troopers from First Platoon don't need to ask for directions or further orders. They spread out and strengthen the firing line with their three full squads, thirty-six fresh troops with full ammunition loads and two MARS launchers per squad.

Behind us, the drop ship rises into the sky again. The position and warning lights on the ship paint red-and-orange streaks on the snow. Ten meters off the ground, the pilot retracts the landing skids and soars off to take position above and ahead of our firing line. The winds are shaking the Dragonfly, but the pilot holds station and turns on all his forward-mounted lights to cut through the swirling white mess in front of us. The weather is getting less hospitable with every passing minute, and the more the visibility drops, the less time even the drop ships will have to bring their weapons to bear. To me, it feels like Greenland all over again, only magnified fivefold.

I check my TacLink screen and see that we aren't the only platoon in contact with the Lankies. The southern perimeter at the far end of the airfield is deployed in battle line and firing into a large group of Lankies approaching out of the storm from the southwest. The platoons from Bravo Company made it down to that end of the base just in time to shore up the defense there as well.

Guess you owe me a bottle of booze, Major, I think.

I know how to read the flow of a battle on TacLink, and I don't like what I see. Even with our two extra companies on the ground and more on the way, we aren't enough to hold off attacks from the north and south simultaneously. The perimeter is simply too large. If we get another push by the Lankies in one of the lightly defended sectors, they'll bull right through the line and split our forces in two.

"We need reinforcements on the northern perimeter," I send to the Major. "Whatever you can send, as soon as it comes out of the drop ships, or you'll have Lankies on the airfield in ten minutes."

"Understood. We have a flight landing right now. I don't know what the fuck the things are they're unloading, but I'll send them your way."

Exos. I grin into my helmet and watch as eight icons representing augmented armor units pop up on the airfield one by one. Whoever is in charge of loading the drop ships on *Ottawa's* flight deck right now deserves a medal for that decision.

"We have armor coming," I tell the platoons on the north perimeter. "Hold the line until they get here."

"Contact front!" one of the sergeants from First Platoon bellows. The visibility has dropped to only two hundred meters at most, and there are familiar tall shapes emerging from the squall again. The snow is now coming in sideways, and the wind is in our faces. I check the loading status of my rifle and find that the bolt is frozen shut. I smack the charging handle with the edge of my armored glove, and the bolt retracts halfway to reveal an armor-piercing round.

The drop ship opens up again, this time with both the hull-mounted cannon and the smaller-caliber chin turret. A hail of copper-plated steel casings rains down onto the snow in front of our position. Every fifth round in the rotary chin turret gun is a tracer, and the gun is set to such a high rate of fire that it looks like the gunner is working over the advancing Lankies with a laser beam.

The entire firing line opens up with rifles and MARS rockets. The Lankies blend into the swirling snow eerily well for creatures their size. The lights from the Dragonfly illuminate the battlefield and add to the surrealism.

In front of us, several Lankies fall to the concentrated fire from the drop ship and the rifle platoon, but more are behind them, and they stream around the fallen bodies and advance. The engines of the drop ship increase in pitch as the pilot fights the eighty-knot headwind to stay on station. He's only a hundred meters in front of the advancing Lanky line, barely visible in the polar maelstrom. Then one of the Lankies rises up from its crouched walk and swings a long arm toward the drop ship. The creature gets half a dozen cannon rounds to its chest almost instantly, but one of the huge four-fingered hands brushes the nose of the Dragonfly. Engines screaming, the ship rotates around its vertical axis and tilts to starboard. The Lanky goes down with a wail, but the drop ship is very obviously in trouble. The pilot tries to right it and swing the nose back around. My heart stops for a second when I see the nose of the Dragonfly dropping as the ship picks up speed.

The pilot almost clears the dome of the nearest greenhouse, but only *almost*. I hear a dull cracking sound as the nose of the Dragonfly pierces the polyplast dome two or three meters underneath the observation platform at its top. Then the drop ship's belly armor crushes the alloy lattice framework underneath, and the Dragonfly falls into the greenhouse dome at sixty or seventy knots of forward speed with a thunderous crash that sounds like the sky falling down.

The Dragonfly smashes out of the other side of the thirty-meter dome and then plows into the dome right next to it before hitting the ground with a resounding metallic thunder. Then something ignites— external ordnance, fuel tanks, maybe both—and the second dome goes up with a cataclysmic bang and a huge orange-black fireball. Burning parts of drop ship and greenhouse structure start raining down on us. I can't feel the fireball's heat through the face shield of my sealed armor, but the temperature readout on my visor jumps up well into the positive Celsius range for a few moments.

The closest Lanky is a hundred meters in front of our defensive line when the ground around it starts erupting, dozens of impacts throwing up snow and ice geysers. A second later, I hear the deep, sonorous roar of a Shrike's multibarrel cannon. The Lanky stumbles under the hammer blows of armor-piercing rounds that can cut through a mule from front to back. The Lankies are advancing into a ferocious volume of fire, rifles, and MARS rockets from our firing line and cannon fire from overhead, but they keep pushing on. In another twenty seconds, they will overrun our line with sheer mass and momentum.

The snow in the air and on the ground muffles most sounds, so I don't see the first exos charging through our line until they are already almost right behind our position, striding toward the approaching Lankies and kicking up geysers of snow with every step.

"Armor passing through," the warning comes on our tactical channel.

"Make a corridor," I warn my troops. "We have exos coming in from the rear!"

The exo striding past me aims an arm-mounted cannon at the approaching Lankies and lets rip with a short burst. The muzzle blast blows a dish-shaped hole three meters across into the snow in front of the exo. In front of our line, a Lanky crashes into the snow, felled by superdense twenty-five-millimeter slugs. The exo pilot wastes no time acquiring a new target. I watch as the gun arm swivels from Lanky to Lanky with computer precision—three rounds, swivel, three rounds, repeat. More exos are coming out of the gaps between the buildings, almost unencumbered by the meter-high snow, and the noise picks up tenfold as they add their own weapons fire to the fusillade. All the systems on the exos are networked, so unlike panicking SI troopers with hand weapons, the exos don't waste a shot by engaging the same target twice. It's a marvelous display of power-augmented efficiency. In front of us, the Lankies are falling to the sudden large-caliber precision fire much faster than they succumbed to our rifle shots. In what seems like only seconds, the exos are past our defensive line and right between us and the attacking Lankies. The jackhammer sounds of the arm-mounted cannons are interspersed with the whooshing report from MARS launchers.

"Hold fire," I send to my platoon, but the warning isn't necessary. Every trooper I see is watching the spectacle in front of us. The Lankies are still much bigger than the exos and probably a dozen times stronger, but the exos are stronger and faster than my unprotected troopers, and their guns hit a lot harder. It's like someone crossed the offensive attributes of a drop ship with the mobility of an infantry soldier.

"Frostbite Actual, thanks for the support," I send to the major. "That was in the nick of time."

"Still don't know what the fuck they are," the major replies. "But if they're working, I hope they send a hundred more."

The merciless firing line of exos pushes forward, guns blazing, until we can barely see the orange warning strobes on top of the frames. The fire slacks off slowly as more Lankies fall and fewer volunteer to push up and die next to their species mates.

So many last-second rescues, I think. *So much riding on twenty seconds of borrowed time.*

Up ahead and to the right of me, I see the glow of the burning greenhouse shimmering through the snow squall.

"TacOps, we have a drop ship down," I send up to *Ottawa.* "Don't bother with a SAR flight. His external ordnance cooked off on impact."

"Copy that. We read the crash beacon."

"At least he was already empty," I say, and instantly feel terrible for feeling glad that only three people died instead of forty. "You got ID markers on the pilots?"

"That bird was Eagle 05 from ATS-11, sir. Captains Fisher and Beals."

The recognition of the name sends an unpleasant shock through my body. Once upon a time, I would have found some satisfaction in Captain Beals's death, late justice extracted for the pilots and SI troopers his strafing run killed on Arcadia. But he died in the defense of our platoon, flying impossibly close-air support in unsafe weather, and I feel my hate for him evaporating like snowflakes on a hot gun muzzle. Whatever he did before, and however I felt about him, he earned a measure of redemption for this.

———

The exos emerge from the squall again a few minutes later, walking through the deep snow in an orderly battle line. There are eight of them, and they just held off an advance that almost overran a reinforced platoon of unaugmented SI. I am reasonably sure that this settles the question of whether four of them are worth ten times as many SI riflemen on a dropship.

"The Lankies halted their push," the exo platoon commander says on the tactical channel. "I don't want to pursue so we don't stumble into an ambush."

"Can't say I disagree," I say. "Thanks for bailing us out."

The storm slacks off a little, precisely ten minutes too late to do us any good. The glacier field in front of our position is littered with at least two dozen dead Lankies, although it's hard to get a good count because of the sheer size of their bodies. Behind us, the fire started by the crashing Dragonfly is still burning. The greenhouse dome right behind us is smashed comprehensively, and the one next to it is completely destroyed, a twisted mess of charred support arcs and melted polyplast. Both of the surviving domes have blown-out polyplast panels all over their northern quadrants. We won the skirmish but failed our mission, even if the Lankies never got to within swinging range of these domes, all because of one well-placed Lanky arm swipe and a pilot who was three feet too low. I know that the pilot wasn't Halley because her squadron is in charge of the reserve battalion, not mine. But the flaming wreckage nearby is a stark reminder that the pilots live every bit as dangerously as the squishy grunts on the ground.

"Reload, and let's keep our eyes peeled," I tell my platoon. "I don't think they're done with us yet. They want this place too badly."

"Retreat to the northern defensive line, five hundred meters to your south," Major Coburn says when I inform him of the loss of the greenhouse complex. "With the domes gone, there's nothing to defend there, and you're in front of the line and exposed. Let those exoskeletons screen your redeployment. Reinforce the northern perimeter with those things and hold that line until the weather lifts and we can bring close air to bear again."

"Aye, sir." I cut the channel and relay the major's order to First Platoon's lieutenant.

"Well, that was a fucking waste of effort," the lieutenant grumbles when I'm finished.

"Tell that to the garrison squaddies we just bailed out," I reply. "We pull out by squads. Bounding overwatch. Two squads cover; the others move. It's half a klick, and we don't have a ride anymore. Let's get out of here before they decide to come back for seconds."

"Make it quick," the exo platoon leader says. "We just burned over half our ammo stopping that push. Reloads are all the way in orbit."

A few minutes later, we start our run back to the relative safety of our own defensive line at the edge of town. With the exos drawn up in a defensive line in front of our old positions, we leapfrog back across the glacial plain in pairs of squads, switching off the running and covering tasks every hundred meters. The snow on the glacial plain is knee-deep, and even with the power assist from my armor's servos working at maximum output, the half-kilometer run back to the town is one of the most physically demanding tasks I've ever had to do. By the time we pass the defensive line and get into the cover of the first buildings, I feel weak and drained from the exertion. I stop to catch my breath.

"First Platoon of Alpha Company is back inside the perimeter," I send to Major Coburn once I am no longer panting, even though he probably knows this information from our data links if he keeps even half an eye on his TacLink screen.

"Copy that," Major Coburn replies. "Reinforce the line in that sector and hold. I am sending a platoon from Charlie Company your way, too."

I turn around to look back at the greenhouse complex we just abandoned to the next Lanky advance. The fires set by the crashed drop ship are still burning, casting the white haze in the distance in an orange glow. The remaining domes are almost invisible in the weather from this range. If the nuclear bombardment of the Lanky crash site didn't doom this colony, the loss of one of their main food sources probably sealed that fate unless we can scrape the Lankies off this moon completely. And right now, without the full power of our air and space support and only eight exos on the ground so far, it's likely that *we're* the ones getting scraped off New Svalbard instead.

CHAPTER 21

—— **SECOND NEW SVALBARD** ——

The lull in the storm doesn't last very long. Ten minutes after Charlie Company's fourth platoon arrives to reinforce our position, visibility is back down to under two hundred meters. The heaters in my suit have to work so hard to keep me alive that the battery level is dropping at a concern-inducing rate. This is the harshest environment I've ever experienced, and having to fight in it seems like suicidal madness. But we are the defensive line against whatever lurks in that storm, so we settle down in our hastily prepared positions and wait for the onslaught.

"The southern perimeter defense stopped the Lanky advance cold," Major Coburn reports when I update our status. "We can pull off a platoon or two to help shore up the northern perimeter, but they'll have to ride in mules or walk your way. Weather's too bad for safe drop ship ops."

"Understood," I reply. "Send up whatever you can. We are stretched mighty thin on the flanks, and visibility is shit. One good push by the Lankies, and they'll break right through our line."

"Radar says we'll get a break in the weather soon. The storm should slack off in an hour."

"That's fantastic news," I say. "Let's hope the Lankies will do us a favor and wait until then."

With the arrival of the new platoon, our sector is now the most well-defended one on the northern perimeter, so when the Lanky push from the north comes fifteen minutes later, it's naturally in a different sector. I hear the small-arms fire and rocket launches to our left, but the driving snow muffles the sounds so much that I couldn't even begin to guess the distance. The TacLink screen is unambiguous, however. As soon as the first Lankies come into view of the defending unit to our west, their orange icons pop up on the map. They are coming right at the center of the northern perimeter line, five hundred meters from our position. In the blinding storm, and with knee-deep snow to contend with at every move, five hundred meters may as well be fifty miles.

"Center is under attack and getting pushed hard. Can you redeploy and flank the enemy spearhead?" Major Coburn asks over the company command channel.

"Negative," I reply. "Not without vehicles. It'll take us half an hour in this shit. It'll all be over by the time we get there, and we'll leave the right flank open if we do. Redeploy the exos."

"Already did, but they're low on ammo. The bastards are hugging our belt buckles. Cover the front, but watch your left flank if they manage to get through."

The distant weapons fire from our left increases in intensity until it sounds like a mad minute at the range where everyone empties their magazines at the berm as quickly as they can reload their guns. The sharp reports from M-95 rifles are interspersed with explosions from MARS rockets and the shrieking wails of stricken Lankies. Overhead, I see four Shrikes and two drop ships circling the battlefield, but our troops are already intermingled with the Lankies at point-blank range, and any bombing or strafing run would take out more friendlies than hostiles. Two of the Shrikes dive in anyway and drop canisters of tungsten darts and cluster bombs in front of the defensive line in hopes of catching unspotted Lankies in the open and blunting the main body of this advance. But whatever they are hitting out there, it's not enough to make a difference. A few minutes later, the gunfire ebbs. I see on the TacLink screen what's happening even before the leader of the platoon to the west confirms the situation on the company channel.

"The Lankies have broken through our defensive line. Thirty-plus individuals, moving south along the northern access road. We are falling back to the west to regroup."

The bright orange icons on the TacLink map are piercing the blue defensive line in numbers. As they move south and out of sight of the troopers on the perimeter, their color fades to pale orange. With the rest of the defending forces concentrated to ward off the southern push, there's nothing and nobody keeping the Lankies from walking right into the middle of New Svalbard.

"Alpha One and Charlie Four, fall back to the admin center at grid square Bravo Foxtrot One-Seven and defend the perimeter," Major Coburn orders. "We have to pull back the northern line, or they'll outflank you and crush your position from two sides. We have a company arriving from *Ottawa*. I'm sending them in to form a defensive line across the north-south axis at grid line Bravo Charlie."

An hour ago, we were confident that our reinforcements would turn the tide and crush the Lankies. Four strike squadrons, two full battalions, orbital fire support. But the weather and the need for an overextended static defense line have cost us all our advantages, and with the Lanky breakthrough in the northern center, we just lost the initiative as well.

The admin building looks just like I remember it. It's a tall, windowless concrete structure shaped like a bread loaf. All the buildings on New Svalbard are designed to withstand the ferocious winter weather here, but the admin building is overbuilt even for local conditions. I've been inside many times, and I know that the walls are several meters thick. The whole thing is so massive that it would take a bunker-busting nuke to take it out.

We redeploy and set up hasty defensive positions on both west-facing corners of the building. Without any close-air support to direct, I have very little to do, and the two lieutenants in charge of their platoons can run their own shows, so I step into the entrance vestibule of the admin center. The corners of the building still bear the pockmarks from Shrike cannon fire, inflicted by the attack craft of *Midway* five years ago when they tried to suppress our little mutiny. So much has happened since that day that it feels like those events were lived out by someone else.

When the inner doors open, the sudden gust of warmer air makes my helmet visor fog up instantly. I raise the visor and step into the atrium of the admin building. The atrium is packed with cargo crates and pallets, and several civilians are busy carrying more crates out of adjoining rooms. At the far end of the atrium, a very tall and familiar-looking man in a dark colonial police uniform and light body armor is talking to a small group of civvie techs. He turns around when the inner doors close and the safety bolts latch into place again with a loud metallic clanking sound. I nod at him, and he comes walking over, cradling a well-worn M-66C fléchette carbine that looks distinctly toylike in his arms.

"What's the word, Trooper?" he says.

"Good to see you again, Constable Guest," I say, and his eyes narrow a little in surprise.

"Do I know you?"

He looks at the name plate on my armor, but when I look down, I see that it's caked with snow and ice. Instead of brushing it off, I just pop the latches on my helmet and pull it off my head.

"Well, I'll be damned," colonial constable Guest says. "Staff Sergeant Grayson. Never thought I'd see you around here again."

Constable Guest extends his hand, and I shake it. Even though I'm wearing armored gloves and he isn't, my hand disappears in his enormous paw. The constable is the tallest and most massive person I've ever seen at well over two meters tall. His chest circumference more than matches his height, and nothing about him is delicate in any way except for his carefully measured handshake.

"It's Captain Grayson now," I correct him. "They roped me into pinning on stars."

"I am not surprised," Constable Guest says with a smile. "Cream always rises to the top."

"Yeah, so do other things," I reply, and he grins. "I just got here with two platoons of infantry. They're setting up defenses right outside. The Lankies have broken through our defensive perimeter and into the town."

"I knew we weren't going to be able to hold them off the moment the Fleet ship told us we had three seed ships on the way." Constable Guest shakes his head and sighs. "Why now? They've left us alone for almost ten years. Never showed any interest in this moon. Not even after they took the SRA colony five years ago. I thought we'd be able to fly under their radar indefinitely."

"How many civilians are left down here?"

"A little less than two thousand. We wound down operations over the years. What's left is only essential personnel. Most everyone else evacuated back to Earth."

"What about your family?"

"They go where I go," he says. "We moved everyone into the tunnels before the Lankies made orbit. Wasn't much of a logistical effort. Winter's about to set in down here anyway."

"Is the ops center still where it used to be?"

"Yes, it is. Let me go with you." He turns and gestures for me to follow him.

I have the strangest feeling of déjà vu as we walk through familiar corridors to the secured ops center in the middle of the first floor. During the rebellion on New Svalbard, I spent entire days and nights in that room, staying in touch with *Indianapolis* in orbit and coordinating the defense of the town. Everything looks the way it did half a decade ago, but just like in the control tower on the airfield, there are more signs of wear and infrequent maintenance. I guess when you live on a moon that's actively trying to kill you most of the time, keeping the wall paint freshened up is low on the list of priorities.

The ops room has more people in it than I remember seeing in here on my last stay. Everyone looks over to the door when Constable Guest and I walk in, and I nod at the room in general.

"Captain Grayson, this is the administrator, Director Maynard. Director, this is Captain Grayson with the Fleet. He helped us out five years ago during the troubles with the garrison."

"Captain," the administrator says. "What can we do for you?"

"I have a detachment of SI outside to defend the building. The Lankies have broken through and are now advancing into the town from the northern access road. I'm sorry to say that your greenhouses are gone. We tried to hold them back, but then we had to withdraw to avoid getting flanked."

"The ground commander at the airfield gave me the rough sketch," Director Maynard says. He's lean and wiry and slightly scruffy like most of the settlers here, and he's wearing a faded blue cap with the logo of the Colonial Administration. "Now that you've killed their ships, what are the chances of us pulling out of this and getting rid of our uninvited guests?"

"The way things are looking right now, not so good, sir."

"I appreciate your candor, Captain. Bill, come over here and tell the Fleet officer what you told me before they walked in."

Another civilian engineer detaches himself from his console and walks over to us.

"Bill Cunningham," he introduces himself as we shake hands. "I'm the chief meteorologist in this facility."

"Andrew Grayson. I'm the special tactics officer of the Fleet detachment. Please tell me we have a stretch of good weather coming. Our close-air support is all but grounded in this mess."

"Well, I have good news and bad news for you, Captain." Mr. Cunningham waves me over to his console, and I follow him. He sits down in his chair with a sigh and brings up his terminal screens. Then he flicks through a few screens and brings up a radar map.

"That's the situation on this part of the continent," he says. There's a light pen next to a half-empty coffee mug on his desk, and he grabs it and turns it on. "We are here. That bunch of red coming in from the north is the first big winter storm of the season."

"You mean that isn't a winter storm outside right now? We can barely see a hundred meters."

Mr. Cunningham shakes his head with a smile.

"No, that's not a winter storm. Those are just flurries. That red band, *that's* a winter storm. You're looking at three-hundred-kilometers-per-hour windspeed."

"Holy shit," I say. "How long is that going to last?"

"Two weeks, maybe three."

"Three *weeks*?"

"If it's not an overly energetic system, yes. We've had longer ones."

I run a hand through my hair, which is damp with perspiration. "What's the good news, then?"

"There is a patch of good weather. Relatively speaking, of course. The winds should slack off to about fifty kilometers per hour within the next thirty minutes according to our weather station network. It won't pick up again until a few hours before the main front of the winter storm gets here."

"How long is that break in the weather?"

"About two and a half hours. It's going to get progressively worse after that."

"Oh, that's just fucking *fabulous*." I look at the angry-looking storm front that's forming a red sickle shape to our north on the radar. There will be nothing taking off or landing from the airfield in winds of that strength, not even with a fully automated AILS landing system.

"Excuse me for just a moment. I need to talk to the garrison commander."

I put my helmet back on and switch to the command channel.

"Frostbite Actual, this is Tailpipe One."

"Tailpipe One, go ahead," Major Coburn replies after a few seconds.

"Sir, I am at the admin center. We are in defensive posture. The meteorology crew here at the facility are mapping an incoming storm on radar."

"Stand by for one." The channel goes quiet for a minute as Major Coburn undoubtedly consults his own terminal for the latest feed from the weather radar.

"I see the storm front. Looks like we don't have much time to clear the town and reestablish the perimeter."

"Sir, that's pointless," I say. "We need to get out of here before that storm gets here, or we're not going anywhere for a long time. There's no way we'll last three weeks defending this place in three-hundred-klick winds."

Next to me, Mr. Cunningham shakes his head.

"No, sir. It'll be total whiteout," he says. "You'll walk face-first into buildings because you won't be able to see where you are going. That's if the wind doesn't blow you halfway across the continent."

"We need to evac all the civilians and ground troops while we still can," I say. "This colony is lost, sir."

Next to me, Constable Guest and the two civilians are sucking in breaths as if I had just committed a particularly rude and offensive form of blasphemy.

"You propose to evacuate two thousand civilians and a thousand troops in under three hours, Captain?"

"*Ottawa* has two squadrons of drop ships, plus half a dozen spares," I say. "We can do that in two flights. Forty-five minutes per flight, fifteen minutes for each flight to load."

"I will not give up this colony," Director Maynard says firmly. "We can wait them out underground. See how they like three-hundred-klick winds and negative one hundred degrees."

"They'll burrow in the ice and make your tunnels collapse," I say. "I've seen them dig a five-hundred-meter tunnel and a cave into bare ice on Greenland in just a month. And that was just a dozen of these things. Sir, your colony is lost. We need to get your people out of here before we all get buried in those tunnels together."

Constable Guest shrugs at the administrator. "Hate to say it, Sam, but the captain has a point. And with the greenhouses gone, our goose is cooked anyway. By the time the storm has passed, they'll have smashed the fusion plant, too."

"God*dammit*." Director Maynard takes off his blue cap and smacks it against the frame of the meteorology console. "Nine years of backbreaking fucking work, and it comes to *this*."

"All right," Major Coburn says on the command channel. "I'll contact *Ottawa* Actual and let them know our intentions. I am ordering all military personnel on this moon to retreat to the airfield and establish a perimeter for evacuation. Transmit to all units."

"Copy that," I reply. Then I look at Director Maynard.

"Sir, the commander on the ground has ordered the evacuation. I strongly suggest you follow suit and get your people to the airfield.

Once that storm comes in, we won't be able to protect anyone or go anywhere. I'm sorry, but we've lost this one."

Director Maynard nods, but I can see the muscles flexing on the sides of his jaw.

"I want to disagree, but I don't have the right to make that gamble for two thousand people," he says. Then he walks over to another console and picks up a headset. A moment later, his voice comes from the overhead speakers.

"All colonial personnel, this is the administrator. We are evacuating this facility. All personnel, make your way to the airfield via express tunnel Broadway in a calm and orderly fashion and obey all directions from military personnel. Only take your essentials. We will not have space for luggage or cargo, so don't bring any. We've drilled for this, people. I'm sorry to say that this is not a drill. Good luck and Godspeed, everyone."

He takes off the headset and drops it on the console in front of him. Then he rubs his beard stubble with one hand and looks around the control center.

"What a waste," he says, and shakes his head. "What a goddamn waste."

"Alpha One and Charlie Four, abandon your position and come inside," I send to the platoon commanders in front of the admin center. Constable Guest and I are on the way back into the atrium at a fast walk, the constable outpacing me easily.

"Sublevel three for the tunnels?" I ask, and the constable nods.

"I never had a chance to go to that bar in the Ellipse one more time," I say. "What was it called again?"

"On the Rocks," Constable Guest replies. "Damn, I'm going to miss that place. My daughter had her first job there. Best drinks on this moon."

"I got the worst hangover of my life here."

"Lousy food, rough crowd, but man, do they know how to mix a cocktail." Constable Guest changes course slightly and walks over to one of the offices attached to the atrium. It's the little two-room police station he has been manning for the last ten years. I follow him inside and look around, unsurprised to see that it has changed very little from the way it looked in my memory.

Constable Guest walks to the comms unit on the wall and picks up the microphone.

"This is the boss. All officers, head down into Broadway and do traffic control, please. We don't need any pushing matches. Tell them there's no need to hurry. We have plenty of time to get on the ships. Phelps and Martin, make a sweep of the Ellipse and make sure nobody's lagging behind because they want to make sure the alcohol doesn't go to waste. Thank you all, ladies and gents, and I'll see you on the ship."

The officers send their acknowledgments back, and Constable Guest hangs up the handset.

"Well, that's that, I suppose." He looks around in the office. His diplomas and pictures are still hanging on the walls just like they did five years ago, and he makes no move to take them down.

"You're not packing those?"

"Oh no," he says. "I can always get new printouts. I'm not much of a materialist."

Outside in the atrium, the inner door opens, and a bunch of SI troopers from First Platoon come in from the cold, their armor encrusted with ice.

"I'll give you a minute," I tell Constable Guest. "I'll have to show the grunts how to get to the tunnels."

"I'm good," he replies. "Got all I needed. Not exactly how I pictured my last shift here to end, that's all."

"Sorry about that."

"All good things must come to an end, and all that. At least it's a rescue. Could be worse."

"It could always be worse," I agree, remembering the dead settlers on the streets of a colony named Willoughby and thinking of the bodies the Lankies dragged into their holes on Mars.

Down in the Ellipse, the civilians are streaming toward the tunnel intersection for Broadway, the long, straight express tunnel that goes from the main underground district of the town straight to the admin building on the airfield. At the intersection, two cops are standing guard to funnel the stream of people into a single line. The mood down here is somber, but not panicked. I don't see anyone with children in the crowd. The personnel that remained on New Svalbard after the waves of exodus over the last few years are the toughest and most hard-bitten miners and technicians. When I was here before, it felt like a proper colony, with families and small kids. Now it looks like any other mining outpost in the solar system, hard people living hard lives.

"I'm going to stay here and make sure everyone gets out," Constable Guest says as we leave the concourse and enter the express tunnel. I stop and turn around to face him.

"Just as long as you don't have any heroic notions of going down with the ship," I say.

"I'm not an idiot," he grins. "My wife and daughters will be super pissed at me if I get killed over a few million cubic meters of ice. Bet your ass I'll be on the last ship out."

"I'll hold you to it," I say and shake the constable's hand. "See you topside."

In the Broadway tunnel, we pass the civilians at a trot. They give us curious glances as we run by, loaded down with battle armor and weapons. I remind myself to tell Hansen that I finally found a scenario for which all that running on the track proved to be good preparation. The Broadway tunnel is five meters wide and almost perfectly straight for the whole kilometer of its length.

When we're halfway between the Ellipse and the airfield, there's a loud booming sound overhead, and the floor of the tunnel shakes. Some of the civvies shout out in concern. There's another boom, this one stronger than the first, and ice particles fall from the ceiling and drift to the floor of the tunnel. The line of civilians starts moving faster, and so do we. If I am going to turn in my tags today, I don't want it to be because I got buried alive under twenty meters of ice. I tell myself that once I am out of this tunnel, I'll never step into another one for the rest of my life.

The end of the tunnel has been upgraded since I went through here last. Instead of a ladder, there's a metal staircase leading up to the exit doors. At the top of the stairs, two SI troopers in battle armor are standing guard at the doors. The doors let out into the sublevel of the control center underneath the tower, and we spill out into the vestibule beyond the doors. As soon as we pass through the doors, we hear the rumbling of regular gunfire above, no longer filtered and insulated by thousands of tons of ice. With nothing to block the wireless signal, my TacLink screen updates again, and a jolt of fear goes through me when I see how small the perimeter has become. The Lankies have free run of the town from the Bravo Alpha grid line to the admin center on the eastern end, and the frontline is just a hundred meters from the edge of the airfield.

"Go and reinforce the line," I shout at the lieutenants with me. "Keep them away from the landing pad if you want to go back to the ship today."

Upstairs in the control tower, Major Coburn somehow looks even more drawn and haggard than he did just an hour or two ago.

"We have two thousand civvies in the tunnel," I report. "The admin center is clear."

"The fuckers already tore down the main antenna array over there," Major Coburn says. "They'll have a grand time trying to get into that ugly-ass bunker."

Overhead, a flight of unseen Shrikes thunders by at low altitude. A few moments later, the Shrikes fire their guns into the town and release their ordnance pods blindly. Everything to the east of the Bravo Alpha grid line is now a free-fire zone, even if the attack birds can't see any individual targets.

"They're like fucking locusts," Major Coburn says.

"I've never seen them go for close combat like this. It's like they know that we can't use our airpower if they're right up in our faces."

"Maybe they can sense the storm, and they know they'll have to get under cover before it hits," the major suggests.

I have an unnervingly good vantage point up here in the control tower. There's a defensive line of troops strung across the runway to the south of the hangars and fuel tanks, and another on the outer edge of the airfield facing toward the east. I get glimpses of Lankies in the driving snow, advancing toward our lines and being met with withering defensive fire. Our beachhead has shrunk to a small patch of ground maybe three hundred meters across, and there are orange icons in every direction now. Mars was bigger in scope, but this feels worse somehow, more concentrated and vicious. Someone has set up two autocannon crews on the roof of the tower, and they're sending out bursts of tracer rounds every time they spot a Lanky in the near-whiteout conditions to our east.

A flight of drop ships comes soaring out of the low cloud ceiling directly above the airfield. From their even intervals and precise maneuvers, I can tell they're flying hands-off, with their computers locked on to the AILS beam of the landing pad. I check the markings on their tails and feel my heart doing a little jump when I see that the Dragonflies setting down right now belong to ATS-5, Halley's squadron. One by one, the drop ships set down on the pad and lower their tail ramps. But instead of unloading more troops, each ship disgorges four troopers in exos. The heavy exoskeleton suits stomp down the steel ramps and onto the ice-covered concrete, where they kick up little puffs of white with every step.

"Someone going to let me in on what the deal is with those new toys?" Major Coburn asks.

"Experimental gear," I say. "Power amplification combat system. We brought some with us on *Ottawa*. They kicked royal ass on the northern flank half an hour ago. A few dozen more of those, and we could clear the moon."

On the landing pad below, the exos group up, then pair off. Each pair walks toward the perimeter in a different direction. The ones heading to the east and west edges of the airfield soon disappear from sight behind hangars and maintenance sheds. I watch the pair of exos stomping off to the north perimeter, faster with their casual-looking bouncy walk than a lightly loaded trooper can sprint.

"Drop ships are ready for pax," the leader of the flight sends on the command channel. It's not Halley's voice, so I know she isn't behind the stick of any of those ships.

The SI troopers downstairs start running people from the building to the waiting drop ships. The crew chiefs are standing at the bottoms of the ramps and counting people into their birds by hand. Even with all that gunfire and the shrieks from the Lankies nearby, the ice miners keep remarkable discipline. Everyone moves quickly, but nobody rushes the drop ships. The pilots don't wait for the whole flight to be loaded up. As soon as the first Dragonfly on the far end is full, the ramp goes up, and the pilot pulls the ship up into the lead-colored sky at full throttle. The second one follows, then the third and fourth.

"Next flight ETA one minute, twenty-five seconds," TacOps sends.

"Copy that. Keep sending them down as quickly as you can get them out of the clamps. We have over two thousand pax waiting down here, and the neighborhood is getting unfriendly. And, Garcia?"

"Go ahead, sir," Garcia replies from the TacOps station hundreds of kilometers overhead.

"Next time I tell you to let me take your spot on a drop, punch me in the crotch," I say.

Sergeant Garcia laughs.

"To be fair, sir, you asked to get put on a drop ship to Shitsville if you ever got too comfortable behind this console."

"A fair point," I concede.

CHAPTER 22

REQUIEM FOR A COLONY

I've never admired the piloting skills of our drop ship crews more than now.

For the next two hours, the two assault transport squadrons do the most coordinated high-risk aerial ballet I have ever seen. They come in like clockwork, a flight of four every few minutes, setting down and taking on passengers and taking off again to climb up to *Ottawa* and make space for the next flight to land. At least twice, I think I spot Halley's ship. Most of the Dragonflies unload their cannons into the Lankies before they do their final approach, and the withering fire from so many barrels seems to have an effect. Slowly and laboriously, our SI troopers are pushing the Lankies back from the eastern edge of the airfield and back into the town, until we have a no-man's-land of sorts stretching two hundred meters into the settlement. I know we're taking casualties because there isn't a single flight leaving without SI medics loading at least a few wounded troopers onto the departing birds. I share combat controller duties in the tower with Sergeant First Class Kaneda, and there are so many drop ships and attack birds in the sky overhead that we're both at the limit of our mental bandwidth.

MARKO KLOOS

"All civilians are loaded up and away," the departing flight from ATS-11 finally sends almost two hours later. The winds have picked up again, and the angry red line on the weather radar has advanced to within fifty kilometers of the town. I can't see the clouds in the distance because of the whiteout conditions, but the sky has noticeably darkened over the last hour.

"All units, the civilians are away with no casualties," Major Coburn sends on the local defense channel. "Start a clean fallback and contract the perimeter. We will have overhead cover fire until the last ship leaves the ground."

The SI platoons pull back toward the airfield slowly. A fighting withdrawal to a waiting drop ship lift is called "letting the air out of the balloon," and the troops on the airfield show the quality of their training by keeping control of the perimeter even under the insane stress of facing twenty-meter enemies that can flatten a whole squad with one blow if they manage to close the distance. The PACS crews are the cornerstones of the shrinking defensive line. They move up and down the line, filling gaps in the fire coverage and stopping threatening breakthroughs with accurate and effective cover fire from their cannon pods. The old salts in the Fleet and SI usually make fun of the idea of combat exos, but I've decided that my skepticism was misplaced. They have many of the advantages of fighting vehicles with none of the weight or bulk penalty, and as I watch them tear up the Lankies on TacLink, I wish we had about a thousand of them in the inventory. And all through the battle, the drop ships keep coming down through the increasingly shitty weather, unloading their cannons to strafe the area beyond our defensive line and putting down to pick up troops. Every time a drop ship departs, 45 more troopers are on the way back to *Ottawa*, 180 grunts ferried to safety with every four-ship flight.

"Time to pack it up, Captain," Major Coburn says to me when the outer line of defense is a mere fifty meters to the east of the control center, and the reports from the exos' autocannons shake the window panels in the tower. We have three hundred troops and sixteen exos left on the ground, few enough to fit into two flights of Dragonflies. A four-ship formation thunders up the runway and over the formation of SI troopers and exos holding the line on the south end of the hangars. The ships pop up over the last hangar and set down on the pad in manual mode, barely wobbling despite the wind that has picked up to eighty-plus knots again.

Sergeant Kaneda and I make our way downstairs and onto the landing pad. I watch a squad from the eastern perimeter rush over to the pad and start boarding the ship, leaving a last squad and two exos to watch their backs. A Lanky comes stomping out of the blinding whiteout ahead to follow them, then falters when the two exos open fire with single shots each, and the SI troopers add a MARS rocket for good measure. The Lanky is only a hundred meters away when it falls and flattens one of the residential domes. Half a dozen dead Lankies are already laid out in front of this squad, and I'm sure there are more further out in the snow where I can't see them. Technically, we kicked their asses. And yet they've once again scored the overall victory, because we are leaving this place and they are not.

Over on the flight pad, one of the drop ships has finished loading, and the Dragonfly lifts off the ground and retracts its skids. I can see that the winds are buffeting the ship, but the pilot corrects coolly, with a smoothness that tells me the ship isn't on automatic takeoff. The departing Dragonfly raps out another burst from its cannons toward the Lanky-held area and then roars into the cloud cover.

I run up to the nearest drop ship, which has just lowered its tail ramp. I see the markings for ATS-5 on the tail assembly and look over at the cockpit, where the pilots wear their names and call signs stenciled right under the frames. This one says "MAJ HALLEY 'COMET,'" and I bark a relieved laugh into my helmet.

Halley is anonymous behind her helmet visor, and I suppose my armor does the same for my appearance. Another squad is waiting to board, and I enter the ship with them and make my way to the forward bulkhead seat designated for unit leaders and combat control specialists. More troops come running up the ramp and dropping into seats, stowing their rifles and buckling up in a hurry. There's absolutely nothing that lights a fire under a grunt's ass like having to board one of the last battle taxis out of a hot LZ.

The exos are the last to retreat to the landing pad. The three drop ships that have already taken off are hovering overhead and emptying their magazines to cover the exoskeleton pilots as they unlock their harnesses, drop out of their machines, and come sprinting over to Halley's drop ship. I realize that even if we had the space, there'd be no way to load up the exos under these circumstances without endangering the drop ships tasked to pick them up. The exoskeleton crews run up the tail ramp and find empty seats. The last one to board the ship is Major Coburn, who has been waiting at the foot of the ramp to make sure he's the last SI trooper off the moon he was tasked to defend for so long, the moon for which his men bled and died before we arrived. Behind him, the exos stand in a ragged line on the airfield, millions of Commonwealth dollars' worth of gear destined to be expensive scraps very soon. I know they're just machines, but it feels like we're abandoning a bunch of faithful guard dogs. They were the most effective equipment we brought into the ground battle, experimental kits that performed even better than expected, and we're leaving them behind.

What a waste, I echo the words of the colony administrator in my head. *What a goddamn waste.*

"Loading complete," the crew chief shouts into his helmet mike as he pushes the button for the tail ramp mechanism. "Go, go, go!"

Halley pulls the ship up and turns it around to swing it into the wind. I see the glass windows of the tower flash by through the narrowing gap in the tail hatch and the pile of discarded autocannon munitions containers on the roof. Then we are high enough that we're out of reach of even the most audacious and long-armed Lanky, and the relief I feel makes my knees shake.

I do my usual check-in with the pilot, eager to hear Halley's voice.

"Tailpipe One, in the back, requesting permission for operational control of the sensor suite," I send to the cockpit. "And you're a damn show-off for wanting to be the last bird off the ground."

Halley's inflections are different when she's in her pilot mode, and she talks in the same slightly exaggerated drawl all pilots use for some reason, as if it's a mandatory class at Drop Ship U.

"Says the knucklehead who just absolutely had to wait *until* the last bird," she replies, and I smile when I hear the relief in her voice.

I'm always tired after a mission. There's a special fatigue you feel after the adrenaline from battle wears off. Your body is tired and shaky, and your brain feels like it has just been wrung out and hung up to dry. But this time, I'm even more drained than usual. When we get bounced around in the atmosphere on the way up into orbit, I barely notice and hardly care. I don't even feel hunger or thirst, even though I haven't eaten since before we left *Ottawa*. All I want right now is a bunk and about three days of uninterrupted sleep, and I'm not even sure if that will be enough.

Maybe I am getting too old for this shit, I think. And now I fully understand why all the senior podheads like Colonel Masoud always look a lot older than they are.

Despite my request, I don't bother accessing the sensors of the ship for my customary pre- and postbattle sightseeing. New Svalbard is covered in clouds anyway, but even if the skies were clear, all that's down there now is a former colony that's broken and violated, crawling with beings that use our bodies for building material. I've always liked the place despite its harsh environment, and I've even toyed with the idea of picking it as my destination after I retire from the service and get that free relocation ride to a colony. But that's all irrelevant now, because Fomalhaut will have no human presence anymore after we transition out of the system. Instead of looking back at what is once again a graveyard, I rest my helmet against the soft spall liner on the bulkhead and fall asleep, and I only wake up again when the automatic docking clamps deposit Halley's Dragonfly on the flight deck of *Ottawa* thirty minutes later.

———————

Halley is still in her cockpit shutting down avionics when I walk off the tail ramp of her ship. Impossible as it seems, the gigantic flight deck of *Ottawa* feels overcrowded for the first time. Two thousand civilians are milling around or sitting on the deck, many of them looking as shell-shocked as I feel.

"Request permission to take a week off, Captain," Sergeant Kaneda says next to me, and I grin weakly.

"Go check in with the OOD and make a beeline to your stateroom, Sergeant. And if you see anyone else from the CCT, tell them the same. Don't come out again until you've had a shower and at least eight hours of uninterrupted sleep. That's an order."

"Aye, sir," Sergeant Kaneda says. "With all due respect, you should do the same. You look like you've been run over with a mule, sir."

"That's the very next thing on my agenda, Sarge. Now go hit the rack."

I walk around the Dragonfly's portside wing and to the front of the ship. Halley looks up from her screens when she notices me. The Dragonfly is a low-slung ship, and when it's standing on its skids on the flight deck, the pilot's head is only very slightly above a standing person's head level. I walk up to the armored window panel, take my helmet off, and rest my forehead against the window. Halley pulls her own helmet off and does the same on the other side, and we remain like this for a little while, until the maintenance crew comes around the front of Halley's bird and starts hooking up service umbilicals.

Despite my fatigue, I only manage to sleep for two hours before the watch-change announcement wakes me up again. I allow myself the luxury of yet another shower, even though I already took one before I hit the rack. Then I change into the uniform of the day, the blueberry suit, which feels decadently soft after half a day in battle armor. I decide that the new uniform is not so bad after all, even if it does look a bit like a space leisure suit.

I relieve Sergeant Garcia in CIC, who most likely had the busiest watch of his entire deployment, even if it wasn't half as exciting as mine or Sergeant Kaneda's. The entire CCT was assigned to SI companies, and Sergeants Taggart, Wilcox, Winters, and Graff spent three hours in ready-to-go drop ships until First Battalion's drop was canceled. The other combat controllers, Sergeants Kaneda, Hernandez, and Lang, were on the surface and are now under standing orders to spend the next watch cycle in their bunks. We took a lot of casualties on New Svalbard, but I am beyond glad that I didn't lose any of *my* team. Other commanding officers will have to attend funerals and write letters to the families of young men and women just like I had to do after Arcadia, but I won't have to add that to my list of worries today at least.

The plot still shows us in geostationary orbit above what used to be New Longyearbyen, now Population: None. The *Michael P. Murphy* is flying in close formation off to our starboard side. The destroyer has recently patched holes in the hull that are unmistakably Lanky penetrator impacts from her earlier engagement, but she's still largely in one piece. For what we destroyed and killed in the exchange, we all got off light, which makes the loss of the colony doubly painful. Victories shouldn't hurt like this.

"The flight deck is clear, ma'am," the XO says to Colonel Yamin. "The civilians have been checked in and assigned bunk space. One thousand nine hundred thirty-three."

"Where did the quartermaster find extra space for almost two thousand people?" Colonel Yamin asks.

"We've put them on the running track, ma'am. With field shelters and sleeping bags."

"I see." Colonel Yamin raises an eyebrow. "Whatever works, I guess. At least they're not clogging up my flight deck."

She turns her attention back to the holotable and sighs with emphasis.

"That leaves only one thing to do before we leave this shithole of a system."

"Yes, ma'am," the XO replies.

"Weps, open Hades silos five and six. Nuclear-fire mission authorized. Target is the city of New Longyearbyen. Set the warheads for ground penetration, maximum yield. Let's glass the bastards and get out of here."

"Aye, ma'am. Opening silos five and six. Target programmed and locked. Ready for launch on your mark."

The big screen on the forward CIC bulkhead shows a big slice of the equatorial region of New Svalbard, so I have a ringside seat to Armageddon. The missiles from *Ottawa* streak moonward and enter the atmosphere, far faster than any drop ship or Shrike could. There's heavy cloud cover over New Longyearbyen again, so I don't see the moment of impact directly. But when it happens, it's hard to miss. A sun-bright flash lights up the clouds from below, and a minute later, the mushroom cloud from the twenty-megaton thermonuclear explosion rises through the clouds, roiling black and red, ash and fire. And then everything down there is no more. Everything we risked our necks for five years ago, willing to throw away our careers and our freedom so the colonists could stay in charge of their own world, all scattered into the moon's stratosphere and irradiated for the next hundred years or more.

The fate of New Svalbard was sealed the moment the three seed ships made orbit above the colony. There is no way we could have reclaimed it from the Lankies after a week of landings. They had already begun to dismantle our terraformers, and even if we had been able to scrape them off the moon, the colony would have died of cold and starvation without their fusion plants and food sources. But it's still demoralizing to know that the weapon that killed the scrappy little colony for good came from our own launchers. It was a mercy killing, but a killing nonetheless. And as I look at the boiling, angry-looking cloud rising from the impact site as if it's trying to reach us in orbit, I remember something I said to Halley in the aftermath of another battle, this one almost nine years ago on a far-off colony world named Willoughby.

If this is a victory, I'd hate to see what it looks like when we get our asses kicked.

EPILOGUE

Ottawa and *Michael P. Murphy* transition back into the solar system sixteen hours later. We set course for Daedalus Fleet Yard and the ride home, which won't be as fast as our express passage through the solar system a few days ago because *Murphy* can't keep up with the battlecarrier at full speed. That gives me seven days of thinking time, and I don't mind that at all right now.

The civilians are quartered on our running track, so there's no running laps for the remainder of our deployment. On the second day of our transit to Gateway, I go up to the track nonetheless, to go see someone I know.

The ice miners and engineers have managed to adapt to their temporary living arrangements with admirable speed and thoroughness. We've issued everyone field shelters and sleeping bags from the ship's SI equipment inventory, and they've used it to make an orderly tent city on the kilometer-long running track. The shelters take up one lane of the track, and the New Svalbarders left the other lane open to facilitate easy movement. They organized screen dividers from somewhere on the ship to have some sections of the tent city walled off for privacy. All in all, it looks remarkably well organized for a makeshift refugee camp that has to share the head and showers of the attached gym among almost two thousand people.

Constable Guest is easy to find wherever he goes. His family has set up their shelters in the far bend of the track. When I come around the bend, he is standing by his open shelter, engrossed in conversation with two other colonists. He gives me a friendly wave when he sees me coming around the loop.

"How do you like your temporary digs?" I ask.

"It's not bad at all, actually. Kind of cozy when you close the flap. Like going camping." He gestures to the shelters next to his. "Wife and daughters are off to the mess hall to get some lunch. They love the food on this ship. I may have a hard time weaning them off it again."

"I'm not going to tell you it's as good everywhere in the solar system. When's the last time you've been back to Earth?"

"Ten years. Before all that Lanky business. The kids have never been. They are New Svalbard born and bred. I still haven't told them that we can't go back, but they know. They're smarter than me by half."

"No, there's no going back," I say. "We made sure of that before we left."

"Nukes?"

I nod. "Twenty megatons, underground burst."

"Yeah, it's as gone as gone can get, then." He sighs.

"Are you going to be okay?" I ask.

"Yeah. I'll be fine. I have colonial law enforcement certification. I'll apply for a new job with the Colonial Administration. Not that we have a lot of colonies left. Push comes to shove, I'll go private and do mining security or something. It was time for a change anyway."

"How do you think your girls will handle Earth?"

"They're coming from a place with ten thousand people on it, and they're going to a place that has a hundred billion. I think it'll be a bit of a culture shock. But they'll adapt."

"I wish I could refer you to someone, but I don't know anyone important in the civilian administration. But if you need anything while you're on this ship, let me know. Just ask for the STO."

Constable Guest extends his hand, and I shake it firmly.

"Thank you, Captain Grayson. For what you did back on New Svalbard. And for helping us again."

"Andrew," I say.

"I'm Matthew," he says. "And wherever we end up, you're welcome anytime."

"I will take you up on that."

I shake his hand again and make my way back around the bend and toward the gym. I like the big, friendly constable, and I am a little shamed by his gratitude and his offer of friendship. All the corps has ever done for him was to turn his colony into a battleground and then nuke it into oblivion. We are damn sure not in the helping business, no matter what the recruiting vids say.

On the way back to Daedalus, I notice a profound change in the atmosphere on board, even more drastic than the attitude jolt the crew got when it was clear that we were headed for battle. There's less chatter in the passageways, less laughter at mealtime in the officer's wardroom, and even the RecFac is quieter. I recognize the mood because it's common among grunts after battle. A large percentage of *Ottawa*'s crew were green before this deployment, and nobody really expected to see action on a shakedown cruise. Now they've seen battle, felt the stress and the fear of death, pushed the buttons that launched the warheads. Whatever happens next, I know that none of the junior enlisted on this ship will ever slack off during an Abandon Ship drill again. But it's the SI grunts who bore the true burden of this battle, especially the seventy-two members of the Seventh Spaceborne Infantry Regiment who are making the transit home to Gateway in airtight and fluid-resistant olive-green Fleet body bags.

There's a funeral ceremony for our SI and Fleet fallen the day after our transition back into the solar system. It's not a real funeral because the Fleet will deliver the bodies of the dead to their families for proper incineration and burial, but the ceremony is tradition because it gives their comrades a chance to say good-bye properly. The disposable coffins with the dead pilots and troopers are lined up on the flight deck in seven neat rows of twelve. Each coffin has an NAC flag draped over it and a little easel with a picture of the lost trooper and their hometown and awards underneath.

I didn't check the casualty lists right after the battle because I had other things on my mind. I haven't seen Hansen since we left, and I wrote it off to the fact that we no longer have a running track on which to bump into each other. Maybe I didn't want to check the lists even after everything calmed down after the battle because I was afraid of what I would find. But right before the ceremony, when we have time to walk the rows of coffins to say our private good-byes to friends and comrades, I see her picture on one of those easels, and it's like someone parked a fully loaded drop ship square on my chest.

Nicole Anna Hansen was born in a 'burber enclave near Atlanta, and she was only a month older than me. She served in the Territorial Army and then the Spaceborne Infantry, climbing all the way to the rank of captain. In her nine-year service career, she received three Bronze Stars, two Purple Hearts, a Silver Star, and a bucket of other awards. She died on New Svalbard, a backwater ice moon in the Fomalhaut system, holding the airfield perimeter at New Longyearbyen with the command platoon of her company until the Lankies broke through and wiped out half the platoon not a hundred meters from the spot where my squad emerged on the surface to lead the civilians to the waiting drop ships. She died to defend a moon that would be turned into a frozen radioactive wasteland a little over an hour later. She died so nineteen hundred civilians could make it off, doing what the grunts in the SI are trained to do. We were squad mates once, and we both almost bought it in that bloody and furious night in Detroit eight years ago. If her career went anything like mine, we both rolled the dice a few hundred times in those eight years. And now her number came up, and my old squad mate—what's left of her—is riding home for the last time, back to a family who doesn't even know about the grief that's about to consume their lives. And I am here, reading her obituary printout and learning things about her I should have known for years.

I run my fingers over her portrait and feel the tears burning in my eyes. Maybe this hurts so much because she was the only trooper I've known for as long as I've known Halley, and because I liked her from the beginning. And maybe it's because I know that it could be me or Halley in that coffin just as easily. Maybe Hansen's death is such a gut punch because it shows me once again that life in the corps is random and capricious, that there are no guarantees any of us will make it through this.

I spend the rest of the deployment mostly with Halley in my time off. We alternate staterooms every night and bunk together, in continued flagrant violation of regulations. We are officers and understand the need for obedience in a military organization, but we are also husband and wife, and we're in our early thirties. Maybe it's the experience that comes from having lived through this war together for ten years, or the knowledge that finding and keeping someone who fits you is harder than almost anything when you're serving. But it seems to us a pointless dumbshit rule that has a married couple sleeping in separate parts of a ship when their jobs have them risking their lives almost every fucking day. There are seventy-two of our comrades down on the flight deck who can't live out their lives anymore, and if nothing else, I feel that we owe it to them to live our own the best way we can.

"What would you do if we weren't in the Fleet anymore?" I ask Halley one evening as we get comfortable in the confines of her bunk.

"What do you mean? What are we going to do when we retire? I thought we had that all sorted out."

"No, not that. I mean quitting the service. Resigning our commissions."

Halley props her head up and looks at me quizzically.

"You are not serious about that. Lose the retirement bonus? And the health care?"

"We'd still get the payout, just without the bonus. It would still be enough to do something else with our lives."

"What brought that on?" she asks.

"This big bucket of shit," I say and knock against the bulkhead with my fist. "The Destroyonator class."

"What about it?"

"We have all this shiny new tech. Most advanced ship in the Fleet. And it's still built around the old battle plan. What are we going to use it for? Going after Lankies outside of the solar system? We just tried that, and we couldn't even defend a single one-town colony. What's the point? Once they have settled on a colony, they flip the atmosphere anyway and tear down all our terraformers. We're never getting those colonies back, with or without Avengers."

Halley doesn't reply. Instead, she just looks at me with an ever so slight smile on her lips.

"But you know they're going to use them because they're there. And because it's the fucking plan. So we'll spend the next ten years hopscotching between a bunch of interstellar graveyards until we bite off more than even a Destroyonator can chew."

I roll over onto my back and look at the paint on the deck above Halley's stateroom.

"Ten years," I repeat. "We'll be forty when we get out. *If* we get out. If we don't end up in a coffin on some flight deck. Or as frozen carbon particles in hard vacuum over some shit moon at the ass end of space."

"So you want to just drop everything and move into the mountains of Vermont?"

"I don't know. Maybe. Or do something else. Have some time to figure it out. And spend time with you."

I turn to face her again.

"We've been in a relationship for ten years. How much time have we had together? Six months?"

"Probably less."

"Yeah. And I really want to see what it's like to have a life with you. Not just spending two weeks a year on leave."

"The corps needs experienced people, Andrew. Half the force is green. We can't just quit and leave them hanging."

"I think we've done our share. And the green ones did all right at Mars. We did, too, when we were green."

"Oh God, can you even imagine just being a civilian again?" Halley says. "Sleeping in every day for a month. Eating meals that don't get served on a plastic tray. Going out for a two-day hike just because you fucking feel like it. Not having to worry about that infernal PDP going off in your pocket, telling you the world's about to end, and would you please show up for your first-row seats?"

"They need pilots in the civilian world, too, you know."

"I don't know, Andrew," she says. "I'll need time to think about that. What on Earth brought that on anyway?"

I'm silent for a little while. Halley bumps my shoulder lightly with her fist.

"Hmm? Come on, spill the beans."

"It's the guy I knew back in New Svalbard," I say. "Big constable, named Guest."

"What about him?"

"He made it off the rock with his family. They're up in Tent City on the running track right now. Wife, two daughters. And they just lost their home. His job for the last fifteen years. Their whole lives. And he shrugs it off because his family made it out with him, and they are with him. We just nuked his *hometown*. And he has already come to terms with having to start over. Because they matter more to him than his job or his home."

Now it's Halley's turn to stay silent for a bit.

"Must be nice," she says after a while.

"Yeah," I agree. "Must be."

For the last half million klicks, we get an escort from the Fleet. News of our rescue of the settlers of New Svalbard has traveled faster than *Ottawa*, and the Networks are sinking their teeth into the juicy red meat of this particular story. So we glide into Gateway instead of Daedalus, exactly three and a half months after we left for our shakedown cruise, and nineteen days after our return from the Fomalhaut system. The two Hammerhead cruisers that accompany *Ottawa* and *Michael P. Murphy* into the berths have the new high-visibility paint scheme and full Christmas tree lights blinking, to give the myriad of news cameras on the observation deck of Gateway something to see. We haven't had any victories to celebrate in the last three years, and I suspect that the rescue of a colony from annihilation is going to be used as proof that the money for the Avengers was well spent.

After a two-day stretch of debriefings, medical checkups, press tours, and visits by what seems like every general officer in the corps, the entire crew of *Ottawa* is granted a special five-day leave, sandwiched between two weekends for a total of nine days of liberty. As officers, Halley and I are among the first group to leave the ship, and we successfully dodge most of the reporters and curious brass waiting for us out in the main concourse to hitch a ride down to Earth at the transfer desk.

"Where do you need to be?" the sergeant at the desk asks as he checks his shuttle schedules. From the way he glances at us when he thinks we're not paying attention, I can tell that he's not familiar with the new blueberry uniforms.

"*Burlington*," we both say at the same time.

"NCAS *Burlington*," he repeats. "Shuttle 802, departs at 0700 from docking collar Bravo 95."

"Thank you, Sergeant," Halley says.

"We can be in the Falls by nine and get some decent breakfast at the chief's," I say to Halley as we walk down the main concourse toward the Bravo gates.

"My thoughts exactly," she says, and I feel content for the first time since we got off New Svalbard by the skin of our teeth.

On the shuttle down to Earth, Halley leans against me and kisses me on the cheek as I watch Gateway and the massive docked *Ottawa* recede in the distance above us.

"If you want to resign, I'll do the same."

"If you really want to stay, I'll stay in with you," I counter.

She punches me on my biceps.

"That's not how it works. You're supposed to let me be gracious and appreciate the offer of sacrifice."

Halley puts her head against my shoulder and closes her eyes with a sigh.

"We can figure all of that out later. But first I want a good cup of coffee and a long hike in clean air."

"I'm with you all the way on that," I say.

"Never doubted it," Halley replies. "Never will."

ACKNOWLEDGEMENTS

After writing dedications for six Frontlines novels, I always feel like I'm saying the same things every time, and yet I know that I invariably forget to thank someone.

As always, thanks are due to my awesome 47North crew—Adrienne, Jason, and Kristin—who take care of me and tolerate my habitual deadline offenses. Thanks also to Britt, who moved on to Kindle Worlds from 47North.

Thank you to my agent Evan Gregory, who keeps on being awesome and keeps me on the right track as far as long-term career plans go.

I'd like to thank my developmental editor, Andrea Hurst, for helping me, once again, make the novel better and cut out all the stuff that people tend to skip.

Thank you to all my writer friends and colleagues, my Viable Paradise posse, and George R. R. Martin and the Wild Cards rogues. Professional validation is nice, but friendships are better. (Both put together are best, of course, and I get to have "best" in spades these days.)

Thank you to the Royal Manticoran Navy for welcoming me at MantiCon and HonorCon, inviting me back year after year, and voting for me so I could take home the Rampant Manticore for Best Military SF Novel and the H. Beam Piper Memorial Award last October at

HonorCon in Raleigh. You're a great crew, and I'll have Shockfrosts with you anytime and anywhere.

Thank you to my wife Robin for doing all the household heavy lifting and making it possible for me to retreat to my office so I can put on the magic no-noise headphones whenever I need to. There's no way I could do what I am doing without you.

And lastly, thank you to all my readers. You make it possible for me to do this full-time, and it's the best job on the planet, as far as I am concerned.

 Marko Kloos was born and raised in Germany, in and around the city of Münster. In the past, he was a soldier, bookseller, freight dockworker, and corporate IT administrator before he decided he wasn't cut out for anything other than making stuff up for a living.

Marko writes primarily science fiction and fantasy—his first genre love ever since his youth, when he spent his allowance mostly on SF pulp serials. He's the author of the bestselling Frontlines series of military science fiction and is a member of George R.R. Martin's Wild Cards consortium.

Marko resides at Castle Frostbite in New Hampshire with his wife, two children, and a roving pack of vicious dachshunds. His official website is www.markokloos.com. He can be reached at frontlines@markokloos.com and found on Twitter (where he spends way too much time) @markokloos.